'Good,' Tolan said. 'So what I want to know, Phil – and you better tell me, like – is the names of those you've most recently sold weapons to and, in particular, the names of any blow-ins you've sold to. That's what I'm here for, Phil.'

Wilson's grey gaze, formerly steely, widened and glazed over with fear because he knew that if he admitted selling to blow-ins, which was forbidden by Tolan, he would be as good as a dead man . . .

'I've never sold to no blow-ins,' he said . . .

'Let's make sure you're tellin' the truth,' Tolan said, stepping back and nodding at Curran who, blinking repeatedly, turned on the blowtorch and set it alight as Donovan, grinning wolfishly, pinned Wilson to his chair and O'Hagan picked up the hammer and nails.

Wilson took a long time to break, but he broke in the end.

Green Light

Shaun Clarke

CORONET BOOKS
Hodder & Stoughton

Chapter One

He awoke just before dawn, breathing like a beast in its dark lair, inhaling and exhaling in slow, ravenous gasps. His wife Mary lay beside him, still sleeping, her fleshy hip pressing against his spine, making him writhe with impatience, not lust. His thoughts were still permeated with the fleeting images of his nightmares: the fiery pits of hell, phantom demons in the flames, the faces of old friends and enemies just visible through the smoke, either begging for their lives or spitting words of contempt before the sound of gunshots (imagined in his nightmares, though all too real in his actual past) reverberated through his head, through his private cosmos, to jerk him awake. Now, conscious at last, his gaze hardening as daybreak brightened, he was pleased to see the morning light slanting in around the edge of the curtains over the bedroom windows. His only torment was sleep.

He sighed. 'Shit,' he whispered, shocked by the ravaged timbre of his own voice, which was due to his boozing during the evening before in the kind of club, in his case republican, supposedly closed down with the coming of the so-called 'peace'. *Fuck the peace*. Who needed it?

Sighing again, he pushed himself upright, rubbed his

unshaven chin with one hand, then withdrew a cigarette from the packet on the bedside cabinet and lit it, using a fancy Ronson lighter. He inhaled and coughed, inhaled again, coughed again. His wife groaned, rolling onto her back and opening her eyes. She glanced at him, as if not really seeing him – no light of love in her gaze at all – then stared up at the ceiling. He, her husband, Pat Tolan, smoked and waited, knowing what was to come.

'Jesus,' Mary said, 'at the fags already and you not yet out of bed, let alone had yer breakfast. You'll be doin' yer lungs in for sure if you don't show more sense.'

'Shut yer gub,' Tolan replied, exhaling smoke as he spoke, having heard what he had expected to hear since he heard it most mornings, 'and get down there and cook me up some breakfast. Sure I've a long day ahead of me.'

'Doin' what?'

'Wouldn't you like to know? Ask no questions an' I'll tell you no lies. Now get down there and put on the kettle an' let me get m'self ready.'

'Don't set fire to the bedclothes,' Mary said as she flipped the blankets back and swung her heavy legs, more like ships' mooring bollards, off the soft, springy bed. 'Sure you could burn the house down.'

'We're insured,' Tolan said.

He watched his wife getting dressed, not admiring what he saw, wondering how the healthily plump, grand-to-feel black-haired lass he had married twenty-odd years ago could have changed into this tub of shapeless lard with darkly shadowed eyes and greying, stringy hair that was cut almost as short as a man's. In fact, two years ago, in a fit of hysteria over one of his other women, she had shorn off her long hair with kitchen scissors, thus depriving him of the last shred of her former femininity and ensuring that his waning desire for her was killed off entirely. It had worked. Tolan had not laid a hand on her from that day to this and she seemed a lot happier for it. They had gone off each other sexually a long time ago; now, in their early fifties, with the kids married and living elsewhere, one in West Belfast, another in Cornwall, they were content to lead separate lives while keeping up the front of a solid marriage. Tolan had his other women and Mary knew about them, but Mary, he assumed, being Catholic and serious about it, stuck to nights in the bingo hall with her female friends and regular visits to the local church. Now, as Tolan studied her, breathing out his clouds of cigarette smoke to stink up the small bedroom, he concluded, given the size and shape of her, that she couldn't even recall what it meant to be admired by a man. Naturally, he had a much higher opinion of himself, though it wasn't an opinion shared by many others; he didn't see what they saw.

He was, at least, slim, which he noted with appreciation when Mary flip-flopped out of the bedroom in her dressing gown and slippers, leaving him to stub out his cigarette, roll off the bed and admire himself in their new bathroom mirror. Though they were living in the Catholic enclave of Ballymurphy, in what had once been a two-up, two-down terraced Housing Executive home, all the houses in the terraced street had been renovated with government grants, courtesy of the ever-helpful European Community, keen to retain the so-called 'peace' in the province in this, the Year of our Lord 2002. Now the houses had extensions to the bedrooms, which included a small en suite bathroom with all mod cons. Thus Tolan could admire himself in his new bathroom mirror and see that he was almost as slim as when he had been a teenager. This particularly pleased him because he was only five feet, six inches tall and his slim figure made his lack of height less noticeable. He wasn't a handsome man – he knew this and accepted it – but he certainly didn't look as old as his fifty-odd years and was, in fact, often mistaken for someone ten or fifteen years younger. Nevertheless, he had a face that was pared to the bone, as ascetic as that of a monk, with a cold grey gaze and thin, downturned lips, the countenance humourless and actually frightening to many. Tolan assumed, however, that the fear was respect and imagined himself as the spitting image of Eamon de Valera – a great man in Tolan's view, even if he had, in his final days, betrayed the cause, as they all did in the end.

I betrayed the fucking cause, Tolan thought as he ran hot and cold water, in equal measures, into the spotlessly clean enamel sink. *I betrayed it and I'm a lot better off for it, so fuck the cause anyway. These days life's for the living.*

He shaved himself with an electric razor, then washed his face in the sink, splashed water under his armpits (he only bathed once a week), cleaned his teeth (the thought of dentists gave him the shivers) and put on a pair of faded denims, an open-necked sky-blue shirt and a pair of rubber-soled, lace-up leather boots. Feeling almost like a new man, his nightmares fading, he left the bathroom and made his way downstairs. Reaching the ground floor, he had to cross a small living room in order to enter the kitchen. The living room was clean and tidy, with brightly flowered chairs and sofa, a patterned carpet bought cheaply in the lower Falls Road, a few gaudy paintings on the walls, and Virgin Marys and other religious bric-a-brac on the walls and mantelpiece, Tolan's wife being a deeply religious woman.

Even before reaching the kitchen, Tolan smelt frying food and heard the sound of the TV. They had another TV, a bigger one which Tolan watched in the evenings, in the living room, but Mary had a smaller set in the kitchen, kept it on all day and seemingly watched it out of one ear or the other, since she rarely actually focused her gaze upon it. Entering the kitchen, Tolan did indeed see that the TV set was on, with another talking head going on about national and local news while Mary focused on the bacon and eggs frying in the pan. She scooped the food out and put it on a plate as he took his seat by the table.

'Quare good mornin',' Tolan said, gazing out the window to see sunshine falling on the terraced houses at the other side of the street. It was a modest enough street for a man like him to be living in but he found it useful to be viewed as one of the hoi polloi, though a knowledge of his true worth would have raised the eyebrows of his neighbours and none of them knew about his fine house in the country. It was best to be normal, like. 'Looks like a right sunny day,' he added.

'Ack aye,' Mary responded, putting two fried breakfasts on the round table beside the mugs of tea already steaming there, then taking the chair at the other side. 'Sure we could do with some sunshine.'

They both tucked into their fried breakfasts, which included eggs and bacon, black sausage, baked beans and fried bread, the standard start to the day – which, when Tolan thought about it, explained the weight of Mary and of many of the other women in Belfast. They ate a lot of fried foods, bread and potatoes and they also, like Mary, drank stout. The weight came from all that scoff.

'So what are you up to today?' Tolan asked Mary as she was forking up bacon and egg on a piece of fried bread.

'Wouldn't you like to know?' Mary retorted, getting back at him by repeating what he had said to her when she had asked him that same question. 'Ask no questions and I'll tell you no lies.'

Tolan offered a thin smile. 'Let me guess,' he said. 'First you'll do the dishes and tidy up the kitchen.'

'Someone's got to do it,' Mary said, 'and you certainly won't.'

'Next,' Tolan said, ignoring her remark, 'you'll take yourself off for a wander down the Falls, stopping into shops here and there just as an excuse for a bit of crack.'

'No shame in that,' Mary said. 'I have lots of friends down there.'

'Next,' Tolan continued with thinly veiled contempt, 'you'll go into the bingo hall to play a couple of games with your girlfriends.'

'Nice wimmen, all,' Mary said between mouthfuls of food. 'And I find a bit of bingo relaxin'.'

'Next,' Tolan said, also while eating, 'you'll join some of those girlfriends in a pub for a spot of lunch – say, Irish stew or shepherd's pie with lots of chips on the side and a couple of pints of stout to wash it down. Sure wouldn't that be correct, now?'

Mary raised her eyebrows, then rolled her unhealthily shadowed brown eyes. 'What if it is?' she replied. 'Sure don't you like a wee drop yourself – an' more than that if you ask me!'

'Next,' Tolan said, ignoring her again, 'you'll wander back up the Falls, stopping here and there for more crack, then come back here and have an afternoon snooze. Finally, you'll spend the rest of the evening watching TV, no matter what's on, good, bad or indifferent. You'll be in bed before I come home, your snores shakin' Black Mountain.'

'You snore as well,' Mary said defensively.

'No, I don't.'

'You moan and groan a lot,' Mary said. 'All them nightmares you have. A bad conscience, is it?'

'Shut yer gub,' Tolan said. Then he methodically finished off his breakfast, ignoring her, while she silently watched him. When he had finished and was lighting another cigarette to have with what was left of his tea, Mary said: 'Actually, today I'm going to see Ruth. I'll be having my lunch there.'

Ruth was their only daughter, now twenty-seven years old, living in Andersonstown, another Catholic enclave, located south of Ballymurphy at the far side of Turf Lodge, and upgraded with the help of EC money. She was married to Mike Reilly, a thirty-year old garage mechanic who, while never taking an active part in the Troubles – or 'the War', as the republicans called it – had serviced and disguised stolen vehicles for Tolan's wing of the Provisional IRA. Now, though Tolan was in another kind of game, Mike still did similar work for him, albeit for different reasons. He and Ruth had two children, both girls, one five and one six, Edna and Moira respectively, and they seemed to get on well together. Though Tolan rarely showed his affections, he was fond of all of them. He wasn't so fond of his twenty-eight-year-old son Liam who, also married and with three children of his own, had always resolutely refused to join the paramilitaries, openly despised his father for what he was now doing, and had gone to live in Cornwall, England, to get away from it all. These days they rarely communicated, which didn't bother Tolan though it had certainly upset Mary and might have contributed to the distance between them. Tolan tried not to think of that.

'So,' he said, sighing, exhaling smoke, 'I'd better be off then.'

'Aye,' Mary responded, standing up to gather the dishes together, 'you take yourself off. Sure a man has his work to do an' the less said the better.'

'That's sensible,' Tolan said.

Letting her get on with it, keeping his still burning cigarette between his lips, he checked his wristwatch and saw that it was just after ten. If he walked, which he liked to do, always keen on the exercise, keeping the figure trim, he would get to the lower Falls by opening time. Feeling calm under the circumstances, as invariably he did, he went back across the living room to the hallway, put on his coat, left by the front door (he had often had to leave by the back) and stepped into the narrow, sloping, sunlit street.

His house was halfway along Divismore Park in Ballymurphy, on the lower slopes of the Black Mountain. Though the name 'Divismore Park' made the place sound fancy, it was just another street of terraced houses in the tangled web of similar streets that made up the estate. Nevertheless, Tolan could never pass Number 11 without glancing at it and recalling that his old friend Gerry Adams had lived there for part of his childhood. Though Tolan and Adams had long since gone their separate ways, with Adams no longer called a 'terrorist' but now a famous 'man of peace', perhaps even on his way to a Nobel Peace Prize, Tolan, in spite of himself, despite his deep resentment of the present-day Adams, often looked back fondly on their childhood together, a very pleasant time indeed, when it was safe to play in the streets or explore the many paths and streams that criss-crossed the mountain that loomed over the estate. Of course, as Tolan and Adams had both learnt later, their idyllic childhood on the mountain in no way reflected the real life of the estate on its lower slopes. In those days, the houses had been damp and cold, the estate had had no shops, church hall, community hall or even school, half of the adults were out of work, subsisting on state handouts, and bored teenagers were already into the kind of vandalism that would spread its ugly reach even wider during the Troubles – or, as the Catholics would have it, the War. In those grim days, Protestants and Catholics had shared the estate, but its bad reputation – the unemployment and vandalism – gradually drove the Protestants, always favoured by the Unionist authorities, to get themselves homes on better estates. Eventually, every single one of the Protestants had moved out, most transferring to the exclusively Protestant New Barnsley estate across the Springfield Road, leaving Ballymurphy totally Catholic, as it was right now. And that, at least according to Tolan, was as it should be. He wanted no truck with Loyalists.

Turning out of the street, he looked up at the green and brown slopes of the Black Mountain, a few white clouds drifting above them, though the summer sky higher up was sheer blue, recalling how he and his school friends, including Gerry Adams, had clambered up those hills to fish for tadpoles, using nets and jam jars, and to play Tarzan or Cowboys-and-Indians and generally enjoy the panoramic view of the city below. Now, alas, given the building boom encouraged by the tentative peace and the financial assistance of the European Community, houses were spreading ever higher up the slopes to obscure, or at least diminish, the Black Mountain's original grandeur.

Disgusted by this turn of events, even though it was certainly profiting him, Tolan headed along the Whiterock Road, passing the City Cemetery where many old friends lay buried, though the true 'comrades', as distinct from mere old friends, lay in honour in the Milltown Cemetery located at the upper Falls Road. Eventually reaching that very road, though well above the Milltown Cemetery, Tolan turned left, in the direction of the Grosvenor Road. Though EC money in huge amounts was being pumped into Northern Ireland, it appeared to have had little effect on the Falls Road which, though lively and thriving, was still an unsightly clutter of new and second-hand furniture shops with the furniture laid out on the pavements, bookie shops, grocery shops, video shops, pet shops, hardware stores, quick-food takeaways, cafés and, of course, pubs – an impressive amount of pubs. As usual, working-class people of all ages were keeping the pavements busy, children were playing unchecked by the side of the traffic-laden road, women were entering and leaving the many shops, the men, young and old, almost certainly unemployed, were darting in and out of the betting shops or hanging about on street corners, smoking, sharing a bit of crack, both conversational and otherwise, and in general trying to pass the long day. Indeed, the only difference between now and the good old days, which many thought of as the Golden Days, was that the side streets were no longer blocked off with barricades manned by armed British troops and the roads weren't filled with armoured cars and troop carriers. This made the place a safe haven for the likes of Tolan – and well he knew it.

Just before reaching the Royal Victoria Hospital, where so many of his friends and comrades had received medical attention for broken bones, bullet wounds and the bloody or bruised results of various forms of torture, Tolan turned and entered a doorway over which was a sign stating TOLAN'S TAXIS. In fact, his 'taxis' were the half-dozen minicabs parked legally in a makeshift garage on waste ground out the back (this business had to be legal so that the others could have 'legs') and their drivers, mostly young and otherwise unemployable, were lounging on the black plastic-covered benches inside the reception area, within sight of Tolan's secretary, the flirtatious artificial blonde Annie Jordan who gazed out from a glassless opening and counter set in a wall with a locked door.

As Tolan entered the reception area, its walls done in golden pine and, the floor covered in linoleum designed to look like Italian tiles, a young man, Tommy Doyle, who had been flirting with Annie, blushed and smiled nervously at him, then hurried back to his chair. Tolan stared steadily, almost threateningly, at the twenty-year old Doyle, then at the twenty-two-year old Annie. While the former blushed more brightly and averted his green gaze, running his fingers nervously through his thick, unruly brown hair, the latter offered her customary big, vacuous smile as she pressed a button hidden from sight, letting the door click open. Tolan pushed the door farther open, walked in, then closed the door firmly behind him, locking himself into the cluttered office that he shared with Annie and his bookkeeper, Liam Hennessey. Annie was seated on a high stool, attending to the phone bookings and to customers coming into the reception area personally to order a taxi; Hennessey was seated behind his surprisingly uncluttered desk, studying his new computer instead of poring over old ledger books. This was the modern age, even here in the Falls.

'Mornin', boss,' Annie said, glancing sideways at him, then flashing a flirtatious smile to someone out in the reception area, almost certainly Tommy Doyle. Perched on the high stool, wearing a tight skirt and sweater, she was something to see, being slim and big-breasted and with a curvaceous backside that encouraged bad thoughts. Tolan had those thoughts now.

'Mornin',' he replied, then turned for distraction to Liam Hennessey, baby-faced and bald-headed at forty-five years of age, dressed in a twenty-year-old grey suit with a buttoned-down shirt and striped tie. Hennessey was homosexual and open about it, confident in the certainty that he was good at his job. 'So how's the numbers man this morning?' Tolan asked him.

'Not bad,' Hennessey replied. 'Sure the numbers are lookin' pretty healthy, so I'm feelin' good too.'

The 'numbers' were the pounds sterling and Euros earned from Tolan's various criminal activities. He had first engaged in those activities to help finance the IRA's war against the Brits and Loyalists, but by the time peace, albeit precarious, had come to the province, Tolan, like a lot of leading paramilitaries on both sides of the divide, was so entrenched in crime as a way of life that the idea of dropping it was unthinkable to him. Therefore, once he was no longer needed by the Provos, supposedly now engaged in the slow, always doubtful process of decommissioning their weapons, he had continued using the skills learnt during, as he would have it, 'the War' to keep himself busy and in business. The taxi company was only a front for that business (though a nice wee earner in itself), with a lot of his illicit income being laundered through it as well as through the many local social clubs specializing in entertainment and booze and one-armed bandits in which he had become a silent partner. Tolan had his fingers in many pies and they all tasted good to him.

'If a wanker like you feels good,' Tolan said, 'then I feel good as well. Though there's never enough, I always say, when there's more for the takin'. Any messages for me?'

'Annie's got all yer messages,' Hennessey replied, lighting a fag and coughing like an old-fashioned steam train before managing to clear his lungs. 'I only do the books, boss.'

'Sure that's fair enough,' Tolan said. 'Try not to cream your pants as you watch that computer screen. I'm told it can have that effect.'

'I should be so lucky,' Hennessey retorted, exhaling

a stream of cancerous smoke. 'Ya have to key into the Internet for that and there's some weird shit on offer.'

'I hope you haven't been keying in on my time.'

'Sure he's got me to look at,' Annie said, speaking over her shoulder. 'There's things that happen under that desk when he looks at me that make me blush to my roots.'

'Lying bitch,' Hennessey said without rancour, his gaze still fixed on his computer screen, calculating the numbers. 'What she has, I don't want.'

'You poor sod,' Annie said.

'So what are my messages?' Tolan asked, speaking to the back of Annie's neck into which he had fantasized about sinking his teeth more than once in desperate attempts to revive his waning libido. He was starting to show his age and he knew it but could not quite accept it.

'Just one,' she replied, tearing the top page out of her notebook and handing it to him. Tolan read it with care, then tore it up and opened his right hand to let the pieces fall into Annie's waste-paper basket. 'That's one of the two I wanted,' he said. 'Have you heard from the Russian yet?'

''Fraid not,' Annie said.

'Okay, I'll see you two later. Call me on my mobile if you actually hear from that Russian.'

'Will do,' Annie said.

'Right, I'm makin' tracks.'

Annie grinned at him. 'You work a long day, boss,' she said saucily.

'Watch your tongue,' Tolan retorted as he opened the door that led out to the garage. 'Some day you might lose it.'

He passed through the doorway and entered the garage located at the rear of the building, its exit leading past the gable end of the first house in the adjoining street. Not wanting even Annie or Liam to know what he was up to, he left by that exit and walked further down the Falls until he had reached the entrance to the Royal Victoria Hospital. Entering the parking lot of the hospital, he walked around until he saw a red Ford Cortina with three men sitting in it, one in the driver's seat, the other two in the back. The driver was Mick Curran. The two in the back were Jack Delaney and Ralph Farrell. All three were in their early forties and had been in the Provisional IRA before the laughable weapons-decommissioning. Tolan took the seat beside the driver then closed the car door.

'I got your message,' he said. 'Are you sure it's him?'

'Yes, boss, I'm sure,' Curran responded. 'The info came from an impeccable source. He's the invisible man behind the competition and there's no doubt about it.'

'How well is he protected?'

'He isn't. He's so convinced of his invisibility, he doesn't even have bodyguards at his farm.'

'And bodyguards would only attract attention. He's a smart one, all right.'

'Ack aye, he is that, boss.'

'He has a wife and kids, doesn't he?'

'Aye, boss. Two girls and a boy, the oldest twelve or so. So we won't have much resistance if they're home.'

'Okay,' Tolan said. 'Let's make an example of the bastard. Make what happens to him a warning to anyone else thinking of doing the same. Hit the road, Mick.'

Curran drove them out of the hospital car park, turned down the lower Falls, picked up the Westlink and left the city by way of the M2 motorway, with Belfast Lough stretched out on their right. The sky darkened as they moved on, choppy water to their right, gloomy green fields to the left, the earlier white clouds now replaced by rain clouds, and the wind picked up as they followed the signs to Larne. By the time they had reached Carrickfergus, the first drops of rain were falling; when they left that town behind them, the rainfall had become a deluge.

Glancing out of the car window, Tolan saw lightning flashing, silvery, skeletal fingers clawing at the black, boiling clouds, making him recall his nightmares with a sliver of dread. He forced those visions from his thoughts, battened the hatch on his fear, concentrated on what he was about to do and felt a lot better for it. About fifteen minutes later, somewhere between Carrickfergus and Larne, Curran turned along a narrow road that snaked through green countryside, the hills gently undulating, and soon led them to the extensive grounds of a fenced-in farm with a big whitewashed house in the middle, sur-rounded by barns.

Thunder roared, the wind howled. Curran drove through the gates of the rainswept grounds around the farmhouse and braked to a halt just outside the house. Instantly, Tolan and the two men in the back, Delaney and Farrell, clambered out of the vehicle to be pummelled by the wind and lashed by the rain as they hurried around to raise the lid of the boot. From the boot, each man withdrew a Browning 9mm High Power handgun, a Standard Sterling Mk 4 9mm sub-machine gun and a spare 34-round magazine for the Sterling. Farrell also grabbed a long-handled sledgehammer. Then the three men walked resolutely through the pouring, wind-whipped rain towards the whitewashed farmhouse.

The three men stopped at the front door of the large farmhouse, a solid oak door with a mock-Victorian brass door handle and letter box. Farrell slung his sub-machine gun over his right shoulder and prepared to swing the sledgehammer. Delaney released the safety catch of his Sterling and got ready to charge into the house. Tolan stepped right up to the door, aimed his sub-machine gun at it, then squeezed off a short burst that tore the lock to hell, sending chips of wood flying off in all directions. Instantly, Tolan stepped to the side and Farrell swung viciously at the door with his sledgehammer, hitting it with a resounding blow that smashed the wood and tore the door from its hinges. Even as the door was crashing inward to the floor, Tolan and Delaney were rushing into the house and Farrell, after dropping the sledgehammer, unslung his own sub-machine gun from his shoulder and released the safety catch as he followed them in.

The rest happened quickly.

Frank Murphy and his family had been having a late lunch in their kitchen when they heard the roaring of the sub-machine gun and the front door crashing to the floor. Even as his wife and children were jerking their heads around, trying to ascertain what was happening, Murphy, more aware, was leaping out of his chair and racing to the kitchen door to slam it shut. He was too late. The door, which was open, was kicked open even wider as Tolan rushed in to slam the stock of his Sterling into Murphy's face, breaking his teeth and making him stagger backwards. As Murphy's wife screamed and protectively grabbed her two daughters, one nine years old, one ten, Murphy was still falling backwards, spitting teeth from a bloody mouth, and Tolan fired a short burst from his sub-machine gun into the man's kneecaps. Murphy screamed and collapsed, flopping face down, then rolling onto his back, as the twelve-year old boy at the far side of the table kicked his chair back. Before the boy could do anything, Farrell had rushed along the table to grab him by the hair and brutally slam him, face first, into the wall. The boy's mother screamed again, hugging her daughters close to her, and Farrell fired a deadly burst into the boy's back, making him convulse and slide down the wall.

'No!' Murphy bawled from the floor. His wife's scream, now inhuman in pitch and seeming to go on forever, was drowned out by the shrieking of the two girls.

Outside the thunder roared. Delaney's sub-machine gun blasted away in the kitchen. Murphy's wife and two daughters were torn apart in the hail of bullets as Murphy, now helpless, his kneecaps shattered, looked on in appalled disbelief. He opened his mouth to protest, either to Tolan or to God, but no sound emerged; then Tolan and Farrell grabbed him under the armpits, roughly hauled him to his feet and slammed him down onto a wooden chair.

As Murphy looked down in horror, his wife groaned and one of his daughters twitched, both lying in expanding pools of their own blood. Murphy's eyes widened. He glanced to the other side of the table at his dead son as Farrell swiftly looped a towel around his mouth, tugged it tight and then tied it to the back of the chair. He then pulled Murphy's arms around the back of the chair and tied both wrists together, preventing him from moving, but forcing him to look down at his groaning wife and daughter as Delaney knelt beside them, glanced up with a crooked grin, then blew their brains out with his Browning 9mm High Power handgun.

When Murphy started struggling wildly, dementedly in the wooden chair, unable to break free and almost choking himself, Tolan grabbed the chair to steady it and Farrell, having withdrawn a hammer and nails from the side pocket of his jacket, nailed Murphy's feet to the floor.

Murphy was obviously trying to scream, but the towel over his mouth kept him silent.

Delaney had raced out of the kitchen after giving Murphy's wife and the twitching daughter the *coup de grâce;* now he returned, carrying a can of gasoline. While Murphy looked on helplessly, his gaze shocked and glazed, tremors rippling through his body and sweat pouring down his face, Delaney poured the contents of the can first over Murphy's dead son, then over his dead wife and daughters. When the can was empty, he threw it to the floor and looked across at Tolan. When his boss nodded at him, he and Farrell hurriedly left the kitchen, taking their weapons with them.

Tolan approached the bound, pinioned Murphy, leaned down over him and stared into his wide eyes. Murphy was sweating profusely and he smelt like an animal. He had shat in his pants.

'Sure ya tried to fuck with me,' Tolan said, 'and this is the price you pay. What's happened here will be a warning to all the others. Now go to hell, Murphy.'

Tolan went to the kitchen roll that was fixed to one of the walls, tore a sheet of paper from it and knotted the paper tightly. Then, as Murphy looked on, his terrified stare now close to madness, Tolan set the paper afire with his cigarette lighter and threw it to the floor between Murphy's dead wife and daughters. The gasoline exploded into a rising, expanding sheet of yellow flames and boiling smoke, instantly enveloping Murphy's wife and female children and spreading out to cover his dead son, then setting fire to the curtains and gradually making its way towards Murphy who, still tied to his chair and nailed by his feet to the floor, could do nothing but await his dreadful fate.

Seeing that everything was as it should be, Tolan turned away and hurried out of the blazing kitchen to leave the house by the front entrance, stepping over the smashed door. Farrell and Delaney had already replaced their weapons in the boot of the car and were sitting in the back. Tolan put his guns in the boot too, then again took the seat beside Mick Curran, who had remained in the car throughout the massacre. Tolan glanced back at the farmhouse. Already heat had made the kitchen windows explode and smoke was pouring out of them. Soon, Tolan knew, the fire would engulf the whole house and incinerate everything, everyone, inside it, including that treacherous bastard Murphy.

At a nod from Tolan, Mick Curran turned on the ignition, made a sharp U-turn and raced back the way they had come, heading for Belfast. Tolan removed his cellular phone from his jacket pocket and put a call through to Annie.

'Has that Russian called in yet?' he asked.

'Yes,' Annie said.

Chapter Two

Boris liked the British summer. He liked *any* kind of summer. Sitting on the balcony of his luxurious apartment in Canary Wharf, London, gazing across the River Thames as the sun sank behind the converted warehouses at the far side, he thought of all the Russian winters he had endured and was glad to have them behind him, even if only temporarily. These days he craved warmth and England was good that way, since even its rain was like a warm shower on skin used to the freezing cold. Right now, however, the only cold he felt came from the chilled vodka he was drinking, pouring it from a bottle into a tiny glass that he would empty once every five minutes in a single, quick gulp. This was the only way to drink vodka, as any Russian would tell you.

Boris was naked. He enjoyed the feel of being naked. As his balcony could not be seen from the adjoining flats – there were high walls on either side – and as only someone with binoculars would be able to see him from the far bank of the river, he was sitting nude in his chair, his legs spreadeagled, sipping vodka while Lara, on her knees between his heavy thighs, worked her wiles on him. Boris held his glass of vodka in one hand while gently massaging the back of Lara's blonde head with the other. He was instructing her with the movement of his fingers and she knew what he required.

Lara wasn't exactly naked. She was wearing a string bikini of the kind she would not have dared to wear in her home country until a few years ago. One of the New Russians, young and amoral, she really only knew of the former Soviet Union by hearsay, and took for granted, as Boris never could, the many pleasures that Russia now offered to those with money or the willingness to earn it. At forty-two years old, Boris could still recall just how dreary the former Soviet Union had been, how seriously short of even the basic necessities, never mind personal freedom. Before the fall of the Soviet Union, Moscow had been a graveyard, the streets poorly lit, the architecture oppressive; now it was filled with fancy shops, restaurants and clubs of all kinds, illuminated at night with neon signs that shed their garish light on a riot of expensive, imported cars and on the so-called New Russians, those who had ruthlessly exploited the new economic freedoms to make themselves rich at the expense of the poor and who boasted about it with Western clothes and jewellery, taunting those in the gutters.

Lara was one of those New Russians, a child of the nightclubs and discothèques, a peasant girl who had fled from her village to Moscow, dyed her auburn hair blonde, mixed with the *biznessmeni*, the new entrepreneurs, and moved adroitly from one bed to the next on a trajectory of hard-headed, even ruthless, upward mobility. These days there were lots of women like Lara in Moscow, available to men of means, men like Boris, but he had been attracted to her in an unusually strong way from the first moment he saw her. It was in a Moscow nightclub, one specializing in drugs and strippers, though Lara had been at the bar, fully clothed, as just one of many unattached female customers looking for a good time. Boris had given her that and more, lavished money and gifts on her, and within days she had become his regular mistress, which was why she was with him now. She was down there, on her knees, between his heavy, outspread thighs, working her magic. When she was done – or, more precisely, when he had come – she looked up with a warm, wicked smile, cleaning her lips with the same tongue that had excited him.

'That should keep you satisfied for a bit,' she said in Russian. 'We can go travelling now.'

'Yes,' he responded, also speaking in Russian while trying to get his breath back and let his spasms subside. 'That's what we're here for.'

'Ireland,' she said. 'First Paris and London, now Ireland. I can't believe this is happening.'

'The times have changed,' Boris told her, now breathing more evenly and pouring another tot of chilled vodka into his tiny glass. 'The old days have gone for good. When I was your age, I never thought I'd see the day. You wouldn't understand that.'

'Maybe I do, Boris. Certainly, never in my wildest dreams, did I ever imagine I'd have the freedom to come here. Not to Paris, not to London – not anywhere. So maybe I *do* understand.'

'Perhaps,' Boris said, though he didn't really believe it. She was only half his age and, despite her own hardships, which must have been considerable, she couldn't possibly comprehend what life in the former Soviet Union had been like. She would have been a child then, wrapped up in her child's world, not aware of anything outside it, protected from the deprivations and fears of communist rule. The world that she had matured in, the more liberated Russia, with its eager adoption of Western culture, its hedonism and freedom, its rock music, drugs and free sex, was a world she would have taken for granted. Men like Boris – certainly Russian men his age – could take *nothing* for granted.

'So are you feeling more relaxed now?' Lara asked him, still down on her knees. 'Are you ready to go?'

'Yes. Though we'll have to make a stop on our way to the airport. I have to talk to some people.'

'What people?'

'Our friends in Soho,' Boris said.

'Ah, yes, *those* friends.' Lara stood upright, a heavenly vision, her slim-waisted, broad-hipped body emphasized by the string bikini, her blonde hair framing perfect features and a steady, amoral, azure gaze, her full lips forming a slight smile that could have been mocking. Despite her possible mockery, she had the ability to take his breath away without doing a damned thing. 'Well?' she said in English.

'Well *what*?' Boris asked, also reverting to English, which he, like Lara, spoke almost perfectly.

'Shall I shower and get dressed?'

'*Da*,' Boris said, using the Russian word for 'Yes'. 'Give me a call when you're finished.'

'The sun's going down.' Lara frowned like an actress, less concerned than she looked. 'You should put your dressing gown back on before it turns cold.'

Boris nodded. 'Yes, I suppose I'd better wear something. Though in truth I rarely feel cold in this country.'

'You have the body heat of an animal,' Lara informed him. 'Slightly higher than normal.'

'I *am* an animal,' Boris said. 'We all are at bottom.'

Lara smiled and shook her head from side to side. 'Not me. I'm still human.' After picking his dressing gown off the floor, she threw it playfully over his head – like one of the hoods he had often used on his victims when blowing their brains out. '*Now* you're respectable,' Lara said. 'Maybe even more human. I'll give you a call when I'm finished.'

Boris listened to her footsteps padding into the apartment behind him, then he removed the dressing gown from his head and stood up to slip into it. After tightening the belt around his expanding waistline, his legacy of good living, he lit a cigarette, poured another glass of vodka and went to lean on the wall of the balcony, cradling his drink as he watched the sun descending, a white ball with yellow tendrils (this being the height of an unusually fierce summer), behind the high, renovated warehouses on the far side of the river. Like Moscow, London was changing rapidly, becoming addicted to anything 'New', amoral in its devotion to material success, its ruthless division of the populace into the 'haves' and the 'have nots'; and what Boris saw across the river illustrated that change. Brand new apartment blocks, vast towers of steel and glass, now soared arrogantly above those areas where the working classes had formerly slaved for poor wages in warehouses and sweatshops. Those workers had been forced out of the area long ago, their modest homes torn down, to make way for those new, luxurious apartment blocks and the nouveaux riches who dwelt in them.

The nouveaux riches of London and the New Russians of Moscow had a lot in common, notably their greed, and this was something that Boris, himself a greedy man, understood. Now, as he gazed across the river, watching darkness descend and the lights wink on in the numerous apartments to cast their lights on the black river, an inverted liquid sky filled with stars, Boris, feeling secure in this city that he could not have visited during the Soviet years, thought with gratitude of the collapse of the former Soviet Union and of the easing of travel restrictions throughout the European Community, which had enabled him and his *mafiya* friends to spread their nets far and wide.

During the 1990s, the Georgian gangs, of which Boris was one, and the Chechen *mafiya* had fought relentlessly, brutally, for control of organized crime in Moscow. An accommodation had, however, been reached between them in the year 2000 and now they were operating together as just one even more powerful *mafiya*. This rapidly expanding criminal organization was controlled by a committee of six men and Boris was one of the six. He was therefore a powerful man and, like a lot of men who had clawed their way from humble origins to the top, he was quietly proud of this fact.

About fifteen minutes after Lara had left the balcony, she called out to Boris, letting him know that the shower was free. Strolling back into the apartment, then the bedroom, he found her seated in front of the dressing table, stark naked, removing the plastic shower cap from her head and shaking her long blonde hair loose. Though almost instantly aroused by the sight of her, which was surprising, he felt, for a man of his age so soon after she'd brought him to orgasm, he entered the bathroom to have his shower. Once he had completed his ablutions, he returned to the bedroom to find Lara dressed in her standard travelling clothes of blue denims, open-necked shirt with a silk scarf dangling down its front, and flat shoes. Her blonde hair was pinned up on her head. Before they left, he knew, she would put on a light windcheater jacket with plenty of pockets. What she couldn't carry, in the pockets, she would carry in a leather shoulder bag. She was a practical lady.

'All set to go, I see,' Boris said in English as he started to dress himself.

'*Da*,' Lara replied as she slipped a cigarette between her full, sensual lips.

'Speak only English from now on,' Boris cautioned her.

'Okay,' she replied.

'I'll be out in five minutes.'

While Lara sat in the adjoining lounge, smoking her cigarette, Boris put on a light grey suit, a sky-blue shirt with a button-down collar, a flamboyant yellow-and-red patterned tie, and immaculately polished black patent-leather shoes. Before putting on the jacket of the suit, he strapped a flick knife in a quick-release holster to his right wrist: it was hidden when he put his jacket on. After checking that he had his passport and wallet, he went into the lounge to join Lara. She was sitting in a deep green leather armchair, her long legs crossed and shapely in the denims. When she saw him enter, she stubbed her cigarette out and stood to put on her light windcheater jacket and pick up her shoulder bag. Her smile was like dawn light.

'It's so nice to go travelling,' she said. 'Are we both ready to leave?'

'The suitcases are already in the car?'

'Yes. Mikhail took them down half an hour ago and he's waiting there for us.'

'Then let's go,' Boris said.

Leaving the apartment, they took the elevator down to the vast basement garage where they found Boris's chauffeur and personal bodyguard, Mikhail Kulinich, sitting patiently behind the driving wheel of a silver-grey BMW. Mikhail had a frail physique, the lean face of a starving poet, blue-grey eyes that would melt a mother's heart, and a total dedication to the *mafiya* and its bloodiest ways. The instant he saw Boris and Lara approaching, he jumped out of the car and hurried to open the rear door for them. When they were inside, he actually touched his forefinger to his forehead, just like an English chauffeur tipping his cap (Mikhail loved being in England and revered the English class system). Then he slipped back behind the steering wheel and drove them up out of the garage, into the soulless sweep of the high apartment blocks and empty roads that now filled Canary Wharf. Within minutes he was out of there and heading for the West End.

It was night-time. The city was awash in neon lights, choked with traffic and pollution, deafening if they had not been inside the car with its bulletproof metal body-work and double-glazed windows. Boris was grateful for those benefits since Britain, like Russia, was no longer a safe place and he had enemies everywhere. Gazing out of the rear window, feeling the reassuring pressure of Lara's fingers on his thigh, he saw the derelicts sitting on the pavements with their pitiful signs declaring I AM HOMELESS or I AM DYING FROM AIDS or I HAVE A MENTAL DISORDER AND MY HOSPITAL HAS BEEN CLOSED. The sight of them helped him appreciate just what he had in this inhospitable day and age when the poor died from lack of assistance while the rich, reaping the wealth that had once been channelled into welfare, grew richer and less concerned every day. Boris was, of course, fully aware of the fact that he, formerly a poor person, was now one of those crass exploiters. But, given his own background, not an easy one by any means, survival, whatever his personal moral reservations, was all that mattered to him.

Not that the roads were any safer than the pavements, filled as they were with biker gangs and hot-rodders who were notorious for cruising the evening streets to harass, rob and even kill anyone not to their taste, though most often they picked on people in Lamborghinis, BMWs and Mercedes-Benzes. Naturally, since he, Boris Vasilyovsky, was travelling through the West End in a BMW, he had good reason for concern, but he consoled himself with the knowledge that his chauffeur, Mikhail, was every bit as skilled and ruthless with defensive – and offensive – weapons as he, Boris, was. Ah, yes, survival was everything.

Having already been briefed on his first port of call, Mikhail made his way into Soho, where the traffic was insane, and parked illegally in Gerrard Street, propped up on the pavement between the high brick wall of the rear of a cinema and the road, thus blocking access to pedestrians. The neon-lit street was awash with the nouveaux riches and the derelicts begging from them as they entered and left the increasingly expensive Chinese restaurants. All of life, Boris thought, the good and the bad, was lived out on this one street. The world was full of such streets.

'You two stay here,' he said to Lara and Mikhail as he slipped out of the car. 'If I come out in what seems like a hurry, you, Mikhail, prepare to drive off and you, Lara, give me covering fire.'

'Right,' Mikhail said as Lara nodded affirmatively. 'No problem, boss.'

Boris turned away and crossed the road to where two Chinese youths, both wearing jeans and black leather jackets, were keeping watch outside a door set in the wall between two Chinese restaurants. The youths, Boris knew, were members of 'Jimmy' Lee Wong's fearsome Golden Dragon triad gang, which controlled Chinatown and other parts of London with extortion, protection rackets, prostitution, drugs and violent, appallingly brutal retribution against informers and other enemies. Boris's present task was to expand the *mafiya*'s own activities in all of those areas by gradually taking over triad territories in London, Manchester, Birmingham and Glasgow, and, ultimately, the former paramilitary territories, now gangster-controlled, in Northern Ireland. Now he was about to have a final talk with Jimmy Wong before flying to Belfast for talks with the new crime barons of that still troubled city. Wong's HQ consisted of a couple of rooms above the two restaurants and these young men were guarding him. When Boris stopped directly in front of them, they stared at him with flat, unfriendly eyes.

'I have an appointment with Mr Wong,' Boris said. 'The name's Boris Vasilyovsky.'

'Boris . . . *what*?' one of the young men said.

'Vasilyovsky,' Boris repeated patiently. 'It's a Russian name.'

'Oh,' the young man said. 'You have identification?'

Boris nodded, then silently withdrew his illicitly acquired EC driving licence and genuine Russian passport from his jacket pocket. The young man studied both items carefully. Then, after handing them back to Boris, he turned away to press the button on the intercom at the side of the door. When a distorted male voice responded with 'Yes?' the young man announced that Boris had arrived. 'Send him up,' the male voice said. When the intercom buzzed, the young man pushed the door open and bade Boris enter. Boris did so. The door was closed behind him. He walked up the narrow, dark staircase until he came to a brightly lit landing with rooms on either side. Another triad bodyguard was sitting on a chair on the landing, reading a Chinese newspaper, but when he saw Boris he put the paper down and stood up in front of him.

'Spread your legs and raise your arms in the air,' he ordered.

Boris did as he was told, though he only held his arms out to his sides, dead level, not above his head, to ensure that the sleeve of his jacket would not fall back and reveal the flick knife strapped to his right wrist. The bodyguard frisked Boris by running his hands around his body and legs, all the way up to the crotch, even under the armpits, but he didn't think to check his wrists. When the bodyguard had finished and was satisfied that Boris was unarmed, he jerked his head to the left.

'In there,' he said.

Boris entered the room to his left and found Jimmy Wong seated behind a large, cluttered desk. The room was bare except for lots of bookshelves, all stacked with thick, dusty files, probably unused these days since Wong had a computer on his desk and doubtless ran most of his business from it.

'Close the door and take a seat,' Wong said.

Boris closed the door behind him, then sat on the hard wooden chair in front of Wong's desk. A handsome man in his late thirties, Wong was dressed formally in a black suit with a white shirt and striped tie. His brown gaze was steady and direct, absolutely fearless, displaying neither malice nor warmth.

'Can I get you anything?' he asked.

'No,' Boris said. 'I'm fine. I'm on my way to the airport and I don't have much time.'

Wong sat back and clasped his hands under his chin. 'You're going away?'

'Only for a few days.'

Wong smiled bleakly. 'Ah, we're not getting rid of you.'

'No,' Boris said.

'Too bad. But we're still *hoping* to get rid of you.'

'I'm sure you are,' Boris responded. 'But I don't think you will.'

'If we have to, we will. The triads still control this city, my Russian friend, and don't make the mistake of thinking otherwise just because you've muscled in on our territory. That won't last too long.'

'We've only muscled in because you won't cooperate – and we'll stay there as long as we want to. However, it would be better for all concerned if we worked together. Surely you must see that, Mr Wong.'

'What I see is a bunch of Russian barbarians asking us to give up the territory we've been controlling for years. We don't need *mafiya* help. We're doing fine on our own, thanks. We've been here for years and we're staying here and you won't push us out. Try and you'll get more than you bargained for. Triads don't give up anything.'

'You don't *have* to give up anything. We can do more together, our strength doubled, than either of us can do alone. If we amalgamate as I suggest, we can, between us, become the most powerful criminal organization in the world. That's what the *mafiya* is aiming for. It's a logical step.'

Wong was unimpressed. 'Triad honour would not let us give up anything to anyone. As for your so-called logical step, if you think it's so logical, why not let the triads into Moscow on the same terms? Are you willing to do that?'

Boris smiled and shook his head from side to side. 'No, I don't think so. Once we let you in, you'd try to take control of everything and we can't allow that.'

Wong nodded affirmatively. 'And once we let *you* in, you'll try to take control of everything *we* own – and we can't allow *that*. Do you think we're fools, Mr Vasilyovsky?'

'No,' Boris said, 'I don't think you're fools. I just think you're misguided.'

'Not so misguided that we'd take the word of the *mafiya*. Not so misguided that we can't give you sound advice.'

'Which is?'

'Stop trying to muscle into our territories. If you persist, we'll simply wipe you off the map. This is no idle threat.'

Determined not to be intimidated, Boris deliberately

glanced at his wristwatch. Wong saw the gesture and smiled thinly. 'Ah, yes,' he said. 'You're on your way to the airport. So where are you going?'

'Northern Ireland.'

'You think you can do with those mad Paddies what you can't do with us?'

'Yes, I think so.'

'You're being foolish,' Wong said. 'Getting involved with those Irish bastards is always a mistake. Their peculiar way of mixing organized crime with politics and religion makes them unpredictable. If, like our triads and your *mafiya*, they stuck solely to crime for profit, we could, perhaps, read them more clearly. But too many of them are still motivated by sectarian hatreds, twisted patriotism and personal power-mongering – a confusing mixture that renders them unreliable. So if you *mafiya* want in there, you're welcome to it. We triads will stick to the mainland – and we don't want you on it.'

'We're here already,' Boris said, 'and we're not going to leave, so why not come to an accommodation with us, as I've just suggested?'

'I've already told you: we triads work only with our own kind. We deal only with Chinese. We've said "No" to you repeatedly, I'm saying "No" again now, and if you don't pull your men out of the West End, we'll make war against you.'

In fact, a war was already being waged between the *mafiya* and the triads because the Russian gangs had moved prostitutes and drugs into former triad strong-holds all over England and were also beginning to extract protection money from Chinese restaurants and other Chinese businesses. While this had not yet led to what could be termed an all-out war, it *had* been the cause of a lot of deaths on both sides – punishment and vengeance killings – and, in a couple of instances, to actual firefights between heavily armed *mafiya* and triad gangs. It was not Boris's intention to let the deaths of his own men deter him from his course, which was to turn the *mafiya* into the biggest, most powerful criminal organization in the world – bigger even than the original Mafia – by either amalgamating with or removing from his path competitors such as the triads and the former paramilitaries who were turning Belfast into a crime city. Belfast was his next stop, but right now, having already made inroads into triad territory, he fully intended completing what he had begun in London, no matter how extreme the measures required.

'We're not frightened of war,' Boris said. 'You already know of our reputation. If we don't get what we want, we'll just take it and to hell with your triads. If we have to do that, if you refuse to cooperate, we will indeed have a real war on our hands and it will be a *bloody* war.'

'My triads aren't afraid of shedding blood, even if it's their own. They're fanatically loyal to the organization and, therefore, to me. So long as I preside over the Golden Dragon, they will never give in to you.'

'Then we'll make you our first target,' Boris said. 'Cut off the head and the body withers. So we get rid of you and take over while your precious Golden Dragon is rudderless.'

Wong smiled and then unclasped his hands to spread them, palms upturned, in the air, as if making an offering. 'Then why should I let you leave this office alive?'

'Because you can't stop me.'

'No? I'm afraid you're mistaken. One word from me and the man sitting on that chair outside my office will blow your brains out.'

Boris made his move with shocking speed and efficiency, springing out of his chair, releasing his hidden flick knife by simply twisting his wrist and gripping its handle in the palm of his hand even as he flopped belly down across the desk and let the blade snap out. He cut Wong's throat from ear to ear with one quick, savage slash, then rolled to the side and off the desk before the blood spraying out of the triad boss's cut throat could splash his immaculate clothing. As Boris straightened up again, he saw Wong still sitting upright in his chair, a hand to his bloody throat, his eyes wide with shock, their light rapidly dimming as the blood poured out of him, spraying through his fingers to soak his clothing and form a dark pool on the desk.

Wong didn't fall. He died sitting up straight, He was, however, just about to topple sideways when Boris hurried around behind him, straightened him in the chair then pushed forward to jam the corpse between the chair and the edge of the desk, thus keeping Wong's body upright. That done, Boris padded across the room, opened the door and stepped out onto the landing where the bodyguard was still reading his Chinese newspaper. As the bodyguard lowered his paper to glance into the room where his boss was still sitting upright, though visibly dead and bloody, Boris stepped around and behind him, slashed his throat with another quick, expert movement, then grabbed him by the shoulder, held him in the chair, and lowered the chair backwards to the floor where he could die without making a sound.

Leaving the quivering, rapidly dying man on the floor, his blood spreading out around him, Boris checked his own clothing, was relieved to note that there wasn't a stain on it, then walked down the stairs and opened the front door. The two other bodyguards were still standing outside. They stared flatly at Boris as he stepped out between them, closed the door behind him and crossed the road to the parked BMW. Slipping into the rear of the car beside Lara, Boris glanced back across the road and saw that the unsuspecting bodyguards had already lost interest in him.

'How did it go?' Lara asked him.

'No problem at all,' Boris said, 'but we'd better get out of here. Get going, Mikhail.'

The chauffeur turned on the ignition, put the car into gear, made his way out of Soho's Chinatown, then drove on to Heathrow Airport.

Next stop: Belfast.

Chapter Three

He had reached the stage where he no longer knew if he was awake or simply dreaming. The darkness was total, the silence absolute. Pain was everywhere. His thoughts turned and glided, a series of fleeting images, linking the past to the present with no future in sight. He was losing his mind. At least, that was his greatest fear. To break the silence and return him to reality, he rattled his chains, banged his handcuffs on the stone floor, bellowed as loudly as he could, then fell backward, exhausted. He had lost track of time.

Hang in there, he told himself. *Don't let the bastards see you crack. Force yourself to think, to remember. Concentrate your thoughts. If you don't, you'll cave in.*

How many days had it been now? How often had they thrown him in here? This was his third time – no, his fourth – and they still hadn't broken him. Contempt was his best weapon. His rage at all the beatings. The pain was everywhere – in his arms, in his legs, across his back – where they had used their batons on him. This was not a soft prison, it was a new-style modern hell-hole, one of the many being built at great speed to house the growing number of criminals in a country where the gap between rich and poor was growing wider each day. He was one of those criminals, a former soldier turned bank robber, and they had punished him by trying to break his spirit, though they hadn't succeeded.

Not yet, he thought.

And thought of other things as well, trying to hold on to his senses, hearing the voices of his past in the silence of his head, haunted by the ghostly images of old friends and enemies: his wife Peggy, blonde and green-eyed, their two children, Don and Marilyn, ten and nine respectively (Jesus, when had he last seen them?); then the wardens, smirking at him, their faces flushed as they beat him up, saying, 'Take that, you cunt!' before throwing him into solitary, this black hole, for another period of hell. They were trying to break his spirit, though his contempt for them sustained him as he visualized them one by one, memorizing them for future reference, for possible vengeance, close encounters in a dark street. Then he gave way to sexual fantasies, first of himself and Peggy together in the days when it had worked, before the separation, her hard nipples and flat belly sweat-slicked against his own body, the soft slapping sounds of sex; then his string of other women, the blondes and the brunettes and the redheads and the blacks (Christ, what were their names?), followed by a variety of female movie and pop stars, those wet dreams for the masses, of whom he was one; then his own anguished moaning breaking the silence of the black hole's cold darkness.

Fuck them, he thought. *Fuck the bastards. They won't break me this way.*

It would have helped if he could have told just how long he had been in here, but his initial attempts to calculate passing time had long since collapsed. The darkness was so complete that he couldn't see a thing, could not count the scratches that he had started making on the wall, could not discern the difference between night and day.

He had hoped to do so with his meals, measuring the time by their regularity, but the guards had fucked that up by not being remotely regular and sometimes failing entirely to deliver meals. He was convinced too that they were trying to further disorient him by sometimes bringing him meals in the middle of the night or by following one meal with another after a few minutes while insisting that four hours had passed. So the calculation of passing time was now virtually impossible – and that, more than anything else, was what was likely to break him.

'So don't *let* it break you,' he said aloud, feeling the need to break the silence. 'They can't keep you here for more than a month; it's against the rules.'

Rules? he thought. What *fucking rules? They don't have rules in this prison. They threw away the book when they built it. You have no fucking* rights *here.*

He closed his eyes, replacing one darkness with another, and recalled the police smashing down his door and hauling him out of his bed. Luckily he'd been alone, no screaming woman to contend with, though the cops had given him a bad beating before hauling him out. They were the new-style cops, paramilitary cops, heavily armed and authorized to shoot to kill at their own discretion, which gave them a lot of edge. So he had offered no resistance, was allowed to remain in one piece, and got to court – without too many bruises – to be sentenced to ten years. He was not a model prisoner. Too much bottled-up anger. He'd only been here six months and in that time he'd been thrown in solitary three (or was it four?) times. He had taken everything the bastards had dished out and he still wasn't broken.

Suddenly, he heard footsteps and the jangling of heavy keys just outside his door. Jerking his head up, he saw the viewing hole in the door being opened, letting light in. Though it wasn't much, it almost blinded him, forcing him to close his eyes briefly. When he opened them again, he saw another pair of eyes framed in the viewing hole, then someone spoke to him. It was that bastard, Sergeant Warden Roy Adair.

'You okay in there?' he asked.

'Yeah,' Coogan replied.

'You've got a visitor,' Adair said. 'Stand up when I turn on the light, then turn your face to the wall.'

'What visitor?' Coogan asked. 'I thought I wasn't allowed any visitors.'

'This one's big,' Adair said. 'We just couldn't say "No" to him. Now stand up and face the wall.'

Adair switched the light on, dazzling Coogan again. Coogan blinked and rubbed his eyes with his fingers, letting them adjust to the light as he clambered to his feet and faced the stone wall of his damp, cold cell. His handcuffed hands were in front of him and his feet were chained together, so he couldn't move very much at all. Behind him, he heard the key turning in the lock, the bolt being withdrawn, then the steel door being pulled open on rusty, squeaking hinges. Sergeant Adair entered the cell and came up behind him.

'Turn around and face me,' Adair said.

Coogan did so. Adair, a barrel-chested man with red hair, steely blue eyes and a constantly flushed, angry-looking face, was staring straight at him. Adair was wearing the prison staff's standard jungle-green coveralls, had a Glock-19 handgun holstered at his waist, and was holding a wooden baton in his right fist. He was accompanied by a young guard also wearing green dungarees and armed with a Sterling Mk 4 sub-machine gun.

'What the fuck are you guys worried about?' Coogan said, rattling his chains. 'I'm not about to run anywhere.'

'Some animals can't be trained,' Adair replied, 'so we're taking no chances. You're going to the visitors' room, Coogan, so let's fucking move it.'

'I can hardly move with these chains on my ankles.'

'You can hop, skip and jump.'

'You fucking arsehole,' Coogan said.

Adair slammed him in the stomach with his baton, making Coogan double over, gasping for breath.

'Now hop, skip and jump,' Adair ordered.

Still gasping, Coogan shuffled out of his grim cell, then advanced by hopping along with his feet still chained together, his hands still handcuffed in front of him. His prisoner's overalls were filthy from the damp walls and floor of his cell and he knew that he stank from lack of hygiene. Not allowed to shave or comb his hair, he had a long beard and was otherwise altogether dishevelled.

As he advanced along the basement corridor, which had a low, curved brick roof and walk interrupted only by the solid steel doorways of other cells used for solitary confinement, he was prodded repeatedly, painfully, by the tip of Adair's wooden baton. The young guard, he noted, was keeping his sub-machine gun aimed at him. Coogan couldn't believe the stupidity of them. Here he was, hopping, skipping and jumping awkwardly in his chains and *still* they felt threatened by him. This knowledge made him feel better.

The corridor led to an elevator with an open door. Adair rammed his baton into Coogan's spine, causing him more pain and forcing him onward. Once he was in the elevator, Adair and the bodyguard followed him in. The lift began its descent as soon as the door closed.

'How come you've such fancy friends?' Adair asked of Coogan.

'Didn't know I had,' Coogan replied. 'You mean the one waiting to see me?'

'Yes.'

'Who is he?'

'You'll find out soon enough. But he's a fancy one, all right. More fancy than the likes of you deserve. God works in mysterious ways.'

The elevator came to a halt. Adair pressed the button to open the door. The guard stepped out first and turned back to aim his sub-machine gun at Coogan. Adair grabbed Coogan by the shoulder and practically dragged him out of the elevator, then brought the baton down hard across his shoulders, saying, 'Move your arse, you animal.'

Coogan's instinct was to swing around and smash his handcuffs into Adair's face, but he resisted it in the interests of self-preservation. Instead, he let himself be prodded along the short corridor that led to a ceiling-high gate of steel bars manned by another armed guard. At a nod from Adair, this guard punched the button that made the gate rise electronically, allowing access to a walkway that led across a vast rectangular four-storey hive of barred cells linked together by more walkways. As Coogan, prodded brutally onward by Adair under the watchful eyes of the armed guard, advanced awkwardly across the central walkway, the inmates of those four storeys of cells – murderers, rapists, cyberterrorists, common terrorists of all ethnic persuasions and diverse millennial psychopaths – started whistling, applauding and beating tin cans on the floors, paying tribute to someone whom they imagined was one of their own.

Despising them, Coogan ignored their racket as he hopped, skipped and jumped across the central walkway, his chains rattling and chafing his already bloody skin, until he had reached the far end. Coming off the walkway, he was faced with another short corridor that led to yet another solid steel door. This was, he knew, the entrance to the visitors' room. Prodded continually by Adair, he made his way to that door and then stopped in front of it. Another guard was seated on a wooden chair beside it, his sub-machine gun resting across his lap. At a nod from Adair, he pressed a button on the control panel fixed to the wall and the steel door made a loud clicking sound. Stepping around in front of Coogan, Adair pushed the door open and said, 'Get your shitty arse in there.' Coogan made his laborious way into the room that contained a lot of booths, each with a single chair, a toughened glass window and a two-way microphone that allowed contact between the prisoner and the visitor at the other side of the window. In the whole of that room, the size of a school classroom, there was only one visitor.

'That's him,' Adair whispered reverentially. 'Take the chair in that booth.'

Coogan hopped over to the booth and let Adair help him into the chair in front of the toughened glass window. Sitting on the other side of the window was a patrician gentleman with ageing matinée-idol good looks, dressed in a pinstripe suit and 'old school' tie and with a neatly folded white handkerchief sticking out of his breast pocket. He was smoking a filtered cigarette and smiling a slight, mocking smile. Coogan grinned back at him.

'Well, well,' Coogan said into the microphone, recognizing his old MI5 friend and occasional enemy Sir Daniel Edmondson. When in the Special Air Service (SAS), just before it had been disbanded, Coogan had been involved in a few covert missions, both on the mainland and in Northern Ireland, organized by Edmondson. He had good reason to respect the man's intelligence – and his ruthlessness. Edmondson, in his civilized way, could be worse than some criminals.

'My, my,' Edmondson replied sardonically, speaking into the microphone on his side of the window while shaking his head from side to side in histrionic despair. 'What on earth has happened to you, Coogan? You look an absolute . . . *mess.*'

'The amenities here aren't the best,' Coogan replied, deadpan. 'A man can't even get a cigarette.'

Edmondson glanced at the cigarette smouldering in his right hand, raised his eyebrows in mock surprise, then smiled, shrugged and exhaled a cloud of smoke against the glass on his side of the window. 'Sorry I can't help you, old boy, but even *I* can't break the rules here. I'm afraid you'll just have to suffer.'

'Yeah, right,' Coogan said. 'So what brings you here?'

Adair had taken up a position a few feet behind Coogan and was listening in on the conversation. Instead of replying to Coogan, Edmondson nodded at Adair and said, simply, 'Sergeant?'

Realizing that he wasn't wanted, Adair said, 'I'm not supposed to let the prisoner out of my sight, sir.'

'You can in this instance and *you will.* I'll call when I need you.'

Adair sucked his breath in, let it out in an angry sigh, then shrugged and turned away, nodding at the armed guard standing behind him. Both men left the room, leaving Coogan and Edmondson alone, facing each other through the toughened glass window. Perhaps as an act of mercy to Coogan, Edmondson stubbed out his cigarette, then folded his hands under his chin and smiled brightly.

'Good to see you again, Coogan,' he said.

'Is it?'

'Of course!'

'So what's the occasion?'

'How long have you been in here now, Coogan?'

'Six months.'

'With how many years to go?'

'Nine and a half.'

Edmondson clucked his tongue in sympathy. 'That's terrible, Coogan. By the time you get out, you'll be ready to be pensioned off. That's not the fate for a man like you.'

'Rob banks and get caught and that's your fate. A man takes his chances and pays his dues, so I'm not about to complain.'

'Still, Coogan, if you could get out, you'd take the opportunity, wouldn't you?'

'What does that mean? Is it some kind of offer or am I dreaming?'

'It could be an offer,' Edmondson said. 'Things aren't so good on my side of this window. These are desperate days.'

'What could be so bad that they'd let you spring me from this place? I can't credit this, Edmondson.'

'You don't even look excited,' Edmondson said, pretending to be hurt. 'I'm disappointed, Coogan.'

'Don't shit me,' Coogan replied. 'What the fuck is this, Edmondson? I'm not about to build up my hopes until I know the whole picture. Paint that picture for me.'

Edmondson sighed. 'All right,' he said. 'I will . . . It's Northern Ireland again.'

'Shit,' Coogan responded. He knew Northern Ireland well. In fact, his own problems had begun in Northern Ireland. He had robbed banks and post offices there, working for former paramilitaries who had turned to crime when the 'peace' came, leaving them unemployed and, worse, feeling unimportant. The gangsters of the province were the hardest men that Coogan had ever dealt with. Indeed, contemporary Belfast was, in his view, a murderous cesspit and he wanted no part of it. On the other hand, if it could get him out of this place . . . 'So what's happening there?' Coogan asked. 'I thought the Troubles were over.'

'They are,' Edmondson said. 'At least, politically speaking. But though the Troubles are over, the peace remains uneasy with neither side trusting the other. Even the individual paramilitary groups are divided amongst themselves, with some arguing for peace and others making wildcat attacks against their own kind in order to precipitate total breakdown. So while the peace is official, Northern Ireland remains a violent province – and our biggest headache.'

'You're telling me nothing new,' Coogan said.

'What's new,' Edmondson retorted, 'is that the hard men in the province, frustrated because they have nothing to do, are presently making contact with the Russian *mafiya*, which has recently emerged from Europe to spread its own kind of brutal crime throughout the British Isles.'

'The *mafiya* are even worse than the gangsters of Northern Ireland. Those fuckers are even worse than the Chinese triads.'

'Correct.' Edmondson sighed again. 'The *mafiya* are the worst of a rotten bunch. Which is why, for the past few years, we've been concerned by the extent of their infiltration into the criminal underworld of the mainland. However, we've just learnt, to our horror, that the *mafiya*, growing more powerful and ambitious every day, has been in touch with former Belfast terrorists, Catholic *and* Protestant, with a view to amalgamating with them to form between them the biggest, most ruthless criminal gang in Europe.'

Coogan gave a low whistle of appreciation. 'That's some thought,' he said.

'Isn't it?' Edmondson responded tartly. 'I mean, the

mafiya have already turned the streets of our major cities into battle zones with their ongoing bid to take over triad territories. Right now, to have a meal in Soho's Chinatown is to risk life and limb. Customers of uncooperative restaurants have been sliced up with machetes, some restaurants have been firebombed, and gang members on both sides are being shot down in the streets. So, naturally, the very thought of the *mafiya* in Northern Ireland gives us the shivers.'

'"Us" being the British government.'

'Correct,' Edmondson said. He reached into his jacket pocket to find his packet of cigarettes, then, perhaps in deference to Coogan, changed his mind. 'Even worse,' he continued, 'according to our sources, this dangerous link-up between the *mafiya* and the former paramilitaries in Northern Ireland is to be sealed by the handing over to the Russians of at least half the vast number of IRA and Prod weapons that were never surrendered to the British government. It is, further, our belief that this link-up – and the handing over of the weapons – is due to take place at an unknown location in the province only six weeks from now. We simply can't let that happen.'

'Does this mean what I think it means?' Coogan asked, allowing himself a little hope at last and being rewarded.

'Yes,' Edmondson said. 'We want you to go in there and ensure that the link-up never happens, if necessary by neutralizing the major figures proposing it.'

'Why me of all people? I am, after all, a convicted criminal, doing eight-to-ten. Why not someone already on the outside?'

'A couple of reasons,' Edmondson said. 'One: we don't want the results of this operation to be traceable back to the British government, so it has to be absolutely covert. Two: when you were in the SAS, before the regiment was disbanded, you were one of the best men they had; you also worked undercover in the province – so you know it well. Three: when the SAS was disbanded and you turned to post office and bank robberies, you pulled most of your jobs in Belfast under the wing of the very paramilitaries we're now so concerned about. In other words, you know the men in question, you know how they think, and you also have a personal motive in seeing at least one of them put down.'

'A *personal* motive?'

'Yes.'

'What the fuck would that be?'

'Pat Tolan.'

Coogan knew Tolan. A hard man. The hardest of the hard. Formerly an IRA paramilitary, Tolan had turned to organized crime with the coming of peace and, when Coogan had known him, had been into bank and post office robberies, drugs, protection rackets, extortion, money laundering, and the sale of arms obtained illic- itly from former paramilitaries and British soldiers to overseas criminals and terrorists. Coogan knew Tolan because it was Tolan whom he had originally worked for when the SAS was disbanded and he, like a lot of other prematurely retired troopers, found himself unemployable and had turned to crime out of boredom *and* financial necessity. Having spent so much time in the province doing undercover work for the 14th Intelligence Group before the coming of peace, Coogan knew Belfast like the back of his hand, knew which of the hard men had turned to organized crime, and knew that it was easier to get away with crime in that troubled city than it was anywhere else in Europe. So Coogan, when he had decided to use his specialist SAS skills for criminal purposes, had taken himself off to Belfast, had got in touch with the most powerful criminal there, Pat 'Paddy' Tolan, and had spent a couple of post-millennium years robbing post offices and banks with his assistance, then letting him launder the stolen money. Eventually, however, Coogan had been arrested by the Special Branch and had ended up in this English prison. Clearly Tolan was still a free man and doing well for himself.

'He's still in charge of the Belfast gangs?' Coogan asked.

'Protestant *and* Catholic,' Edmondson replied. 'In charge of the whole show and growing more powerful every day. If you bother him, you get eliminated. It's as simple as that.'

'He's still as ruthless as ever, then?'

'Ruthless beyond belief,' Edmondson said. 'Only a few days ago, he put the fear of God into the hearts of everyone under him by making an example of Frank Murphy. Murphy's only sin was that he was selling drugs for Tolan and systematically fiddling his books to keep more of the profit than he should have done. To punish him – and also to make an example of him to anyone else considering a similar foolishness – Tolan slaughtered Murphy and his wife and three kids, then burned their house down with them in it. He only did this after nailing Murphy's feet to the floor and forcing him to watch his wife and kids die.'

'Jesus!' Coogan exclaimed automatically, genuinely disgusted.

'Naturally, as usual, we have no solid proof to pin on him – only the word of our reliable tout – but the word is that Murphy supervised the foul deed himself. So, yes, he's in charge of all the gangs and, as you can gather from my tasty story, he rules with an iron fist.'

'Well,' Coogan said, 'given my knowledge of Tolan as well as what you've just told me, I certainly have no doubts that if the *mafiya* want to amalgamate with the former paramilitaries, Tolan is the one they'll have to approach first . . . But why would I want to neutralize him? I mean, the guy just employed me.'

'And shopped you,' Edmondson said.

'What?'

'You know damned well that someone had to have shopped you in order for the RUC to arrest you and get that conviction. You just didn't know who was behind it because the RUC's source was kept secret and the evidence was given behind closed doors. That is, of course, strictly speaking, illegal, but we do things in the province that we'd never be permitted to do here.'

'I'll *bet* you do,' Coogan said.

Edmondson grinned and shrugged. 'Life isn't always a birthday cake.'

'But you're sure it was Tolan who shopped me?'

'Absolutely. You and he were having a few disagreements, as I recall from the evidence, with Tolan demanding more of your profits for his assistance and money laundering, which made you accuse him of exploiting you. This reached a head when you more or less told him to go to hell and then started robbing banks in his territory without paying the great man his dues. It was shortly after the second such robbery that the RUC broke into your flat in Belfast and hauled you off to the brig. That was Tolan's doing.'

Thinking about it, Coogan realized that it had to be true. No one else in Belfast would have possessed the knowledge needed for him to be arrested successfully and subsequently imprisoned. Also, it was indeed true that he and Tolan had fought bitterly those last few months and that Tolan, when Coogan had said he was going it alone, had threatened to put a stop to him. At the time, Coogan had taken that as a threat of violent retribution and had, accordingly, kept on his guard thereafter. What he had not anticipated or been prepared for, however, was the possibility of Tolan, himself a master criminal, shopping him to the Special Branch. Now the knowledge that Tolan had done so filled him with a quiet but all-consuming rage.

'Okay,' he said. 'You've just given me two motives. One is to get the fuck out of here; the other is to get that bastard Tolan. When do I do it?'

'Immediately,' Edmondson said. 'I've come here with the necessary papers and you can walk out of here an hour from now.'

'Because we only have six weeks,' Coogan said, 'before the paramilitaries hand over their pile of illicit weapons to the *mafiya*.'

'Exactly. And it's our belief that the *mafiya* will then use those weapons, not only for more crime in the province, in cahoots with the paramilitaries, but also to engage in an all-out war against the triads of London. If that happens, all hell will break loose, causing a public scandal and possibly even bringing down a government already in great disfavour with the electorate because of the escalating crime wave. So you walk out of here an hour from now and, yes, then you have just six weeks.'

'What about the *mafiya*?' Coogan asked him.

'The man you'll be looking for – and he too has to be neutralized – is Boris Vasilyovsky. If anything, he's even harder than Tolan. It's Vasilyovsky who's been personally responsible for bringing the *mafiya* into the EC and for starting a war with London's triad community. With regard to the kind of amalgamation that he's planning in Northern Ireland, we believe that he's already tried to get a similar deal with the triads and been roundly rejected, since the triads only work with their own kind.'

'What makes you think he approached the triads?'

'Because we've had him under surveillance and he's made quite a few visits to Jimmy Lee Wong, the leader of the Golden Dragon group in Soho, even as his men and Wong's men were cheerfully slaughtering each other. A couple of days ago, however, Wong abruptly vanished and four buildings known to be owned by the *mafiya* – a casino, a nightclub and two restaurants, all in the West End of London – were firebombed in what appear to have been vengeance attacks by the triads. According to one highly reliable source, Wong was, in fact, killed in his own office by Boris Vasilyovsky and the triads, not wishing the police to be involved, simply spirited his corpse away and then launched a war of vengeance against the London *mafiya*. So now, more than ever, Vasilyovsky needs those paramilitary weapons. If he gets them, we don't doubt for a second that the streets of London – *and* other British cities where the triads have a presence – will be turned into war zones.'

'Where's Vasilyovsky right now?'

'He flew to Belfast a couple of days ago in the company of his Russian mistress Lara Tokhonova and his driver and bodyguard Mikhail Kulinich.'

'Where's he staying in Belfast?'

'The Europa Hotel, though we suspect, if he remains over there for an extended period – say, until the para-military weapons are handed over – he'll move into a more secure private residence.'

'So what's our deal?'

'A complete, albeit unofficial, pardon that will remain in force as long as you don't talk. The *official* line will be that you traded information for your freedom and were placed under a Witness Protection Programme at a secret location in Australia, where you'll remain for the rest of your life. This official line will be spread far and wide, including throughout Belfast, to ensure that it reaches Tolan's ears. Meanwhile, you'll be inserting yourself covertly into that very city in order to carry out your task.'

'Do I get any help?'

'False identification papers and a Belfast bank account which will be opened by us in your false name.'

'Limitations?'

'Once you're in Belfast, we'll wash our hands of you – total deniability – so we can hardly impose limitations. Just do what you have to do.'

'And if I fail?'

'Assuming you're still alive, we'll seek you out and throw you back in here. You'll do the whole ten years, Coogan.'

Coogan smiled. 'I should have expected that. So what's the drill when I walk out of here?'

Edmondson withdrew a key from his jacket pocket and handed it to Coogan. 'That's the key to a bank deposit box somewhere in central London. The number of the box is shown on the key. In the box, you'll find money – a lot of it, all in cash – and details of a West End hotel where you can stay until you're ready to leave for Belfast. You'll also find your false-identity papers, a new passport, bank books and everything else you'll need for your six weeks in the province, including up-to-date dossiers on Tolan and Vasilyovsky. No weapon. We can't risk you being searched while entering Belfast. Once there, you'll have to find what you need as best you can – I'm sure you know all the sources – and in general play the whole thing by ear. Once there, as far as we're concerned, you no longer exist. Do you have any more questions?'

'I don't think so,' Coogan said.

Edmondson smiled. 'Be a good boy until you get out of here,' he said. 'Don't aggravate anyone.' He pressed his foot on the buzzer switch on the floor, letting Adair know that he was finished. Seconds later, the exit door opened and Adair and the armed guard walked in, the guard automatically aiming his sub-machine gun at the still seated, still heavily chained Coogan. Adair advanced across the room and stopped beside Coogan's chair. 'Take this man back to his cell,' Edmondson said with a deliberate display of chilly authority. 'Thank you and goodbye.' Then he pushed his chair back, stood, turned away and left the room by the front door.

'Some fucking friends you've got,' Adair said flatly when the front door had closed behind Edmondson. 'Okay, back on your feet.'

Coogan stood upright, moving awkwardly in his chains, and Adair made him hop, skip and jump all the way back to his black hole of a cell in the solitary-confinement wing.

'Get in there, you fucking animal,' Adair said, slamming Coogan in the spine with his baton, causing pains to dart through him, and pushing him forward with his free hand. 'Fancy friends or no fancy friends,' he added with relish as Coogan hit the cold, damp stone floor and rolled over onto his back, 'you're going to turn *into* a fucking animal before you get out of here. Have sweet dreams, you lump of shite.'

When the cell door had closed behind him, wrapping him once more in total blackness and silence, Coogan huddled up on the floor and closed his eyes, again replacing one darkness with another.

One hour to freedom, he thought. *This time let's make it permanent. Either that or die trying.*

An hour later, Coogan walked out of the prison, a free man again.

Chapter Four

'This could be the big day for us all,' Tolan said enthusiastically to his second-in-command Bobby Meehan, as they drank pints of stout in a private room above a pub in the lower Falls with some of their men. 'Tying up with the *mafiya* could really make us unbeatable when it comes to conflicts with the RUC and the British authorities. It could remove all limitations from our planned expansion, so I say it's a good thing.'

'I'm not so sure,' Meehan replied. He was a small, stocky man with red hair, ice-bright blue eyes and lips that formed a thin, straight line. He had never been known to smile at anyone. 'As things stand, we take orders from no one, we answer only to ourselves, and we don't have to look over our shoulders. Why spoil this by inviting someone else in?'

'Because no matter how easy it is for us at the moment,' Tolan explained, 'we're still limited to the six counties – and the *mafiya* can help us go worldwide. I mean, those bastards are all over the fucking place – not only in Russia, which is now practically run by them – but in every country in the EC, in the Balkans and now even in Sicily and Italy, where they've even got the original Mafia on the run. If you can't beat 'em, join 'em, I say. Let's grow as they grow.'

'We can grow without them,' Jack Delaney said. He was over six feet tall, huge in every respect and still believed, despite all evidence to the contrary, that he was at war with the Orangemen and the Brits. Crime, according to him, had nothing to do with it. 'We can tighten the knot we've already tied around the Dublin underworld and gradually take over this whole country – and we can do it without the help of the *mafiya* or any other outsiders.'

'Right,' Sean O'Hagan added, scratching at his thin, acne-pitted face with dirty fingernails and exhaling smoke from his cigarette. 'We're all Irish here. What the fuck do we know about Russians? What do the Russians know about us? I say we stick to our own kind and we'll continue to do all right.'

'Yeah, we can trust our own kind,' Jack Delaney said. 'Or, if we can't exactly *trust* them, we can at least *understand* 'em and guess what they're likely to do, then act accordingly. We won't be able to do that with the Russians. Those boyos are as alien to us as Martians would be. They're impossible to read and unpredictable, so my thumb remains down on this one.'

'Anyway,' Meehan said. 'Your Russian friend, this Boris whatsisname—'

'Vasilyovsky.'

'Yeah, right . . . The word's out on the grapevine that he tried to make a similar deal with the London triads, an amalgamation with them, and was turned down flat. If the triads don't want to join up with the *mafiya*, why should we?'

'That's just hearsay,' Tolan said, starting to feel annoyed by their lack of enthusiasm for his proposal. 'We *don't know* that he approached the triads and, if he did, we don't know if he was actually refused. I mean, come on, boyos! If they agreed to get together, they'd hardly advertise it to the worldwide media, would they?'

'They approached the triads and they were turned down,' Meehan, always a hard-head, insisted. 'We can take that as fucking read. The word's out that the last person to see Jimmy Lee Wong alive was your friend, Boris . . . whatsisname . . . who visited him a few times in London, obviously to discuss *some* kind of deal, and who certainly paid him a visit a week ago. That's when Wong disappeared – approximately a week ago. And while the official line is that Wong has simply gone undercover, it's pretty well known throughout the London underworld that he was found in his office in Soho with his throat slashed from ear to fucking ear – and that the last person to visit him in that office was your good friend Boris. Now, as we all know, the triads of London have gone on a rampage against that city's Russian *mafiya* – clearly for revenge. So do we want to get involved in all that shite with the very people who caused it?'

'Ackay, we do,' Tolan said. 'Because the biggest threat to our own organization is the triads.'

'How come?' Sean O'Hagan asked, being none too bright.

'The triads have already shown an interest in the growing drug trade over here,' Tolan explained, 'and they'd certainly be interested in expanding their extortion and protection rackets in Belfast. So the Russians, whether knowingly or not, have done us a big favour by getting rid of Lee Wong and giving the triads something else to think about. My thought, then, is that we *should* make this link-up with our Russian friends and work with them until we decide that we no longer need them.'

'Until we no longer *need* them?' Meehan asked doubtfully.

'Yeah, right,' Tolan said with relish.

'What does *that* mean?' Meehan asked.

'What it means,' Tolan said, 'is that we work with

the *mafiya* until we're set up, with their help, in the EC and their other major territories. Once we're well established there, we can drop the fuckers and go it alone. More immediately, though, they're desperate for weapons to use in an all-out war against the triads and we're gonna give them the weapons they need as part of our deal with them. So we simply give them the weapons, then sit back and let them fight it out with the triads. When they've put down the triads, we can make inroads into the London underworld and spread out from there. Eventually, growing stronger as we expand, we'll reach the stage where we can drop the *mafiya* altogether.'

'Pretty fucking neat,' Meehan said, 'except for one thing.'

'What's that?' Tolan asked him.

'Once you make a deal with the *mafiya*,' Delaney said, 'you won't be able to drop 'em that easily. I mean, those fuckers don't like to be messed around with. They like to keep what they have.'

'Right,' Meehan affirmed.

'Ah, for Christ's sake, lads . . .' Tolan interrupted himself long enough to have another slug of his stout and wipe his lips with the back of his jacket sleeve. 'No one likes to give up what they have – sure, aren't we the same that way? – but we won't break away from the Russians until we know that we're strong enough to tackle them without too many worries. Believe me, boyos, that day will come – and when it does, when we turn against the *mafiya*, when we beat 'em, which we will, we'll take over their territories, recruit what's left of their members, and become the biggest thing on the fucking planet – even bigger than the Italians and Sicilians. We can do it, believe me.'

His friends glanced at one another, clearly nervous about his theory, not certain that they should tie up with the *mafiya*, let alone plan to turn against them one day – which could be suicidal.

'So when do we meet the Russian?' Meehan eventually asked Tolan, breaking the silence.

'This afternoon,' Tolan told him. 'Two o'clock this afternoon in his room in the Europa Hotel. He arrived in Belfast this morning.'

'Seven days to the day that Jimmy Lee Wong had his throat cut,' Meehan said. 'Time to wash the fucking blood off his hands.'

They all laughed at that one. 'Yeah, right,' Sean O'Hagen said. 'He can come to us with nice clean hands and his Russian gaze poetic and all innocent, like.'

'You've got it,' Delaney said to O'Hagen. 'That's his ticket, all right. So,' he said, turning to Tolan, 'who goes to the meeting?'

'Me and Meehan here. You two stay down in the lobby and keep yer eyes peeled.'

'You think he's brought some watchdogs?'

'No, I don't think so, though he might bring some later.'

'What makes you think he hasn't brought some with him?' Delaney asked.

''Cause we already have the Europa under surveillance and our boyos saw Vasilyovsky arrive – him and some blonde doll and a chauffeur. There was no one else.'

'What kinda car did they arrive in?' Meehan asked.

'A BMW,' Tolan said.

'The car companies at Belfast City Airport don't rent out BMWs,' the sharp Meehan reminded him. 'That means he must have had someone waiting for him here in Belfast – either a helpful local or one or more of his own men sent on ahead of him.'

'Jesus,' Tolan said, at once admiring and resenting

Meehan's intelligence, 'I'll admit, I never thought of that, boyo.'

'So he *could* be here with some of his cowboys,' Delaney said.

'Right,' Meehan said. 'So while Tolan and I talk to this Boris whatsisname, you three will stay down in the lobby and keep yer eyes peeled.'

'Will do, boss,' O'Hagen said.

'Okay,' Tolan said, satisfied with how the meeting had gone and pleased that there were no more arguments against his proposal, 'let's make our way slowly down to the Europa, dropping in here and there on the way to shake a few hands or rap some knuckles. We should have enough to do to keep us busy until two o'clock. So finish yer drinks and let's go.'

He led the way by knocking back the rest of his own pint, sighing with pleasure, then wiping his wet lips with his jacket sleeve while kicking his chair back and climbing to his feet. The rest did the same, hastily finishing their drinks and then following him down the stairs, out through the busy pub and along the lower Falls Road, heading in the direction of the Grosvenor Road in the grey light of an overcast morning, an unseasonably chill wind blowing fiercely. While pretending to modesty, Tolan secretly enjoyed the recognition he always received, either respectful or fearful, when walking along the Falls with his entourage, past furniture shops, video shops, betting shops, fruit-and-vegetable shops, off-licences, churches, clubs and social halls, many of which looked as grim now as they had during the Troubles. Tolan, however, did not see the place as grim, he viewed it as the vibrant centre of his expanding criminal empire, which he ruled with an iron fist.

To some of those he knew personally, either house-wives out shopping or unemployed men loitering around pubs and bookies, he either gave a nod of recognition or called out friendly greetings. To others he was distinctly chilly, letting them know that they were in his bad books and keeping them on edge because they didn't quite know what they'd done wrong and so had to wonder what their fate might be if he decided to punish them. Many a man would have nightmares at the very thought of Tolan's punishments (the kneecappings and batterings with baseball bats; the breeze-blocks heaped on the belly; the burnings with lit cigarettes; the temporary cruci-fixions, hands nailed to pool tables or walls) and those nightmares, Tolan knew, would be enough to keep them in line. In other cases, however, the punishments were not imaginary and were, indeed, dispensed on the spot, as it were, when Tolan deemed them necessary. Now, as he worked his way through the late morning and early afternoon, checking on his various business enterprises, his mood swung between pleasure and rage, with pun-ishments meted out to those who provoked his wrath.

You couldn't trust anyone. Tolan had learnt this during the Troubles, when betrayals were commonplace and dirty deeds were practised on all sides. He knew it to be true when he entered Tom Slattery's video rental shop by the back door and found Tom, who rarely served in the shop, leaving that task to his weary wife, hastily doing his sums at the kitchen table. Almost bald and always looking like a startled rabbit, Slattery was in the dark ages when it came to running his business and still used an old-fashioned hardback ledger book instead of a computer. He was scribbling into that ledger book when Tolan stomped in with his three hard men. Slattery looked up in surprise, not having expected them, then started sweating immediately.

'Tolan!' he exclaimed, his quavering voice revealing his fear. 'I wasn't expecting you. Is this—?'

'No, it's not fucking Thursday,' Tolan said. 'It's only Wednesday, you dumb fuck. But someone whispered in my ear, so I thought I'd come a day earlier before you got a chance to cook your books. Let me look at that ledger.'

With sweat popping out on his high forehead, Slattery gave his ledger book a fearful glance, then looked up at Tolan. 'Cook the books? What are ya talkin' about, Tolan? Sure, I've never cooked the books in my life. I swear on my mother's grave.'

'Your fucking mother isn't dead,' Tolan said. 'Now let me look at that ledger book.'

'I haven't finished yet,' Slattery insisted. 'The figures won't make sense to you 'cause I haven't finished yet. Why not . . . I mean . . . Like, why not come back in an—'

'I'm not coming back in a fucking hour, that's for sure,' Tolan said. 'Now let me look at that book.' He snatched the ledger book off the table and stood there, thoughtfully perusing it, moving his lips as he counted silently, seeming to take for ever, letting Slattery sweat even more and gradually start visibly trembling. Finished with his reading, satisfied that he had been short-changed, Tolan slammed the ledger book shut, then swung it viciously at Slattery's head. The hard edge of the book split Slattery's temple open and propelled him sideways off the chair, blood spurting from the deep cut.

'Fucking thieving cunt!' Tolan bawled, then started kicking Slattery as the man huddled like a foetus on the floor, knees pulled up to his chin, arms folded over his face. 'Take that, you wee shite!'

'No! Please!' Slattery cried out piteously. 'No, Tolan! Please don't!'

Tolan kicked him once more, breaking a couple of ribs,

extracting a cry of anguish. Then he turned away in disgust and said to Meehan, 'Get rid of the customers, send his missus back in here, close the front door, take whatever you find in the till, then make a mess of the shop. You stay here, O'Hagan.'

'Right,' Meehan said. Then he and Delaney left the kitchen and entered the shop that had originally been the front lounge of the house. Looking down at the kitchen floor, Tolan saw Slattery crawling towards the back door on his hands and knees, still sobbing piteously and dripping blood. 'Pick that stinking turd off the floor,' Tolan said to O'Hagan, 'and put him back in that chair.' O'Hagan did as he was told. Once Slattery was in the chair, wiping blood from his cut temple and sniffing back his tears, Tolan slapped his face and said, 'I know you don't put yer money in the bank, so where the fuck *do* you hide it?'

Slattery opened his mouth to speak but was distracted by a woman's screaming emanating from the shop out front, followed by the sounds of video cases and cassettes being swept off the shelves and onto the floor. 'Get yer fuckin' hands off me,' Slattery's wife said defiantly as she was propelled through the kitchen door and came to a halt beside the kitchen table, where she saw her bloody, terrified husband, with Tolan and O'Hagan looming over him. 'You dumb bastard!' Mrs Slattery snapped at her husband. 'Have you been fiddlin' the books again? Christ, if these two don't do you in, sure I'll do it m'self.'

'Please!' Slattery sobbed, gazing wide-eyed at Tolan. '*Please*, Tolan, I—'

'Where do you hide your money?' Tolan said to Mrs Slattery, who was fat and ugly and aggressive. 'Either tell me or I'll chop your face to shreds with that fucking bread knife.'

'Which wouldn't make the bitch less ugly,' O'Hagan said, with a wide, evil grin.

'Jesus!' Mrs Slattery said, more outraged than fearful, walking away from the table to open the door of a wall cupboard and pull down a battered biscuit tin. 'Jesus Christ!' She handed the tin to Tolan and said, 'Whatever that dumb bastard stole, it'll be in there. But leave me at least enough to get me through the next week and let me put the shop back in order. He won't do it again, I promise you that, Mr Tolan.'

'Good woman,' Tolan said, taking the tin off her, opening it and withdrawing the thick stack of banknotes that he found inside. After counting the notes, he took a decent amount and put it back in the tin, which he handed back to Mrs Slattery. 'This is for you,' he said. 'Not for him. The next time, if we catch him at any nonsense, we'll firebomb the whole place.'

'You won't have to,' Mrs Slattery said. 'I'll make sure of that, if I have to kill this dumb bastard m'self.'

'Good woman,' Tolan repeated. Then he looked down at the trembling, sweating Slattery and said, 'You hear that, Slattery? Even your wife thinks you're a fuckin' bin-lid. You ever try to cheat me again; it'll be the last time. Okay, boyos, let's go.'

Delaney and Meehan had returned from the shop, which they had thoroughly trashed, and so, with an appreciative nod to Mrs Slattery, Tolan led them out of the premises, once again by the rear door. When they were back in the Falls, they continued on their journey, interrupting it each time they passed a pub that was paying them protection money, this being the day when they collected it. Most barkeepers paid up and were meticulous about it, fearful of Tolan's punishments. But occasionally, as with Slattery, Tolan found barkeepers trying to fiddle him out of some cash by understating their takings. In each such instance Tolan and his boyos made the culprit pay the price, either by wrecking the bar completely or by smashing up the tables while the customers were actually sitting at them, thus discouraging them from returning to those particular premises. This ensured, obviously, future damage to the owner's business.

In another case, they found a former dicker (one of the teenage youths who had kept watch for the security forces during the Troubles), now thirty years old and jobless, selling skag without Tolan's permission. So they marched him up an alley, took the skag off him, then held him against a brick wall while Meehan, who particularly enjoyed this kind of thing, fired a 9mm bullet from a silenced Glock-19 handgun into his left kneecap, causing him considerable pain while leaving him free to hobble on his right leg back to the Falls and, with luck, a passing taxi that would convey him for treatment to the nearby Royal Victoria Hospital.

In yet another instance, down near the bus station and international airport terminal, they found an ice-cream vendor who had set his van up there without clearing it with Tolan first. When they tried to discuss this with the vendor, he told them to piss off, so Tolan's men entered the van by the rear door before the vendor could lock it. Meehan and Delaney instantly attacked the man with their fists, hammering away at him in that cramped space while O'Hagan closed the side of the van, then unzipped himself and urinated into each of the urns of ice cream in turn. By this time, having been kicked on the shins and kneecaps as well as battered by the fists of his two assailants, the unfortunate vendor was stretched out on the floor, at the base of the ice-cream urns, bleeding profusely from his nose and ears, so Meehan and Delaney unzipped themselves and urinated over him as well. Only when the three men had zipped themselves up again and left the van did Tolan enter the vehicle to lean down over the bloody, urine-soaked, shivering vendor and say, 'You have till Friday to come and have a talk about how much you're to pay on a weekly basis. If I don't see you, I'll come looking for you. I'll be off now. God bless.'

For the most part, however, they had an easy morning of it and were able to stop just before 1.00 p.n for an hour's lunch break. Lunch consisted of soup, Irish stew and Guinness in a booth in the Crown Liquor Saloon in Great Victoria Street, opposite the Europa Hotel. With its Victorian gaslights, mahogany and stained-glass doors, ornamented woodwork and tiles, the pub was now a leading tourist attraction and so always busy at lunchtime. But Tolan and his boyos were early enough to get a booth which, with its closed doors, gave them the privacy they needed for their crack.

'Christ,' O'Hagan said in fake disgust as they commenced their lunch, 'this is soup you could top a battery with.'

'That's why I'm not having it,' Delaney replied. 'This stew will do fine.'

'Nothing wrong with the soup,' Meehan said, spooning his up with relish, 'so I don't know why you're complaining. But sure I thought you were the kind who could eat a tomato through a tennis racket. You could eat your own cock, like.'

'I've never tried,' O'Hagan replied, 'though I *do* like Ma's sausages.'

'Say, boyos,' Tolan interjected between mouthfuls of Irish stew, having already polished off his soup, 'do ya remember the times when our kind wouldn't have dared to come in here, when this was a Prod place? The times have changed right enough.'

'Sure we're all in the same boat now,' Delaney said. 'All

left unemployed by the peace plan, Prods and Catholics alike, and now just in it for what we can get out of it. When you're betrayed by your own kind – that fuckin' peace plan – then what else can ya do? Sure you sleep with the enemy.'

'They're sleepin' with us,' Tolan said. '*That*'s for fucking sure. Out there in the bar, for instance, is that quare bastard, Bobby King, who used to be a leading light in the UVF and was responsible for more atrocities against us than you can count with a fucking calculator. I'd still like to kill the cunt, but we can't do without him now, since he's the one liaising between us and the English gangsters that supply the skag we sell in the streets. Yeah, we're all in the same bed now.'

'At least we're all Irish,' Meehan said, as solemn as always, 'which is more than we can say for the bastards we're about to have talks with.'

'Stop it now,' Tolan said with a grin. 'Sure don't we all know you're a wee racist, Meehan, who has no time for anyone but yer own. When it comes to the Prods, I can understand it; but the Russians are different.'

'How?' Meehan asked.

'Sure they've no particular grudge against us, like the Prods have despite their big Orange smiles, and their only ideology is money, which should make them straightforward to deal with. The fucking Prods, now, they're shining prisms of treachery, though we need them right now. If we snuggle up tight to the Russians, the day might come when we can not only get rid of our Prod brethren – it's an unnatural marriage, like – but actually crush them out of existence and then take over the whole friggin' country, including down south. Sure you can only do that if you're as big as we'll be when we amalgamate with the *mafiya*. Think of it that way, Bobby, and you'll feel better when we cross that road to have our wee talk. So let's finish our grub and get to it. Sure I can't wait to meet them.'

Thirty-five minutes later, with their lunch finished and a lot of lively crack shared, they left the pub and crossed the traffic-heavy, windblown road to the Europa Hotel. Entering the building, the most frequently bombed in the world, they scanned the spacious, modern lobby, trying to ascertain if Boris Vasilyovsky had any of his men planted there amongst the genuine clientele.

'That fucker doesn't look Irish,' O'Hagan said, gazing at a portly middle-aged man in a grey suit with shirt and tie, standing near the stairs that led up to the Gallery Bar.

'How the fuck would you know?' Meehan responded brutally. 'Sure you've never left this country in your fucking life and wouldn't know what a foreigner looks like.'

'He's a stranger, that's for sure,' O'Hagan insisted.

'So are half of the people in here,' Delaney reminded him. 'I mean, this is a place for *tourists*, right? So *most* of this lot are strangers to us. Christ, O'Hagan, you're dumb!'

'All right, lads, knock it off,' Tolan said, though he too was casting his gaze around the lobby, trying helplessly to ascertain if any of the men looked either like Russians or seasoned bodyguards. 'If he *has* anyone down here, they may not necessarily be Russians; they could be local hard men out for hire. If, as Meehan said, he was picked up in a BMW, that suggests he had someone waiting here for him. Not that it makes a damned bit of difference, since we're just here for a talk. He's hardly likely to want to assassinate me, is he? If anyone tries that, it's going to be a local enemy: some Prod or one of our own carrying a grievance. That's why you boyos accompany me everywhere; it's not because of the Russians.'

Tolan took a deep breath and let it out again in a nervous, gasping sound. 'Right, you, Jack, and you,

Sean,' he said, turning to Delaney and O'Hagan, 'take a seat down here and keep your eye on those comin' in and goin' out. We shouldn't be much more than an hour or so. Bobby,' he said, turning to the grim-faced Meehan, 'you come with me.'

As Delaney and O'Hagan wandered off to find seats giving a good view of the whole lobby, Tolan led Meehan across to the reception desk, where a well made-up uniformed blonde smiled brightly at him.

'Yes, sir?'

'You got someone called Vasilyovsky – Boris Vasilyovsky – staying here? If so, I've got an appointment with him. We're meeting up in his room.'

The girl checked her computer screen and nodded affirmatively, then picked up the telephone and looked inquiringly at Tolan. 'Can I have your name, please?' When Tolan gave his name, the girl rang through to Vasilyovsky's room and announced that a Mr Tolan had arrived for his appointment. Nodding affirmatively again, she placed the phone down, smiled brightly again at Tolan and gave him the number of the room. 'Fifth floor,' she added.

'Thanks,' Tolan said.

He knew where the lifts were because he had been here before, both for business meetings and for sweaty sessions with one or other of the whores that he had working for him in Belfast and was therefore able to use for free. He gave the first lift a miss because other people were entering, but he took the second and pressed the button to close the door before anyone other than himself and Meehan could get in. *Better safe than sorry, like.*

'Bet you never thought you'd see the day,' he said jokingly to Meehan, standing beside him in the lift, 'when someone like you, a working stiff from the upper Falls, would find it natural to be in a hotel like this.'

'I *still* don't feel natural in a place like this,' Meehan responded without the trace of a smile. 'It just isn't my style, like.'

'Intimidated by the monied classes, are you? All them nice bits of sophisticated fluff with their scented cunts and noses in the air. Make you feel inadequate, do they, Bobby boy?'

'No,' Meehan lied. 'I've just never been comfortable in hotels and that's all there is to it. It's the same with fancy restaurants. I'm a working-class man and proud of it. I have no pretensions, like.'

'That sounds like a right load of blarney to me. If you're so keen on the working classes, what the fuck are ya doing running around with the likes of me, given what I get up to?'

'*You*'re working class,' Meehan said. 'That's why you joined up with the Provies. Joining up was a form of working-class solidarity against British imperialism and Orange rule.'

'It *was*,' Tolan said, 'but it isn't any more. As for me, I wouldn't mind rubbin' my nose in scented cunt and I'll sure as hell be doin' it some day. Oh, oh, here we are.'

The lift door had opened and they walked out onto the fifth floor, checked the layout of the rooms, then walked along in the direction they required.

'Fucking nice, eh?' Tolan said, admiring the decor as they advanced along the corridor.

'It's all right,' Meehan said.

'We'll all be livin' like this in the near future if things go as I plan. There it is. That's the room.' He stopped in front of the door of Boris Vasilyovsky's room and stared silently, nervously at it for a while. At first he didn't know what was making him nervous – he was frightened of few men – then he realized that it was the simple fact that he had never met a Russian before and was wondering what they were like. Meehan had been right about that, at least: it was best to deal with your own kind. On the other hand, there could be no advance that way, so new directions were called for.

'Let me do the talking,' he said to Meehan. Then he rang the door bell.

When the door opened, he found himself staring at a green-eyed, blonde-haired bit of fluff wearing an open-necked blouse and skintight blue denims. A real beauty to take your breath away.

'Mr Tolan?' she asked in a husky, sensual voice, with just the trace of a Russian accent.

'Yes,' Tolan said.

The woman offered him a dazzling smile.

'Welcome,' she said.

Almost overcome at the sight of her, Tolan stepped into the room and caught a glimpse of a man seated in a deep armchair by the window, hazed in striations of sunlight. Meehan came in behind Tolan and stopped beside him. Tolan was about to return his gaze to the woman, when something cold and hard – the barrel of a handgun – touched the back of his head.

'Don't make a move,' someone said.

Chapter Five

Boris could see that the Irishman was livid, but trying hard not to show it. Boris didn't blame him. He had come here in good faith and now he was standing there with a handgun to his head. Who *wouldn't* be mad?

'What the fuck kinda greeting is this?' Tolan said, not raising his hands in the air, but not moving either.

'Sorry, Mr Tolan,' Boris said, 'but one can never be too careful in this business. Please stretch your arms out by your sides and let Mikhail frisk you. You, too,' he said to the other, shorter Irishman.

'Jesus Christ,' the second Irishman said in disgust, though he, following Tolan, stretched his arms out to his sides and prepared to be frisked for hidden weapons.

They were frisked by Lara who was not remotely embarrassed to have to slide her hands over their bodies and between their legs, patting them swiftly as high as the crotch. She was quick and expert.

'Don't damage the goods,' Tolan said without humour, gazing down upon her as she knelt in front of him, her hands sliding up his inner thighs.

'I won't,' she said, unfazed. Finished with Tolan, who had no weapon on him, she turned to Meehan and repeated the process. Meehan was obviously fighting to control himself, torn between acute embarrassment and rage, and he did so by glaring at Tolan, blaming him for this indignity. Naturally, Lara found the Glock-19 handgun holstered at Meehan's waist, hidden at the small of his back. She withdrew it from its holster, walked away from Meehan and laid the weapon down on Boris's desk. Boris picked it up and studied it with interest.

'Austrian,' he said. 'Very good. I trust, however, that it wasn't meant for me.'

'Don't be fuckin' daft,' Tolan said, still holding his hands out by his sides. 'We came here to discuss a fucking merger, not to have a firefight. Can we lower our arms now?'

Boris nodded. 'Please do.' When Tolan and Meehan had both lowered their arms to their sides, Boris indicated the two chairs in front of his desk. 'Please,' he said, 'take a seat.' Mikhail lowered his pistol to his side as both men sat in the chairs. 'Would you gentlemen like a drink?' Boris asked.

Before Tolan could reply, Meehan nodded at the pistol in Boris's right hand. 'We don't talk until I get my weapon back. I feel naked without it.'

Boris smiled. 'I know you people don't approve of decommissioning.'

'Fuck you,' Meehan said.

Boris smiled more broadly, then nodded and leaned across the desk to hand the pistol to Meehan. 'Sorry about that,' he said, 'but by now it's an instinctive reaction. I just didn't think.'

'It was unnecessary,' Tolan said.

'I'm sure it was,' Boris said. 'Even if your intentions weren't good, that weapon wouldn't help you.'

'Why not?' Meehan asked.

Boris nodded at Mikhail, who was standing behind the two Irishmen, holding his pistol by his side and prepared to use it. 'My bodyguard,' Boris said.

Both Irishmen glanced back over their shoulders, then turned back to the front. Meehan still looked quietly outraged but Tolan was grinning. 'Ackay,' he said. 'Naturally.'

'So can I offer you a drink?' Boris asked.

'Why not?' Tolan replied, glancing around the large, opulent suite and taking in Lara standing by the doorway, svelte in her open-necked blouse and skintight blue denims. Tolan could hardly take his eyes off her, but he forced himself to do so. 'I'll have a neat whisky,' he said.

'Me, too,' Meehan said.

Boris nodded at Lara, who immediately disappeared into another room, obviously going to the minibar. Tolan watched her departing, then he looked around the suite again and eventually returned his gaze to Boris. 'A very nice wee habitat,' Tolan said.

'Not bad,' Boris replied.

'You *are* Boris Vasilyovsky?' Tolan said.

'Yes,' Boris replied. 'And I know who *you* are, but . . .' He turned to Meehan and raised his eyebrows inquiringly.

'Meehan,' Tolan's henchman said without the trace of a smile. 'Bobby Meehan.'

'My second-in-command,' Tolan explained with an air of self-importance.

'Very good,' Boris said. 'Pleased to meet you at last.'

'Sure yer English is real good,' Tolan said, breaking into a grin. 'Even better than mine.'

'Thanks,' Boris replied. 'Where I come from languages are important, with English the most important of all. So the three of us here, including Lara and Mikhail, all speak good English.'

'Just as well,' Tolan said, 'since I don't know a fucking word of Russian.'

'That's no problem, my friend.'

At that moment, Lara returned with four drinks on a tray. She handed the whiskies to Tolan and Meehan, placed a glass of neat vodka in front of Boris and took the remaining one for herself. Leaving the tray on a small table beside the desk, she went to sit on the sofa, where she crossed her long legs and lit a cigarette. Tolan cast her a quick, furtive look, then studied his glass of whisky with elaborate, histrionic intensity before looking up again, grinning at Boris. 'Very generous,' he said. 'I trust ye're not trying to get us drunk to give you an advantage.'

'Why not try?' Boris responded with a smile. 'It's all in the game. But in truth, we Russians are renowned as big drinkers, so that measure comes naturally.'

Tolan nodded. 'Right. I can see that's a good wee drop of vodka you've got there in yer hand. Well, here's to you.'

They raised their glasses in the air and drank, then Boris leaned back in his chair and thoughtfully studied the two Irishmen. Neither man struck him as being sophisticated, though Tolan was possessed of a kind of animal cleverness and Meehan was clearly tough and streetwise. Both were grim specimens. Though Tolan had grinned a few times, it had merely made him seem like a wolf, since there wasn't a hint of real humour in his lean, ascetic features and direct, cold grey gaze. Meehan, who was approximately the same size as his boss but looked smaller because he was so stocky where Tolan was slim, had a face carved from granite and lips that formed a thin, taut line. Tolan's weakness, Boris sensed, was vanity and that could be useful. Meehan, on the other hand, had no vanity at all and obviously was suspicious of anyone not of his own kind. Neither man could be trusted.

'So,' Tolan said, trying to open the negotiations in a casual, conversational manner, 'when did you get in?'

'This morning,' Boris lied. In fact, he had arrived in Belfast a week ago (mere hours after slitting the throat of Jimmy Lee Wong) and moved into a suite in the Hilton Hotel, located beside the magnificent concert hall and with a soothing view of the River Lagan. He had moved in there with Lara and Mikhail, all using assumed names, in order to spend a week spying on Tolan, both personally and with the aid of a former RUC officer, Phillip Greene, who specialized in illegal surveillance for business organizations and criminal elements that were based on the mainland but wished to move into the province. It was one of Greene's men who had picked up Boris and the others at Belfast City Airport a week ago and transported him in a BMW to the Hilton. It was Greene himself who had supervised the surveillance of Tolan during that week and driven Boris around when he personally wanted to follow Tolan's movements. In truth, then, while they had certainly checked into the Europa only this morning, Boris and his colleagues had merely moved across town from the Hilton.

'So you haven't even seen the city yet,' Tolan said.

'No.'

'Pity. It's a real nice wee town. A lot nicer than you'd glean from what you see on them blatherin' British TV programmes.'

'I'm sure I'll see it soon enough, Pat – can I call you "Pat"?'

'Ackay. First names all round, like.'

'And certainly, if we can put together a package, I'll be hanging around until it's complete and will then have plenty of time to explore the city.'

'A package is what we're here to discuss and I'm sure we can wrap it up. I mean, we've already agreed to most of it either over the phone or through your intermediaries – those boyos you sent over here before – so it's just a matter of deciding who gets what and when it all starts.'

'You suggested six weeks from now,' Boris said. 'Six weeks to the handing over of the weapons. Can you do it in that time?'

'Guaranteed,' Tolan said. 'Conditional upon coming to an agreement about what you get here in the province and, eventually, in all of Ireland and what we get in England, then in the EC, in return.'

'I'm sure we can work something out,' Boris said. 'That's what we've come here to do.'

'Then let's get to it,' Tolan said.

They talked for a couple of hours, working out a deal that would allow Boris to insert a set amount of his *mafiya* men into the province to work hand in hand with Tolan's men in the latter's ongoing local rackets, notably drugs, extortion, protection, bank and post office robberies and a limited amount of prostitution, concentrated on the city's best hotels, with Boris's organization receiving forty per cent of all profits. In return for this, Tolan would be able to do the same in the London territories controlled by Boris's men, also receiving forty per cent of all profits. This agreement would commence with the handing over to Boris, six weeks from now, of a specified amount of the weapons not surrendered to the British government through the laughable decommissioning process. In return for this, Boris would supply double the amount of drugs that Tolan was presently selling in the province, given his normal difficulty in obtaining them, and would ensure their safe delivery to the province. This initial agreement would last for one year. If, at the end of that period, both sides were happy with each other, Tolan would then help the *mafiya* extend their Northern Ireland operations into the south, notably in Dublin, and Boris would help Tolan extend his London operations to *mafiya*-controlled territories in the EC. If, at the end of another year, they were still happy with each other, Boris would invite Tolan's organization into Russia and Tolan, in return, would aid Boris's infiltration of the United States, where Tolan's organization already had strong interests. By which time, if all went well, the two outfits between them – Boris's *mafiya* and Tolan's former paramilitaries – would have become the single biggest criminal organization in the world.

That, at least, was what they agreed upon. Boris, however, had other ideas. By now, after a week's thorough surveillance of Tolan's movements, some of it done by direct eyeballing, some with the aid of high-tech bugging equipment, Boris was convinced that Tolan was something of a loose cannon, firing with devastating effect but also in all directions, motivated more by vanity than logic and extremely crude in how he went about things. From what he had observed during his week of secret surveillance, Boris was convinced that Tolan was more courageous than intelligent – or, more precisely, was too vain to imagine himself failing at anything – so was taking extraordinary chances when he did his rounds of the Falls, beating up someone here, wrecking a bar there, collecting protection and extortion money in person, shoving the money into his pockets . . . In other words, ruling his small empire with an iron fist but in full view of too many witnesses and ignoring the possibility that the police might eventually catch him at it. Tolan, therefore, was not a man to be trusted in the long term, though he was, in the short term, vitally necessary to the *mafiya*'s plans to infiltrate, first, the so-called Six Counties, then the whole of Ireland.

It was Boris's decision, therefore, after a couple of

hours of negotiation, which included a lot of Irish blarney from Tolan, that he would cooperate with these former paramilitaries only for as long as he needed them – six weeks, in fact – and then, when he had the weapons he needed for his all-out war against the London triads, he would not only wipe out the triads but also turn the weapons against the very people who had given them to him . . . namely, Pat Tolan and his fellow no-hopers. In short, he would court Tolan for six weeks, then wipe him off the map with his own weapons. What could be sweeter?

'So,' Boris said when most questions had been dealt with and the conversation was running down, 'we send you the first supply of snow in four weeks' time and the handover of the weapons takes place six weeks from now. Can we have a definite date?'

'Ackay,' Tolan responded, playing the hearty but crafty Irishman. 'Assuming the snow arrives on the date agreed, I'd be able to guarantee delivery of the weapons any day you want during the first week of August.'

'Where?' Boris asked.

Tolan offered his humourless smile and tapped his forefinger a few times against his nose. 'Well, we can't be tellin' you that now, can we, until we actually receive the snow. Now wouldn't *you* think that foolish?'

Boris smiled in return. 'Yes, Pat, I must confess that I would, so we'll drop that question for now. Just guarantee that, in return for our drugs, we can have the weapons in six weeks.'

'Guaranteed,' Tolan said.

'Shall we shake hands on it?'

'Ackay, let's do that.'

They both stood up and Boris walked around the desk to shake Tolan's hand. Lara, still sitting cross-legged on the sofa, drinking and smoking, lightly clapped her hands in what was, perhaps, mock applause. Tolan glanced at her, then returned his gaze to the front as Boris also shook Meehan's hand, which he found to be unusually cold, just like his visage.

'Very good, gentlemen,' Boris said. 'A constructive meeting. Shall we have another drink to seal the agreement?'

'Why not?' Tolan said, taking his seat again, preparing to settle in for the afternoon.

'I think we should be getting back, boss,' Meehan said softly while remaining on his feet. 'I mean, we've got a lot of business to attend to and—'

'Aye, right,' Tolan said, sounding annoyed. 'I suppose we'd best make tracks all right.'

'Pardon?' Boris said.

'Make tracks,' Tolan explained, still sounding annoyed and casting a brief, resentful glance at Meehan. 'It just means "get going". Like a train: making tracks.'

'Ah, yes,' Boris said, hoping that they would indeed make tracks but not wishing them to know he felt that way. 'Naturally, if you must go . . . But if not a drink, can I offer anything else by way of celebration?'

Tolan glanced at Lara, still sitting on the sofa with her long legs crossed, their exquisite shape emphasized by the skintight denims. Her blouse, which was unbuttoned almost to her midriff, was showing what she had under it. Tolan looked away quickly.

'Well, now that you ask . . .' he began tentatively.

'Yes?' Boris replied blandly.

Tolan nodded in Lara's direction. 'Is she . . . ?'

'Pardon?' Boris responded, knowing just what was being asked, but stringing it out for all it was worth.

'Is she . . . ?'

'No,' Boris said. 'I'm afraid not.'

'She's with you?' Tolan ventured.

Realizing that Lara could be the key to unlocking Tolan, Boris said, lying blatantly, 'No, not in the way you're implying. We don't have that kind of relationship. It's more of a business relationship. You understand? I get what I pay for.'

Tolan's nostrils positively dilated. 'You mean, she might . . . I mean, under certain conditions . . . I mean . . .'

Boris shrugged, as if helpless. 'She might,' he said. 'She's the one who picks and chooses. If you're interested . . . Well . . .' Here Boris shrugged again. 'You and I will be meeting frequently over the next few weeks, which means that you'll be meeting *her* often as well. I don't care one way or the other. It's entirely up to you.'

'No offence meant, I assure you, boyo.'

'And none taken,' Boris said, despising the low-life shit.

'Well, great,' Tolan said. 'I mean, as long as we're clear between us about it.'

'We are,' Boris assured him.

'Great,' Tolan repeated. 'Brilliant.' Expanding his vocabulary. Then he sighed, as if relieved of a great burden, and added, 'Well, I guess, as Bobby here pointed out, we'd best be makin' tracks. A good meeting all told.'

'Absolutely,' Boris said.

Everyone stood up. Boris walked around the desk as Lara rose from the sofa and crossed the room to join them. Mikhail, still standing by the front door, kept the pistol in his hand but diplomatically held it behind his back. Lara gave Tolan a gleaming smile, then placed her empty glass on Boris's desk, spreading her fingers as she raised her hand again. She was standing mere inches from Tolan, her breasts practically touching his chest. Tolan, though avoiding eye contact with her, was breathing too deeply. Boris was satisfied.

'So,' Boris said, taking Tolan by the elbow and walking

him to the door of the suite, 'we haven't wasted our time. May I suggest that we meet at least once a week until the weapons have been handed over and the deal is complete?'

'Good idea,' Tolan said.

They all stopped at the door, Mikhail hanging back, his handgun discreetly out of sight, Lara positioned invitingly close to Tolan, Boris at the other side of him, while Meehan, slightly apart from the general group, kept his steely gaze fixed on Mikhail and, more precisely, on where his arm curved behind his back, keeping his pistol out of view. Boris, who noticed the direction of Meehan's gaze, decided that Meehan was the one who could be the most threatening. Still smiling, Boris nodded at Lara and she opened the door, stepping aside to let Tolan and Meehan leave.

'I'll be here for another few days,' Boris said, 'until I find a decent place to live in.'

'I can fix that up for you,' Tolan said quickly.

Boris waved his hand gently and shook his head, as if embarrassed by Tolan's display of generosity. 'It's all right,' Boris said. 'I've already found a house up off the Ormeau Road, near Queen's University, but I can't move in until next week. In the meantime, you can get in touch with me here and I will, of course, send you details of my new address. Do you have e-mail?'

'Ackay,' Tolan said. 'Naturally. All the mod cons here, don't you know?'

'Then send me your e-mail address, care of this hotel, and I'll e-mail my details back to you.'

'Great,' Tolan said. 'Well . . .' Here he gave a melodramatic sigh while throwing a quick, hungry glance in Lara's direction. 'I guess it's *really* time to be making tracks. We'll be in touch real soon.'

He and Boris shook hands. Boris shook hands with

Meehan. Tolan shook hands with Lara and had trouble in letting her go, though he finally managed to do so. No one shook hands with Mikhail.

'Sure we'll see you real soon,' Tolan said.

'Absolutely,' Boris said, then started closing the door as Tolan and Meehan stepped backwards into the corridor. 'Meanwhile, we'll e-mail you.'

'Right,' Tolan said.

Boris closed the door and turned around to lean his back against it. He looked at Lara, then smiled and sighed melodramatically. Lara grinned and then giggled.

'What a pair!' she exclaimed.

'Sleeping with the enemy,' Boris said, 'isn't *always* a thrill. Pat Tolan is extremely self-absorbed and obviously thinks he's wonderful. The other one is the smarter of the two, but neither of them recognizes that fact. The other one . . . What was his name?'

'Meehan.'

'Yes, Meehan. Bobby Meehan. He could be deadly. But we'd better keep our eyes on both of them until this is over.'

'They're not to be trusted,' Mikhail said as he placed his handgun back in its holster. 'I'd be careful with those two.'

'I will be,' Boris said, pushing himself away from the door to be closer to Lara. 'I'll be keeping them under constant surveillance until we no longer need them.'

'When will that be?' Lara asked.

'When they hand over the weapons,' Boris said. 'Once they do that, we can annihilate the triads, bring more men into London, then use those same weapons for a war against Tolan's men right here in Belfast. Before the year's out, we'll be ruling the criminal world of the whole province and can use it as a springboard to the south. Dublin, here we come!'

He picked his glass of vodka off the desk, raised it to Lara and Mikhail in a mock toast, then had a sip of it and placed the glass back where it had been. Excited by what was happening, he was also becoming sexually aroused at the sight of Lara, whose breasts were practically tumbling out of her blouse.

'You can go now, Mikhail,' Boris said. 'Take the afternoon off, but be back by six.'

'Right, boss,' Mikhail said.

When Mikhail had left the room, Boris took Lara into his arms, pressed himself close to her, sank his teeth gently into her neck, then said, 'That pig Tolan has the hots for you.'

'I noticed,' Lara replied.

'That could be useful to us. I'll keep him out of your bed if I can, but you might have to endure him.'

'I'll do what I have to do.'

'The very sight of you excited him.'

'Like you're excited right now.'

'Yes,' Boris said, pressing his hardness against her belly, which was soft and yielding. 'Like I'm excited right now.'

'*Why* are you excited? Is it the thought of Tolan wanting me? You always seem to get excited when you see other men lusting after me. Is that what this is now?'

'Yes,' Boris confessed, rubbing his belly against her belly, arousing himself even more, 'I suppose so. I think of all the things he's imagining doing with you right now and, yes, that excites me.'

'Making *you* want to do those things?'

'Yes,' Boris said.

'Then do them, Boris darling, do them . . . because that's what I'm here for.'

Boris pushed her back across the desk and started removing her clothing. They wrecked the desk and then progressed to the bedroom where they stayed for a long time. The more Boris worked at Lara, the more he thought of Tolan doing the same and those thoughts made him even more excited. In fucking Lara, he was actually fucking Tolan, though not from any straightforward homosexual inclinations. He was fucking Tolan by doing what Tolan wanted to do with Lara. He was fucking the woman that Tolan wanted to fuck. He was fucking Tolan as he would fuck him in the future when he turned his own weapons against him and wiped him from the face of Northern Ireland. He was excited by that thought.

Chapter Six

Coogan sat fully clothed on his bed in a hotel in west London, once more reading the dossiers on Pat Tolan and Boris Vasilyovsky that he had found in the bank deposit box in central London, along with money, false identity papers, a new passport and details of his account in a bank in Belfast. Coogan had read the dossiers at least twice a day for the past five days and now felt that he nearly knew them off by heart. Nevertheless, he had felt obliged to read them one last time before going to meet his potential collaborators in a pub in Kensington High Street, mere minutes away.

When he had finished reading them, he sighed and put them back into their folders, then swung his legs off the bed. Standing up, he placed the dossiers back in the drawer of the bedside cabinet, glanced at the bed where he had fucked a whore last night, then put on a windcheater jacket and left the room. He went down the stairs, nodded at the girl behind reception, then walked out into the bright light of noon on this warm summer's day.

After walking the length of the leafy side street where his hotel was located, he turned the corner into Kensington High Street. The road was packed with traffic and the pavements were crowded, but the sight of so many young women, some wearing miniskirts or bare-bellied, taking advantage of the sun, was compensation for the heat, dense traffic and jostling crowds. Besides, he didn't have far to walk. About five minutes later, further along the High Street, he entered the bar where he was scheduled to meet Nick Wright and Barry Newman, two of his best friends and both former SAS buddies.

They were already standing at the bar when Coogan entered, both with pints of bitter in their hands. Since this was just after noon, the bar wasn't crowded yet and both men had a lot of elbow space. They were deep in conversation and didn't see Coogan until he was actually standing in front of them.

'Halfway through your first pints already,' Coogan said. 'It doesn't take you two long.'

Both men looked around and grinned at him. They were both six feet tall, two inches taller than Coogan, and as solid as rocks. Wright had jet-black curly hair, cut short at the back and sides, whereas Newman had his auburn hair, thinning on top, tied in a short ponytail at the back, giving him the appearance of a hippy. Both men were wearing denims, open-necked shirts and casual jackets.

'Well, if it isn't fucking Coogan,' Wright said, 'last seen entering Pentonville Prison. How the hell did you get sprung?'

'Friends in high places,' Coogan replied.

'I believe you,' Newman said. 'Only someone placed as high as the Post Office Tower could have got you out of that place. I still can't believe it.'

Coogan raised his hands in the air and grinned. 'Believe it! Here I am, boys. I'm not a ghost. This is me. And, believe me, I'm thirsty. Who got the first round?'

'Me,' Newman said.

'I'll have the same,' Coogan told him.

Newman indicated to the barman that he should serve them another pint of bitter, then he turned back to Coogan and pinched his arm, checking that he wasn't a ghost. 'Okay, I believe it,' he said. 'He's flesh and blood, Nick.'

'Fucking miracles never cease.' Wright held his pint up in the air in a mock salute. 'Cheers,' he said.

'I'm still waiting for my pint,' Coogan said.

'I'll drink to you anyway.'

Wright and Newman both sampled their bitter, then lowered their glases again. 'So,' Newman said, wiping his wet lips with the back of his hand, 'what are you going to do with yourself now that you're out?'

'*How* did you get out?' Wright asked. 'I mean, what did you offer them?'

'I didn't make the offer,' Coogan said. 'They did. They made me an offer I couldn't refuse, which was why I called you guys. I've got a job for you.'

Wright and Newman glanced at each other, surprised, then both returned their gaze to Coogan.

'A job?' Newman asked.

'I thought you'd called us together just to celebrate your freedom,' Wright said. 'Now you say this is business.'

Coogan nodded. 'Yes.' He was about to say more when the barman put his pint of bitter down in front of him. Feeling the heat, thirsty, Coogan instantly picked it up, had a good drink, then lowered the glass but kept it in his hand. 'Let's grab a table, order some food and discuss it over lunch.'

'Right,' Newman said. He reached along the bar for a menu, studied it, said, 'Shepherd's pie for me,' and handed the menu to Wright who said, 'I don't have to look at it. I don't like big lunches, so I'll just have the ploughman's.' He passed the menu on to Coogan who perused it and decided on fish pie. He ordered the three meals and paid the barman for them while Newman grabbed a table and Wright fetched three sets of eating utensils wrapped in sky-blue napkins. This being his business meeting, Coogan then ordered three more pints and carried them to the table, where the other two were finishing off their first pints. Taking the spare chair, he glanced about him and was pleased to note that the tables were spaced well apart and that few of them were taken, since it was still early.

'So we're actually here to discuss a job?' Wright asked.

'Yes,' Coogan said.

'I could do with a job,' Newman said. 'I'm bored shitless right now.'

'I'm not bored,' Wright said sardonically. 'I'm too busy fighting with my missus over my lack of a future and our mutual lack of a decent income. So, no, sir, it ain't boredom!'

'It's the curse of the Regiment,' Coogan said.

'Damned right,' Newman added.

Like a lot of former SAS men, Wright and Newman had found it difficult to get a job (not many people wanted to hire prematurely retired professional soldiers) and rarely held a job for long when they *did* get one, usually being fired for bad timekeeping or insolence. Also like a lot of former SAS men, they were too restless for routine work and too addicted to danger to be satisfied with normal civilian life. Other former SAS men, in the same boat, had drifted into crime or succumbed to drink. A few had managed to pick up jobs, either in the UK, or overseas, as security consultants, but those were the lucky ones. Wright and Newman, both Londoners by birth, had remained in the city and managed to survive, though they had drifted restlessly from one routine job to another and were always on the lookout for something more challenging than what they were generally offered. Coogan was hoping that what he was about to offer would stir their interest.

'It's Northern Ireland,' he said.

His friends glanced automatically at one another, both raising their eyebrows in surprise. When in the SAS, they had both worked with Coogan on covert operations in the province at the tail end of the Troubles so, like him, they knew the place well. Having glanced at each other, registering their surprise, they turned back expectantly.

'Really?' Wright asked.

'Really.'

'I thought all that shit was finished over there.'

'Not quite,' Coogan said.

'If they sprung you for Northern Ireland,' Newman said, 'it must be something big.'

'It is,' Coogan said. 'It's a planned merger between former paramilitaries, now professional criminals, and the Russian *mafiya*. My job is to prevent that merger from happening.'

'Wow!' Newman exclaimed. 'A merger between the Paddies and the *mafiya*?'

'That's what I said, Barry.'

'The *mafiya*?' Wright asked. 'I've read a bit about them, but I'm not clued up on them that much. I mean, isn't the *mafiya* based in Russia?'

'Not any longer, Nick. Since the early 1990s, the *mafiya* and the Chechens have been the fastest-growing crime organizations in the world – and they haven't confined themselves to Russia. In fact, according to Russian police estimates, they're conducting their business in over thirty countries, making arrangements with local criminals where necessary. For instance, in Italy it's the foreign *mafiya* who control organized prostitution, having reached an accommodation with the old Mafia over the distribution of drugs in Russia. Here in London, the East End sweatshops are paying protection to Russian mobsters, while Russian-controlled prostitution rings are to be found not only here but also in provincial towns like Peterborough and Northampton, with the profits being laundered through non-existent timeshare operations. From what I've read in the dossiers I was given, courtesy of MI5, the *mafiya* are presently washing money in London and the other European capitals on a grand scale. That money has been acquired through drugs, fraud, prostitution and extortion, often with the participation of former KGB officers.'

'So how do they launder all that money?' Newman wanted to know.

'Right now, at least in London, they're using property deals and a three-stage process known as placing, layering and integration. In other words, they move money into a small firm, mix clean money with it, then move it into totally clean stocks or into larger companies. That way the money gets washed clean.'

Nick Wright was about to make a comment when the arrival of a barmaid with their food made him shut his mouth. The barmaid was short and curvaceous, dressed in a black skirt and white blouse, with her auburn hair pinned up on her head and her lips brightly painted. As she laid their plates on the table, leaning across it, Newman automatically raised his right hand to give her rump a gentle pat. Then he thought better of it and lowered his hand. Straightening up, the waitress noticed the movement and grinned at Newman. 'You just did the right thing,' she said, then flounced off, her full hips swinging like a metronome.

'Oh, boy!' Newman exclaimed softly, longingly.

'You obviously need some distraction,' Coogan said as

he removed the napkin from his knife and fork, preparing to eat. 'I think this job's just the ticket.'

'Absolutely,' Wright said as he buttered his bread roll and cut up some cheese. 'So let's get back to it . . . You say the *mafiya* are going to move into Northern Ireland to tie up with the criminal gangs there and that your job – maybe *our* job – is to stop that from happening. How do you plan to do it?'

'By neutralizing the top dogs on both sides,' Coogan said after swallowing his first mouthful of food.

'*Neutralizing* them?' Wright asked.

'Yes.'

Wright gave a low, brief whistle.

'Who are they?' Newman asked.

'The Irish gang is headed by Pat Tolan, whom you may remember as one of the most ruthless heads of the Provisional IRA at the tail end of the Troubles.' With their mouths full of food, Newman and Wright both nodded silently to indicate that they did, indeed, remember Pat Tolan. 'So, Tolan is now the head of a criminal organiz-ation that's composed of former Catholic *and* Protestant paramilitaries – the ones who turned to crime when the peace came in and left them unemployed and, of course, unemployable.'

'What do you do when peace comes,' Newman said, having swallowed his mouthful, 'and you've no skills other than those you learnt with the paramilitaries? What *can* you do, except carry on using the skills that you've learnt? And what are those skills, my dear friends? Kneecapping, kidnapping, bombing, doorstep assassin-ation, the collection of protection money and, of course, the robbing of banks and post offices.'

'Don't mention that last activity,' Wright said. 'Coogan might be embarrassed.'

'Fuck you,' Coogan said. 'But I can see you're on the

right track. A lot of the freedom fighters on both sides, rendered unimportant and unemployable by peace, turned to crime as their only alternative. And now their nominal head is Pat Tolan.'

'And he's the one setting up this deal with the *mafiya*,' Wright said.

'Correct, Nick. He's the one. He's hoping that by amalgamating with the Russians, his own organization will become twice as strong as it is now, with a much longer reach – all the way from Ireland to the rest of the EC and, perhaps, even to America. So that's Tolan's master plan.'

'And the other side?' Newman asked.

'A gentleman – though that may be the wrong description – called Boris Vasilyovsky.'

'That's a right fucking mouthful for a start,' Wright complained.

'That's his name and we're stuck with it.'

'Sorry, Coogan. Continue.'

'Vasilyovsky—'

'Can we just call him "Boris", for Christ's sake?' Wright interjected. 'I mean, I'll *never* be able to pronounce that fucking name!'

'Okay,' Coogan said, 'Boris.'

'Perfect,' Wright said.

'The *mafiya*,' Coogan continued, 'is presently under the control of six heads, each with his own territory. Boris is one of that all-powerful six and his organization is scattered all over Europe and moving into the UK at great speed. Here, in London, he specializes in drugs, fraud, money laundering and prostitution. In Italy, he's into drugs, prostitution and illegal immigrants. In Belgium and Germany, it's stolen cars, drugs and money laundering. In Albania, it's drugs, weapons and fraud. In the former Yugoslavia, he's supplying arms to

Serbs and Muslims alike. He's also sending prostitutes from Bulgaria to the Middle East. Last but by no means least, he's known to have close ties with the Colombian drug barons and is moving his supplies through the Caribbean to Europe.'

'Some smart cookie,' Newman said.

'Absolutely,' Coogan said.

'We can take it, then,' Wright said sardonically, 'that our Russian friend Boris isn't exactly a boy scout.'

'You can take it as read. He's absolutely fucking ruthless. His reprisals for so-called "bad faith" are instant and take place worldwide. Here in Britain we've had to suffer a whole spate of murders, with people shot on their own doorsteps, or when driving their cars, or after being abducted and taken to some lonely spot for torture followed by execution. The bodies have turned up all over the place, from London to Manchester and Birmingham. Boris has eyes and ears everywhere, he's utterly ruthless, and his ambition would appear to know no limits. Recently, he turned the streets of Soho into a battleground when he moved into the drug-dealing areas normally controlled by the triads and it's believed that he's about to engage in an all-out war with them.'

'So what's he doing trying to set up a deal with the crime barons of Northern Ireland?'

'Simply extending his territory,' Coogan said, 'to make his *mafiya* even more powerful and far-reaching. Since he's already controlling half of Europe's underground, he wants the British mainland as well – thus his present conflict with the triads – and then Northern Ireland *and*, I'll bet, eventually the south. This man is ambitious.'

There was silence for a moment as the ex-SAS men all thought about this while continuing with their lunch and sipping from their pint glasses. Eventually, with a satisfied sigh and a histrionic patting of his taut belly, Newman said, 'So the job you've been assigned is the neutralizing of at least Tolan and Boris, with perhaps a few others thrown in.'

'Yes, that's it,' Coogan said.

'Who gave you this job?' Newman asked him.

'I can't tell you that, Barry.'

'If he got you sprung from Pentonville,' Wright said slyly, 'he has to be someone in a top-level position with the government.'

'You said it, Barry, not me.'

Newman grinned. 'I'll assume that's agreement. So how do you propose doing this dicey job?'

'Let me just say that according to certain intelligence reports—'

'Ah, ha!' Wright exclaimed. 'Intelligence! It has to be MI5.'

'I didn't say that,' Coogan said.

'Of course not. Please continue.'

'According to certain intelligence reports,' Coogan continued, 'the deal between Tolan's organization and Boris's *mafiya* will be sealed when Tolan hands over a pile of weapons to the Russian about six weeks from now.'

'Where?' Newman asked.

'That's for me to find out,' Coogan said, 'when I get to Belfast.'

'But you're pretty sure that the handover is due to take place in approximately six weeks from now?'

'Yes.'

'That means the first week in August.'

'Exactly. And though we don't know where the handover is due to take place, it's pretty certain that it won't be in Belfast itself, so our bet is the "bandit country" that we old hands all know so well.'

'Armagh,' Newman said.

'Exactly.'

'So your task,' Wright said, pushing his unfinished lunch aside, 'is to insert covertly into Belfast, find out just where and when this handover is to take place, then neutralize the organizers, namely Tolan and Boris, before they can complete their planned merger.'

'What a bright boy you are.'

'You've only got six weeks,' Newman said. 'That doesn't give you much time.'

'No. Not much.'

'So when do you plan to go to Belfast?'

'At the end of this week. I only waited to speak to you two guys. So . . . are you in or out?'

'What's the deal?' Newman asked.

'You mean money?'

'That would help.'

'A year's SAS wages for six weeks' work, payable half up front, the second half when the job is finished.'

'What if we don't make it back?'

'Since theoretically this job doesn't exist, we can't pay anyone other than you two individually, so if you don't make it back, the second half of the payment isn't made.'

'Charming,' Newman said sardonically. 'But what the hell, I'm signing on the dole at the moment and the boredom is awesome, so I'm coming aboard.'

'And you?' Coogan asked Wright.

'Barry here's okay – he's separated from his missus and can just disappear; but I'm still living with Maxine, so how can I explain a six weeks' absence when I can't actually tell her where I'm going or what I'm up to?'

'Are you working at the moment?'

'No. Like Barry here, I am presently unemployed, which has my missus going apeshit.'

'Okay. Tell her you've got temporary work on a building site in Frankfurt, Germany. I'll give you the address of a German friend who'll forward any letter she may send you.'

'She never writes,' Wright said.

'A dying art,' Newman observed.

'Good,' Coogan said. 'So during your time in Belfast, you ring her once a week, using a cellular phone, and pretend that you're calling from Germany. It's no problem at all.'

'If I give her the money you give me up front, she may wonder where it's coming from.'

'Don't give it to her,' Coogan said. 'Just stick it in an account that she doesn't know about and keep it for an emergency. I mean, this isn't really about money, is it?'

'No, I guess not,' Wright said. 'Okay, fuck it, I'm in. What's the game plan?'

Coogan pushed his plate aside and lit a cigarette. He didn't smoke much these days, but he still liked the odd one, particularly after a meal or when drinking. 'We all arrive in Belfast separately, taking different routes and arriving on different days during the same week.'

'Next week,' Newman said.

'Yes, next week. I'll fly there at the end of this week and fix us up with accommodation so that each of us has our own separate pad in the city. You, Barry, will fly to the Isle of Man and take a Steam Packet Company ferry from Douglas to Belfast, arriving next Tuesday. You, Nick, will take the train to Stranraer, Scotland, and take a Sealink or P&O ferry to Larne in County Antrim, then rent a car and drive to Belfast from there – a twenty-mile journey. You should plan to arrive no later than next Thursday.'

'How do we find you when we get there?' Wright asked.

'When I've settled into Belfast, I'll phone you with details of where you'll be staying in that city. You'll both call me, using cellular phones, just before you leave London, giving me your exact date and time of arrival. When I know that, I'll make a point of being at your address when you get there, to hand over the keys, give you money for your expenses – that's separate from the first half of the fee – and fill you in on the lay of the land as I see it at that point. When all three of us are settled into Belfast . . . well . . .' Here Coogan shrugged. 'We just play it by ear. Do you have any questions?'

Wright and Newman glanced at each other, then shook their heads from side to side.

'No questions,' Wright said.

'Me neither,' Newman said.

'Good,' Coogan said. 'Glad to have you both aboard. I'm sure we're all in for a bumpy ride, which is just what we need.'

'Fucking A,' Newman said.

After finishing their food and drink, the three men went their separate ways.

Chapter Seven

Tolan could feel the lure of her even before he arrived at the big house in the Ormeau Road. He knew the dangers of women as much as any man could, knew how distracting they could be, but the very thought of Lara was enough to get him all agitated: loins on fire, heart racing. Tolan was convinced that Lara was a woman who liked the thrill of danger, who could be seduced by powerful men – men such as himself – and though he couldn't be too sure, he had the feeling that she fancied him, was attracted to his power, and that she would make herself available if that bastard Boris wasn't standing between them. He had seen it in her fleeting smiles, in the way she always seemed to move in close to him, in the way that, when she laughed at something, she would thoughtlessly reach out to lay her hand on his arm or, perhaps, let her shoulder brush his. When he was in the same room with her, even when Boris was also present, he seemed to feel her presence all around him, felt himself consumed by her. Knowing women (as he thought he did), Tolan was convinced that he could not be mistaken and that she would have been his for the asking had it not been for Boris.

Fuck, he hated that Boris!

Arriving near the Ormeau Road house, recently rented by Boris and located in one of the quieter tree-lined streets of the lively university area, Tolan clambered out of one side of his Honda Accord while Meehan, who had been driving, slipped out the other side. They had deliberately parked the car in the street a short distance along from Boris's detached house with its high red-brick wall, steel gates and electronic surveillance systems.

'Sure he's turned the place into a fuckin' fortress,' Tolan said. 'You think he's expectin' unwanted guests?'

'You never know,' Meehan said.

In fact, as Tolan was well aware, this kind of security was not uncommon in Belfast these days. Since the coming of peace, the city had been awash with money pouring in from the EC and from foreign investors even as the crime rate had soared. So people with money – and there were more of those than ever – were obsessed with security. This was to Boris's advantage, as no one would think his own obsession with security was unusual.

Walking along the lamplit street to the main gate, they saw the infrared video camera automatically following their movements. They stopped at the gate. Glancing between the iron bars, they saw a couple of bodyguards, both wearing dark suits with shirts and ties, sitting on folding wood-and-canvas chairs at the far end of the short gravel driveway, one at each end of the building, with the front door between them.

Tolan pressed the button on the intercom beside the gate. A male voice, distorted by static, asked him what he wanted. Tolan announced himself and the video camera above the gate angled downwards to identify him. Then the gate made an audible clicking sound and Tolan was able to push it open. As he and Meehan walked up the driveway to the front door, watched stonily by the guards in the folding chairs, both of them heavily built and almost certainly armed, the main gate closed automatically behind them. When they reached the front door, which was made from solid oak, Tolan had to ring another bell. The door was opened by a man in what was beginning to seem like the regulation dark grey suit with shirt and tie – obviously another armed bodyguard. He didn't say a word but merely nodded, indicating that Tolan and Meehan should enter, which they did. The entrance hall led into a spacious square-shaped reception area with stairs leading up from it to a first-floor landing running around three sides of it, past the doors of what were obviously bedrooms.

The bodyguard closed the front door again, then led Tolan and Meehan across the reception hall to an open door. He motioned for them to enter. This time they found themselves in a large living room with a Victorian fireplace, antique furniture, thick magnolia-coloured carpets and matching curtains. Lara was sitting on the sofa, wearing a figure-hugging dress with a high hemline, her elegantly crossed long legs sheathed in sheer stockings, her feet in stiletto-heeled shoes, her long blonde hair hanging loose: sex incarnate. Tolan had to force himself not to ogle her and only managed to do so by returning her fleeting smile and then turning instantly to Boris, who was standing in front of the fireplace in which no fire was burning, drinking a brandy and smoking a cigar. Boris was smiling, though it wasn't a smile that Tolan could trust.

'Ah,' Boris said, 'you got here! All set for your big night?'

'Ackay,' Tolan said.

'You know, you really don't have to come if you don't want to . . . I mean, if you're worried that there might be some kind of trouble.'

'I'm not worried,' Tolan said. 'I'm used to trouble. Sure

I can deal with any trouble that comes along. That's why I rule this town.'

'So long as you're happy, Pat. Would you like a quick drink before we leave?'

'*If* it's quick,' Tolan said. He didn't really want a drink, but he did want to be around Lara a bit longer. He glanced at her as she uncrossed her long legs and stood up to approach him. She seemed to be moving in sensual slow motion and he saw every curve of her. She stopped directly in front of him, her breasts rising and falling under his gaze. He raised his stare to her warm smile.

'What will it be?' she asked, her voice husky and oddly suggestive, as if she was whispering in bed in the darkness of midnight.

'A whisky. Neat.'

Still smiling, she nodded at him, then turned and gazed more coldly at Meehan. 'And you?'

'The same,' Meehan said, scarcely able to hide his detestation of her . . . of her and all foreigners.

'Right,' Lara said. Turning away from them, she walked to the bar, as curvaceous from the rear as she was from the front, forcing Tolan to fight to keep his concentration. Trying to appear indifferent, he glanced around the spacious, elegant living room.

'A nice wee place,' he said. 'A few years back, you'd have been hard pressed to find anything like this in Belfast. Sure things have changed right enough.'

'Foreign money,' Boris said. 'EC grants and heavy investment. Right now, Belfast's more prosperous than London and its property values are still rising. This is certainly the place to be these days if you want to make a killing. We're going to do that between us.'

'Let's hope so,' Tolan said.

'Please,' Boris said, looking at Meehan and indicating the armchair facing the sofa. 'Take a seat.'

'Thanks,' Meehan said and sat down.

'And you,' Boris said, indicating the sofa where Lara had been sitting.

'Right,' Tolan said, sinking into the sofa and glancing across the room to where Lara was bending over the drinks cabinet, her back turned to him, her gorgeous arse clearly defined in the skintight dress, thrusting out invitingly in his direction. Tolan felt that he was breathing hot air and heard his own voice from faraway.

'You're sure they'll be bringing it in tonight?'

'Absolutely,' Boris said.

'Well, I'm not frightened of trouble, like I said, but I don't go lookin' for it, so I hope you can trust the men you're using. No blabbermouths, like.'

'Pardon?'

'Blabbermouths – careless talkers.'

'No,' Boris said. 'Their silence is guaranteed. I personally guarantee it.'

'Good,' Tolan said.

They were silent for a while, uncomfortable, still strangers, not trusting each other. Then, thankfully, Lara returned with the drinks. After handing a glass to Meehan, she sat on the sofa beside Tolan, gave him the second glass, then crossed one long, shapely leg over the other, revealing a silken thigh in sheer stockings, her foot curved in the high heels. Tolan had never known a looker like this before and, in truth, he could scarcely deal with it. Yet he had the feeling again – the way she smiled warmly at him and the way she had placed herself (close to him, practically breathing in his face) – that she was subconsciously putting herself at his disposal. *If it wasn't for Boris* . . .

Tolan had a sip of his whisky and glanced blindly around the room.

'Is it all right?' Lara asked, her voice making him think of a wet tongue sliding over his belly.

'What?' he said, staring at her, seeing himself twice reflected in her big green steady cat's gaze.

'The drink. Is it all right?'

'Oh, right,' he said, realizing that he felt hot and was blinking too much as he held up his drink and stared at it. 'Ackay, it's fine.' Without thinking, he raised the glass to his lips and knocked it back in one gulp. Gasping, wiping his lips with the back of his hand, wanting Lara so much he was actually desperate to get away from her, he handed the glass back to her and climbed to his feet. 'I think we should make tracks,' he said. 'It's a fair wee drive to where we're going.'

'That's true enough,' Boris said. He finished off his brandy, threw the still-smouldering butt of his cigar into the grate of the fireplace, then nodded at the bodyguard near the door. Lara rose from the sofa to stand beside Tolan, again, perhaps deliberately, close to him. He fought to keep his hands off her.

Meehan finished his drink as well and placed the tumbler on the table in front of him. Then he stood up, preparing to leave with them. He cast his flat gaze from Tolan to Lara, then turned to face Boris.

'What do we go in?' he asked.

'My car,' Boris said. 'Some of my men will follow us in a van. Both vehicles are down in the garage.'

'Right,' Meehan said.

'You're not a man to talk too much,' Boris noted.

'No, I'm not,' Meehan said.

Boris smiled, then glanced from Tolan to Lara, who were still standing close together. 'Well, let's go,' Boris said.

Lara smiled at Tolan, a dazzling smile, as he turned away with reluctance and followed Boris and the others out of the living room, along a couple of short corridors and into the adjoining garage that was at the rear of the building. Boris's rented BMW was parked beside a lime-green transit van. Boris used a hand control to open the electronically controlled door of the garage, which rose upwards and pivoted backwards until it was parallel with and just below the ceiling. As Boris and his bodyguard, who was also acting as chauffeur, were slipping into the front of the BMW and Tolan was taking his place beside Meehan in the rear, four other men, all wearing dark blue overalls, came into the garage and entered the transit van, two in the front cabin, the other two in the rear.

'Okay, Yuri,' Boris said to the bodyguard driving the BMW, 'let's go.'

That's a Russian name, Tolan thought as the BMW hummed into life and moved out of the garage into the shadowy lamplit street that ran parallel to the rear of the house. *That means those bodyguards in front of the house are probably Russian as well. He's moving his men into Belfast real quick, like. I'd better watch out for that.*

It was good, in a sense, to have something to think of other than that sexy bitch Lara. Tolan, despite his vain belief that he understood women, had only known *Irish* women, including his unattractive wife and his whores. His obsession with Lara was, therefore, not only based on her remarkable beauty, her almost palpable sensuality, but on the simple fact that she was *foreign*, something different, and he had never sampled that kind before. Thus, when he imagined fucking her, his imagination ran riot, producing outrageous, tormenting scenarios of the most extreme, even perverse eroticism. Those fantasies were, to put it mildly, highly distracting and he had to fight to suppress them.

'So how are you finding Belfast so far?' he asked Boris

as the vehicle moved at a steady clip through the university area, heading for the northern side of town and the M2 motorway. 'Is it very different from Moscow?'

'A lot smaller,' Boris said. 'A lot warmer, though I know you think it's cold. Believe me, you don't know what cold is until you've been to Russia.'

'But it's summer here,' Tolan said, just trying to keep himself distracted. 'Sure it gets as cold as hell here in the winter, what with the winds and all.'

'Nothing compares with Russia,' Boris said, 'except, maybe, Antarctica.'

'You've managed to see a bit of Belfast?'

'Is there really that much to see? I think you can cover Belfast in a day and have nothing left to see. Of course, I look at places that have been in the news – at the Falls and the Shankill – trying to imagine what it was like here during the Troubles. The Falls and the Shankill are practically shoulder to shoulder, the Catholics and Protestants living on top of one another. No wonder the Troubles lasted so long. This place is too small for such conflicts.'

'That's the advantage, like. It may be too small for that kind of conflict, but it's grand when it comes to the likes of me needing to control it. Sure, it's so small, you can practically eyeball the whole of it and that makes life easy. Count yer blessings, I say.'

Boris made some kind of reply, but Tolan hardly heard him, being distracted by images of that Russian whore, Lara, who was definitely getting under his skin and making his balls itch. He was convinced she fancied him – it was pretty obvious, really – and his only problem was what to do about Boris. On the other hand, it was possible that no problem existed, since Boris had actually intimated that he and Lara weren't that close, that they had an . . . *arrangement* . . . and that what she did, who she did it with, was entirely up to her in the end. The way these foreigners thought was morally disgusting . . . but it was also exciting. Tolan felt that excitement.

He and Boris kept up a kind of general, meaningless conversation throughout the journey to Carrickfergus and beyond, simply trying to fill up the silence. As they neared their destination, however, which was, as Boris had explained to Tolan, a small cove located about half-way between Carrickfergus and Larne, the talk tapered off and Tolan contented himself with gazing out of the window of the car at the rolling moonlit fields and, beyond them, the dark, white-streaked carpet of the sea, which was calm this evening.

'Have we arrived yet?' Meehan asked, speaking for the first time in the whole journey.

'Almost,' Boris said. 'Just a few minutes more.'

Meehan nodded, as if talking to himself, and said no more as the car continued on its journey, seeming to drive itself as expertly driven cars did, and eventually brought them to a cove where the sea lapped quietly upon the rocks and its gently undulating surface was rippled with moonlight. The Russian driver, Yuri, braked to a halt at the bottom of a winding track that led out to the horseshoe-shaped cove, with strips of sandy beach to the east and the west. The light wind that was blowing into the cove made an oddly mournful sound.

'This is it,' Boris said.

When they were out of the car, Boris led them down to where the water lapped against gargoyle rocks. A short jetty thrust out into the sea and a large motor launch was anchored to it. As Boris led them towards the launch, the transit van that had been following them pulled up in the cove, parking beside the BMW, and the four men in overalls emerged from it. Two of them,

Tolan noticed, were carrying canvas bags that obviously contained either rifles or sub-machine guns.

'What the fuck are they for?' he asked of Boris.

'Better safe than sorry,' Boris replied. 'But, really, there's no need to worry. Let's all get in the boat.'

Tolan glanced at Meehan and caught his hard, suspicious stare. Refusing to share Meehan's paranoia about all foreigners, or *aliens* as Meehan called them, Tolan simply moved his right hand to the left-hand side of his body, under the jacket, checking that his Browning 9mm High Power handgun was still there. Satisfied, he withdrew his hand and stepped down off the jetty into the motor launch. Boris was already there, standing beside Yuri who was preparing to take the boat out. Meehan and the other four men soon followed. When they were all in the motor launch, Yuri started the engine and the launch surged forward, heading out to sea.

It did not go far. Within minutes, Tolan saw the outline of a large fishing vessel, obviously at anchor and silhouetted against the starry, moonlit sky.

'That's it?' he asked.

'Yes,' Boris replied.

'It came here all the way from Dublin without being searched by the Coast Guard?'

'Almost certainly it was searched,' Boris replied, 'but the cocaine – nearly one thousand kilograms – is in waterproof plastic bags fixed below the waterline onto the bilge-keel of the boat, undetectable except by a diving team. Those bags have been repeatedly transferred from one boat to another, all the way from Colombia to here, always by the same method.' He checked the luminous dial of his wristwatch. 'They're expecting us,' he said, 'so they'll be pulling the bags up right now. Let's go and collect them.'

As they approached the fishing vessel, looming ever

larger in the moonlight, Tolan felt the familiar tightening
in his gut that was a mixture of anticipation and wariness. He glanced at Meehan and saw the shifting of his
gaze as he took everything in, as silent and as watchful
as always. Glancing around him, Tolan saw the black
sheet of the sea, the gentle waves white-capped, almost
silvery in the moonlight, and the four men in the overalls
silhouetted against the starry sky. The motor launch
pulled up beside the fishing vessel and the anchor was
lowered.

Tolan saw three crew members on the fishing vessel,
all leaning over the starboard side and looking down as
two divers in the gently undulating sea removed the last
of the plastic bags from the hull below the waterline
and handed them to the crew member who was in a
rowboat that was anchored between the fishing vessel
and the motor launch. That rowboat was piled high with
plastic bags.

'Are they Colombians?' Tolan asked, indicating the
men in the water and on the fishing boat.

'No,' Boris replied. 'Irish. Dubliners. As I said, the
merchandise has been transferred repeatedly from ship
to ship en route. The last stop was Dublin.'

'Those fellers are from the Dublin underworld?'

'Yes.'

'How do you know you can trust them?' Tolan asked.

'I don't make mistakes,' Boris said.

There was little that Tolan or Meehan could do except
look on while the last of the plastic bags were held up
by the divers in the sea to be taken by the single man
in the rowing boat. When one of the divers stuck his
thumb in the air, indicating that there were no more
bags attached to the hull, the man in the rowboat started
rowing towards Boris's motor launch and the divers
made their way back to the fishing vessel. As the man in

the rowboat anchored his vessel by the side of the motor launch, two of the men in dark blue overalls threw nets over the side. The man in the rowboat filled one net with plastic bags, then, as the net was hauled up, he started filling the other one and this, when it was full, was also hauled up. This process was repeated again and again until all the bags had been transferred from the rowboat to the motor launch where they could be counted and weighed personally by Boris.

Meanwhile, the two divers had clambered up the side of the fishing vessel and were removing their diving outfits with the help of the three men who had remained on deck. The man in the rowboat, having passed up the last of the plastic bags, started making his way up the rope ladder that was dangling down the side of the hull. Reaching the top, he gripped the brass railing, preparing to haul himself up onto the deck, obviously expecting to receive the rest of the payment for his valuable cargo.

Tolan, his gut still tight with anticipation and wariness, was glancing across at the fishing vessel, watching the divers wriggling out of their kit, when he heard the sudden, sharp crack of a pistol, followed by the savage roaring of sub-machine guns.

Oh, Christ, he thought, *the Russian bastards are killing us!*

Even as he reached instinctively for the handgun hidden under his coat, he saw that one of the men in blue overalls had withdrawn a handgun of his own and fired a bullet into the head of the man from the rowboat – his corpse now splashing into the sea – and that the other three overalled men had unwrapped their sub-machine guns and were spraying the fishing vessel with a hail of bullets. The noise was catastrophic, a savage splitting of the former silence, and Tolan saw the men on the fishing vessel scattering, bellowing, convulsing and collapsing as the bullets tore through them, ricocheted off metalwork, shattered the glass of portholes and caused pieces of splintered wood to fly out in all directions.

It was all over in seconds. When silence descended again, there was no movement from the fishing vessel and the body of the man in the rowboat was sinking into the black sea.

Boris turned to stare steadily at Tolan.

'I told you,' he said, 'I don't make mistakes. If those men couldn't be trusted before, they can be trusted now.' He turned to two of the men in overalls. 'Okay,' he said.

Without a word, one of the men picked a waterproof satchel up off the deck, then both men clambered over the side and made their way down the rope ladder to the rowboat. They rowed across to the fishing vessel. When they reached the fishing vessel, the man with the waterproof satchel clambered carefully up the side of the hull, keeping a grip on the rope ladder with one hand and holding a pistol in the other, while the second man, still in the rowboat, kept his pistol aimed at the deck, preparing to fire at anything that moved. In the event, nothing moved.

When the first man had made it to the deck, he leaned down, briefly disappeared from sight, then straightened up again and raised his thumb in the air, confirming that all of the crew were dead. He then disappeared into the central cabin of the fishing vessel, obviously going below decks, while the man in the rowboat holstered his pistol and sat back to wait, letting the crossed oars rest on his legs. After about five minutes, the first man reappeared, clambered over the railing and made his way down the rope ladder to the rowboat. He was rowed back to the motor launch and both men clambered back up onto the deck. When they were safely aboard, a third man in over-alls fired a sustained burst from his sub-machine gun at the rowboat, peppering it with bullet holes until it started sinking. Eventually, the rowboat sank completely.

'Let's get back to shore,' Boris said.

The motor launch roared into life and headed back to shore. Five minutes later, it had docked at the short jetty and the men in overalls started transferring the plastic bags to the parked transit van. They had just completed this task when there was a thunderous explosion and the fishing vessel out at sea exploded in a jagged sheet of silvery-yellow flames and clouds of black, boiling smoke. It was a fearsome explosion, lighting up the night and briefly blotting out the stars, and when the echoes of the blast subsided, which did not take very long though it seemed like an eternity, the fishing vessel was almost destroyed, the remains of its still blazing, smoking hull sinking into the sea. Eventually, like the rowboat, it sank under the waves and vanished completely, leaving only a few pieces of debris floating on the surface. When the smoke cleared away, the starry sky reappeared in all its glory.

Falling in beside Boris, Tolan and Meehan went to look into the rear of the transit van where the four men in blue overalls were now seated, two on each side, facing each other over the high pile of plastic bags filled with cocaine. Tolan had never seen so much of it before and he was truly impressed.

'Sure this is a grand day indeed,' he said on an emotional impulse, turning to face his new friend Boris. 'The dawn of a new era, like. I think we should shake on it.'

'You hand over the weapons two weeks from now?'

'Ackay,' Tolan said.

They shook hands at this dawn of a new era, then made their way back to Belfast.

Chapter Eight

Knowing how important it was to keep in shape, Coogan went through his daily routine of rigorous exercises. Then, sweating profusely, he showered and dressed in casual clothing suitable to the unusually warm weather of this summer in Northern Ireland: blue denims, open-necked shirt, zip-up light windcheater jacket and rubber-soled brown suede shoes. When he was dressed, he sat on the fold-down table in the kitchen-diner of this white-walled holiday cottage and had a high-calorie fried breakfast while looking out at the green fields of this secluded glen in Country Antrim.

So far, everything had gone according to plan. Exactly seven days ago, Coogan had flown into Belfast City Airport. Renting a car, using his false driving licence for identification, he had driven straight to County Antrim, where he had soon found this holiday cottage being let through an estate agent in Antrim city, where he had never been before and was not known. Coogan had decided that he could not stay in Belfast because too many people there knew him. Instead, he was staying out here in the green glens of Antrim, in an area filled with holiday cottages, where unfamiliar faces would not be thought unusual, and was driving into Belfast only when strictly necessary. He had, however, put Nick Wright and Barry Newman in Belfast, Wright in a studio apartment in Fitzroy Avenue, Newman in Rugby Avenue, only a couple of blocks away, both addresses in the university area where Catholics and Protestants mixed freely and where, again, because there were so many tourists, strangers' faces would not be considered unusual. He had also put them there because, as he had found out through a friend who was presently acting as his eyes and ears in the city, Boris Vasilyovsky had recently moved out of the Europa Hotel and into a large, secure house in the same area.

Coogan was going to see that friend at lunchtime.

Finishing his breakfast, he methodically cleared away the dishes and placed them in the dishwasher, which he only used about once a week because of his dismal bachelor existence. Finally, since there were no random police searches in Belfast these days, though the city could still be dangerous to him, Coogan strapped a holstered Brown 9mm High Power handgun, his old SAS weapon, to his waist, positioned to the left of the small of his back to enable him to make a quick cross-draw if and when required. Then he left the house.

Stepping into the silvery-grey early light of this fine summer's morning, he walking to the Ford Cortina parked in the tree-lined road at the end of the garden. The road, which here was more like a country track, surrounded by gently rolling green hills, led in one direction to the shore of Lough Neagh, located three miles west of here, and, in the other direction, to Antrim city, where it merged with the M2 motorway to Belfast. Coogan headed off in the car in the direction of Antrim city.

It truly was a lovely country, he thought, not for the first time, as he drove through the undulating green hills, under a sky filled with clouds that were streaked with striations of sunlight and resembled drifting pieces of candy-floss. It was hard to imagine how many bodies were still lying out there in unmarked graves, in those lovely green fields, under that candyfloss sky, the remains of the victims of brutal sectarian murders.

Coogan thought of the hills in that way because of his previous time in Belfast, working covertly for the British Army's supposedly disbanded 14th Intelligence Unit during the tail-end of the Troubles in the late 1990s. At that time, Coogan, an SAS sergeant, and others from the Regiment had been tasked with neutralizing the breakaway terrorist groups that were attempting to disrupt the fragile peace on both sides of the divide. It had been an unpleasant task, requiring duplicity, occasional blackmail and the taking of lives, exposing Coogan to a side of the conflict not normally reported in the press, with viciously dirty tricks being played by both sides. Now, when he looked at the beautiful hills and glens on both sides of the road he was driving along, Coogan could only recall the unfortunates who had been tortured, killed and buried secretly out there. A few of them had been shot by him, though certainly those had not been tortured before being executed.

When he bypassed the city of Antrim and picked up the motorway to Belfast, where the traffic was more dense, he began to feel slightly but helplessly uneasy, as he had done all week each time he had ventured into that familiar though rapidly changing city. His discomfort was due to the fact that he could not avoid going in but knew that a chance encounter could lead to his recognition by an old friend or enemy. In fact, he was going to see an old friend now, though that was by choice. But what he most feared was being seen either by someone who had cause to dislike him – a former paramilitary, say, with whom he had 'interacted' during his SAS days – or, even worse, by one of Pat Tolan's men.

Some of Tolan's mob had met Coogan when, after the SAS was disbanded, he had returned to Belfast to work for the gang boss, robbing post offices and banks on both sides of the border. The decision to do so had probably been the worst that he had made to date. He had made it when his military career had come to an end, his marriage was breaking up, he was bored, frustrated and drinking too heavily, and his inability to find a job that could hold his interest had driven him to the edge of breakdown. Coogan's eventual drift into crime in the province was not something that he felt particularly proud of, though he knew that he would do it again under similar circumstances. Even now, back here to 'neutral-ize' Pat Tolan and Boris Vasilyovsky – in other words, to kill them and, if necessary, their friends – he could not deny that he was excited by the challenge. Nevertheless, he was also aware that he had to be careful when moving around the familiar streets of Belfast. Too many people knew him there and most of them were Tolan's friends.

Arriving on the outskirts of the city, where the Black Mountain loomed above the new high-rise buildings to the west with Cave Hill, the cliff edge known as Napoleon's Nose, clearly visible, he drove past the pedestrianized centre of town, now greatly modernized with office devel-opments and shopping arcades, bypassed the imposing City Hall with its soaring copper dome, and drove on to the university area. There he patiently searched for, and eventually found, a free parking meter. Leaving the car, he walked the short distance to the Botanic Gardens and went straight to the Ulster Museum. Frank Cooney was waiting there for him.

A former journalist with the *Belfast Telegraph*, a Union-ist newspaper, Cooney had, in the past, assisted Coogan and other undercover operatives with helpful information about the terrorist groups on both sides of the divide. Though a Protestant who had lost his daughter during a shoot-out in an abortive IRA bank robbery many years ago, Cooney had few religious or political prejudices and strongly believed in the peace process. He had therefore been keen to assist Coogan when the latter told him about the proposed amalgamation between Pat Tolan's criminal gang and the *mafiya*. It was Cooney who had informed Coogan that Boris Vasilyovsky had moved out of the Europa Hotel and into a house in the university area. Hopefully he had been, as instructed by Coogan, checking Pat Tolan's movements over the past few days.

When he saw Coogan enter the museum, Cooney advanced across the reception area to greet him and said, 'Let's go back outside for a walk. I could do with some fresh air.'

'Right,' Coogan said, turning away and leaving again, Cooney coming out behind him. Once outside the building, Cooney fell in beside him, lit a cigarette and smoked as they wandered around the Botanic Gardens' colourful array of flower beds.

'Best to talk out here,' Cooney said. 'Too many bloody tourists in there these days.'

'This is the first time I've ever met you here,' Coogan said. 'We used to meet way out at the Giants' Causeway.'

'I was younger then,' Cooney said with a wry smile. 'I drove out of town a lot in those days; walked the cliffs and so on. I'm not so energetic these days. Besides, the Troubles are over and despite the rising crime figures, we don't have the same need for secrecy that we used to have. No British Army or police foot patrols. No paramilitary spies or assassins. We should be okay here. So how's life out in Antrim?'

'Boring,' Coogan replied. 'Naturally, I'd rather be staying right here in the city, but I can't take that chance.'

'No, I suppose not. You're okay in this area, but you're liable to run into old friends and enemies if you go to your old haunts. They all go to the same places these days, so you could be spotted by either side.'

'You mean the Gallery Bar in the Europa?'

'Yes. *And* the Crown Liquor Saloon. Even Tolan uses those places these days, so you'd better stay out of them.'

'I will,' Coogan said.

'What about your friends? Are they here yet?'

'Yes. They're living in separate apartments not far from here.'

'A nice anonymous area,' Cooney said. 'And not far, I gather, from where your Russian is living.'

'That was the idea,' Coogan said.

'So you only come into Belfast when strictly necessary and let your friends do most of the legwork?'

'Right. Particularly when it comes to surveillance work in the Falls. I'd be recognized up there in an instant whereas they'll be viewed as just two more tourists.'

Grinning, Cooney shook his head from side to side in mock disbelief. 'Who'd have believed it? Guided tours of the Falls and the Shankill. Tourists taking photos of Sinn Fein headquarters and buying old UVF propaganda posters to take home and hang up on their walls. We've certainly come a long way since the Troubles, though we're still on a knife edge.'

'What does that mean?'

'The dramatically rising crime rate. All the former paramilitaries now out of work and with skills only suitable to crime. The likes of Tolan and now, so you tell me, the *mafiya*. It doesn't bear thinking about, does it?'

'We can put a stop to it,' Coogan said, 'and with your

help, we will. Have you been checking up on Tolan as I requested?'

'Yes,' Cooney said, exhaling a stream of cigarette smoke and distractedly patting down his still abundant silvery-grey hair. He had aged a lot in the past few years, though he was still a handsome man with great charm. He still attracted the ladies. 'Not much to report, though. So far, he hasn't been seen doing anything unusual, other than visiting your Russian friend in his new house only a few streets from here.'

'That confirms that he and the Russian are, at least, talking,' Coogan said.

'Quite. And there *is* a lot of talk in the pubs about something big coming up – something to do with Tolan. No one knows what it is, but the general feeling is that Tolan is involved in something bigger than usual. Though it's only a rumour, that rumour has to have a basis in fact and it certainly lends support to your contention that Tolan is preparing to tie up with the Russian *mafiya*.'

'No doubt about it,' Coogan said.

Approaching Palm House, the curvilinear glasshouse and cast-iron conservatory at the centre of the Botanic Gardens, Cooney spotted an empty bench. 'Let's sit down,' he said and went straight to it. When they were sitting side by side on the bench, watching the passers-by – men, women and children, tourists and locals – Cooney said, 'I tire easily these days. A few problems with the breathing. A few months back, virtually overnight, I suddenly felt old. Went to see the doc about it. "You're old," he informed me. "You drink and smoke as if you're still a young man and now you're paying the price. Stop smoking and cut down on your drinking or your days will be numbered." So did I stop smoking? Did I cut down on my drinking?' Cooney held his cigarette up in front of his face and gazed at it, smiling dreamily, then shook his head despairingly from side to side. 'Of course not. Why prolong your life if you can't enjoy life's little pleasures? So I tire easily these days . . . Where were we, Coogan?'

'You were telling me that, according to local gossip, something big is coming up – and what it is, almost certainly, is the merger between Tolan and the Russian.'

'Ah, yes,' Cooney said, exhaling another stream of cigarette smoke. 'That was it.'

'So what do you think of the possibility of those two working together successfully?' Coogan asked.

'I'd say it might be fraught with difficulties. Tolan, after all, is not renowned for his loyalty to his own kind, let alone to strangers; and the *mafiya* are notorious for controlling all they own with an iron fist and for not sharing anything with anyone. What's in it for them on a long-term basis? In the short term, Tolan can help them get their foot in the door in Northern Ireland; in the long term he'll be an anchor around their necks, draining off half their profits, so sooner or later they're going to want to get rid of him. Tolan's bound to know that. He's an animal, but he's not dumb. He won't trust them an inch and he's bound to be thinking already of how he can use them and then dump them. He's always been an ambitious brute. Some even think he's psychotic. Either way, he's not the sort to share power for very long – no more than are the *mafiya* – so my bet is that Tolan and Boris will eventually go for each other's throats. That's something you may be able to use, so you should watch out for it.'

'For a rift between them?'

'Correct,' Cooney said.

The sun was shining over the gardens, turning the flower beds into a riot of colour against which the passers-by were sharply outlined. Most of them looked carefree, enjoying this rare good weather, as if magically untouched by the past Troubles or the crimes of the present. Of course, looks could be deceptive, hiding all kinds of trauma, and Coogan knew from his previous experiences in this city that it was not all it seemed. Despite the peace, it was still a troubled city, still riddled with sectarian hatreds, ancient suspicions, lasting animosities, and now it was being consumed in a crime wave of unprecedented proportions. Behind the scenes, despite the posturing of politicians, Tolan was ruling this city with a combination of intimidation and brute force. If not checked, he would, with the help of Boris Vasilyovsky's even more brutal *mafiya*, turn the city into a cesspit. Right now, though, as Coogan gazed around the sunlit park, it was difficult for him to accept that this could be so. Sunlight made the world seem sweet.

'Do you have much time?' Cooney asked.

'No,' Coogan replied. 'According to our informant, the handover of weapons will take place in about five weeks from now – in early August. That's all the time I have.'

'Do you know where the handover is going to take place?'

'No. But we're pretty sure it won't take place in Belfast. It'll have to be somewhere well outside the city, but that could be anywhere. If I knew where it was going to happen, my job would be a lot simpler. Have you any ideas, Frank?'

'Well,' Cooney said tentatively, 'most of the terrorist weapons that haven't been surrendered are known to be buried in bunkers scattered around the old bandit country.'

'In County Armagh.'

'Correct. And since Tolan has a big house in County Armagh, he may well use it as his base when he's collecting the weapons to be handed over to the Russians.

So if you place his house in Armagh under surveillance, you may come up with something.'

'Where is it, exactly, in Armagh?'

'Just south of Keady, very close to the border. It's a big old manor house in its own grounds, surrounded by high brick walls. It hasn't been confirmed, but it's widely believed in certain circles that Tolan shifts a lot of material, including weapons and, possibly, drugs and other contraband, in both directions across the border, through Monaghan and Cavan and, ultimately, of course, all the way to and from Dublin, which is where, increasingly, arms and drugs are coming into the country. As I said, it's a big house – the biggest in the area – so you can't really miss it. It's off the road leading out of Keady on the way to the border.'

'I didn't know he had that house,' Coogan said. 'I always thought he was falsely modest, still living in his simple two-up-two-down in Ballymurphy to impress everyone with his working-class origins. Now you say he has a big house in Armagh. That's useful to know.'

'Place it under surveillance,' Cooney repeated, 'and you might come up with something.'

'I'll do that,' Coogan said. 'Anything else?'

'Nope. I don't think so. That's it for now, though I'll keep my eyes peeled and my ears open.'

'Great,' Coogan said. 'Who leaves this place first?'

'I do,' Cooney said. 'Give me five minutes to get lost.' He sighed and rose to his feet, glanced distractedly around him, then looked back down, grinning at Coogan. 'Coogan and Cooney,' he said. 'Sure wouldn't we make a good vaudeville team?'

'I can't sing or dance,' Coogan said.

'Too bad. I'll call you if I come up with anything else. Until then, you be careful.'

'I will. Thanks, Frank.'

'My pleasure,' Cooney said.

He turned and walked away. Coogan watched him departing. He waited until Cooney had left the gardens by the front gate, escaping into University Road, then gave him another five minutes before he himself stood up and wandered off in the opposite direction, eventually leaving the gardens by the rear gate. From there he walked to the end of Agincourt Avenue, which was empty and quiet, turned left into the Ormeau Road, which was noisy with traffic, continued walking for another few minutes, then turned up one of the side streets on his left. It was an elegant street, lined with trees and detached or semi-detached homes, most with expansive gardens, and he walked along until he saw Boris Vasilyovsky's house at the far side of the road. He didn't stop walking, but scanned the house as he passed it, taking note of the closed gates, the surveillance cameras above them, the two bodyguards sitting in chairs at the end of the drive, one at each gable end of the house.

It won't be easy to get in there, he thought, *but certainly it would not be impossible and we might have to do it.*

He kept walking. When he reached the end of the street, he turned another corner and found himself in Fitzroy Avenue. After walking about halfway along the street, he stopped at the front door of one of the terraced houses and rang the doorbell. Nick Wright's voice, distorted and metallic, came out of the speaker fixed to the door, 'Yes?' Coogan announced himself. Nick told him to come on up and Coogan heard the door click. He pushed it open and went inside, closing it securely behind him. Coogan walked up the stairs to see Nick Wright and, he hoped, Barry Newman. Wright had spent the past couple of days in the Falls Road, keeping Tolan under surveillance, while Newman had being doing the same with the Russian. Between them, they might have learnt something valuable.

Coogan needed something valuable. His time was already running out and the tension was rising.

'Hi, boss,' Nick Wright said.

Chapter Nine

'The dawn of a new era!' Boris exclaimed in disgust, repeating Tolan's words. 'Doesn't it make you want to puke? The only new era for him will be eternity, which he'll get once he hands over his weapons. God, that man is a fool!'

'Fools of a certain kind can be dangerous,' Mikhail said, 'and that man is only a fool in certain areas of his activity. That makes him a serious danger to us. Also, he knows this city better than we do and that makes him even *more* dangerous. We must tread carefully here.'

They were facing each other across the long table in the dining room of the house in Belfast, having a meal of fried bacon and eggs, with potato farls and soda bread – a real Irish breakfast – though they were washing it down with iced vodka instead of Guinness. Lara, wearing an open-necked shirt and tight blue jeans, with her long blonde hair tumbling loose, was seated beside Boris, but she had only nibbled at biscuits and cheese and was now smoking a filter cigarette. Her full lips, touched up with a moisturizer, made Boris feel horny, even though they'd had sex only an hour ago. Lara made him feel younger than he was and that was no bad thing these days.

'You're always so serious, Mikhail,' he said. 'So suspicious of everything. This man, this Paddy Tolan, is no more than a jumped-up hoodlum with delusions of grandeur. We will use him and then put him in his grave, so you have no need to worry. Once the Irishman is out of the way, we can move against the whole Irish underworld and make it our own.'

'Hopefully,' Mikhail said, forking up a piece of bacon, some egg and a piece of potato bread. 'But what makes you think he's not planning for you what you're planning for him?'

Boris thought about that as Mikhail popped the food in his mouth and proceeded to chew it. Boris glanced at Lara, whose lips were forming an 'O' to blow a series of smoke rings while her green gaze, as fathomless as a cat's, roamed about the room. When her gaze eventually came to rest on him, she gave him a slight smile. He returned the smile, then gave his attention to the always solemn Mikhail.

'You think he might be planning that?' he asked.

'Why not?' Mikhail replied. '*You* are.'

'But he has more to gain from us than we have from him. All we gain is Northern Ireland—'

'The gateway to the south,' Mikhail interjected quickly.

'—While he stands to gain a share in our territory. That territory is now as large as the Italian Mafia's and soon will be even bigger than that. He's joining up with us because that's what he imagines he's going to gain, so why would he risk it?'

'Because he doesn't trust us,' Mikhail explained. 'Because he knows the *mafiya*'s reputation and suspects that we won't be satisfied with what he is giving us. He's a fool, my friend, but not *that* kind of fool. He knows that once we have our foot in the door, we'll kick it open and charge into the room. He knows that when we have a piece, we'll want it all and that will mean getting rid of him. He doesn't trust us one inch.'

Boris gazed sideways at Lara. She had crossed her long legs and was raising and lowering her left foot, making the muscles along her thighs ripple under the denim. The sensual movement of those thighs gave him an erection and forced him to look away. He concentrated on Mikhail.

'So what do you think he's planning?' he asked, always having had great respect for Mikhail's judgement. A lot of people thought Mikhail was only his bodyguard and driver, but in truth he was much more than that. Mikhail was the shadow that either stretched out in front of Boris or trailed out behind him. Mikhail was Boris's other half and not a man to be messed with.

'I think he'll give us the weapons and let us move into Belfast, then wait to see how much of our overseas territories he gets in return. Once we open a few doors in Europe, he's bound to want more and that, if he isn't planning to do it already, is when he'll turn against us.'

'"If he isn't planning to do it already?"' Boris asked, repeating Mikhail's words. 'What does that mean?'

'He's not an absolute fool, but his greed overrides his judgement and he's likely to be so suspicious of us that he's close to paranoid. If that's the case – and since he now has his supply of drugs – he might decide to get rid of you, by which I mean all of us, while we're still here in Belfast.'

'What good would that do him?'

'No good at all, but that wouldn't concern him. He'd only be thinking of the threat to his own life and decide to get rid of it. Also, we gave him more cocaine in one transaction than he'd normally receive in a year – and that supply will stretch a great distance and open a lot of doors that were formerly closed to him. Without us here to control him, he could sell or trade that coke anywhere, using it, instead of using us, to get into other criminal territories, perhaps through the Mafia or the triads – even the Yakuza in Japan. We've boosted his worth tremendously in one evening and he might want to use it. Those drugs would give him a lot of muscle where he thinks he most needs it – not here where he's already powerful, but in Europe and elsewhere. So we can't trust him, Boris.'

'We have to trust him at least until he hands over those weapons,' Boris said. 'We need them for our war against the triads in London; we'll also need them for our activities here.'

'I merely suggest that we be careful until he's handed over his weapons. Let's keep a tail on him. We have to know what he's thinking, what he's planning, on a day-to-day basis. That's all I'm saying here.'

'I understand,' Boris said. 'And you're making sense as always, Mikhail. I'll do something about it.'

'When?'

'As soon as humanly possible.'

'I think that's wise,' Mikhail said. He glanced at his wristwatch. 'Do you need to go anywhere today,' he asked, 'or can I have the day off?'

When Boris glanced at Lara she shook her head from side to side. 'I've no special plans,' she said. 'Just a bit of shopping, maybe, and I can either walk or take a taxi for that.'

'So be it,' Boris said, returning his gaze to Mikhail. 'You can have the day off. Any special plans?'

Mikhail shrugged, pushed his chair back and stood up. 'No,' he said. 'No special plans. Like Lara, I just want to wander about, have a look at the town, find out what's happening.'

'Keep out of trouble,' Boris said.

Mikhail smiled. 'I'll try to. See you both later.'

He left the dining room. Less than a minute later, they heard the front door opening and closing as he left the house. Boris smiled, leaned sideways, took hold of Lara's chair and tugged it towards him, until her knees were touching his. Leaning forward even further, he pressed his lips to the side of her pale, smooth neck, then straightened up again, sighing.

'Very nice,' he said. 'I could make a meal of you.'

'You often do,' Lara said.

'That's because you're irresistible. I can't think of any man who could resist you – except, perhaps, for Mikhail, who doesn't react to you one way or the other.'

'Maybe he dislikes me.'

'If he did, you'd soon know it. No, it's just that he's an exceptionally private man who rarely shows his emotions or desires. He must like you, because he's comfortable with you. He simply doesn't desire you.'

'Has he ever desired anyone?'

'A few times,' Boris said. 'But he doesn't take sex lightly. When he's serious, he's very serious indeed and that certainly applies to his women. I don't think he can pick them up casually.'

'Not like you.'

Boris smiled. 'No, not like me.'

'But you're married,' Lara said. 'You must have been serious about your wife at one stage, no matter how you feel now.'

'I feel about her now as I felt about her when I proposed. Olga's a decent, moderately attractive, middle-class woman who was born to be a devoted wife and mother. I recognized that as soon as I met her. I didn't love her then and I don't love her now, but a man needs a home and someone to look after it, a social life and someone to take care of it, a respectable front for society and someone to maintain it; and Olga was simple-minded enough to give me all of that without complaining that she hardly ever saw me. In return, I gave her three children and a big house in the country to keep her busy. As long as I treat her decently, as long as I'm kind to her and the children, she'll be as happy as that type of woman can be which is, after all, happier than most women are. Now, Mikhail, being *serious* . . . well, he married for love, or lust, perhaps confused between the two, and he had a couple of children and then the marriage broke up because his wife, disgusted by his devotion to the *mafiya*, his constant absences from home, couldn't take it any more and eventually asked him to leave. Mikhail, you see, though a criminal and a trained killer, still can't have a relationship with a woman if he doesn't think it's serious. That's his weakness, not mine.'

'You're the hardest man I've ever known.'

'That's my strength.'

'And even I'm not your weakness?'

'No. I like you and I certainly lust after you, but you're still not my weakness. Our relationship is physical, not emotional, and when the physical side of it dies, I won't want you any more. I'll be decent to you – I'll make it worth your while to leave – but you'll certainly have to go. Our relationship is, when you really get down to it, a business relationship. No other kind makes sense to me.'

He saw the shock in her face, though she was trying to conceal it, and he felt a fleeting twinge of remorse that took him by surprise. It was possible that he cared for her more than he had imagined – or, perhaps, more than he could admit to himself – but despite that, he felt it best to tell her the brutal truth rather than let them both live with a lie.

'You treat me like a whore,' she said abruptly.

'Because that's what you are. You were whoring when I first met you in Moscow and don't call it otherwise. You may not have had a pimp, you may not have been a complete professional, but you always went out looking for men with money and you never failed to find them. Did you ever go to bed for the sake of love? No, of course not! You told me so yourself. Your early life was too harsh to permit love as a luxury, so you gave yourself – I won't say you *sold* yourself – to the men who gave you the most in return. When you met me, I gave you more than all the others and that's why you're still with me. I treat you better than most whores are treated. What more could you want?'

'Maybe a proper home and children,' Lara said.

'You're not cut out for that,' Boris said.

Lara stared steadily at him, her green gaze unrevealing, then she smiled, inhaled on her cigarette and blew a few more smoke rings. She watched the smoke rings dissolving.

'Tolan likes you,' Boris said.

'What does that mean?'

'It means that his eyes crawl all over you like spiders. He has to fight to keep his sweaty paws off you.'

'That's not unusual,' Lara said. 'As you more or less said yourself, I make a lot of men react that way, so what's the difference with Tolan?'

'I want you to be nice to him.'

'I *am* being nice to him. You asked that of me before I met him. You told me to make him think that I found him attractive and that's exactly what I've been doing.'

'I know,' Boris said, 'and doing it very well indeed, but now I want you to do a bit more.'

Lara raised her eyebrows in a questioning manner, then stubbed her cigarette out in the ashtray. 'You mean . . . ?'

'If necessary, yes.' Boris turned around in his chair until he was facing her, then he leaned forward to take her hand and pull it into his lap. 'As Mikhail pointed out, we can't trust Paddy Tolan and so I have to know exactly what he's thinking. You can find that out for me. You can make the man talk. It's pretty clear that he's never had a woman like you – a foreign woman, a real beauty, a mystery and a magnet to him – so you wouldn't have any problems in getting him into your bed.'

'*Our* bed,' Lara said sharply.

'Okay, *our* bed. So don't take him to our bed. Actually, you *can't* take him to our bed because I live here and he won't do it in front of me. Just seduce him, Lara. Arrange to meet him somewhere else. Let him fuck you in some fancy hotel and you'll be stroking his ego even more than you would with sex in *his* bed. That man is trash with pretensions. He has a yearning for the good life. His idea of the good life is a woman like you, to him exotic and strange, in a bed in a fancy hotel with a minibar and TV and room service. Let him have that, Lara, and he'll soon be besotted with you, lose his common sense in your presence, feel the need to confide in you – he'll run off at the mouth like a babbling brook. So please get him into bed and make him talk his head off.'

'You want me to have sex with that piece of slime?' Lara asked disbelievingly.

Boris nodded. 'Yes.'

'I don't think I can do that.'

'Yes, you can. You've done it before.'

'Not with garbage like that.'

'You can manage it, Lara.'

'I don't want to.'

'You have to.'

'What if I say "No"?'

'If you say "No" our relationship is finished and you go back to Russia.'

'You'd really do that?'

'Yes.'

'You're a cold bastard, aren't you?'

'I am what I am,' Boris said, 'and you know what that is. Now will you do it or not?'

'Will you still want me in your bed, Boris, after that piece of slime has been all over me?'

'Of course, Lara. Why not?'

'How could you possibly still want to touch me when that scumbag has left his stench on me?'

'I have a poor sense of smell.'

Lara didn't smile. 'So I get him into bed and make him talk. Talk about *what*?'

'What his plans for the future are.'

'What makes you think he'll tell me?'

'The man's a Belfast Catholic with a limited sex life, so if you let him experience what he'd only imagined before—'

'In other words, fuck his brains out,' Lara interjected brutally.

'Correct,' Boris said. 'If you fuck his brains out he'll become addicted to you, want you ever more desperately, and eventually include you in his future plans. When he gets to that stage, he'll start confiding in you, whispering into your sweet ear, and you'll report every word back to me.'

'I repeat: I don't think I can do this.'

'Yes, you can,' Boris said. 'I *know* you can do it.'

'I'm not a whore,' Lara insisted.

'But you've bedded men for profit.' This was true enough, he thought, though there was more to her than that. She was a woman with guts, a woman shaped by harsh experience, and she had done what she did out of necessity. Boris could understand and respect that.

'So what?' she retorted, her eyes bright with anger. 'I was born in abysmal poverty, grew up with few expectations, but had the luck to become a young beauty. I attracted men from an early age and soon learned that they would pay handsomely for me. So, yes, in one sense I *did* whore – but in a personal, private way. I never used a pimp or walked the streets. Instead, I went where the money was, to hotel bars and nightclubs, and let myself be picked up by men with money. There were no one-night stands, no back-alley fucks. I always made the man court me before I went to bed with him and then, if I respected him and he asked me, I became his mistress. That always lasted until he tired of me or I tired of him, in which case we would part with no hard feelings. In short, though I've certainly used my body for gain, I've never – at least as far as *I*'m concerned – prostituted myself . . . And certainly I've never gone to bed with a man I detested, which is what you're now asking me to do.'

'You don't detest me?' Boris asked out of detached curiosity.

'I didn't until today. I don't particularly like the things you do for a living, but I've certainly never detested you – and, indeed, I've always felt comfortable with you. If I detest you right now it's because of what you're asking me to do. Pat Tolan makes my flesh crawl, so please don't ask me to fuck him.'

'I'm not *asking* you,' Boris said quietly, implacably. 'I'm *telling* you. You *will* fuck that piece of slime, Paddy Tolan, on a regular basis and report everything he says back to me. If you don't, you'll find yourself back in Russia. The choice is all yours.'

'All right, I'll fuck him, but don't ask me to pretend that I'm enjoying it.'

'I won't,' Boris promised.

Lara stared steadily at him for a moment. Then she sighed, as if weary, shook her head despairingly from side to side, pushed her chair back and stood up.

'When do I start?' she asked.

'From the next time he comes here,' Boris replied.

'And when's that?'

'I'm going to invite him for drinks tomorrow evening. Please wear something slinky.'

'Anything you say, Boris.' She stared steadily, contemptuously at him. 'Can I go shopping now?'

'Of course,' Boris said. He sat on in his chair, his erection subsiding, watching her as she turned away from him and walked, her arse a treat in the tight jeans, to the door of the dining room. Just as she reached the door, he called out, on an impulse, 'Would you like me to come shopping with you?'

She stopped in the doorway and turned back to face him, her gaze steady, her lovely face expressionless. 'Not unless you really want to. It's not been my experience that you like shopping and I really feel like wandering here and there, just taking my time. A girl's day out, I guess. But if you'd *really* like to come . . .'

'No,' Boris said quickly. 'Not really. I have to make, and receive, a lot of phone calls, so I think I'd be better off staying here. You go out and enjoy yourself. Come back when you feel like it.'

'I will,' Lara said.

Boris watched her turn away and walk out of the room. Then he sat back and smiled to himself.

'Good girl,' he whispered.

Chapter Ten

'Have you guys settled in okay?' Coogan asked, facing Nick Wright and Barry Newman over the small table in the kitchen-diner of Wright's studio flat. Nick had opened three bottles of stout and they were all sipping from them.

'It's hunky-dory with me,' Wright said, grinning. 'This is a great little area to be in. Lots of sexy female students – *young* flesh and wine bars and restaurants. I'm even thinking of moving here when this job's finished. A man could do worse.'

'I don't think Maxine would appreciate moving to Belfast,' Coogan said, referring to Wright's English wife, presently living in Enfield. 'I don't think she'd appreciate the Golden Mile as much as you do.'

'Probably not,' Wright said, looking crestfallen.

'So what about you, Barry?'

'I've settled in okay and I've been doing as you asked: keeping my eye on the Russian's house just a couple of streets away, so I haven't even seen the centre of town yet.'

'Not much to see,' Coogan informed him. 'The City Hall's worth a look, but apart from that, it's mostly modern shopping centres. Even the old Smithfield Market's virtually gone. You're actually better off out here.'

'Except that I'm sitting outside that Russian's house, fucking night and day. Now that's boring. *Real* boring.'

'Okay,' Coogan said. 'Let's take you one at a time. You've been keeping Tolan under surveillance, Nick. What have you seen so far?'

'Quite a bit,' Wright replied. 'He's pretty easy to follow. Cocky enough, or mad enough, to do what he does openly, obviously thinking that he rules the roost here. The first day, I went by car to Tolan's street and parked there from eight in the morning, a good way down from his house. He didn't come out until late in the morning, just before opening time, and he walked all the way to his taxi company in the lower Falls. I followed him on foot, then watched him from across the road. The good weather was a help. I could buy a beer in the pub opposite and drink it outside on the pavement, just like one of the locals or tourists. Nowadays, with the Troubles over, there are plenty of strangers in the Falls and a lot of people are drinking outdoors, getting their suntans, so no one gave me a second glance when I stood outside, drinking. Tolan usually turned up just after the pubs had opened because doing the rounds of the Falls pubs – obviously collecting his protection money – was part of his daily routine. At least, he did it both days I observed him.'

'You followed him all day?'

'Yep. The first day, when he'd walked to his taxi company, he spent about an hour in there, maybe doing his administration, making phone calls and so on, then went out with some of his men to do his rounds. One of the men was his second-in-command, Bobby Meehan, and the others were Jack Delaney – a big bastard – and Sean O'Hagan. I recognized them all from the photos included in the intelligence dossier on Tolan.'

'Good,' Coogan said. 'Keep talking.'

'So I followed the whole gang when Tolan was doing his rounds. He dropped into pubs, video shops, betting shops and social clubs; and always came back out smiling, sometimes so bold as to actually be holding money in his fist, licking his thumb and counting it as he walked on. In one instance – this was at a lower Falls social club – I heard a lot of noise inside and saw people streaming out of the place in a panic, so I assume that Tolan and his three musketeers were wrecking the joint as punishment for some real or imagined offence. This also happened in at least one pub. So Tolan and his boyos spent the whole afternoon doing their rounds, collecting their blood money. Then, about five-thirty, the happy hour, ho, ho, they went into a pub and stayed there for a long time. Eventually, assuming that they were boozing, I entered the pub and saw them doing just that. I hung around until they left, which wasn't until closing time, then I followed them out and watched them all go their separate ways. This time, Tolan only walked as far as his own taxi company in the lower Falls, where he had one of his own cabs drive him home. Since I was on foot I couldn't follow him but, as my car was still parked in his street, I walked all the way to his place in Ballymurphy. There were a couple of kids hanging about outside, talking, smoking, his bodyguards, so I just walked past them and went to my car and drove back here without being bothered.'

'The bodyguards were just kids?'

'Tough kids,' Wright clarified. 'Not the kind to take for granted. They were like those dickers we used to have to deal with during the Troubles – the ones who'd watch out for the security forces in the hope of eventually being given something better to do – hardly out of their teens, but hard as fucking nails and almost certainly well trained in the use of weapons. They were bodyguards, all right.'

'Did they keep Tolan company when he walked to the lower Falls?'

'At a discreet distance – yes. Two out front and two in the rear. They kept well away from him, though – probably letting the dumb arsehole think he was being brave – but they were always there, front and rear, ready to close in at a moment's notice.'

'Okay. The next morning?'

'Pretty much the same routine all day, ending, as it did the day before, at approximately five-thirty, when they all had a few pints in the same pub that they'd been in the evening before. This time, however, Tolan and Meehan left the others and went back together to Tolan's taxi company. When they came out, they did so by the side entrance, in one of the cars, with Meehan driving, and took off towards the centre of town. Naturally, having left my own car up in Tolan's street in Ballymurphy, I wasn't able to follow them and had no idea of where they were going. So I lost them that evening. Then, as it turned out . . .'

Wright glanced at Newman who said, 'They went to visit Boris Vasilyovsky in that house that he has a few blocks from here. I know because I was keeping his house under surveillance at the time, sitting in my own car parked just along his avenue. Tolan and Meehan pulled up in their car, slightly further along the road, about fifteen minutes after Nick here saw them driving away from Tolan's premises on the lower Falls. As I watched them, they entered Boris's house. I contacted Nick immediately on my cellular phone, told him what was going on, and asked him to come on over to watch the front of the house while I drove around to the rear, where the exit to their garage was located. I mean, I didn't know what they were planning, but I knew that if Boris took Tolan anywhere, he'd leave by that garage – and that's just what he did.'

'Nick had joined you by this time?' Coogan interjected.

'Yes. Nick grabbed a taxi in the Falls and was over here ten minutes after I called him. He stayed in the street to eyeball the front of the house while I drove around to the back. I got there just in time to see Boris's BMW come out of the garage at the rear of the house. Boris was in the car with Tolan and Meehan. A transit van followed them out. I followed both vehicles all the way to a cove beyond Carrickfergus. When they stopped there, Boris, Tolan and Meehan, along with Boris's driver and four men from the transit van, got out of their vehicles and took a motor launch out to sea. I watched them from a rocky ridge overlooking the cove. I used my binoculars. The men in overalls were carrying parcels that looked like weapons wrapped in plastic sheeting. It was night, but I could see another boat, not too far from shore, outlined against the sky. Boris's motor launch went out to that boat and stopped close to it. They were there for about thirty minutes. Even with the binoculars, I couldn't see that much – it was pretty dark out there – but I heard gunfire coming from that direction. Eventually, the motor launch returned to the cove and the men in overalls, now with sub-machine guns slung over their shoulders, transferred a lot of plastic bags, almost certainly drugs, from the motor launch to the transit van. They had just completed this task when the ship out at sea exploded. Boris and the others then returned to the BMW, the men in overalls piled back into the transit van, and both vehicles returned to Belfast.'

'To Boris's house,' Coogan ventured.

'No,' Newman said. 'I followed them again. Just outside Belfast, in a lonely road that led from the M2 to Cave Hill and points north, the BMW and the transit van pulled into a lay-by where a Ford Cortina was parked. The driver and the four men in overalls got out of the transit van, carrying their weapons but leaving the plastic bags in the transit van, then got into the Ford Cortina, one in the front and the other four crushed up in the rear. The Cortina then took off in the direction of the North Circular Road, clearly taking them back to Belfast, and the BMW, with only Boris and his bodyguard in it, followed immediately. When Boris and his men were gone, Tolan and Meehan clambered up into the cabin of the transit van and Meehan drove them away.'

'I hope you followed them again.'

'I did. I followed them all the way back through Belfast, around Ballymurphy and Andersonstown, then on to Lisburn, and from there to Lurgan, Portadown and Armagh, finally arriving, in the early hours of the morning, at a big house just outside a place called Keady, near the Armagh–Monaghan border. The house had a high brick wall all around its extensive grounds. The transit van entered the grounds, but I couldn't follow for fear of being seen. I did, however, park just down the road from the entrance to the house, perfectly safe in darkness, and waited until Tolan and Meehan came out again. They didn't do so until about six the following morning and they didn't come out in the transit van. This time they were in a Volkswagen Golf, with Meehan once more doing the driving. He drove them back to Tolan's house in Ballymurphy, dropped Tolan off there, then went on to Andersonstown, where he parked the car in front of his own house. Meehan then entered his own house, doubtless to have a few hours decent kip, and I returned to my place for the same.'

'By which time,' Wright added, 'I was already back here, having received a call from Barry, telling me that he was following the BMW out of Belfast and that I might as well go on home. Which I did, of course.'

'Tolan's country house,' Coogan said.

'What?'

'I learnt earlier today that Tolan has a big country house located exactly where you were. Bit of a secret. Doesn't tell many about it. He's not even registered as the owner. According to the records, it's still formally owned by a retired businessman from the town of Armagh, a Catholic who's known to have had involvements with the IRA during the Troubles. The house was probably some under-the-counter payment from him to Tolan for protection or other services offered. It remains formally in his name, but only Tolan has the use of it. Clearly, then, assuming those plastic bags contained drugs, the first part of the transaction between Boris and Tolan has been completed. What you witnessed, almost certainly, was the delivery to Tolan of his promised drugs, brought in by sea and transferred from the smuggler's ship to Boris's motor launch, then transferred again into the transit van to be driven by Meehan back to Tolan's country house for storage.'

'What about those shots I heard out at sea?' Newman asked. 'And the ship that was blown up and sank?'

'Although the *mafiya* were in charge of the drugs, they probably used local criminals – by local, I mean from Dublin – to ship the drugs to that cove in Carrickfergus. Boris is a ruthless bastard who doesn't even trust his own men, so he's hardly likely to put his faith in the silence of a bunch of hired Irish criminals. He probably had them shot by those men in overalls, once they'd handed over the drugs contained in the plastic bags.'

'Then he had their ship blown up,' Newman said, 'so it couldn't be traced.'

'Correct,' Coogan said. He took another slug of his

beer, then glanced down through the window at the brick-walled backyard of the terraced house. The sun was still shining. Even the backyard looked cheerful. It was difficult to believe in the existence of men like Tolan and Boris when the sun was making the world seem so sweet. But Tolan and Boris existed, the shadows in the sunlight, poisonous to all that they touched, accepting no limits. Coogan prided himself on his own toughness, his ability to be ruthless, his general lack of fear, but when he thought of Tolan and Boris, what they did and could do, he felt almost soft. They were the hardest of the hard men, convinced that might was right, capable of any kind of violence, and willing to go to any lengths to get what they wanted. Coogan himself had that quality to a certain degree – indeed, he shared their criminal traits – but he had his limits and that could prove to be his weakness when it came to the crunch. He could not let that happen, had to make sure he survived, and so he tried to remind himself that Tolan had shopped him, landing him with ten years in prison, and that the need for revenge could be his saving grace in this sorry affair.

He couldn't feel that sort of personal hatred for the Russian – Boris was still an abstraction – but he knew, when he thought back on the man's dossier, that he was, if more sophisticated than Tolan, no less ruthless and brutal. His day would come, too.

'Anyway,' Coogan continued, 'if the *mafiya* have handed over their drugs, as clearly they have, that means their deal with Tolan is ongoing and the next step is the handing over of the Irish weapons. That gives us slightly less than five weeks to get rid of Tolan and the Russian, thus putting a stop to the rest of it.'

'So how do we do that?' Newman asked.

'We start by neutralizing either Tolan or Boris – and

right now Tolan seems the easier choice. Boris's house is well secured and he never travels anywhere by foot or without his bodyguards wrapped tightly about him. Tolan, on the other hand, is living out in that quiet street in Ballymurphy and he travels into the Falls a lot. He's either dumb enough, or arrogant enough, to do it on foot with his dickers ahead and to the rear, in both cases a good distance away. That could make him a pretty good target if we do the job properly.'

'We'd have to be in and out quickly,' Wright said, 'to avoid interference from the dickers.'

'A hit-and-run job from a passing car,' Newman suggested. 'That would seem the obvious way to do it.'

'We can certainly try it,' Coogan said. 'At the same time, we'll have to keep Boris *and* Tolan's house in Armagh under surveillance.'

'Aw, shit!' Wright exclaimed in disgust.

'I was hoping you wouldn't say that,' Newman added, grinning at Coogan. 'Doing that kind of job on your own is an absolute bastard.'

'I'm afraid it might be unavoidable,' Coogan said. 'Two of us will have to stay in Belfast to track Tolan and Boris simultaneously while the third does the OP job in Armagh.'

'A fucking OP on your own,' Newman said, referring to the loneliness of being in an observation post without company, 'is truly the pits. Not recommended, pal.'

'We *have* to keep our eye on that house in Armagh,' Coogan insisted. 'We have to find out if Tolan is moving weapons in and out of there. If he is, it means that the handover of weapons to the Russians will take place either there or somewhere in that area. So an OP it has to be.'

'Before considering an OP in Armagh,' Wright argued, 'I think we should all stick together, at least until we've tried to neutralize Tolan. For that, we really need one man to drive the car, a second man to fire the weapon, and a third man watching the killing zone with a line of communication to the hit-and-run vehicle. That's three men; not two.'

'Yeah, you're right,' Coogan conceded. 'Thanks for reminding me. We need that man at the killing zone. I just don't like the idea of leaving that house in Armagh unattended. That place could make or break this operation.'

He was enjoying himself. This informal conversation about tactics, taking place over the kitchen table, with three bottles of beer to hand and the sun shining into the terrace's backyards below the window, reminded him of the so-called 'Chinese Parliaments' he had attended during his days with the Regiment. Those Chinese Parliaments were informal meetings held by the commanding officers of SAS patrols, troops or squadrons before an operation to discuss the plan of action. During such discussions, despite the fact that the CO might have his own initial plan, the lower ranks were free to suggest ideas, which were discarded or adapted according to the situation. Coogan had appreciated the Chinese Parliaments because they had always reminded him that he was in an organization in which the idea of class distinctions was not tolerated. So this free exchange of ideas with Nick and Barry was taking him back to the good old days.

'The proposed handover of weapons,' Newman insisted, 'isn't scheduled to take place until about two weeks from now. That means we can afford to ignore the house in Armagh for at least another few days. Why not use those few days to set up an assault on Tolan? Let's just do it and get it over with. If it fails, then we can try something else.'

'And if it succeeds?' Wright said.

'What does that mean?' Newman asked him.

'What it means,' Coogan explained, 'is that if we succeed in neutralizing Tolan, we'll be leaving the field open
for Boris and his men to take over Tolan's rudderless
gang and thus take control of Northern Ireland's underworld.'

'So we have to strike at the Russian as well.'

'Correct,' Coogan said.

'That should be easier to do,' Newman insisted, 'if
Tolan's out of the way.'

'Not necessarily,' Coogan said. 'Once we attack Tolan,
whether or not we succeed in neutralizing him, we'll
alert Boris to the fact that someone is interfering with
his plans.'

'He might not necessarily think that way,' Wright said.
'He might just assume that the attack on Tolan was
made by one of the many enemies that vicious bastard
has amongst his former paramilitary buddies.'

'Even that thought would be enough to make Boris
take extra precautions,' Coogan said. 'He would assume
that the man who killed Tolan would try the same against
anyone taking over Tolan's position – and that possibility
alone would certainly encourage him to look over his
shoulder. Also, the death of Tolan, or even an attack on
him, might be blamed on Boris and that could lead to a
range war between his *mafiya* and Tolan's men, which
would make it a lot more difficult to get to him.'

Newman shrugged. 'What's the difference? We're here
to get them both and we have to start with one of them.
And, as you just said yourself, Tolan is the easiest target
– so let's target the bastard.'

'As soon as possible,' Wright added. 'Then, if we fail,
one of us risks losing his marbles through boredom in an
OP keeping that big house in Armagh under surveillance
while the other two keep their noses to the wind right
here in Belfast.'

'Agreed?' Coogan asked of Newman.

'Agreed,' Newman said.

'So what about the groceries?' Wright said.

'I'll get the groceries,' Coogan said.

Chapter Eleven

'It's absolutely perfect,' Lara said to Mikhail as they lay side by side in a bed in a single room in the Europa hotel, both sweat-slicked from the rigours of love. 'It means we can see each other even more. He's insisting that I seduce Tolan, screw him regularly in a hotel room here in town, and report back everything he tells me. So I repeat: it's absolutely perfect.'

'What's perfect about it?' Mikhail asked, feeling sick to his stomach at the thought of Lara making love to Paddy Tolan. He despised Boris for demanding that she do it.

'Because it means we can see each other more often and more safely than we've ever been able to do before. Boris wants me to meet Tolan as much as possible, every day if possible, which means that I won't have to use the occasional shopping expedition as an excuse to get out on my own. He's going to expect me to be out nearly every afternoon, screwing Tolan in some hotel room or other. Instead, I'll be seeing you.'

It could indeed be a blessing, Mikhail thought, recalling how difficult it had been for him and Lara to get together during their past year in London; how they had only been able to do it once every few weeks when Lara was able to persuade Boris, until recently a possessive man, that she simply needed a day out on her own to dawdle in the shops, buy clothes and make-up, have lunch and generally do 'women's things'. Now they had the same problem in Belfast. To be able to have her to himself more than that, two or three times a week instead of once a fortnight, would be like heaven to Mikhail. On the other hand, given Tolan's involvement, it could be truly dangerous.

'But you're going to have to do what Boris wants,' Mikhail said. 'I mean, Boris is no fool. He wants you to get Tolan to talk about his plans and you're going to have to do that.'

Lara sighed. 'I know. But I don't have to see Tolan *every* day. I can see him once or twice a week, tell Boris I'm seeing him every day, and instead see you on my free days. At least, I'll be able to get out most days of the week and see you a lot more.'

'Naturally, that would be wonderful,' Mikhail said. 'It's just the thought of you and Tolan together. I—'

'It upsets you?' Lara asked him.

'Yes,' he said.

'Then it should upset you that Boris is making me do it.'

'That upsets me as well. I already loathe the thought of Boris making love to you. But this . . .' Mikhail visibly shuddered. 'It's nearly unbearable.'

Lara pressed her naked body to his and tightened her arms around him. He felt her moist, full lips on his cheek. 'It's all right,' she said. 'Tolan won't have me in spirit. My mind will be elsewhere when he touches me. I'll be thinking of you.'

Mikhail closed his eyes. Instantly, he had a vision of Lara lying under Tolan, legs and arms wrapped around him, so he quickly opened his eyes again and gazed up at the ceiling.

'That bastard,' he said.

'Who? Tolan?'

'No. I meant Boris. I've been in his shadow so long, always secondary to him, the real brains behind him but not recognized as such, and if I already loathed him for that I now loathe him even more because of what he's asking you to do. Some day . . .' Mikhail clenched his right fist. 'Some day . . .' he repeated.

Lara kissed his cheek again, letting him feel the warm softness of her breasts, the hardened nipples, the smooth skin of her pale limbs. 'Yes, Mikhail, some day. Your day will come. And who knows? The information that I'll be getting out of Tolan could be useful to you. Every word that I pass on to Boris, I'll pass on to you too. If necessary, I can even be selective in what I pass on to Boris. I could, for instance, tell you first and let *you* decide what I should tell Boris.'

'In other words, control the flow of information.'

'Yes, Mikhail, exactly.'

Mikhail liked the idea. The control of information was the most effective way of controlling any country, corporation, organization, situation or individual: it could certainly be a useful tool in Mikhail's secret plot to eventually get rid of Boris without overt personal involvement and have himself elected by the other five leaders to the six-man team that ran the worldwide *mafiya*. Mikhail had been with the *mafiya* since 1985, when he had been only eighteen, and had spent the next five years as a bootlegger, helping to build up the organization's sales of illicit alcohol during Gorbachev's anti-alcohol campaign which, just like Prohibition in America, had made fortunes for the illicit booze-runners. He had been introduced to Boris Vasilyovsky in January 1991, shortly after the collapse of the USSR, when the *mafiya* had held a conference to discuss the Government's plans to phase out the rouble note.

Introduced by his local *mafiya* boss as 'the brightest boy I have', Mikhail had made a strong impression on Boris who had promised to contact him soon. In fact, they had met again in March, this time in Warsaw, when the *mafiya* met with Italian organized-crime syndicates. During that meeting, Boris, already powerful within the organization, had elected Mikhail as his personal aide and later, when the conference was over, had asked if Mikhail would be interested in working permanently for him. Mikhail had said that he would and at the end of that year, when the most powerful of the *mafiya* met at Vedentsevo to determine future strategy, Mikhail was there as Boris's secretary.

By the early 1990s, when the struggle for control of organized crime in Russia was between the Chechen *mafiya* and Otari Kvantrishvili's Georgian gangs, Mikhail was tasked by Boris with eliminating as many Georgians as possible and did so, with his team of well-armed men, in a series of bold gun battles, ambushes and bombings that caused devastation among the Georgians. Not content with this, Mikhail then went on personally to assassinate their leader, Kvantrishvili, by shooting him dead with a sniper rifle as he came out of a Moscow bath-house.

Impressed, Boris made Mikhail his second-in-command and placed him in charge of, first, the bottom end of the *mafiya* market (prostitution, protection and robbery), then the second level (money launderers, corrupt police officers on the take and those in the military who sold high-quality protection and weapons) and, finally, the topmost tier: the corrupt businessmen and white-collar criminals, many in superficially legitimate conglomerates that controlled a broad spectrum of criminal activities worldwide. Now Mikhail had only one personal ambition left: to become one of the arbitrators and 'matchmakers' in the *mafiya*'s national council, the *vory v zakonye* – thieves within the code. But the only way to do that was to take Boris's place – and Boris had made it perfectly clear that he had no plans for retirement.

'If we do as you suggest,' Mikhail said to Lara, 'and Boris finds out, you can be sure that he'll kill us.'

'He won't find out,' Lara said fearlessly. 'And if we do it, you could have all the information you need to somehow compromise Boris with the *mafiya* or have him killed by your more immediate enemies, namely Tolan or his former paramilitary thugs. You'd then be automatically promoted by the *mafiya* to Boris's seat on the national council. Then our life would be perfect.'

Mikhail turned his head on the pillow to stare into Lara's eyes, which were green and opaque, drawing him in, as helpless as a fly in a spider's web, to consume him and render him as dust. He was helpless in her presence, not hard as he normally was, not as coldly intelligent, not as strong, and even while he wondered just how far he could trust her, he knew that he had no choice in the matter because he couldn't resist her.

Even now, Mikhail could scarcely believe that he had Lara in his bed, that he had stolen her from Boris (though she was still Boris's mistress) and that despite his misgivings about his previous affairs, not to mention his failed marriage, he could scarcely sleep at nights for thinking about her.

How had this come about?

In truth, Mikhail couldn't really remember. He only remembered that when Boris had first brought Lara to his place in Moscow, his exclusive apartment overlooking Tagansky Square, well away from the home of his wife and children in the countryside, he, Mikhail, had thought her beautiful, as most other men did, but had not been particularly interested in her. His interest had come about gradually, as he came to know Lara more, as he had sensed that they could be friends, when he found himself noticing the way she smiled at him, her warmth saturating him, and the way she would giggle softly when something amused her, automatically placing her hand on his shoulder, on his forearm, his wrist or hand.

It had all begun like that, like an unravelling dream, slowly creeping up on Mikhail as he drove Lara here and there, looking after her for Boris, until the day she suddenly kissed him, as if on an impulse, an almost sisterly kiss, though he seemed to feel her lips on his for days after, smelt her scent, saw her face, was haunted by her presence with every breath he took, and then knew, though he could scarcely believe it, that she was his for the asking. He took her out shopping again, driving the car with her beside him, and she reached out to lay her hand on his thigh and her touch stripped him bare.

'Take me somewhere,' she said.

Mikhail took her to a hotel in the West End of London, the name of which now escaped him. He simply parked near the first hotel they passed and booked a room for the night. In fact, it was only lunchtime. They had a meal in the hotel restaurant. They both drank a lot of wine and were drunk when they went up to their room. Their lovemaking was extraordinary, like nothing he had known before, and when they finished, in the late afternoon, he was hers for the asking.

Their affair had started that day (like Mikhail's whole life, a subterfuge) and throughout it he had felt like a man who had lost his identity. He had once had the confidence of the thoroughly amoral, killing without remorse, taking his pride from his criminal skills, but from the moment Lara came into his life, all that went to the wall. Now he was like a fish out of water, floundering about on hot sand, only aware of the dazzling light that was her presence in his bed, in his thoughts, in the pores of his flesh. Without her, he was nothing.

'We'll have a perfect life,' Mikhail said, 'if we get away with this. But Boris has the instincts of an animal – geared to survival. He can sniff out treachery from a mile away and retribution is swift.'

'Don't be frightened, Mikhail. Put your faith in me. Boris will only sniff my cunt and that will keep him distracted enough not to look too deeply into what I tell him. And what will I tell him, Mikhail? Not *everything* that Tolan tells me. I'll always tell you first what Tolan tells me and you can then select the bits of information that I pass on to Boris. That way we can motivate him, make him dance to our tune, turn this way or that, gradually move in the direction we want, which with luck will lead to his self-destruction. What we want is to set up a situation between him and Tolan where they go for each others' throats in circumstances where Boris will be the first loser and get terminated. Then, since we'll know all about Tolan's movements – since he'll be telling me what they are – we can move against *him* and get *that* bastard out of the way as well. You'll then be promoted within the ranks of the *mafiya* and can take over the Irish underground, which will make you even more powerful. Have faith in me, Mikhail, don't be frightened. We can only win with this one.'

But Mikhail *was* frightened . . . for the first time in his life. His long years with the *mafiya* had made him fearless as a rule but the thought of turning against Boris Vasilyovsky filled him with dread. Boris was swift with retribution and could be unspeakably brutal. Men who stole from him had their fingers chopped off; men who proved to be traitors were blowtorched before being shot; men who went to the police or joined rival criminal gangs were forced to watch their wives and children being raped and murdered before they, too, were put to death, usually after torture. So there were no limits to what Boris might do if he discovered Mikhail's treachery.

Thinking of this, Mikhail, usually a hard man, became as soft as a child. Pressing more closely to Lara, resting his cheek on her warm breast, he choked back a sob and whispered, almost desperately, 'Do you love me?'

'Yes, Mikhail, you *know* I do. But Boris would never permit us to be together – he'd send me away first. That's what he threatened to do if I refused to go to bed with Tolan: he was going to send me back to Russia. He'd do that if we knew we wanted each other. We both know he would, Mikhail.'

'Yes,' Mikhail said bitterly.

'We have to make sure that never happens,' Lara said, 'and there are only two ways to do it. The first is to make sure that he never finds out about us; the second is to somehow get rid of him, so that you, his second-in-command, get to take his position, in which case we would be free to be together. Just think of that, Mikhail . . .'

Lara's voice trailed off, giving Mikhail time to ponder. Then, just as his confidence was waning, he felt her tongue in his ear. She rolled it around in there, exciting him, then she nibbled his ear lobe, before licking down his neck and around his face to put her tongue in his mouth. He kissed her passionately, hungrily, trying to obliterate all doubt, and she rolled over onto his body, her belly pressing down on his. He hardened and felt her melting around him as she sat upright, her breasts above him, thrusting outwards, to come down upon him. He thrust upwards and in, reaching out for her breasts, spreading his fingers to press the palms of his hands onto her hardened nipples, to squeeze and stroke, to feel that softness, her heat, losing himself in the realms of pure sensation. His whole being rushed to join her, to be consumed by her, as his consciousness drained down to the centre of his being, permitting only an awareness of his cock in her cunt, the startling shifts of her flesh, her insides melting around him. She sighed and he groaned as she rolled off him and lay beside him, pulled him to her, on top of her.

Mikhail wanted it all then, letting the beast in himself roam freely, pressing down on Lara, biting her, pummelling her, squeezing her, feeling her squeezing him, legs and arms wrapped around him, moving up and down under him, writhing this way and that, trapping him, enslaving him, making him all her own. Then he cried out and spasmed and came, collapsing in a shuddering heap.

Mikhail felt ecstatic, renewed.

'We'll do this together, won't we?' Lara whispered.

'Yes!' Mikhail gasped.

Chapter Twelve

Wilson was already sitting at a table in the pub in Bangor when Coogan walked through the door. It was just after noon and the pub was almost empty, which explained why Wilson had picked this relatively early hour. Though there were a few men lined up along the bar, Wilson was the only person sitting at a table, framed by a large bay window overlooking a stormy sea. He raised his right hand in greeting when he saw Coogan who waved back as he walked up to him.

'Hi, Phil,' he said, not offering his hand. 'Long time no see.'

'Not that long,' Wilson replied, without a smile. 'Only a couple of years.'

'It seems a lot longer,' Coogan said.

'Not to me, Coogan. But then, I don't travel around the way you do, so time seems to stand still for me. Anyway, here you are. A stranger in a strange town. You ever been in Bangor before?'

'No.'

'I hope you didn't mind coming out all this way.'

'It's no distance in the car,' Coogan replied, 'and I think it was a sensible idea. No one knows me out here.'

'That was my thought,' Wilson said, now smiling slightly, without humour.

'You want another of those?' Coogan asked, nodding to indicate Wilson's nearly finished glass of stout.

Wilson nodded. 'Why not? It's as good a lunch as any.'

'Right,' Coogan said.

He went to the bar and ordered two more pints of stout. As he waited for them to be poured, he studied Wilson in the mirror above the bar: the red hair, freckled face, thin Calvinist lips and steel-grey eyes showing that Wilson was, indeed, a hard man. Though Coogan despised him, he had often done business with him. During the Troubles, Wilson had been responsible for obtaining, hiding and distributing illicit weapons for the UDA, which had placed him pretty high in their ranks. He had, however, also been a tout for the British security services, secretly passing on information about the plans of his UDA pals in return for a handsome remuneration. The fact that he was still alive and, more revealingly, had not even been kneecapped was a fair indication of his skill at being a traitor to his own kind. Coogan, then an SAS sergeant working covertly for the British army's notorious 14th Intelligence Company, was only one amongst many in the security forces who had used Wilson as their eyes and ears in the Protestant terrorist community. He was approaching Wilson again because he knew that, during the interminable peace talks, Wilson had moved his 'groceries' from where he had been keeping them for the UDA to other secret locations outside Belfast. Now, during the uneasy peace, repeatedly broken by both sides, he had started selling the weapons to anyone willing to pay for them. Coogan was only here – he was only speaking to this man whom he despised – because he needed to buy some 'groceries' from him.

When the drinks had been poured, Coogan paid for them and carried them back to the table, placing one in front of Wilson, then taking the chair facing him. He raised his own glass in the air.

'Cheers,' he said.

Wilson finished off his first pint, then picked up the second and lifelessly repeated Coogan's 'Cheers,' before having a sip. 'So,' he continued, wiping his lips with his free hand, 'you're back in Belfast again. Sure I was glad to get out of that fuckin' hole and move down here by the sea. I've given up on all that lot now. I keep to myself these days. Hands clean an' so on.'

'You never see your old mates?'

'Naw. Only by accident, like. Like when I'm in the city doing some business and might run into a familiar face in the pub. Apart from that – nothing. I lead a quiet life here, I keep my nose clean, and I've nothing to do with politics any more. That war against the Brits, it was shite. It was all shite to me. So what are you doing back here? Last I heard, you were doing about ten years in a British prison for armed robbery or something. Was I misinformed?'

'No, you weren't misinformed.'

'Workin' for that bastard Pat Tolan, weren't you?'

'Yes.'

'That must have been a bit of a comedown after being in the glamorous SAS.'

'It was a living,' Coogan said.

'How did you get nicked?'

Coogan shrugged. 'The Northern Ireland Police Service came bursting through my door.'

'Someone shopped you.'

'Yes.'

'Had to be Tolan. That bastard's the kind to do that. Back-stabbing's his middle name. So how the fuck did you get out?'

'Friends in high places,' Coogan said.

'I'll bet,' Wilson said. 'Does it concern what you're doing back in Belfast?'

'I can't answer that question and this meeting between us never took place.'

Wilson offered his crooked, humourless grin. 'Ackay,' he said. 'Right. We're a pair of fuckin' invisible men. That suits me as well, like.'

'So can we do some business?'

'You mentioned groceries on the phone.'

'That's right.'

Wilson removed a notebook and a ballpoint pen from his jacket pocket and prepared to take down the order. 'What kind?'

'Three handguns, preferably Glock nine-millimetres with thirty 15-round box magazines.'

'I have the Glock-19. The box magazines are no problem. Okay?'

'Okay.'

Wilson jotted down the first order, then looked up again. 'What else?'

'A Barrett Light .50 rifle with tripod and a couple of dozen half-inch shells.'

'The Barrett's known as the Sniper's Supergun,' Wilson said. 'The very fact that you want one tells me something about why you're here in Belfast. Am I gonna read about this in the newspapers, Coogan?'

'Maybe,' Coogan said. 'So do you have one or not?'

'Yeah, I have one – and the tripod and the ammo. So what else?'

'A GPMG,' Coogan said, using the abbreviation for a General-Purpose Machine Gun, 'with a dozen belts of the appropriate ammunition.'

'An old SAS favourite,' Wilson said, showing off his insider's knowledge, 'and I've got plenty to hand. When they disbanded the Regiment, a lot of your boyos were so embittered that they went into the business of nicking and selling on the Regiment's weapons. Since most of those selling had formerly served in the province, most of the weapons found their way to me, like. This is beginning to shape up like a major firefight. What else do you need?'

'Three Heckler & Koch MP5 sub-machine guns and three rifles, preferably G41s with 30-round box magazines. Do you have them?'

'Yes to the MP5s. No to the G41s. What about M-16s?'

'What kind of bullets can you supply?'

'What do you prefer?'

'The European SS109.'

'You want 'em, you've got 'em. How many magazines?'

'You've got 30-round magazines?'

'Ackay.'

'Thirty magazines.'

'It's the Battle of Waterloo, is it?'

'Might be,' Coogan said. 'What about a good old-fashioned grenade launcher and the grenades to go with it?'

'Sure that shite's too old-fashioned these days,' Wilson said. 'Take a SMAW instead. I'm sure you know what it is.'

'Yes,' Coogan said. 'A Shoulder-launched Multi-Purpose Assault Weapon with a reloadable launcher that fires HEDP – High-Explosive Dual Purpose – and HEAA – High-Explosive Anti-Armour – rockets.'

'Right,' Wilson said. 'Since these are days of peace, ho, ho, sure ya can't be plannin' to take on tanks or military bunkers, so I'd surmise ye're thinkin' of concrete or brick walls – a private house, for instance – and, maybe, light armoured vehicles or just plain cars or vans. Am I right?'

'Fuck you,' Coogan said.

'You're the one who'll be fucked if you don't take my advice. So is it a pitiful grenade launcher or a SMAW?'

'A SMAW.'

Wilson nodded. 'Good man,' he said. 'Sure I knew you'd see the light. What else, then?'

'Despite the fact that I've dropped the grenade launcher, I still need hand grenades. What have you got?'

'Haley & Weller fragmentation and incendiary grenades. Silent electric fuzes that don't snap or crackle when the handle comes off. Take anyone by surprise, those fuckers would. Real beauties, believe me.'

'Okay, I'll take thirty.'

'I note that you're ordering mainly either in threes or in thirties. That suggests a three-man team. Right?'

'Pull your own cock, Wilson, not mine.'

'Sure ya always were a hard fucker, Coogan. Worse than the hardest of the hard men, truth be told. No wonder ya ended up workin' for that treacherous pig Tolan, only to be shopped by the fucker. So what else can I sell you?'

'Image-intensifying sights?'

'Ackay. Nat'rally. Orion-80 passive night sights for attaching to the MP5s. Davin Optical IRS 281 night-rifle scopes for fitting to the M-16s.'

'Okay. Three of each. Surveillance equipment?'

Wilson grinned. 'No bottom to this well, pal. Just fuckin' ask, boyo.'

'Would you have a tripod-mounted Surveillance Technology Group audio surveillance system, including laser transmitter, optical receiver, eight-millimetre high-grain microphone probe, and lens?'

'The Surveillance Technology Group?' Wilson asked rhetorically, doing his old Smithfield Market-trader bartering bit. 'That's the fucking US of A, Coogan, and it doesn't come cheap, like.'

'Just throw it in with all the rest of it,' Coogan said, 'and give me a round figure.'

'Sounds good,' Wilson said.

'Communications?'

'We *are* talking about Belfast? Local action, like? Not the fuckin' Iraqi desert. Counter-terrorist, close-quarter battle and so on. Nothin' too grand?'

'I think you have the picture.'

'No respirators? No . . . ?'

'No,' Coogan interjected abruptly.

'Okay. Something simple. Compact, lightweight, easy to operate and with a hands-off operational capability that allows weapons to be fired at the same time. Right?'

Coogan closed his eyes and opened them again, a sign of impatience with Wilson's incorrigible self-regard and insistence upon trying to seem clever. 'Right,' he said.

'What about a Landmaster III hand-held transceiver including encoder, microphone and earphones, available in either the VHF or UHF frequency ranges?'

'Too complicated. We—'

'The three of ya.'

'Okay,' Coogan acknowledged, 'that much is obvious. None of the three of us will be requiring encoders, microphones or earphones, despite any noise that might be present. Should the situation change in the near future, I'll get in touch with you again. Meanwhile, all we require are—'

'Radio Systems Incorporated walkie-talkies,' Wilson interjected enthusiastically. 'Ya can't beat 'em for intimate operations, like. You'll be wantin' three, nat'rally.'

'Naturally,' Coogan said.

'I'm makin' m'self a tidy wee sum here,' Wilson said, 'so I'm gettin' pretty excited, like. Anything else?'

'I don't think so,' Coogan said. 'At least not for now, though I may have need to return to you.'

'Just pick up the phone, boyo.'

Coogan was not amused. As he stared into the cold grey eyes of this former terrorist and tout, his red-haired head and acne-scarred face framed by the broad window and wind-lashed, sludge-grey sea, he recalled how, during the Troubles, the man had moved like a shadow between the UDA and the defence forces, shopping his friends even as he was climbing the ladder of their organization. Wilson was a scumbag, a Catholic-hating Loyalist on the one hand, a self-serving criminal on the other, who would sell out his own mother for a deal. Yet despite his double-dealing and, now, his selling of weapons to all comers, irrespective of their motives, he could be trusted to keep a deal once he had made it – and he could also be trusted not to talk to anyone about it. Coogan respected him for this, if nothing else. But no way could he like the man.

'So how do I pick up my groceries these days?' Coogan asked.

'How do I get paid?' Wilson retorted.

'In hard cash the second I check the delivery.'

'That's too late. I need at least fifty per cent before anything's delivered.'

'Anything?'

'Anything.'

'Not even a sample of the merchandise?'

'Nothing.'

'Nothing's too little for me.'

'You don't trust me?'

'No.'

'Okay,' Wilson said, offering that humourless smile. 'You pay fifty per cent up front and pay the rest when you've personally checked the delivery. *I'*ll trust *you* that far.'

'A decent, upstanding Protestant,' Coogan said. 'A man of faith, as they say.'

'Fuck you,' Wilson responded.

Coogan couldn't help smiling at that response. 'How much will all this cost me?' he asked.

Wilson removed a miniature calculator from his inside jacket pocket, then started keying in numbers as he checked the lengthy order written down in his notebook. When he had finished, he put the calculator back in his pocket and slid the notebook over to Coogan.

'There's the figure,' he said.

Coogan automatically whistled, not sure himself whether he was expressing admiration or outrage at what Wilson was demanding. 'That's a lot,' he said.

'Don't shite me,' Wilson retorted. 'You're doing eight-to-ten, you somehow get released, then you turn up here asking for weapons for what has to be a three-man assault team. Only the fucking British government could have fixed that up, so the money has to be pretty grand. You don't want to pay, don't pay, but where else can you go? You want weapons in Northern Ireland, I'm yer man. There's no one else, that's for sure. Pay up or shut up.'

'I'll pay up,' Coogan said. 'So what's the drill? You have to tell me the drill. I'm sure you work differently these days. These being days of peace and reconciliation. I'm sure you know what I mean.'

'Peace, my arse,' Wilson said. 'This city's worse during the peace than it was during the Troubles.'

'How come?'

'Belfast is fucking Kosovo all over again,' Wilson said. 'The Prods are the Kosovars, but they refuse to move out and now they're practically surrounded by the Serbs, by which I mean the Taigs. You know where I come from, Coogan?'

'The Torrens estate in north Belfast, as I recall.'

'Right. The Torrens estate. That estate is strictly Protestant, but now it's virtually surrounded by the Taigs of
Ardoyne even as it's shrinking in size.'

'What does that mean?'

'Before the Troubles erupted in 1969, our estate had
nearly five hundred Protestant families; today, only sixty
remain. All the rest of the Protestant houses are empty
and bricked up like old bomb shelters. Nearby, in Ponsonby
Avenue, which used to be equally balanced between
Prods and Taigs, there isn't a single Protestant left. Ethnic cleansing's the only term to describe what's happening in Belfast. I mean, since the ceasefire, the number
of people in need of relocation within one of their own
communities, either Prod or Taig, has risen from about
two hundred a year to six hundred. And the places they're
being relocated to are becoming ghettoized, with the
people living in constant fear of their neighbours. I mean,
fuck it, man, even children's playgrounds and parks have
become segregated since the so-called ceasefire.'

'You're exaggerating, surely,' Coogan said, already wea-
ried by Wilson's sectarian paranoia and keen to take
the conversation back to the business at hand. Wilson,
however, had other ideas.

'Am I?' he said. 'Well, listen to this, you Anglified
eejit. Until the Balkans reignited over Bosnia, it was
fucking Belfast that experienced the biggest population
shift in Europe since the Second World War with 60,000
people having to relocate to avoid being attacked by their
neighbours. In short, they were moved out of their homes
because they could only be safe in single-religion areas.
Those relocations are still happening, but in even greater
numbers – and most moves are to the benefit of the Taigs.
These days, north Belfast is increasingly Catholic and the
Prods are in a panic because it's them that are gettin'
pushed out or jammed into ghettoes while the fucking

Taigs breed like lice. You think I'm exaggerating? Well, boyo, let me tell you that since 1971 we've lost over a hundred thousand Protestants while the Catholics have increased by 7,000. Even where money rules, in the Malone Road, for instance, where the big houses are, what was once an exclusively Protestant area is now mixed, with more Catholics moving in every week.'

'That's why you moved out here to Bangor?'

'I moved out,' Wilson said, 'when my local Protestant church hall was taken over by Catholics and then used to teach the Irish language to Catholic kids. The front door of that hall used to face our estate. Now the front door's sealed up and the back door, facing the Catholic estate, is the only one that's used. That fucking did it for me, like. I moved out and came here to Bangor, a nice wee respectable, well-off town where a Protestant doesn't feel that he's bein' besieged by fuckin' Taigs. I have a trouble-free life here.'

What really annoyed him about Wilson, Coogan now realized, was the blatant disparity between his criminal activities, which included the betrayal of his old UDA buddies, and his insistence on still talking as if he was a dedicated Loyalist. This kind of hypocrisy was one of the many curses on Northern Ireland in these sorry times. Wilson was only loyal to himself, though, clearly, he liked to think otherwise.

'Well, thanks for the political lecture,' Coogan said drily, 'but as I asked you before, what's the drill?'

Wilson sat back, looking expansive, a man in control of his own patch and enjoying himself. 'When do ya want yer groceries?' he asked.

'Now.'

Wilson raised his eyebrows in enquiry. '*Right* now?'

'Yes.'

'That's a bit short notice, like, even for me.'

'What's the problem?'

'The problem is: Who do I deliver them to and how?'

'I have a transit van, driven by one of my friends, parked just outside this pub. You come out to that van and I'll give you half of the money in hard cash, then we all get in the van and drive to wherever you keep your hidden weapons. You give us what we want, we pay you the rest of the money, then we split. It's as simple as that.'

'You fuckin' kiddin' me, boyo? It's certainly not as simple as that with me. No way are you going to find out where my weapons are hidden. I'll fill yer van with the weapons you pay for, but you don't see where I keep 'em.'

Coogan sighed. 'Okay. What's your suggestion?'

'My suggestion is that we go down to your van. You give me half of the money. Yer friend then gets out of the van and comes back to this pub with you, where you both wait patiently until I come back, which won't take much more than an hour or so. While ye're waitin' here, getting pleasantly pissed or having your cocks sucked by some floozy, I'll drive yer van back to my secret warehouse, load it up with the weapons you've requested, then personally bring it back to a location near this pub. I come in here to collect you and your pal, take you back to the van, which will be parked a few streets away, up an alleyway where it can't be seen, and you can personally check that your order has been delivered. Then, if it's to your satisfaction, you pay me the second half of the money and we split. What say you?'

'I say fine,' Coogan said.

'Grand. Then let's do it.'

He and Wilson finished off their pints of stout, then left the bar which was located along the seafront. The afternoon was grey and a strong wind was noisily tossing the waves out in the sea. Coogan's transit van was parked a few yards up from the hotel. Barry Newman was seated behind the steering wheel. He rolled his window down when he saw Coogan with Wilson.

'What's up?' he asked.

'I need some of that money,' Coogan said.

'How much?'

When Coogan told him the amount, Newman gave a low whistle, expressing either disgust at the outrageous cost or admiration of Wilson's nerve in asking for it. 'I just hand it over?' he asked.

'No,' Coogan said. 'You take it out of that little satchel you've got strapped around your shoulder, lay it in bundles on the seat beside you, then get out of the van, leaving the key in the ignition, and join me here on the pavement.'

Newman raised his eyebrows in surprise, glanced at the hard-faced Wilson, then shrugged and did as he was told. The driver's cabin was so high above the pavement that no passers-by could see what he was doing as he removed the piles of notes from his satchel, counted them off one by one, and laid them on the seat beside him. When he had finished, he zipped the satchel up again, looped the strap over his shoulder and then slipped out of the other side of the vehicle, firmly closing the door behind him.

Coogan turned to Wilson and nodded in the direction of the transit van. 'Okay,' he said. 'In you go. When you've counted the money, you can place it in the plastic bag you'll find on the floor under the seat. We hope to see you back here in an hour or so.'

'You will,' Wilson said.

'We'd better,' Coogan retorted.

As Newman came around one side of the transit van,

Wilson grinned crookedly and went around the other side to clamber up into the driver's cabin. Coogan and Newman waited on the pavement until Wilson had driven off before turning away to enter the pub. Newman still had the leather satchel slung over his shoulder and when they were standing at the bar, ordering two more pints, he glanced left and right at the other customers.

'Christ,' he said, 'if they knew how much dosh was in this bag, they'd all become muggers. So that was your old buddy Wilson, was it?'

'Yep,' Coogan replied. 'Not the most charming of bastards, but he *does* have his uses.'

'Can you trust him to come back with the groceries?'

'Absolutely,' Coogan said. 'He knows that if he doesn't, I'll come after him. Also, he's as sharp as a whip and he knows I might come back for more groceries. Wilson likes steady custom.'

'Let's hope so,' Newman said.

In the event, Coogan was right. Slightly over an hour later, when he and Newman were on their second pints (actually, Coogan's third), Wilson entered the pub, saw them at the table, and jerked his thumb back over his shoulder, indicating that they should come outside.

Leaving the table without finishing their pints, Coogan and Newman followed Wilson out into the street, then a good way along the darkening pavement (black clouds were moving in on a cold wind) and, finally, up a narrow side street where the transit van had been parked with all its doors securely locked. Wilson unlocked the rear door, opened it and nodded for Coogan to clamber in. When Coogan had done so, Wilson closed the door again and said to Newman, 'You get back in the driver's seat.' Newman duly clambered up into the driver's seat and Wilson took the seat beside him. The rear of the van was filled with the 'groceries' and Coogan was checking them.

Wilson didn't say a word until Coogan finished checking the weapons and confirmed to Newman that everything had been delivered.

'Pay him the same as you paid him before,' Coogan said.

'Right, boss,' Newman said. Then he looked at Wilson and said, 'Have you got something to carry this in?'

Wilson nodded and held up a small black-laminate case with coded locks. 'I think this should hold it,' he said.

'Just about,' Newman retorted. Then he opened his leather satchel and proceeded to hand sheaves of notes to Wilson who did not count the individual notes in each bundle, though he counted the bundles off as they were handed to him and transferred them to the laminate case. When the transfer of cash had been completed, he closed and locked the case.

'Right,' Wilson said. 'I'm taking it as read that each bundle contained the proper amount of notes. If not, you'll obviously be hearing from me.'

'I checked them myself,' Coogan said from where he remained in the rear of the van, surrounded by his impressive arsenal of weapons and high-tech surveillance equipment. 'And there's not a note missing.'

'Sure I trust you that far,' Wilson said as he opened the door of the cabin and started slipping out. 'I'm sure I'll have no cause for complaints in that department.'

Coogan opened the rear door of the transit van, hopped out, and closed and locked the door. Then he faced Wilson, who was carrying his black laminate case in one hand, on the pavement beside the van.

'Day's work done,' Coogan said.

'Call any time you need me,' Wilson replied.

'I will,' Coogan said.

They did not shake hands. Wilson simply nodded and

turned away to walk along the pavement, obviously heading for where his car was parked. Coogan watched him go, then clambered up into the cabin of the transit van, taking the seat beside Newman.

'Here,' Newman said, handing Coogan the leather satchel. 'That arsehole charged a lot but there's still a fair amount of dosh in this bag. I'm responsible for driving the van, so you take care of what's left of the cash.'

'My very intention,' Coogan said. 'Now let's get the hell out of here and back to my place in Antrim as soon as possible.'

'Say no more,' Newman replied, turning on the ignition, pulling out from the kerb and easing the van into the solid stream of traffic along the esplanade, hemmed in by the many hotels on the one side and the sludge-grey angry sea on the other. The van headed out of Bangor. Newman drove straight back to Coogan's rented cottage in Antrim where, as the sun became obscured by stormy clouds that started releasing rain, they transferred the weapons from the back of the van into the garage.

'What next?' Newman asked when they were sitting opposite each other in the small diner/kitchen, eating Coogan's bachelor salad (lettuce, sliced hard-boiled eggs, tomatoes and onions) accompanied by buttered bread and washed down with beer.

'The neutralizing of Tolan,' Coogan replied. 'So let's put a call through to Nick and find out what Tolan has been up to. If he's doing the same thing, going the same route, we'll make the attack tomorrow morning.'

Coogan picked up his cellular phone from where he had left it lying beside him on the table, dialled Nick Wright's mobile number and said, 'This is Coogan here. We're thinking of going fishing. Has anything changed?'

'Yes,' Wright replied. 'Everything's changed. The fish aren't behaving as expected. You'd better get over here.'

'We can't get over there,' Coogan said. Meet us at the cottage in Antrim about an hour from now.'

'I'll be there,' Wright said.

Chapter Thirteen

Boris was restless. He was supposed to be communicating by e-mail on his laptop computer with his *mafiya* associates worldwide, but he was having difficulty concentrating, his thoughts drifting away and circling back repeatedly, like ripples on a dark pond. Perhaps it was simply age: he was certainly beginning to feel that. Though only forty-two years old, his sex drive was starting to diminish and, like an old man, he was thinking more frequently about his childhood. His decreasing libido was due, he assumed, to his familiarity with Lara and his secret need for yet another woman to inject some novelty into his jaded sex life. But the recent flood of childhood memories, all reminding him of incidents that had previously been forgotten, could only be explained by his age and a growing awareness of his mortality. Indeed, every morning, when he studied himself in the full-length mirror in the bathroom and saw his expanding waistline, the results of too much expensive brandy and rich food, he was forced to accept that he was no longer young and was, in fact, approaching middle age. The thought depressed him deeply.

A man of mixed Chechen and Slav descent whose maternal grandparents had come from Grozny on the northern slopes of the Great Caucasus, Boris had emerged from a background of extreme poverty to make his way in the Moscow underworld and survive a dangerous, violent life that had made him contemptuous of normal fears, including the fear of ill health and early death. As for his formerly prodigious sex drive, he had led a life of relentless promiscuity and it had never entered his thoughts that he might one day fail to get it up. Recently, however, when in bed with Lara, he had not been able to perform or, at best, had only been able to do so after a great deal of effort on her part. And since Lara was undoubtedly the sexiest woman he had ever known, his inability to respond adequately, despite the rareness of the occasions, had given him cause for concern.

We've been together too long, he decided as he stared, not concentrating, at the glowing screen of his laptop, trying unsuccessfully to compose a short e-mail to the head of the *mafiya* gang in Peterborough. *We know each other too well. What's lacking is the thrill of the unknown. Perhaps I need a new woman.*

It interested him that he had only recently discussed with Lara the possibility of their parting some time in the future. Perhaps that thought had been subconsciously on his mind when he had ordered her to seduce Pat Tolan and report back any information she received from him. In truth, though there was certainly great value in having Lara do just that, Boris also had to acknowledge that he was unusually excited by the thought of her, his mistress, being fucked by a man who disgusted her, as could possibly be happening to her at this very moment in some hotel in the centre of town. Certainly, the previous evening, when Tolan had come around to Boris's house for drinks, Lara had, as Boris had requested, made herself virtually irresistible by wearing a skintight, off-the-shoulder white silk dress that rippled every time she moved and, being slit up the sides like a *cheongsam*, exposed her long shapely legs practically all the way up to the crotch.

Tolan had found it impossible to keep his eyes off her, no matter how hard he tried, and Lara had made it even more difficult for him to do so by making a point of always being close to him, either standing at the bar or sitting beside him on the settee, crossing and uncrossing her legs directly before his wide-eyed gaze. Boris, meanwhile, had deliberately stayed away from them, excusing himself frequently to go into the kitchen on some pretext or other. Finally, when Lara was practically crawling over the agitated Tolan, breathing into his face, making him melt in her body's heat, Boris had told them both that he had suddenly been overcome with extreme weariness, asked them to excuse him for leaving them so early (though he hoped they would stay on and enjoy themselves), and taken himself off to bed, leaving them together in the lounge.

In the early hours of the morning, when Lara had finally joined Boris in bed, she was able to inform him that she had managed to seduce Tolan and, more importantly, had arranged to meet him 'secretly' for drinks in the Gallery Bar of the Europa Hotel the following day.

'In what way did you seduce him?' Boris had asked her.

'I let him kiss me and paw me while we were sitting on the settee. He couldn't keep his hands off me. I pretended to find him irresistible and made it seem that I was practically on heat because of his presence. He was breathing like an animal. Slobbering all over me. He was just about to lose control, practically coming in his pants, stifling his groans and pressing desperately against me, like an inexperienced youth in the back seat of his car, when I pulled away. I looked fearful, glancing deliberately towards this bedroom as if terrified that you'd emerge to catch us at it, then said something like, "No, I can't! Not here! Let's meet tomorrow. Let's go somewhere together." And, of course, he suggested the Gallery Bar of the Europa for our initial meeting and promised that by the time we'd met he'd have found somewhere more private for us to go to. So we made a date for tomorrow, starting off in the Europa Hotel and then probably moving off somewhere else.'

Lara had kept that date and Tolan, after buying her a few drinks in the Gallery Bar, followed by lunch in the Europa's restaurant, had taken her to a house near the Belvoir Golf Course, secluded in an extensive garden, in a quiet, leafy street, explaining that he had rented it especially for them and that they could use it as long as they needed for the foreseeable future. So they had used the bed in that place, that day and more since then, with Lara letting Tolan believe that she was brazenly lying to Boris, telling him she was going shopping when in fact she was meeting Tolan, gradually enslaving him by letting him fuck her and by responding as though she couldn't get enough of him.

Tolan, Lara informed Boris, was over the moon, unable to believe his good luck and growing more hungry for her every time he placed his sweaty paws upon her. More importantly, he was already starting to confide in her, trying to please her by childishly boasting to her, telling her a lot about his underworld operations, about the fear and respect that he inspired. He was even starting to question her relationship with Boris and that, too, was a good sign. He had yet to talk specifically about his present activities or his plans for the future, but Lara was convinced that if she continued to see him, letting him fuck her in that house in that respectable area, he would eventually tell her the kind of things that Boris needed to know. Boris was content.

Yet not fully satisfied.

Something was nagging at him, but he didn't know what it was. Perhaps it was, indeed, just his age, his spreading waistline, his mysteriously weakening sexual drive, these new feelings of mortality, all the memories that were crowding in on him to remind him of what he had been and what he had eventually become. Repeatedly, each time more vividly, he had recalled himself as a child in Zagorsk, a town seventy-five kilometres north-east of Moscow, where he had lived with his parents in an immense, monolithic, depressing apartment building of the modern era, redeemed only by its view of the golden cupolas and pale blue bell tower of the distant Troitsa-Sergyeva Lavra – the Trinity Monastery of St Sergius.

Boris had played with his friends on the concrete stairs of the apartment building, in the rubble-strewn grounds around it, in the snow-covered fields farther beyond, but he had done little else, since his parents didn't have much money and drank away what little they did have (the whole apartment reeked of stale vodka) while having violent, often physical rows. Though Boris himself had not, up to this stage, been actively mistreated by his parents, he had been largely ignored by them and left to fend for himself. He was soon dreaming of making his escape from his dreary, aimless existence to make a new life for himself in Moscow, the fabled city of his most romantic yearnings.

In the event, when he was twelve his mother died after a lingering, painful illness caused by failing kidneys and his father decided to move to Moscow in the hope of finding a better-paying job. There, while the twelve-year-old Boris was adjusting painfully to the loss of his mother and friends, his father got a job as a labourer in the port area of the Moscow-Volga Canal, earning even less than he had done in Zagorsk, spending most of his wages on travel to and from his dreary suburb and going back to heavy drinking for solace. The drinking did not, in fact, bring solace. Instead, it made him violent and his only son became his victim, suffering physical, albeit not sexual, abuse throughout most of his troubled adolescence.

Inevitably, Boris soon started visiting upon others the violent abuse he was receiving from his father. A bully at school, he mixed with a crowd of adolescents renowned for terrorizing the other pupils, extracting money and favours from them, and for robbing local stores and mugging unwary tourists. First failing to get into the Komsomol, or Young Communist League, which would have opened doors to higher education and travel, then also failing to receive the school grades that he required for university, he eventually got a job as a trainee garage mechanic in a violent Moscow suburb. But he drifted deeper into crime in his spare time and was fired for his frequent absenteeism.

To be unemployed in the USSR was a crime, but unable to stand living with his father any more, equally disenchanted with the thought of regular employment, Boris left home, went underground, and became a pimp for a group of amateur Moscow whores whom he ruled with an iron fist. With the collapse of the USSR and the subsequent breakdown of law and order in Russia, he was able to practise his criminal trade more openly and expand his operations to include protection rackets, armed robbery and money laundering.

Eventually, with the aid of a criminal friend, a Moscow-raised Chechen, Boris was invited to join the Chechen *mafiya* and, proving himself to be both clever and ruthless, taking readily to torture, murder and gang warfare against the Georgians, he soon rose to a high position within their ranks. Given the new freedoms of a liberated Russia, he was able to travel extensively for his work and gradually became sophisticated and world-weary, always happiest when living in a hotel.

Now, as Boris sat staring distractedly at the colour screen of his laptop computer, he did not see his e-mail but saw instead the faces of all those he had dealt with in his travels: the drug dealers, fraudsters, money launderers and prostitutes employed in his operations in London and other major British cities; the drug dealers and car thieves in Belgium and Germany; the drug dealers and illegal arms salesmen in Albania; the fanatical Serbs and Muslims to whom he had personally sold arms in still-fractious Bosnia; the innocent girls and hardened prostitutes whom he had personally rounded up in Bulgaria and transported covertly to the Middle East for a life that neither the innocent nor the hardened could possibly have imagined would be their fate; and, finally, the fat-bellied, corrupt drug barons of Colombia and the equally corrupt, often drunken ships' captains who had illegally transported his purchased drugs from Colombia through the Caribbean to Europe. He also saw the smooth, well-fed faces of the white-collar criminals and highly placed members of the law whom he had so carefully cultivated in his climb to the top of the slippery *mafiya* slope to reach his all-powerful position on the national council. He saw the faces of all of those and also the faces of his many victims: those personally tortured and executed by him, their eyes glazed with shock, disbelief or pure pain as they gasped their last and expired in his presence.

Boris saw his past life parading before him and was shaken by it, though he didn't know why. He had never been shaken by it before and this new mystery tormented him.

Did he have a conscience, after all?

No, he didn't believe so.

So what could this be?

It could only be the conviction, still nagging at him, that something was wrong . . . and he always trusted his instincts.

Right now, however, his instincts were betraying him and instead of trying to resolve his problem in a logical manner, he succumbed again to the image of Pat Tolan fucking Lara and was stirred by a mixture of revulsion and excitement.

What was it with Lara?

Thinking about her, he saw her vividly in his mind, but as he had seen her that first night in Moscow: in a notorious nightclub in a former Foreign Ministry building, which was itself near the Lubyanka, the former KGB headquarters. It was a nightclub renowned for its beautiful female clientele, yet from the instant Boris saw Lara in the crowd he couldn't take his eyes off her. Her remarkable beauty had played a part in this, but it had been something more than that – something that had set her apart (and still did) from every other beauty in the place. What was it that had excited him, intrigued him, captivated him? He had not known at the time, but he thought he knew it now: it was the air of danger about her, a feline grace combined with hardness, an air of absolute self-containment and, perhaps, the kind of ruthlessness that he himself practised and had to admire.

Now, thinking about it, still feeling distracted, he realized that she excited him because he didn't trust her and was intrigued by what she might do, which way she would turn.

And turn she surely might, since clearly she resented him making her whore on his behalf and, worse, with a man who made her skin crawl, namely, Pat Tolan. She might turn just for that.

Sighing, Boris got up from his chair, glanced down through the window at the leafy street in the university area of Belfast, surely a long way from home, then poured himself a large brandy and returned to his desk. Sipping the brandy, he stared again at his laptop screen, trying to keep his mind on the business of the day, the e-mails and phone calls to *mafiya* associates worldwide, and instead imagined, yet again, Lara being fucked by Pat Tolan, right now, somewhere near here. Almost instantly, that image was replaced by another: himself fucking Lara that first night in his exclusive apartment overlooking Tagansky Square, where he had lived while in Moscow, which was most days of the week, usually only going to his home in the country at weekends to share some 'respectable' time with his loyal wife and loving children.

His wife and children served a purpose – they were a respectable front for a professional criminal – and he now realized just how coldly, how professionally, he had gone into his marriage, made his wife pregnant and acted the role of loving husband and responsible father. He had done that while fucking Lara and a lot of other women, including some of the whores who worked the streets for him. He'd been convinced that he was immune to retribution. Now retribution could be coming his way, perhaps through Lara, maybe from another source. He had no way of knowing.

Why am I worrying about this? he thought. *Or, perhaps, imagining it? It can't be my conscience, which is something I've never had, so it has to be something else; my survivor's instinct telling me that something isn't quite right . . . Think of work. Concentrate.*

So he tried to concentrate, to ponder what he was doing here, and suddenly he found himself thinking of Jimmy

Lee Wong, head of the Golden Dragon triads, and realized that he might have gone too far with that particular killing. Already, according to the reports that he was receiving by phone and e-mail, the triads had embarked on a massive campaign of vengeance, virtually going to war against the *mafiya* in London and other major British cities. Startled at the extent of their outrage, Boris was forced to accept that his hasty action had stirred up a hornets' nest that would not be as easy to deal with as he had previously imagined. Indeed, according to the reports he was receiving, he would not need Tolan's weapons for a war of aggression but for one of defence in which the aggressors would be an army of triads motivated by fanatical, even suicidal hatred for the *mafiya*. This was not what Boris had intended. Now it was likely that he would have to commit to exactly what he had always tried avoiding: a war on two fronts. In his case, one war against the triads in Britain and the other against the paramilitary-styled criminal gangs of Belfast. Certainly, then, he would need all the weapons he could get from Tolan and he had to ensure that Tolan didn't turn against him before those weapons were handed over.

Thank God for Lara, he thought. *She's my eyes and ears as far as Tolan is concerned. With her help, her insider's knowledge, I should be able to move against Tolan before he tries anything foolish. With her help, I can get rid of Tolan and take over Belfast and, perhaps, the south, before returning, trebled in strength, to England. I think I've made the right move here.*

But had he?

His nagging doubts concerned Lara and the contempt she had shown for him when he had ordered her to share a bed with Tolan. She was doing what he had demanded of her – seeing Tolan every day and reporting back what he told her – but Boris sensed that he had pushed her that little bit too far and that something had now changed in their relationship. Lara was trying to act the same, to be casual with him, but Boris knew that she was hard, that her first concern was for herself, and he sensed that his recent demand had pushed her close to the edge. Though he didn't doubt for a second that she still despised Tolan, that Tolan's touch made her flesh creep, he now suspected that she was looking at him, Boris, as she had not done before and, perhaps, pondering how to get back at him for what he had done to her . . . And when a woman like Lara started thinking that way, all hell could break loose.

Boris finished off his brandy, put the glass back on the desk, and decided that there was only one thing to do. He had to place Lara under surveillance until this business was finished.

Boris picked up his telephone.

Chapter Fourteen

'We use this,' Coogan said, sliding the Barrett Light .50 rifle to the centre of the small table in his kitchen/diner in the rented cottage in Antrim. The rest of the 'groceries' had been stacked up in the adjoining locked garage and Coogan had no reason to think that anyone was liable to come snooping around this isolated property and accidentally find them.

'The so-called Sniper's Supergun,' he continued. 'This little beauty can fire a half-inch calibre bullet at a speed of two thousand miles an hour. The bullets can pierce concrete and have even been known to bring down helicopters. The weapon can be used to kill victims up to a mile away and a direct hit to anywhere in the torso will mean certain death. Even better: you don't even have to be a good shot to use it. Once this particular item is mounted on a tripod and the sights are correctly zeroed, you'd have to be as blind as a bat to miss – and even then you probably *wouldn't* miss. It's that accurate, believe me.'

'We can't use a tripod,' Wright said, facing Coogan across the table and sipping hot coffee, the remains of his late-morning breakfast still in front of him. 'We'll be firing from the back of the car, remember?'

'Yes,' Coogan said, grinning, 'I remember that, Nick. So you'll just rest the barrel on the lower edge of the rear window and steady it that way. It's as good as a tripod.'

'I'm the one doing the shooting?' Wright asked.

'Yes. You were always the best shot in the Regiment, so you're the logical choice.'

'Gee whiz,' Wright said sardonically, 'I'm so thrilled to be chosen.'

'Arsehole!' Newman exclaimed without malice.

'Barry here drives the car,' Coogan said, ignoring what he was hearing. 'I'll be sitting up front beside Barry, carrying a Glock-19 handgun for defensive purposes. In fact, we'll all be carrying handguns.'

He left the table, opened a cupboard by the door and withdrew three holstered Glock-19 pistols and six box magazines. Then he returned to the table and distributed the weapons to Wright and Newman, leaving one handgun and two magazines for himself.

'If Tolan's bodyguards get too close, we might have to shoot our way out but, with luck, that isn't going to happen. On the other hand . . .' He grinned and shrugged, then removed his handgun from its holster and proceeded to check carefully that it was in working order. The other two did the same.

'So let's go over it one more time,' Coogan said as firing mechanisms and magazines were noisily checked.

'Jesus Christ, not again!' Newman complained.

'Just one more time,' Coogan insisted.

Newman and Wright both sighed, but nodded assent.

'Okay,' Coogan continued. 'Tolan has changed his routine. He's stopped walking from his home in Ballymurphy to his taxi company in the Falls and instead is leaving home later, usually but not always in the early afternoon, and getting a car, driven by one of his men, to take him to a house – conveniently for us – next to the Belvoir

Golf Course. Sometimes he goes there directly from his home; other times he leaves home earlier and makes his customary stops along the way – his taxi company, then the pubs, the betting shops and so forth. He's been observed – by you, Nick – entering that house every two or three days. The first time he did so, he was in the company of the woman known from our intelligence photos to be Lara Tikhonova, also known to be Boris Vasilyovsky's mistress. On subsequent afternoons, he and the woman arrived separately, Tolan arriving in the car driven by one of his men, the woman arriving slightly later in a taxi. In most instances, the woman was observed to leave the house before Tolan, again using a taxi; on other days, but rarely, Tolan left with her and gave her a lift in his own car, driven by the same man, always dropping her off somewhere in the centre of town, often in front of the Europa Hotel. He would then either let himself be driven straight home or would drop into his office or other establishments, usually bars or betting shops, along the Falls. So that's his new, more variable routine, right?'

Wright sighed. 'Right, boss.'

'So,' Coogan went on enthusiastically. 'We'd originally planned to hit Tolan as he was walking away from his own home and was about halfway along the street. Now that he's not walking but is, instead, getting straight into his car, always parked outside his home and driven by a man who's certainly also a bodyguard, the time that he's exposed to us has been drastically reduced, which would make shooting him that much more difficult.'

'Right,' Newman said, shaking his head from side to side in mock weariness while throwing a knowing grin in Wright's direction.

'Nor can we fire at him while he's in the back of his car,

en route to that house near the golf course. We can't do that because—'

'The route takes him through areas of dense traffic and crowded pavements,' Newman interjected, having heard all of this before.

'Exactly,' Coogan said, 'so an attack there would endanger other drivers and pedestrians.'

'As well as making the target more difficult to hit,' Wright added, 'because both the attack vehicle and the target vehicle would be on the move and getting the rifle sight properly zeroed would be well-nigh impossible.'

'There speaks our medal-winning marksman!' Newman said, grinning again as he wriggled in his chair in order to strap on his holstered handgun, positioning it to the rear of his left side to enable him to make a quick cross-draw. Wright was doing the same.

'Our marksman speaks with straight tongue,' Coogan said. 'We can't open fire as Tolan's leaving his own home and we can't do it when he's travelling in his car, so we have to do it at the other house, which in fact could be helpful. The house is detached, it's backed by the golf course, and the street itself is helpfully secluded and, as Wright here has noted, not exactly packed with passers-by.'

'Correct,' Wright put in. 'It's one of those streets where the people hardly know each other and generally arrive and leave in their cars. A well-off street, you might say . . . golfers' paradise . . . and empty more often than not.'

'Which is perfect for our purposes,' Coogan said. 'Sometimes he arrives there with the woman, but usually she's the one to leave first unless they both leave together. Correct?'

'Correct,' Wright said.

'Okay,' Coogan said, 'here's how we do it. Nick is in the rear of our car with the Barrett Light .50 rifle. You, Barry, drive the car and I sit beside you, ready to take defensive action should anything untoward occur. We drive to the street this morning and park the car about halfway along it, on the opposite side of the road, to give Nick a good line of sight to the killing zone and also to enable you, Barry, to drive straight forward when the shot has been made and take the first left, almost directly opposite the killing zone, out of the street. Which means we don't have to make a time-consuming U-turn when it's time to get the hell out of there.'

'That's fine by me,' Newman said.

'Good,' Coogan said. 'Since Tolan and the woman arrive separately, with Tolan coming first, we won't try the hit as he's entering the house in case the woman turns up just as we're doing it. Since Tolan usually leaves the house after the woman, we'll commence the attack as he's doing so and when he will, with luck, be on his own, apart from his driver who, as we now know, usually remains in the car for the whole time that Tolan's in his love nest. This is also advantageous in that, given what Tolan is doubtless up to in the house, he's almost certainly going to be a lot less alert coming out than he would be when he's going in.'

'It's disgusting of you, Coogan, to even think of that,' Wright said, grinning.

'He's a dirty old man,' Newman said, 'and knows just what he's talking about. I'm with him on that one.'

'So,' Coogan said, ignoring both jibes, 'we wrap the rifle in a zipped-up golf bag and you, Nick, are in charge of it from then on. We drive into Belfast in my rented car and park it somewhere around Queen's University, in a street that's packed with other vehicles. We hot-wire one of those vehicles, transfer to it with our weapons, and drive on to Tolan's love nest, arriving there just before Tolan normally does. We park the stolen car mere yards along from the left-hand turn that gets us out of the street and we wait there until Tolan and his woman arrive, one after the other. We let them enter the house in turn, unmolested, then we patiently wait for another couple of hours until the woman leaves. Once she's gone, we keep our eyes on the front door. The instant we see it opening, you, Nick, roll down your window and position your weapon for firing while you, Barry, turn on the car's ignition in preparation for the getaway. With regard to the killing zone, you'll have to get him, Nick, as he's walking from the front gate to the car and with luck you can do it in one shot. The instant he goes down, you, Barry, get us the hell out of there, stopping for nothing. Once out of the street, you slow down to normal speed and take us back to a street near to the one our own car is parked in. We ditch the stolen car and you, Nick, give me the rifle, now back in its zipped-up golf bag. You and Barry then go your separate ways – to your flats or a pub or wherever – while I return to my own car, carrying the rifle in the golf bag, and then drive all the way back here. We all relax for a day or two, see what transpires when the word gets out about Tolan's death and then, based on what happens, get together again to decide what we're going to do about our Russian friend, Boris Vasilyovsky. Any questions?'

'More of a statement,' Wright said. 'The only thing against your plan is that Tolan and that woman don't go there every day, so we can't guarantee that they'll *be* there today.'

'That's true enough,' Coogan said, 'but there's no way around it except to go there and hope that they turn up. If they don't, we go back tomorrow and then, if that fails, the day after and so on until they show up. Any more questions?'

Wright and Newman glanced at one another, then both shook their heads, indicating 'No.'

'Then let's do it,' Coogan said.

Having already strapped on their holstered handguns, they each shoved two magazines of ammunition into the deep zip-up pockets of their travelling jackets. When they were on their feet, Coogan went to the walk-in cupboard in the kitchen and emerged carrying a well-used golf bag, which he handed to Wright who carefully placed the Barrett Light .50 rifle into the golf bag, zipped it up, then slung it over his right shoulder. Without saying a word, Coogan nodded in the direction of the front door of the cottage, indicating that Wright and Newman should leave. When they had done so, he followed them outside, locked the door behind him and led them along the path that crossed the small garden and finished at the door of the garage. His car was not in the garage because the garage was filled with weapons; instead, the vehicle was parked in the gravel driveway.

'Put the rifle in the boot,' Coogan told Wright, 'just in case we're stopped in a routine police check.'

'Good thinking,' Wright said. 'Right fucking joke if we were caught by a copper simply checking for out-of-date road-tax discs. Would we ever forgive ourselves?'

Chuckling, he placed the golf bag in the boot and stepped back to let Coogan lock it.

'In the back,' Coogan said and Wright took the rear seat as Newman sat behind the steering wheel and Coogan slipped in beside him. When Newman turned on the car's ignition, Wright started singing softly, 'We're on the road again,' an old Willie Nelson song. Newman put the car into gear and drove out onto the road, turning in the direction that would take them to Belfast. They made desultory conversation as they travelled through the green, gently undulating countryside, pastoral, sooth-ing, filled with the unmarked graves of victims of the Troubles. They stopped talking altogether when they reached the outskirts of the city, where the greenery gave way to the granite ghettoes of West Belfast, webbed with streets of terraced houses, some old, many new, separated by fields of rubble and dominated by gable walls painted with huge sectarian murals and the propaganda that the peace had not erased: IRA, INLA, UDA, UFF, UVF, BRITS OUT, FUCK THE POPE, FUCK THE QUEEN and, most incongruously, a Loyalist sign saying GET THE IRISH OUT OF IRELAND, the 'Irish' being, in this case, the republicans. Not too much had changed here.

'It's so nice to go travelling,' Wright said as Newman drove from Divis Street into Castle Street, 'and see so many exotic sights. It sure beats sitting at home watching TV.'

'Give me the TV any day,' Newman retorted as he began to make his way around the pedestrianized part of the centre of town. 'This province still stinks.'

'I like it,' Coogan said. 'I've *always* liked it. Despite the fact that the Prods and Catholics are so keen to kill each other, I've always found them to be a friendly, lively lot. A man could do worse than live here.'

'You came from here,' Newman said.

'No, I didn't,' Coogan replied as Newman circled around the City Hall and turned south, heading for the Golden Mile and the university area. 'My *parents* came from here and brought me here for a few years when I was still a kid. My parents were mixed, my mum a Prod, my dad a Catholic, and they lived somewhere out on the Ormeau Road and were never touched by the Troubles. They went back to London for purely monetary reasons – my dad got a good job there – and so I was only here for those few years, between when I was about five and ten. I can't remember too much about it, but I *do* know that I was happy enough here and pretty shook up when I had to leave. Then, years later, when I came back with the Regiment, during the tail end of the Troubles, I was surprised to find that the people weren't as I'd been told they would be – a bunch of fucking savages. They were, for the most part – and putting aside the fanatics – a decent and good-natured lot. The Troubles never changed that.'

'That good and decent lot,' Wright said sardonically, 'kill and maim like there's no tomorrow.'

'That's just one side of them,' Coogan insisted.

'So is that why,' Newman asked, 'when you decided to get into armed robbery, you came back here to do it? You wanted to work with good and decent people, like the bastard we're now trying to neutralize?'

'Go fuck yourself, Barry.'

In fact, Coogan had no idea what impulsive or crazy impulse had made him come back here to rob banks and post offices, other than his desperate need for the adventures he had missed ever since the Regiment had been disbanded and he decided to get out rather than serve in the regular army, which he thought was fart-boring. Not wanting to think about it now, he looked out the window and saw that they had just crossed the Donegall Pass and were entering University Road, which was dense with traffic and packed with pedestrians, including students from Queens.

'Take any street on the right,' Coogan said, 'and just go up and down the adjacent streets until you find a parking space.'

'Good as done,' Newman said.

He kept driving until he had passed the Methodist College, then turned right into a long, narrow street of terraced houses. Though the street was packed with cars parked nose to tail, he found an empty space near the far end. When he had parked, they all clambered out and Coogan unlocked the boot to enable Wright to remove the golf bag containing the rifle. Coogan locked the boot again and said to Newman, 'We'll wait here, having a smoke, until you find a nice little number to break into.' Grinning, Newman sauntered off along the pavement while Coogan and Wright leaned against the rented car. Coogan lit up a cigarette, something he did only rarely.

They both watched Newman with interest. He didn't go very far. About twenty metres away, he stepped off the pavement and went around to the driver's door of one of the closely packed cars. Neither Coogan nor Wright could see what model it was, though they could see Newman leaning down to expertly pick the lock. Seconds later, he had disappeared entirely, obviously slipping into the driver's seat to hot-wire the vehicle, then he reappeared to give a hand signal, indicating that they should join them. Coogan had smoked very little of his cigarette but he flicked it away, then he and Wright hurried along the street to find Newman back in the car, a battered and dusty maroon-coloured Ford Cortina, its engine running after being hot-wired. Coogan slipped into the seat beside Newman, who was already behind the steering wheel, as Wright clambered into the rear seat and placed the golf bag across his knees.

'Let's go,' Coogan said.

It did not take long to drive to Tolan's love nest in the leafy street that ran alongside the Bouvoir Golf Club. Newman parked about fifteen metres away from the left-hand turning that would afford them a quick exit from the street. The turning was situated obliquely across the road from the house that Tolan was using for his trysts with Lara Tikhonova. It was a white-painted house with bay windows and a red-tiled roof, set well back from the road in a garden bordered with hedgerows. Nevertheless, from where he sat, Coogan could clearly see the top half of the front door.

'Do you have a good view of the killing zone from there?' Coogan asked of Wright.

'Perfect,' Wright said, still holding the golf bag across his knees but not yet unzipping it.

'No problems for the shot?' Coogan asked.

'No problems,' Wright said.

'Can you turn the ignition off?' Coogan asked of Newman.

'Sure,' Newman said, then leaned sideways and downward to work his magic with the wires that he had jerked out of the steering column. The engine went dead.

'Can you turn it on again when we need it?' Coogan asked.

'Sure,' Newman said again.

'How long will it take?'

'As long as it takes to touch a couple of wires together,' Newman replied. 'As quick as turning the actual ignition key.'

'Perfect,' Coogan said. 'So let's sit here and wait.'

They waited for slightly under an hour and were just starting to think they were out of luck when Tolan arrived. In fact, the street was so devoid of traffic that the first car to pull up, a sky-blue Honda Accord, was Tolan's. They only knew it was Tolan's when the chauffeur, a hard-looking young man in denims and a black leather jacket, emerged from the driver's side and quickly opened the rear door to let his passenger out. Thin as a rake and wearing a black suit with shirt and tie and polished black shoes, Tolan looked like an undertaker. He nodded silently to the young man, then opened the gate of the house, walked up the garden path and let himself in by the front door. When he was inside the house, the young man, judging by his abrupt disappearance from view, again took his seat behind the steering wheel. Within seconds, coils of cigarette smoke were spiralling up from his open window.

'Tolan certainly doesn't live like a king,' Newman said. 'That suit could have come off a rack in the lower Falls and his Honda, according to its registration, is a good ten years old.'

'He likes to keep up a modest appearance,' Coogan said, 'but he's got the money all right. He won't die a poor man.'

'He won't take it with him either,' Wright said, speaking from the rear seat. 'I'll make sure of that.'

They did not have to wait long for the arrival of Lara Tikhonova. She stepped out of a black taxi, slim and long-legged, wearing a cream-coloured, light summer coat that failed to conceal her perfect figure, her blonde hair hanging loose down her spine. Even from where Coogan and the others were parked, they could see that she was truly something special. Newman gave a low whistle of appreciation. The woman paid the taxi driver, walked up to the house and let herself in with her own key, closing the front door behind her.

'Jesus!' Newman exclaimed. 'No wonder Tolan changed his normal schedule. How the hell did a ghoul like him find a woman like *that*?'

'Through Boris,' Coogan said. 'That woman is Boris's mistress. She has a chequered history, and it's possible that she services some of his associates at his request. You know? To soften them up.'

'Either that or she's doing this behind Boris's back,' Wright suggested.

'With that ugly bastard Tolan?' Newman said. 'I just don't believe it!'

'True love is mysterious,' Wright retorted. 'You just never know.'

'I know enough to be sure that a beauty like that doesn't betray someone like Boris for a creep like Pat Tolan.'

'She may have her own reasons,' Coogan said, 'and they could be worth thinking about. They might be useful to us in the future.'

'You're surely not thinking of blackmail,' Wright said.

'You never know,' Coogan said. 'Now let's all be quiet and just watch the front of the house *and* Tolan's driver. He might be watching *us*, after all.'

'He's half asleep,' Newman said.

In fact, they couldn't see the driver. They could only see the back of the Honda Accord and thin streams of smoke coiling upwards from the open car window where he was sitting and enjoying another cigarette. On the other hand, it was clear that because of where their own vehicle was parked Tolan's driver couldn't see them either.

They waited . . . and waited . . . nearly three hours in all . . . and eventually the front door of the house opened.

Coogan stiffened instinctively, straining to see more, as Wright rapidly unzipped the golf bag to pull out the Barrett Light .50 rifle and Newman checked that the exposed ignition wires were to hand.

'Shit!' Coogan exploded.

He had expected the woman to leave first and, indeed, she did, visible from the chest up behind the hedgerows. But Tolan came out directly after her. He closed the door behind him, then fell in beside the woman as they advanced side by side along the garden path.

'Oh, fuck!' Wright exclaimed as he rolled his window down and leaned the barrel of the rifle on the lower edge. 'Tolan's practically glued to her.'

Which was certainly true enough. As Tolan and the woman beside him reached the garden gate, it was clear that they were still close together, possibly even arm in arm. As they came through the open gateway, Tolan's driver jumped out and hurried to open the rear door of the car.

Wright steadied the barrel of the Sniper's Supergun and squinted into the telescopic sights.

'Watch the woman!' Coogan hissed.

'Fuck her,' Wright responded.

Newman touched the car's exposed ignition wires together and the engine growled into action.

At that moment, Tolan's bodyguard saw them.

'Open fire!' Coogan bawled.

Chapter Fifteen

Tolan awoke late that morning, still not believing his good luck. Lying in bed, still drowsy from sleep, he heard his wife moving about downstairs in the kitchen and realized that he liked to sleep late because it saved him from having to watch the fat hag getting dressed. If he had felt that before, he felt it even more now that he had the extraordinary Lara Tikhonova to compare Mary with.

Tolan still could not believe, despite the fear and respect he commanded within his own community, despite the fact that he had often made use of the women who whored for him, that he now had a woman as gorgeous as Lara and, even more exciting, a *foreign* woman at that. Like many a man in Belfast, a small, provincial and narrow-minded city, Tolan had spent a lot of his life secretly fantasizing about overseas places, all the countries he had never been to. He'd included in his fantasies, that endless private movie of wishful thinking, a whole host of beautiful *foreign* women with their mysterious, sophisticated, seductive ways, who would do to him in bed what no decent Irish Catholic woman would even consider. Lara Tikhonova was such a woman. Not like his blowsy wife at all. They were as different as chalk and cheese and Tolan knew what he wanted to taste the most. Not the chalk – his wife – that was for sure.

Sighing, feeling horny just thinking about Lara and the afternoon to come, Tolan rolled off the bed and went into the bathroom to shave himself and then have a bath. He used to only bathe once a week – he was normally satisfied with washing his face in the sink – but now that he was seeing Lara a couple of times a week, he liked to keep himself clean for her. Indeed, he even sprayed deodorant under his armpits and, when he had shaved, applied aftershave lotion to make himself smell nice. Luckily, Mary was always downstairs when he did this and had not so far noticed his change of habit; his new concern for his appearance and how he smelt. If she had done so, she might have wondered what he was up to, but to date she hadn't noticed a thing. Then again, he and Mary hadn't had sex for years – Tolan had quietly gone to his whores and Mary had never asked questions – so she wasn't likely to notice anything remiss there. A lot of Tolan's friends probably lived the same way, but they never discussed it.

As he was dressing himself in clean underwear, newly pressed trousers and a clean white shirt and tie, Tolan felt a certain smug pride in the thought that he was not only fucking a beautiful foreign woman but doing so at fifty-odd years of age. During the past year or so, he had suffered from bouts of depression and lack of confidence because of what he had felt was the waning of his sexual prowess. He had first noticed it when he turned fifty and found that his erotic imagination was waning and his morning erections were less frequent. He had read somewhere that when a man stopped having morning erections, he had started dying, and that possibility had haunted him ever since.

Of course, Tolan had still been able to get it up, to

perform when he felt the itch, but more frequently these days his whores had to use their expertise to arouse him more directly than had been the case before. Indeed, over the past couple of years, Tolan had been shocked to find that he no longer had involuntary erections but could only obtain one when in direct physical contact with a woman. Small wonder, therefore, that by the time he met Lara, he was no longer confident that he could do the necessary unless he was being worked over by a professional. Lara had changed all that. The very sight of her had been enough to arouse him instantly and make him feel like a teenager again, hot and sweaty and dizzy. Even now, as he tightened the knot of his tie and admired himself in the bathroom mirror, he felt that way just thinking about her. Taking a deep breath, trying to keep his face composed, he went downstairs for his breakfast.

Mary was in the kitchen, watching some crap on TV while cooking bacon and eggs, and the smell of the fry-up returned Tolan to normality. He really didn't want to sit here eating her swill when he could be with Lara in an upmarket restaurant, eating a fancy foreign meal of the kind she liked, invariably washed down with champagne. No question about it: his life had changed, all right, and now his patience with his home life was running low. Nevertheless, realizing the danger of showing his real feelings, he let Mary serve him and pretended to tuck into the food with relish. He tried not to rush, like.

'Going to do some business, are you?' Mary said, sitting opposite him at the small table, lighting up a fag and blowing smoke in his face.

'What?'

'Wearing the shirt and tie again,' Mary said. 'All dressed up in the suit, like. That usually means you're havin' a business meeting.'

'Aye, I am,' Tolan lied. 'Sure I'm thinking of expanding, buying another taxi company, and we're gettin' down to the brass tacks this afternoon. The bastard I'm buying from is trying to rob me blind, but you know me, Mary. I can wheel and deal with the best of 'em.'

Mary nodded, not interested. He didn't interest her much at all. Hadn't done so for years. Tolan felt the same way about her. When he studied her – the great bulk of her: the heavy breasts, the sagging chin and jowls, the shadows under her weary eyes – he found it difficult to recall what she had been like when they'd first met. It was at a dance in a Republican club in the early days of the Troubles, but that was about all he could remember. She must have had something about her to attract him, to make him think he was in love with her, or whatever that young man's shite was, and he couldn't even remember the slow change in her over the years.

Studying her now, the massive, slovenly bulk of her, it seemed to Tolan that Mary had always been that way. But she must have been slimmer once, maybe even pretty, and certainly they had managed between them to produce two children, so the sex had certainly taken place – though reluctantly on her part, as he dimly recalled, and pretty desperately on his part, a kind of quick, furtive rape while she lay passively under him. Lara wasn't like that. Lara moved like a snake. Lara responded to his fucking like she couldn't get enough of it, exhorting him to give her more, gasping obscenities into his ear, urging him on until he couldn't control himself and just poured it all into her. Lara made him feel like a real man, like a conqueror, and that feeling kept him inflamed. Sweet Jesus, he wanted her right now.

'We got a letter from Liam,' Mary said, referring to their twenty-eight-year old son who lived in Cornwall with his wife and three kids.

'Oh, yeah?' Tolan responded, feigning the interest he did not have. 'So what's he got to say for himself, then?'

'The letter's on the mantelpiece.'

'I'll read it later,' Tolan said.

'Sure he seems to be doin' fine. Got a raise last week. Wee Cheryl was sick, a bit of the bronchitis, but she's over it already and lookin' forward to startin' school next month. Jim and Catherine are grand and mixin' in nicely with the English kids at their school. He says Jean sends her love.'

'I bet she does,' Tolan said.

Jean was Liam's wife and she couldn't stand Tolan. The three kids were Tolan's grandchildren, whom he'd hardly ever seen because Liam, his only son, despised how his father made his living and had taken his wife and kids to what he felt was a better, less dangerous place. Liam had so-called principles, he didn't believe in sectarianism, and so he had gone to live with the fucking English, the disloyal wee shite. Tolan despised him.

'How's Ruth?' he asked, though his daughter, also married and with two children, only lived in Andersonstown, which was, even on foot, mere minutes away.

'Sure she's grand,' Mary said, always keen to discuss the kids since there wasn't too much else in her life. 'I was over there yesterday. She invited us both over for Sunday dinner, but I said I'd check it with you.'

'Ackay, why not?' Tolan was deeply fond of Ruth, had always spoilt her something rotten, and now spoilt her two daughters, Moira and Edna, the same way. He was happy to go and spend the afternoon there because Sunday was the most boring day of the week and, even worse, was one of the days that he couldn't meet with Lara. Better to spend it with his daughter and grandchildren than have to sit here, staring resentfully at his pudding of a wife. Also, it would give him the opportunity to have a few words with his son-in-law, Mike Reilly, who, though never directly involved during the Troubles, had serviced and disguised stolen vehicles for Tolan's wing of the IRA and now did the same for the vehicles, also often stolen, that Tolan used for his criminal activities. Mike was a grand lad.

'Right, love,' Tolan said, pushing his plate away from him, having rushed his meal despite trying not to. 'I'd best be makin' tracks. Gotta call in at the office and go over the books before I meet the bastard tryin' to rob me blind. That was a good breakfast, love.'

'Sure ya haven't called me that in years.'

'What's that?' Tolan said, surprised.

'Ya haven't used that partic'ler word in years and, come to think of it, I can't remember when ya last praised my fry-ups.'

Shit! Tolan thought in a sudden, unexpected burst of panic. *The bitch is on to me. Better watch what I say here.*

'Haven't I?'

'No, Paddy, you haven't. So what's the occasion?'

Tolan smiled at her. He hadn't done that in years either and it didn't seem natural. 'No idea. It just slipped out, like. Must be feelin' emotional in my old age. Why? Does it bother you?'

'Doesn't seem natural, like,' she said.

'Most nat'ral thing in the world,' Tolan responded, still feeling that odd, unfamiliar panic, wondering if she'd guessed something and surprised that he was so concerned that she might have. 'Sorry if I haven't said it in a long time, but that's marriage, I reckon.' He glanced ostentatiously at his wristwatch. 'Christ,' he said, 'I'm running late. I *really* have to be makin' tracks.' He pushed his chair back and stood up. 'A man's work is never done,' he said.

'Nor a woman's,' Mary retorted, blowing smoke rings and watching them drift away, clearly wanting to follow them.

'That's true enough,' Tolan said. 'So, Mary, I'll see you this evening.'

'Lucky me,' Mary said.

Tolan got out of there. Once out on the pavement, he took a deep breath, released it, then walked to the Honda Accord that was parked on the road, waiting for him, with young Tommy Doyle at the steering wheel. It was a blustery day, but the sun was shining over the Black Mountain that dominated the upper end of the street.

'Mornin',' Tolan grunted to Tommy as he slipped into the rear seat.

'Mornin', boss,' Tommy replied, then turned on the ignition, slipped into first gear and took off. 'Nice day, boss.'

'Aye, not bad.'

Tommy said no more as he turned into the Whiterock Road and drove between Corrigan Park and the City Cemetery, heading for Tolan's office in the lower Falls. Settling into his seat, Tolan stared at the back of Tommy's head, at his thick, unruly, young man's hair, and wondered if he was fucking Annie Jordan. Tolan was convinced that he was and, until recently, the possibility that this might be true had annoyed him. He knew why this was so. It was because he, Tolan, had also wanted to fuck Annie, (she was his secretary, after all, and that gave him certain rights). But each time he had let her know this with a nudge and a wink, she had cheerfully and boldly treated him as just what he was: a man more than twice her age. These days, however, Tolan didn't care so much because he had Lara Tikhonova as more than adequate compensation and even Tommy could hardly keep his eyes off her, knowing class when he saw it. It pleased

Tolan, then, that if Tommy *was* fucking Annie, he was having to do it in the knowledge that his boss, Tolan, a much older man, had the kind of woman that Tommy could never hope to have – and, to rub his nose in it, it was Tommy who had the job of driving Tolan to his trysts with Lara. This thought made Tolan feel good.

Arriving at the taxi company in the lower Falls, Tommy drove into the garage at the rear and was ordered by Tolan to remain there. It pleased Tolan to do this as well because he knew that Tommy, whether or not he was actually fucking Annie Jordan, was dying to see her, have a bit of crack in the office, and Tolan wanted to deprive him of that pleasure. So, leaving Tommy in the car, Tolan entered the building by the rear door to find his baby-faced, bald-headed homosexual account-ant, Liam Hennessey, sitting behind his desk as usual, completely ignoring Tolan's sex-bomb secretary Annie, who was perched as was her custom on her high stool, wearing a tight skirt and sweater that left nothing to the imagination.

'Mornin',' Tolan grunted by way of greeting.

'Afternoon, more like,' Annie retorted cheekily with a big, white-toothed smile.

'So you've come,' Hennessey said, using that peculiar-ity of Belfast speech as a greeting. 'How's tricks, boss?'

'Not bad, like. No great changes since last we met, which was only yesterday, so what's new around here?'

'Not much,' Hennessey replied. 'Annie,' he added, glanc-ing at the sexy dish with lacklustre eyes, 'go and fetch me a cheese-and-onion special from that Chernobyl of a sandwich bar around the corner.'

'An early death,' Annie replied, letting her tight skirt ride up her long legs as she slid off the high stool, clearly grateful to be getting out for a minute. 'Anything to drink with it?'

'No,' Liam said. 'I'll wash it down with a cuppa tea boiled in my own kettle. It's safer that way.'

'Right,' Annie said. 'It's on the tab, is it?'

'Ackay,' Hennessey said. 'Sure I'm good for it there.' When Annie had left the office, he turned to Tolan and said, 'Her tongue flaps like a flag in the wind, so it's best not to talk business in front of her.'

'Fucking right,' Tolan said. 'So how are things around here?'

'Fine, considerin' you hardly stick around these days. In and out in two minutes, like.'

'Just tell me, Liam.'

'Actually, things are grand. The taxi business is doin' fine, the betting shops are paying up, most of the publicans are paying too – only a few out of line and they're bein' taken care of – and all of the money's bein' washed clean and recycled without a hitch so far. So how are things with the Russians?'

'Hunky dory,' Tolan told him. 'They're lookin' forward to the handover of the weapons and keepin' their noses clean while they wait. I don't know how long they'll do that, so I'm having them watched.'

'Only two weeks to the handover,' Hennessey reminded him, being an accountant with a head full of numbers.

'Sure I know that right enough. That's no problem to me. The weapons are bein' collected in small loads every day from our various dumps scattered around Armagh. The material's bein' delivered to the big house down near Keady and it's dry and safe down in the basement. We're bringing nothing across the border. The last delivery should be made Monday or Tuesday next week and we'll hand the weapons over to the Russians at the end of that week – *if* we hand it over.'

'What does that mean?'

'We're dealing with the *mafiya* and those bastards can't

be trusted. That Boris, sure he can charm you when he wants to, but who knows what's behind his smarmy smile? If we can work with the bastard, I'm sure both sides would benefit, but greed is a terrible thing and the Russians have always been a greedy lot. I'm just sayin' that my eyes and ears are open for anything unexpected that might transpire. If Boris given me any cause for suspicion – the *slightest* cause for suspicion – he won't get the weapons.'

'You've already got your half of the bargain,' Hennessey said, 'so if the Russian doesn't get his weapons, all hell could break loose.'

'I'm prepared for that,' Tolan said.

'Are you?'

'What does that mean?'

'You're hardly ever in this office any more,' Hennessey said boldly, 'because you're too busy fucking that Russian's whore.'

'She's not a whore,' Tolan retorted before he could stop himself, not prepared to have his woman insulted.

'Sorry,' Hennessey replied smoothly. 'I apologize. She's not a whore. But she's certainly Boris's woman and now you're fucking her behind his back two or three times a week. That doesn't read good to me.'

'He won't find out,' Tolan said. 'He gives her a lot of freedom. He thinks she's just out spending money – buying clothes and so on. I've no problem with that.'

'I say it's a risk we can't afford.'

'And I say you're my fucking accountant and no more than that. Mind your own business, Liam, and keep your nose out of mine.'

Hennessey shrugged and lowered his gaze, then started shuffling his papers as if dealing cards. 'Anything you say, boss.'

'Right, then, I'll be off. See you later this afternoon, maybe.'

'Yeah, see you later.'

Tolan turned away and stomped out of the office, again using the rear door, feeling hot under the collar as he made his way back to the Honda. Slipping into the rear seat, he said brusquely to Tommy Doyle, 'Sure I don't have to tell you where we're going. Just let's get the fuck out of here.'

'Yes, boss!' Tommy chirruped like a bird.

When Tommy had driven out of the garage and turned along the Falls Road, heading for Divis Street and the centre of town, Tolan sank into the rear seat, took a couple of deep breaths, thought about what Hennessey had just said and hated the cocky wee shite for saying it. In the back of his mind, however, he knew there might be some truth in it (it was true, after all, that since becoming involved with Lara he had spent every second day or so mainly out of the office, neglecting his business). But he couldn't face up to that possibility right now and had only one burning desire: to get his hands on Lara, naked and slippery with sweat, and fuck her like he hadn't fucked in years, with all the passion of youth.

Trying to calm down, letting the image of Lara soothe his soul and excite his loins, Tolan glanced out of the speeding car and saw the many new high-rise buildings slipping past the window, giving way only occasionally to the solid Victorian buildings of the linen manufacturers that had once dominated the city. Now the city was mostly modern, all gleaming steel and glass, so lacking in character, so anonymous, that it could have been any city in Great Britain. Nevertheless, this still remained *his* city, was practically ruled by him, and he wondered if in truth he really wanted to share it with Boris or anyone else.

In fact, Tolan wanted to get rid of Boris, wanted Lara for himself, and he found himself, more and more every day, wondering how he could do it. If he got rid of Boris, he could then get rid of Mary and maybe start a new life for himself – still keeping his criminal activities based in Belfast, where the pickings were good and where he and Lara could live the life of Riley. With Lara, who liked the finer things in life, who knew her wines and champagne and the best places to eat – yes, even here in Belfast – he could really enjoy all the money he was earning and, until she had come along, hardly ever spent. With Lara, he could justify his crimes by living the good life.

'Here we are, boss,' Tommy said as, about fifteen minutes later, Belfast being a small city, he pulled into the kerb outside the house by the Belvoir Golf Club and came to a halt.

'Good lad,' Tolan said. Feeling almost benevolent towards Tommy, who at least had enough taste to cast furtive, covetous glances in Lara's direction (not like that resentful poofter Hennessey), Tolan patted him on the shoulder and added, 'Right, lad. You keep your eyes and ears peeled when she comes and when we're both inside.'

'Wilco, boss,' Tommy responded, using a word he had picked up from one of the many old-fashioned comic books, all of them about World War II, that he read while waiting patiently in the car. 'Will do,' he added for clarification.

'That's grand,' Tolan said. He clambered out of the car, went up the short garden path, and let himself into the house. It was a real classy place, a typical wealthy golfer's house, tastefully done with no stinting, of the kind that Tolan had previously not wanted to live in because his old friends would think he was going toffee-nosed. Now, however, he was looking at it with different eyes, seeing himself in something similar with

Lara – assuming he could somehow get rid of Boris and dump dreary Mary. By then, he would be so powerful in Belfast that he wouldn't have to worry about what his old friends thought. He'd be living the life of Riley with Lara and the whole lot of them could go and get fucked. Maybe even, eventually, he'd move out of Belfast after all to a white-walled villa located somewhere fancy – like Benidorm, say, in the south of Spain. He'd always fancied going there, though he'd never managed to get out of Belfast, but now, with a woman like Lara by his side, all things seemed possible.

Tolan went into the bedroom, undressed hurriedly and put a dressing gown, bought specially for these afternoons, over his still slim, naked body. Being a good Catholic, still an occasional churchgoer and keen on Confession, with lots to confess, he didn't like Lara to see him naked until he was in the kind of state, erect and in a good sweat, where normal inhibitions became redundant. Having put on the dressing gown, he then poured himself a large Bushmill's whiskey and stretched out on the bed, all prepared like. There was a TV set over the bed, angled on a black metal frame attached to the ceiling, and a large pile of videos on the bedside cabinet, with the video set under the top of the cabinet. The video collection was a mixture of golfing documentaries and illegally imported porn movies, courtesy of the pervert who owned the place and was now sunning it up in Torremolinos.

Tolan slipped a porn movie into the video set, switched it on with the remote control and fingered himself distractedly while he sipped his whisky and watched the erotic-action tape. Surprisingly, for a man who could torture and murder without batting an eyelid, he flushed with guilt when he heard the front door opening, signalling Lara's arrival, and immediately switched the video film off. It had, however, served its purpose, since he was now, if not totally erect, at least halfway there. Lara would do the rest.

She entered the bedroom. The very sight of her made him breathless. She was wearing that familiar off-white light overcoat, unbelted at the waist, and when she smiled at him and pulled it open, then let it slide slowly off her and fall to the floor, showing what she was wearing underneath, he felt a healthy twitching down there.

'I always imagine you won't be here,' Lara said for openers in that incredibly sexy, sultry tone of voice, 'and I get in a panic. The panic arouses me sexually – I'm thinking of what I might miss – and then, when I see that you're here, I feel even sexier. I want everything. *Everything!* Dear God, I'm *so wet.*'

No woman had ever spoken to Tolan that way before and he felt his body magically swelling preparing not only for her but for the whole fucking universe.

'Ackay,' he said, his voice unnaturally hoarse, 'I know just what you mean. Sure don't I feel the same way?'

Lara had come to him wearing a figure-hugging dress of artful simplicity: powder blue, teasingly diaphanous, off the shoulder (her shoulders were pure ivory) and with the hemline high above the knees, showing to full advantage the exquisite curves to her long legs that were further emphasized by her high-heeled shoes. She was, to Tolan, like one of those sexy dancers in those old Fred Astaire musicals – Cyd Charisse, say, as the blonde *femme fatale* in The Band Wagon – and Tolan, whose sexual tastes had been dictated by such movies, could not resist a single inch of her. Thus, when she slowly stripped the dress off, smiling teasingly at him, any will-power that he might once have possessed immediately vaporized.

Lara's underwear consisted of a string-bikini number,

also diaphanous, showing her tits and bush, and Tolan stripped it off her before he knew what he was doing. Whether he entered her, or whether she drew him in, was a question that he did not care to ask. He did things to her or she did things to him (he couldn't be sure of that either: of who was in command here) and when they were finished, when he had come, filling her with his potency, groaning, 'Oh, fuck, fuck, *fuck*!', Lara started all over again, not able to get enough of him, and he, still not believing his good luck, swelled again with pride and male arrogance. Two hours later, when his sweat made him feel that he was melting in Satan's furnace, he groaned and gasped as if asphyxiated and finally gave up. Lying beside her, trying to get his breath back, Tolan comprehended, for the first time in his life, just how empty his existence had been.

'Oh, Jesus!' he whispered.

Lara stroked his wilting cock with what seemed like true affection and smiled with the allure of a Cheshire cat. 'You're so good,' she murmured throatily. 'So surprising. So . . . *fuckable* . . . I've never really liked sex before, not even with Boris, but with you, I have to tell you, I'm on fire. I can feel you inside me even now, as if you've left your brand on me. Which, in a way, you have. Because I'm now possessed by you. There's nothing you could ask that I wouldn't do. I can't believe that I'm saying this.'

Neither could Tolan. He couldn't quite believe it, but he *wanted* to believe it, *needed* to believe it, *had* to believe it. So, having no other choice, he believed it completely and, resting a hand on her breast, said, 'What *about* Boris?'

'Pardon?'

'Boris? What do we do about Boris?'

'What do you mean, darling?'

'I want you,' Tolan said. 'Sure you're all I've ever wanted.

You're every woman I've ever wanted rolled into one and I can't let you go. Do you want me that way?'

'God, yes,' Lara whispered.

'So what do we do about it?' Tolan asked. 'I mean, what happens when I hand over my weapons and Boris, satisfied, leaves his men here to interfere with my operation and takes you back to London with him? I mean, what happens then, love?'

Lara sighed. 'I don't know.'

'Will you go?'

'I'd have no choice.'

'Why not?'

'Because Boris would kill me if I refused. He'd kill you if he knew we were involved with each other. That's how Boris operates.'

'Fuck Boris,' Tolan said. 'I'm not frightened of Boris. You and me, we'd have a good life together if it wasn't for him. I want you to stay here.'

Lara sighed again and wrapped herself around him, arms and legs, soft breasts and hot belly, a warm and soft drowning pool. 'I want to stay here as well,' she whispered. 'I want to stay here with you. You've no idea how badly he treats me, the things he does to me, but if I told him I wanted to stay here with you, he would . . .' She shivered, as if terrified by the very thought of it. 'No, darling, I can't.'

'Because of your fear of Boris?'

'Naturally. Yes.'

'You don't have to worry about that fucking Boris. I'll take care of the bastard.'

Lara raised her head from his chest to gaze at him with large, glistening, green eyes. 'How, darling? *How*?'

'I'll put the fucker's lights out.'

'You mean . . . ?'

'I mean I'll make him disappear. He'll turn up ten years

from now in an unmarked grave in the green fields of Antrim. He'll be yesterday's news.'

'But what about your deal with him? I thought that was important to you. What would happen if you . . . ? No, I can't bear to even think about it. Boris is too clever, too experienced, to let you or anyone else . . .'

'Are you saying I'm not as bright as he is?' Tolan interjected abruptly, his pride cut to the quick.

Lara gave him a hug. 'Of course not, darling. I'm not saying that at all. I know that if you wanted to, you could . . . But, no, I shouldn't even say such things. I'd better get dressed and go back to him. Oh, please, darling, don't . . .'

'Fuck him,' Tolan said, feeling explosive with anger. 'I won't let that bastard interfere with us. This is Northern Ireland – *my* territory, not his – and if I want him to disappear, he'll disappear. Just give me the word.'

'Oh, darling, I . . .' But Lara had been rendered speechless, choked up with emotion, and when she leaned forward, almost sobbing, to take Tolan's cock into her mouth, there was nothing that he wouldn't have done for her, short of going to hell. When she had finished (when he had come) he knew exactly what he would do – because what she was doing to him, which was renewing him, left him with no choice. Fuck Liam Hennessey and all his other old, unimaginative comrades – he would now live his own life.

'I'll get you away from Boris,' he promised. 'Don't worry about it. Go back to him and keep a smile on his face and I'll do all the rest.'

Lara's eyes were wet with tears. 'Don't do anything dangerous, my love. Not for me. I'm not worth that much.'

'Yes, you are,' Tolan assured her, already wondering how to get rid of his missus, Mary, and clean up this whole mess. 'Sure it's only a matter of a week or so. Trust me. I'll sort it out.'

'You're so strong,' Lara said. 'That's what excites me. When I'm with you, I feel that I'm secure and have no need to worry. Apart from that, I feel overwhelmed and can't even think straight.'

'I'll do all the thinking for you,' Tolan said, swelling up with chauvinistic pride. 'Now just go back to him, love.'

'I will,' Lara said.

Sighing despairingly, which made Tolan feel brilliant, Lara slipped out of the bed and crossed the room to pick up the clothing she had let fall, so seductively, to the floor. Only when she had gone into the bathroom to clean and dress herself did Tolan gain the nerve to stand again and, not bothering to clean himself, since he wanted Lara's smell to linger upon him, put his clothes on in preparation for leaving. When Lara emerged from the bathroom, looking like a million dollars in her powder-blue diaphanous dress and high heels, with her long blonde hair hanging loose down her back, she picked her light overcoat off the floor and put it back on also, making herself look like one of those high-class models, stinking of wealth. Fully dressed for her journey back to Boris, she smiled at Tolan with what he imagined was a touch of genuine sadness.

'Well,' she said, sounding breathless, almost sighing, 'I suppose I'd better be going. Can you call me a taxi?'

Normally, Tolan would have done just that. But this time, even more committed to her than before, he couldn't let her go that quickly and instead said, 'Sure why don't I drop you off in town instead? We could have a quick drink in the Europa and then you can get a taxi out front.'

'If we go to a hotel, even for a drink,' Lara replied, 'I may find myself trying to keep you there – and that would be foolish.'

Tolan's pulse quickened at the compliment, agitating his loins despite his previous exertions. 'Just one drink and then we'll go our separate ways. A wee one for the road.'

'You're so persistent,' Lara said with what seemed to him to be helpless admiration.

'That's because I don't see you enough,' he responded. 'Only two or three times a week, never more than that. Sure a man like me, with my sexual drive,' he added, unconsciously boasting, 'needs to see you a lot more than that.'

Lara sighed again. 'I've tried, darling. Believe me, I've tried. But Boris always get suspicious if I try to go out two days in a row, so right now, I fear, it just isn't possible.'

'I'm going to solve that problem,' Tolan said in a determined manner, straightening his shoulders and then putting on his jacket, preparing to leave with her. 'You can depend on me, love.'

'I will,' Lara said humbly.

They left the house. Lara stayed close to Tolan, taking hold of his elbow and squeezing it as they walked down the garden path. Tolan felt really chuffed. He knew that Tommy was watching. He wanted Tommy, who might have fucked Annie, the sexpot secretary who had repeatedly rejected Tolan, to envy him for having a *real* woman, the kind of woman that only the privileged could have. When they reached the end of the garden path, as Tommy opened the rear door of the Honda for them, Tolan saw the young man's eyes widen involuntarily at the sight of Lara. That made Tolan feel grand.

Then a car started up farther along the street and Tommy's head jerked around.

'Fuck!' Tommy bawled. '*Get down!*'

He threw himself in front of Tolan and Lara as the first shot rang out.

Chapter Sixteen

Shouting a warning, the young bodyguard threw himself instinctively – bravely or stupidly – in front of Tolan and the woman, simultaneously pushing them to the ground, just as Wright fired his first shot. The half-inch shell struck Tommy instead of Tolan, making him jerk epileptically and throw his hands up in the air. He was crumpling to the ground as Tolan pushed Lara back into the garden and followed her in, practically falling on top of her, seeking protection behind the low wall and hedgerow. The bodyguard slumped to the pavement as Wright, muttering 'Shit!', fired a second shot – too late – and saw part of the wall exploding into boiling clouds of pulverized mortar and flying pieces of brick where the shell had slammed into it.

'*Go!*' Coogan bawled angrily at Newman who instantly put his foot down, sending the car racing forward as Tolan reappeared, rising up from behind the hedgerow, to fire a couple of wild shots from a handgun.

The sudden jolting of the car threw Wright back into the seat, the barrel of his sniper's rifle banging noisily against the roof as he tried to regain his balance and sit upright.

As the car raced towards the escape road, two other

men, both wearing dark suits, scrambled out of a vehicle parked farther along the street, carrying Heckler & Koch MP5 sub-machine guns and preparing to use them.

'Oh, fuck!' Wright explained. 'More bodyguards! Where the hell did they spring from?'

'Jesus!' Newman hissed.

He wrenched at the steering wheel, putting the car into a tight, screeching turn, entering the road almost directly opposite Tolan's love nest, just as one of the sub-machine guns roared and bullets whipped past.

Coogan had rolled his window down and now fired back with his handgun, emptying the fifteen-round magazine with a sustained burst of semi-automatic fire, making a shocking din and striking one of the two bodyguards. The man convulsed and dropped his weapon, arms flung wide, face turned pleadingly to the sky, and staggered drunkenly backwards as his buckling legs gave way under him.

As the car straightened out again, Coogan caught a glimpse of Tolan standing in the garden gate, bawling at the other men and firing his handgun at the same time, though the bullets whistled harmlessly past the car.

'Shit!' Wright exclaimed. 'Damn it!'

Newman drove at high speed away from the killing zone, leaving Tolan and the others well behind. But before he had reached the main road, where he was planning to slow down, a silver-grey Ford Cortina screeched around the corner behind and drove at accelerating speed towards him.

'Fuck, those bodyguards are following us!' Wright exclaimed.

'Keep going!' Coogan snapped as he ejected the empty box magazine from his Glock-19 handgun and snapped another one home. 'Don't stop for anything.'

'I won't,' Newman said.

'They're catching up!' Wright shouted.

'You can't fire your rifle from that position,' Coogan told him, 'so stretch out on your seat, out of sight, before those bastards open fire.'

'Damn it!' Wright exclaimed in frustration, though he did as he was told, placing the rifle alongside him, gaining protection from the gunfire that would undoubtedly soon come from the rear. 'What a fucking waste!'

As Newman approached the end of the street and was forced to slow down, preparing to make his turn into the busy main road, Coogan glanced back over his shoulder and saw that the Ford Cortina was rapidly catching up on them.

'*Brake now!*' Coogan bawled as he grabbed the window frame with one hand, supporting himself, and prepared to fire his handgun with the other.

Newman braked.

The car went into a screeching spin and the Ford Cortina, right behind them, swerved sideways to avoid a crash, then was suddenly racing past them on Coogan's side. Coogan fired another sustained burst from his handgun even as he saw the snout of a sub-machine gun aimed at him. His fifteen shells made a mess of the passing car, smashing the windscreen and a side window, peppering the bodywork with holes, then striking the man aiming the weapon from the rolled-down rear window. The weapon fell from the man's hands, clattering noisily on the road, as the car, with bullets still ricocheting off it, went out of control, the driver now either dead or wounded. It skidded sideways, bounced up onto the pavement, then crashed through the low front garden wall of a semi-detached house, the bonnet screeching and buckling, to become obscured in boiling clouds of pulverized mortar as it shuddered to a halt in the garden, just short of the house front.

Newman put his foot down again, racing on in the same direction. Reaching the end of the street, he slowed down and made a left into the main road, not waiting for the oncoming traffic to give way to him, forcing other cars to brake sharply, with drivers angrily tooting their horns. He kept going for about half a mile, slowing down to normal speed so as not to draw attention to himself, then eventually made a right turn into one of the side streets, nowhere near where they had originally planned to be.

'Fuck it,' Coogan said, slipping his empty handgun back into its holster so that it was once more hidden under his jacket. 'Stop at the first parking space you see and let's get out of this thing. If a witness gives the cops its details, they'll be out looking for it.'

'Then we'd be hung, drawn and quartered,' Newman said, trying to joke to ease the frustration they were all feeling. 'Say goodbye and amen. They'd lock us up and throw the fucking key away.'

'Wright,' Coogan continued, aware that his heart was racing with a combination of excitement, anger and, of course, frustration. 'Zip that rifle up in the golf bag and give it to me. I'll take it back to Antrim.'

'Okay,' Wright said, sounding shaky but sitting upright in the rear and proceeding to do what he had been told.

Newman braked to a halt in the first parking space he came to. He was flushed and breathing heavily. Glancing through the open window, Coogan saw the Queen's Bridge where it crossed the River Lagan. The car was parked at the end of a side street off the Short Strand.

'Phew!' Newman said. 'That was a close one!'

'It was a cock-up,' Wright retorted. 'A right fucking balls-up.'

'That damned bodyguard,' Newman said, shaking his head from side to side in disbelief. 'He threw himself right in front of Tolan and his Russian whore. The things you do when you're young and dumb.'

'Dumb's the only word for it,' Wright said.

'We'll discuss all this later,' Coogan said, 'out in my place in Antrim. Right now, we have a slight change of plans, since we're nowhere near where we're supposed to be.'

'Where your car's parked in that street off University Road,' Newman said helpfully.

'Correct. So . . .' Coogan was breathing as heavily as the other two and his heart was still racing. 'We dump this car here. You, Wright, give me that weapon and I'll take it back in my car to Antrim. While I'm doing that, you two can make your way back to your respective flats – though don't go together; go your separate ways – then pick up your cars and drive to Antrim for an urgent Chinese Parliament. I'll see you there in an hour or so.'

'Okay, boss,' Wright said, opening the rear door of the car and clambering out, holding the rifle, zipped up in the golf bag, in one hand. He was flushed with excitement and perhaps, like Coogan, with frustration.

As Coogan also clambered out, Newman leaned sideways and down to disengage the ignition wires and turn off the engine. 'Nice baby,' he said. With the engine off, he, too, slipped out of the car and joined the others on the pavement. When Wright handed Coogan the golf bag, Coogan slung it over his right shoulder.

'Okay,' he said. 'You, Wright, can make your way back to your place via the Ormeau Embankment, across the Ormeau Bridge and then along the Ormeau Road to University Street. You, Newman, will have to take the long way round: along the Ravenhill Road, back down Annadale Avenue, then across the Governor's Bridge and up the Stranmillis Road. So get going and I'll see you both later.'

Wright and Newman nodded, then walked off, initially in the same direction, but with Newman soon taking the far side of the Short Strand. They would head off in different directions when they reached the Ormeau Park, but meanwhile they would be on opposite sides of the road. Coogan went in a different direction, crossing the Queen's Bridge, then down Oxford and Cromac Streets, across the Donegall Pass and, finally, up University Road.

The complete journey took Coogan about forty minutes and as he walked, carrying the golf bag over his shoulder, he carefully watched the other pedestrians and passing traffic, instinctively looking out for more of Tolan's gunmen. He also found himself listening for the sounds of police sirens, of which there were always plenty in Belfast, even in these days of peace, and each time he heard one he tried to ascertain in which direction that particular squad car was travelling. In the event, nothing came his way and he made it back without incident to where his own car was parked. After placing the golf bag containing the rifle in the car's boot, he glanced left and right to check that he wasn't being watched, then climbed gratefully into the vehicle and drove off.

Boiling mad because Tolan was still alive, Coogan drove back to Antrim.

Chapter Seventeen

'Ah, Lara, my dear, you're back!' Boris said to her when she entered the living room of his rented house that evening. 'So how did your afternoon with Tolan go?'

'I need a drink,' Lara responded. 'A *large* drink. Please make it a brandy.'

Boris raised his eyebrows, expressing his surprise, then studied her thoughtfully. She had already removed her overcoat, hanging it up on the coat rack in the hallway, and she certainly was a ravishing sight in her powder-blue diaphanous dress and stiletto-heeled shoes, with her long blonde hair hanging down her back. She also looked, however, a little shaken as she lit a cigarette and exhaled a cloud of smoke.

'What's the matter, dear?' Boris asked. 'Did something go wrong?'

'Yes,' she replied. 'Please fetch me that drink.'

Realizing that she was indeed shaken, Boris was quick to get off the sofa and pour her a stiff brandy. When he handed it to her, she had a long sip of it, then lowered the glass. 'I needed that,' she said.

'You'd better sit down,' Boris said, taking her by the hand as he lowered himself back onto the sofa, encouraging her to sit beside him. 'So,' he said, 'what was it? Did Tolan make some outrageous sexual demand. Did he—?'

'No,' Lara interjected. 'That would hardly bother me. It was something a lot worse. Someone tried to assassinate him this afternoon as we were leaving that house he uses as his love nest. The one out near the golf course.'

'*What?*'

'You heard me right, Boris. Someone took a shot at him – a couple of shots – with a sniper's rifle. We were coming out of the house together when the shots were fired from a car parked farther up the road.'

'What kind of car?'

'A maroon-coloured Ford Cortina.'

'Okay, continue.'

'Luckily, Tolan's young driver and bodyguard – Tommy Doyle, I think he was called – jumped in front of us just as the first shot was fired and he caught that bullet full in the chest, giving Tolan and me time to take cover behind the garden wall and hedgerow. Tolan had a handgun on him and he fired back at the Ford Cortina as the driver raced away, turning the corner almost opposite the house. As they turned that corner, we were able to see that there were three men in the car: two up front and one in the rear.'

'The one in the rear would have been the marksman,' Boris said.

'I suppose so,' Lara said.

'They got away?' Boris asked.

'Just about. As they were making their escape, two of Tolan's other bodyguards, who had gone there ahead of us and parked facing the house, were about to open fire with sub-machine guns, but one of the men in the car shot first, this one using a handgun, and managed to kill one of the bodyguards. The other bodyguard jumped back into his car, which had a driver, and they followed the Ford Cortina along the street opposite the house. Halfway up the street, someone in the Ford Cortina fired another sustained burst from a handgun, obviously emptying the magazine, killing two more of Tolan's men, including the driver. Their car then crashed through someone's garden wall and came to rest in the garden as the other car, the sniper's car, turned left at the top of the street and disappeared.' Lara hesitated here, obviously still troubled by the incident, then went on: 'Christ, I could have been killed! If it hadn't been for that young man . . .'

'He took the bullet meant for Tolan.'

'And that bullet could just as easily have struck me instead of Tolan. Yes, it was close.'

'Three men in a car,' Boris said. 'Two in the front, one in the rear with a sniper's rifle, which meant that the man sitting beside the driver was the one with the handgun.'

'So?'

'It certainly sounds like a professional hit job. The question is: who organized it? Had Tolan anything to say about this, once he got over his shock?'

'Well, he was in quite a state. Naturally, with a shoot-out in the street, two dead men in front of that house, then two more dead men in a car that was riddled with bullets and crashed through a garden wall, the police were there in a matter of minutes and Tolan had to answer a lot of questions – as did I.'

'I don't like the idea of that,' Boris said. 'What did the cops ask you?'

Lara exhaled a stream of cigarette smoke, then crossed her long legs, letting the high hemline ride up her thighs. Even though he had seen those legs many times, Boris still thought them wonderful. 'They asked me who I was. What was I doing in that house with Tolan?'

'What did you tell them?'

'What else could I tell, them, Boris, except the truth? I gave them my name and told them I was a Russian over here as a tourist.'

'You got away with that?'

'Not quite. The officer interviewing me actually laughed. He asked me where I was staying and I had no choice but to tell the truth again.'

'You gave him this address?'

'Yes. Naturally. It's no secret, is it? You must know that when a man of your reputation comes to a town like this, the police will be keeping track of you.'

'So as soon as you gave this address, the police knew you were connected to me?'

'Yes.'

'So how did the police officer react when he realized you were staying here with me?'

'With a few cynical remarks. Some sexual innuendo. Also some joky comments like, "So you and the notorious Boris Vasilyovsky are visiting Belfast as simple tourists?" When I said, "Yes," he said something like, "And you and Mr Tolan, who's equally notorious in this city, just met in this house as friends?" Tolan feigned anger at that point and threatened to have his solicitor get onto the police for using libellous language in front of me – by which he meant, presumably, the word "notorious". The police officer who'd made the remark just smiled, offered a mock apology for using "notorious", then said, "So how come the *notorious* Mr Tolan was attacked by a hit team while in the company of a lady friend of the *notorious* Boris Vasilyovsky who is reportedly – I repeat: reportedly – a member of the Russian *mafiya?*"'

'That must have thrilled Tolan.'

'He just smiled that icy smile he sometimes has and quietly told the police officer that a man was innocent until proven guilty and that the police officer had better watch his tongue. At which the police officer, certainly not easily intimidated, said, "Excuse me, Mr Tolan, but I have three dead bodies that require explanation and I'm talking to a man who is reportedly – I repeat: reportedly – a leading underworld figure and, more intriguing, who is in the company of a lady known to be a friend of a man reported – I repeat: reported – to be one of the leading figures of the Russian *mafiya*. I would say that gives me grounds to be a little bit loose with my language, wouldn't you, Mr Tolan?"'

'To which Tolan responded with . . . ?'

'"Go fuck yourself, officer."'

'That was bold of him,' Boris said sardonically. 'It is, however, worth knowing that we have such a high profile with the Belfast police force. Now they know that we're here to do business with Tolan and they'll be watching us closely.'

'That's not my fault,' Lara said. 'You're the one who ordered me to go to Tolan's bed and that's what I did.'

'I'm not blaming you,' Boris said. 'And I'm not that concerned. I knew full well that I couldn't enter this country – or, indeed, any other – without being placed under observation. They know we're here to negotiate with Tolan, but they don't know what our business is nor where or when it's to be conducted. When the time comes, we can do what we've come here to do despite their surveillance. We have some leading policemen in our pockets already and they'll help us to elude the surveillance when we need to do so. So what *else* did the RUC officer have to say?'

Lara shrugged, sipped some more brandy, inhaled and exhaled more cigarette smoke. 'That was it, really. He supervised the removal of the dead bodies, had Tolan's love nest turned upside down, told him that he might have to report to Castlereagh for further questioning and then, as a parting shot, told me that I should be more careful of the company I keep while I'm in Belfast. Then he left with the squad car and the ambulance.'

'Which gets us back to Tolan. Did he tell you who he thought might have been responsible for the attempted assassination?'

'Well, as I said, he was in quite a state, really angry, and he said we had to get out of the house immediately. He called for a taxi. While we were waiting for the taxi to arrive, he ranted and raved, first going on about all the enemies he had in the city – rival gangs and the police and old Loyalist enemies – any one of whom could have been responsible for it.'

'Did he mention me?'

'Yes, as a matter of fact, he did. He asked me if I thought it could have been you and I said I didn't think so because you still needed him to fix up the delivery of the weapons. "So why would Boris want to kill you now?" I asked him. "That wouldn't make sense." But he said it might. He said you could have made a deal with a rival gang and might want to get him out of the way. Or you might not trust him; might imagine that he was going to get rid of you to avoid having to pass the weapons over to you and to keep the *mafiya* out of his territory.'

'He said that?' Boris asked, raising his eyebrows and smiling slightly.

'Yes, Boris, he said that.'

Boris nodded, as if talking to himself. 'That's interesting, Lara. If he said that, he must have been thinking of doing it. Do *you* think that's what he's up to?'

'I don't know. I can only confirm that he doesn't trust you. He keeps asking me about you, saying, "Can I really trust him? Can anyone trust the *mafiya*? Do you think he'll betray me?" He wants to know if you ever talk about him, and when I tell him you do he wants to know exactly what you say.'

'And of course you tell him.'

'I tell him what you've told me to tell him and that's *all* I tell him.'

'And, though you've told him that it wouldn't make sense for me to move against him before the weapons are handed over, he still thinks I may do just that?'

'Yes. He's pretty paranoid about it. He thinks you won't be satisfied with sharing what he has but will want to use it as a mere foot in the door, to keep it propped open while you take over Belfast completely.'

'My very intention,' Boris said.

Lara nodded. 'I know.'

'So does he have any other paranoias, rooted in reality or not?'

'Yes. He also said that you might have had me placed under surveillance, found out that we were seeing each other, and decided to execute him for that reason.'

'That's good,' Boris said. 'That means he still doesn't suspect that I was the one who put you onto him for my own purposes. He still thinks your relationship with him is genuine. That is truly *very* good. What about the sniper's car? Did either Tolan or the police talk about tracing it?'

'They both did, but both concluded that it would be useless to try as the car would almost certainly have been stolen and then dumped after the aborted job.'

Boris nodded and smiled. 'So, to sum up . . . Tolan thinks that the attack was arranged either by a rival criminal gang or by me.'

'Yes. And since it wasn't arranged by you, who do *you* think arranged it?'

'That, as they say here in the West, is the million-dollar question. But given Tolan's position in this city which is virtually ruled, albeit illegally, by him, I'd say that it was either a rival criminal gang, a rogue element in the police service, or – and I hate to even consider this – a covert military operation set up by the British government.'

'A rival criminal gang – yes, possibly. Rogue policemen – also possible. But why on earth would you suspect the British government?'

'Because the attack, my dear, had all the hallmarks of a military-style assassination – the kind once often carried out in this province by the discredited SAS Regiment – and that, if it's the case, would certainly get us back to the British government.'

'Why would they order the assassination of someone like Tolan?'

'Tolan, my dear, is no nonentity. He is, in fact, a gang lord so powerful that he's beginning to have more authority in this country than even the North Ireland Police Service. Now, as you've just informed me, the police are aware of the fact that I'm here in the province to have words with Tolan. Finding you in Tolan's company would only have confirmed what they already suspected – and that would certainly give them great cause for concern. If, as is the case, the *mafiya* are going to link up with the Belfast underworld, which is composed largely of highly professional, utterly ruthless former IRA and UDA paramilitaries, they're certainly going to do so only because it would make them even more powerful, even more widely spread, than they are at present. The British government, already concerned with the precarious state of peace in this province, is going to be even more alarmed at the thought of a link-up between the Irish underworld and the *mafiya*. Thus, since they're already losing the confidence of the electorate because of the widely held view that crime in Great Britain is out of control, which it is, a link-up between us and the Irish underworld could be the straw that breaks the camel's back. Would they order the covert assassination of someone like Paddy Tolan and, perhaps, after him, me? Yes, I believe so. I'm not saying that this is necessarily the case, but it's certainly worth considering. That assassination attempt was certainly carried out in the style of the special services, notably the SAS. So whether I'm right or wrong, the important thing is to find out who those men were.'

'I'm sure Tolan thinks the same,' Lara said.

'I'm sure he does,' Boris responded. 'I'm sure he'll try to find those men. And since you were present when they tried to assassinate him, I'm sure he'll keep you informed of what's happening as he slobbers on your breasts. So if he comes up with any interesting information, please keep me informed, dear.'

'I will,' Lara said.

Chapter Eighteen

'A fucking disaster,' Coogan said when he and his two colleagues were seated at the table of the kitchen-diner in his rented cottage, having a beer to cool down and glancing frequently through the window at the rain-drenched green glens of Antrim. Wright and Newman faced him across the table, both drinking beers too. No one was happy.

'Yeah, right,' Newman said. 'A real fucking balls-up.'

'It was the kid,' Wright said, shaking his head disbelievingly from side to side, still pained to have missed his two shots. 'If that damned kid hadn't moved, jumped in front of him, I would have hit Tolan. I was right on the mark there.'

'Don't blame yourself,' Coogan told him. 'You were on the mark okay. The kid jumped the instant you squeezed the trigger to become Tolan's shield. Your aim wasn't off, Nick.'

'Dumb kid,' Newman said.

'Enthusiastic,' Coogan said. 'He probably wasn't even thinking about what he was doing – either he just jumped instinctively, or he was trying to make an impression on his boss, the way these kids do. A lot of the dickers during the Troubles were like that. A lot got killed that way.'

'Which is no help to us,' Wright said. 'Because Tolan's still alive and, even worse, now he knows that someone's out to get him. He'll want to know who that someone is.'

'Right,' Coogan said. 'That's the worst thing about all this. That bastard's still alive and now he'll be more alert than ever. He'll have eyes and ears all over the place and getting close to him is going to be harder than ever.'

'The Russian, too,' Wright said.

'Boris Vasilyovsky?'

'Yeah. When he hears about the attack on Tolan, he'll also wonder who was behind it and be a lot more wary in the future.'

'Come to think of it,' Coogan said, 'that could be to our advantage.'

'Oh, yeah?' Newman retorted sceptically.

'Yeah,' Coogan said. 'Tolan's bound to be wondering who tried to kill him and one of his suspects will surely be Boris, who would have a lot to gain from Tolan's death. Boris, on the other hand, is bound to be equally worried, though for different reasons.'

'What reasons?' Newman said. 'Please tell me. I'm all ears.'

'Well, being smart, Boris is going to know that the attack on Tolan had to be made either by one of his many enemies in Belfast – a rival gang, say, or a Prod with some lingering resentment – or on the orders of someone outside the community, which could only be a British government agency. So that's bound to worry him. Even more important, despite the fact that Boris had nothing to do with the attack, he's going to know that Tolan will suspect him of being behind it and that unless he can prove otherwise, absolutely, their relationship is going to be poisoned.'

'How can he prove otherwise?' Wright asked.

'By finding us,' Coogan said, 'which is next to impossible, since we did the job in a stolen car.'

'They find that car,' Wright said, 'and some poor fucker's going to get it in the neck.'

'I doubt it,' Coogan said. 'Most hit-and-run jobs are done from stolen cars, so if the police or even Tolan find out the number of that car and it turns out to be owned by a student at Queens or the like – someone local, without a record – they're going to know that person wasn't the sniper.'

'What if the car turns out to be owned by someone *with* a record?' Wright asked.

Coogan shrugged, being ruthless enough not to be concerned for the fate of a former or present hard man. 'We can't cover all bases.'

'So,' Wright said, 'to get back to the subject, Boris will now be worried that Tolan, suspecting him of being behind the attack, will try the same number on him – try to put out *his* lights.'

'Beautiful,' Newman said, grinning. 'A potential turf war.'

'Which we could certainly exploit to the hilt,' Wright said.

'Which we could actually make happen,' Coogan corrected him.

The two other men stared at him.

'Make it happen?' Newman asked eventually.

'Yes,' Coogan said. 'We make Boris suspect that what he fears is going to happen *has* happened: namely, that Tolan has tried to assassinate him.'

'You mean,' Wright said, 'that we attack him, as we attacked Tolan today, and, if we fail to kill him, we'll at least make him blame Tolan for the attack.'

'Correct,' Coogan said.

'It won't be easy,' Newman said. 'That fucking Boris

never seems to leave his house and when he's in it, he's protected like royalty. Tight security there, boss.'

'So we don't bother trying to attack him,' Coogan said. 'Instead, we just torment him: set off a bomb or two and maybe take out a couple of his bodyguards during the night. Wake him and his woman up.'

'The girl who's now possibly Tolan's woman too,' Newman pointed out.

'Yes,' Coogan said. 'Now possibly Tolan's woman too – and if that's the case, we could take advantage of that as well.'

'Some looker,' Wright said. 'Even through the sights of my rifle, I could see that she was something pretty special.'

'A fucking movie star,' Newman said.

'That movie star,' Coogan said, 'is supposed to be Boris's woman, but she's certainly meeting Tolan at that house by the golf club, either with or without Boris's consent. If without – and I suspect that it is – she may have turned against Boris and that, too, could be useful.'

'Short of personally asking her,' Newman said sardonically, 'we've no way of finding that out.'

'But if we placed her under surveillance,' Coogan said, 'we could at least find out just *how often* she's seeing Tolan. Also, I think we can take it as read that if she never goes back to Boris's house *with* Tolan, then she must be seeing him behind Boris's back. So let's place her under that surveillance.'

'All well and good,' Newman said, 'but can I just remind you, boss, that we only have two weeks left to the handover of those weapons and that doesn't leave much time for watching the woman?'

'One week will do it,' Coogan said. 'Meanwhile, during the same week, I'll personally give Boris something to think about and one of you – and I'm sorry to have to tell you this – will keep that house in Armagh under surveillance at the same time.'

'Aw, shit!' Newman exploded.

'I knew it was coming,' Wright said. 'Now, given a choice between the house and that woman, who do you expect is going to volunteer for the house? That's going to be a long, lonely stretch and a man could go mad out there.'

'Sorry,' Coogan said, 'but I've got to personally take care of Tolan *and* Boris. So one of you two will have to cover that house in Armagh and the other can play with himself while observing the woman. No volunteers for the house?'

'No,' Wright said.

'No,' Newman said just as quickly.

'Then we toss for it,' Coogan said.

'Why do we have to watch the house?' Newman asked. 'That seems a lost cause to me.'

'We have to watch the house,' Coogan said as he wriggled in his chair, groping in the side pocket of his denims for a coin to toss, 'because, as you kindly reminded me, those weapons will be handed over in approximately two weeks from now.'

'Unless we put a stop to it,' Wright said. 'Or unless Boris turns against Tolan or vice versa and the job is done for us.'

'We have to put out Tolan's lights no matter what happens,' Coogan said, looking down at the pound coin in the palm of his right hand, 'because, apart from his proposed amalgamation with the *mafiya*, he's now got a massive supply of drugs and we can't let him distribute them throughout the province or even down south.'

'We won't necessarily stop that by killing him,' Newman said. 'Those drugs could be distributed without him.'

'Those drugs,' Coogan said, 'are almost certainly being

kept in that house in Armagh. So, apart from putting out Tolan's lights, we'll also have to destroy what's there.'

'How?'

'By neutralizing those inside the house and then blowing it up. So surveillance of the place is mandatory.'

'Aw, shit!' Newman complained. 'I might have known there was no way out of this one.'

'No,' Coogan confirmed, preparing to toss the coin. 'Heads or tails, guys?'

'Tails I get the woman,' Newman said.

'Heads I get her,' Wright said.

'Fine,' Coogan said. He tossed the coin. It came down heads.

'Aw, shit!' Newman said for the third time. 'I've never won a bet in my fucking life.'

'Me, I was born lucky,' Wright informed him. 'I win things all the time. I mean, I try a lot of things for that very reason – you know? Scratch cards, the pools, the lottery, the horses and so on – because I win all the time.'

'Go fuck yourself,' Newman said, disgusted. 'Okay, I get the house in Armagh. So what am I looking for?'

'As you kindly reminded us,' Coogan said, rubbing Newman's nose in it, 'the handover of weapons will take place in about two weeks' time, so we'll need to know if it's going to happen at that house or somewhere else. You'll be able to judge that by the movement of material in or out of the building – and there should be a dramatic increase in such movement over the next week or so.'

'Where do *you* think the handover will take place?' Newman asked.

'Our intelligence reports indicate that the weapons have always been scattered about the fields of Armagh and as Boris intends using most of those weapons for his war against the London triads, he'll find it easier to smuggle them directly out of the south, the same way that he smuggled the drugs in. This leads me to believe that the weapons will be handed over either in that big house near Keady, in Armagh, or in some suitably desolate spot nearby. Certainly they'll be *stored* in that house, which means that Tolan's men will be delivering them there in manageable loads over the next couple of weeks. Obviously, then, I need you to confirm that they're doing so, to ascertain if there's any kind of regularity to the deliveries and to photograph everyone coming or going. Last but by no means least, I need you to let me know if Boris or any of his Russian friends turn up at the house.'

Newman sighed like a man being executed. 'Okay, boss, I lost the fucking toss, so when do I start?'

'Tomorrow,' Coogan said. 'We'll both come out with you in the transit van to help you set up. There'll be radio communication between us and I'll visit occasionally. Apart from that, you're on your own.'

'Charming!' Newman said.

'Just think of me,' Wright said, grinning. 'I'm in desperate need of sympathy. I'm having to follow that gorgeous creature night and day, but I'm not allowed to approach her. Don't you think that's real torture?'

'Fuck off,' Newman retorted.

'Any more wisecracks from you,' Coogan said to Wright, 'and I'll switch your duties around.'

'My lips are sealed,' Wright said chirpily. 'So when do *I* start?'

'The day after tomorrow,' Coogan said. 'When we've helped Barry set up in his OP.'

'I can't wait,' Wright said. 'So what am *I* supposed to be reporting, apart from how often that woman sees Tolan?'

'I want a complete picture of what she does when she's set loose – in other words, when she leaves Boris's place, when she returns, and exactly where she goes and who she meets during that time. I want you to watch her and Tolan carefully for any indications that they *are* having an affair or whether they're meeting for some non-sexual reason.'

'Such as?' Wright asked.

Coogan shrugged and spread his hands in the air. 'Who knows? Maybe she's simply acting as some kind of courier for Boris or as a liaison link between him and Tolan.'

'In a fucking love nest by the Belvoir Golf Club,' Newman retorted. 'Tell me another!'

'The fact that they meet there two or three times a week doesn't necessarily mean that they're screwing.'

'Are you kidding?' Newman said. 'When they get to that house, they stay there for at least two or three hours.'

'Tolan's fifty-some years old,' Wright said, 'and is unlikely to be able to keep it up for that long, so they *could* be just talking.'

'Ho, ho,' Newman said.

'I'm convinced they're screwing,' Coogan said, 'but I could be wrong in that. That woman has a chequered past, she's known to be tough as nails, and she *could* be working out the details of the exchange on Boris's behalf, using both her brains and her beauty to soften Tolan up. Not necessarily screwing him, but charming him as she negotiates. That could explain it. Either that or she's screwing him with or without Boris's permission.'

'You think he'd give his permission?' Wright asked.

'If there was something to gain, he might,' Coogan said.

'And what might that something be?' Newman asked.

'Information. He could have told her to go to Tolan's bed, make his eyes pop and get him to talk his head off in the throes of passion. That could be the case here. Either way, let's find out just where she goes and exactly who she meets when she has those two or three afternoons off each week.'

'One question,' Wright said.

'What's that, Nick?'

'To keep my eye on that woman, I'll have to watch the house from just before lunchtime every day because she sometimes goes out that early.'

'That isn't a question. It's a statement.'

'Right. Well, the question is this: if you're keeping your eye on Boris's movements, won't you be watching his house at the same time as I am?'

'No. Since Boris hardly ever leaves the house, most of the time I'll be keeping my eye on Tolan's movements around the Falls Road and the centre of town. You and I are going to be in contact, using cellular phones, so if you see any movement from Boris – as distinct from his mistress – when you're on watch outside his house, you can call me instantly. If I need you at any time, I'll do the same thing. Apart from that, if I go to Boris's house, which I certainly will, it'll be at night.'

'And that's how I keep in touch from Armagh?' Newman asked. 'With a cellular phone?'

'It's the modern age,' Coogan said. 'Now, is everyone satisfied?'

'Yep,' Wright said.

'I guess so,' Newman said.

'Then let's get a good night's sleep – sleeping here – and then load the transit van tomorrow and drive out to Armagh. I want that OP operational by midnight.'

'Lucky me,' Newman said.

Chapter Nineteen

'It'd be amusing if it wasn't so nasty,' Lara said. 'Boris making me screw information out of Tolan – literally screwing it out of him – and then telling you to keep me under surveillance to make sure that I'm doing it. Boris must be turning paranoid. I mean, he doesn't trust *anyone*.'

'He trusts *me*,' Mikhail said. 'Thank God, he trusts me. If he hadn't asked me to watch you, someone else would have done it and would have noticed that instead of seeing Tolan every afternoon, as Boris thinks you're doing, you're only seeing him two or three times a week and meeting me on the other days. If Boris knew that, we'd both be dead by now, so thank God he trusts me.'

'He trusts no one,' Lara said. 'It simply isn't in his nature. He's been with the *mafiya* for most of his life and he thinks everyone is up for sale. He doesn't know what trust means.'

'He trusts *me*,' Mikhail insisted once more.

'I don't think so,' Lara said. 'He respects you, but doesn't trust you. He's often told me that no matter how close to someone he feels – even someone like you – in the end, he has to treat them with suspicion. He told me that all human beings can be bought and sold, that loyalty has its price, that the best friend of today can be the enemy of tomorrow and that he always has to watch out for that. I mean, I thought he trusted me, Mikhail, until he asked you to watch me. I even thought he trusted Tolan at first, but now we both know better. Of course, Tolan no longer trusts him, so now there's bad blood between them.'

'He never trusted Tolan,' Mikhail corrected her, 'but at least he thought that Tolan would go through with the deal and deliver the weapons we're owed. Now, he's not so sure. He thinks that Tolan might turn against him. Though we had nothing to do with that assassination attempt, Tolan suspects we might have and that's enough to make Boris even more wary of him. I think the sooner we get those weapons the better, because who knows what will happen next?'

'*You'll* happen,' Lara said. 'I know you can do it, Mikhail. You've been treated like Boris's shadow for too long and now it's time to step out. Trust me in this, Mikhail. I can help you in this, darling. Let me continue to tell Boris only what we want to tell him instead of what Tolan's actually told me. Let me deepen the suspicion he already has of Tolan and hope that it makes them both behave foolishly. If we play our cards right, we can pit one against the other and turn the streets of Belfast into a bloodbath. When that happens, you can use the bad blood between them to bring them both down – if they haven't already done that themselves. When that happens, when they destroy each other, when the Belfast underworld is in chaos, the *mafiya* chiefs will want to replace Boris and you're the next in line for his position. *You*'ll happen, Mikhail, believe me . . .'

'I want to believe you, Lara, I do, but I have certain doubts.'

'You doubt me, Mikhail?'

'No!'

'You're frightened of Boris?'

'Yes.'

'Fear's nothing to be ashamed of, Mikhail, but you have no need to fear.'

'I . . .'

'Ssshhh. There's no more need for talk . . . Is this what you like?'

'Ah, God.' Mikhail sighed. 'Yes, that's what I like. Ah, God, Lara, I'm . . .'

'Don't be frightened,' Lara said. 'Take your courage from me. Just think of how well we fit together and the future we could have.'

'Ah, God, Lara, yes!'

'This?'

'God, yes!'

'What about this?'

'Ah, God!'

'Don't be scared. Close your eyes and just . . . *feel* . . . Let me feel you. Feel *me!*'

'Ah, God, Lara . . .'

'This, Mikhail? And this? And this, my darling, and this . . . Yes, Mikhail, yes, yes. Let it come, Mikhail, yes! It's coming and you have to let it come because you don't have a choice . . . You and me, Mikhail, yes?'

'*Yes!*' Mikhail exploded.

Chapter Twenty

At 2200 hours, under cover of darkness, some of the 'groceries' were transferred from the garage of Coogan's rented cottage in Antrim to the dark blue transit van backed up to it. Few motorists passed by Coogan's cottage during the day, let alone at this time of night, but even if they had they would only have been able to catch a glimpse of the front of the van. They would not have seen the transfer of the 'groceries', which included, amongst the bulkier items, a dismantled Surveillance Technology Group (STG) audio surveillance system.

Already dressed and made up for his lengthy sojourn in an observation post overlooking Tolan's big country house in Armagh, Newman was wearing unmarked DPM windproof coveralls, Danner boots with Gore-Tex lining, and a soft-peaked camouflaged combat hat, all of which would make him blend in with the colours of the surrounding countryside, particularly if viewed from overhead by a security-forces helicopter. To ensure that the exposed areas of his skin would not gleam in the moonlight or otherwise be seen at night, the visible parts of his face, neck and hands had been smeared with stick camouflage, also good for blending in with local foliage.

Since Newman would be on his own for the first week

and would run the risk of being seen and captured by Tolan's men, he was taking defensive weapons, including a Heckler & Koch MP5 sub-machine gun with an Orion-80 passive night sight, a Glock-19 handgun, a belt's worth of Haley & Weller fragmentation grenades and plenty of spare ammunition. He was also taking one of his old SAS bergen rucksacks, packed with high-calorie rations, spare water bottles, first-aid kit, sleeping bag, and sundry items such as a pencil torch, cellular phone, spare batteries and binoculars. Because they would be driving Newman to the OP site and had to look perfectly normal, both going there and coming back, Coogan and Wright were not using stick camouflage and were wearing ordinary windcheater jackets and denims.

When the loading of the transit van had been completed, Newman clambered into the rear with his 'groceries', and Coogan closed the doors behind him. Then he and Wright clambered up into the front cabin and Wright drove the van away.

During the uneventful journey to Armagh, neither Coogan nor Wright spoke. Content to gaze out of the window at the moonlit glens passing by, Coogan realized that the silence between them was due to their shared knowledge that time was running out quickly and they had less than a fortnight to complete their task. The four weeks that he had already spent here in the province seemed a lot longer than that, possibly because nothing much had happened until yesterday's abortive attempt to neutralize Tolan. Now, however, with Tolan almost certainly trying to ascertain who was behind the attack and suspecting either Boris, a local enemy or an outside agent, events might move forward at greater speed. Certainly, Coogan was now poised to do his own bit to bring about that particular acceleration.

As they left Antrim behind and circled around Lough

Neagh, the biggest lake in the British Isles, 153 square miles, Coogan gazed across that vast expanse of limpid black water, at once mysterious and ominous, its shore-line hawthorn trees silhouetted eerily against a moonlit sky. He found himself thinking, inexplicably, about his wife and children, wondering why he had left them.

Well, he hadn't quite left them. In fact, Peggy had thrown him out. She had never been particularly thrilled by his work with the SAS, his frequent, lengthy absences from home, whereabouts unknown, and she had certainly not been happy with his insistence upon living like a bachelor even when he *was* home. Coogan's bachelor-style activities, while married, had included a lot of riotous living: fighting in pubs and fornicating with various women, both ways of releasing the tensions that his strongly violent nature created in him. In the early days, Coogan had often wondered about his relentless promiscuity, given that Peggy was a blonde-haired, green-eyed beauty with a figure to kill for and a healthy sexual appetite – terrific in bed, in his view – but he had never come up with any justification for it and in the end simply assumed that it was his nature, as was his undoubted need for excitement and danger.

Unfortunately, it was that need that often got him into trouble, sometimes even into jail, usually for drunken brawling. His violence too, he was forced to conclude, was an ineradicable, unpleasant part of him. Unable to tame it, he had let it get out of control completely when the SAS was disbanded and, refusing to stay on in the regular army, he had returned to Civvy Street. Barely able to hold down a proper job, he had drifted gradually into crime as well as even heavier drinking and ever more blatant affairs. In the end, unable to take any more, Peggy had asked him to leave and he had done so.

Now, when he thought back on his married life, he

found himself wondering if he had ever loved Peggy at all or if he had wanted her only because she was sexy and also good for his ego. As for his children, the ten-year old Don and the nine-year old Marilyn, he had always treated them kindly the few times he was at home. But he had been at home too rarely to judge his true feelings for them and to this day could not say if he had ever truly loved them or not. Indeed, these days he seriously doubted that he was capable of truly loving anyone and was convinced that his need for excitement and danger overrode his other, more conventionally human emotions.

Sometimes he felt like a mutant.

If not a mutant, I'm certainly a criminal, he thought bleakly as he gazed out of the window of the van. They had crossed the unguarded border and were travelling through the lush countryside between Lurgan and Portadown. *Well, fuck it, why not?* he thought. *The saint and the sinner end up in the same place in the end: a six-foot hole in the ground – or, more likely these days, the furnace of an anonymous crematorium. What's love got to do with it?*

Certainly no love had been lost between him and Pat Tolan when he left home and went to work for Tolan in Belfast. Now, engaged to kill the very man he had once worked for, he thought back on those days and realized just how much he had despised himself for what he was doing even as he was doing it. He had, of course, also despised Tolan – more so because he had been working for him – and now, knowing that Tolan had shopped him, landing him with what should have been a ten-year stretch in prison, he despised him more than ever and was grateful for the opportunity to punish him.

Or was he? In truth, right now, as he watched the dark, moonlit countryside beyond Portadown slip past, he could feel no animosity towards Tolan and was moved only by the urge to get the whole job done, which meant neutralizing Boris Vasilyovsky as well.

Just thinking about Boris, however, made the woman spring to mind: Lara Tikhonova, whom Coogan had read about in his MI5 intelligence report. According to that report, Tikhonova was a tough and resourceful lady who had been born in poverty in the bleak countryside outside Moscow, fled home and went to Moscow as a teenager when the fall of the USSR made travel possible, worked her way up the slippery ladder by leaping from one bed to the next, and was believed to have been instrumental in the ruination of several formerly powerful Russian businessmen and criminals. It was the belief of MI5 that she had done so either by employing sexual blackmail to bleed her victims dry or by passing on information about their movements to those enemies who wished to assassinate them. She had become Boris Vasilyovsky's mistress a couple of years back and was suspected of helping him in a similar manner. This could explain why she was seeing Pat Tolan, as Coogan now realized. She could, in fact, be seeing Tolan with Boris's permission in order to spy upon him for Boris.

She could spy on me any day, Coogan thought, sexually aroused by the very thought of Lara Tikhonova. *That's one hell of a looker.*

About forty-five minutes after leaving the house in Antrim, they arrived in the lush countryside around Keady. As the van travelled along the narrow, winding, hilly road that led to the area shown on Coogan's map, passing undulating fields of deep grass and woods of beech, pine, hazel and ash, Coogan surveyed the sublime moonlit beauty of it all and recalled how, when he had first come here during the Troubles, he had found it almost impossible to reconcile the loveliness of the area with the dreaded 'bandit country' so often mentioned by his fellow soldiers. Yet much violence *had* been wrought here and that beautiful countryside, he knew, was filled with the unmarked graves of many men, Brits and Irish alike, who had been tortured, killed and buried out there. That Tolan should choose to hide his stockpiles of illegal weapons in the old 'bandit country' certainly seemed appropriate.

Constantly checking his map, Coogan guided Wright to a crossroads about half a mile from Tolan's country house. Then, instead of going on to the house, he made him take the left fork and follow the narrow road, more like a dirt track, that rose and fell like a helter-skelter as it looped over the hills to the south-west. When they arrived at an area of undulating fields, high above the road they had left ten minutes before, Coogan pointed to the woods on his right and said, 'There should be a track leading into those woods. Find it and go into the woods and park where the van will be well hidden.'

'Gotcha,' Wright said. He drove along the track for another few minutes and came to a gateway that led into another track – one obviously used by a local farmer. When Wright stopped the van, Coogan jumped down and opened the gate. He waited until Wright had driven the van through, then closed the gate again. When Coogan was back in the van, Wright followed the track into the beech and hazel trees of the woods. Once in the woods, he drove on until he came to a spot where he could get off the track and park well away from it, hidden by the trees. He parked, killing the engine. Then he and Coogan slid down from the driver's cabin and went around the vehicle to open the rear doors. The black-faced Newman gratefully clambered out, then glanced about him.

'Where are we?' he asked.

'In the hills high above Tolan's house. About a mile from it. We'll hike the rest of the way.'

'Let me collect my kit,' Newman said.

When Newman had removed his kit from the rear of the van, including the various parts of the audio surveillance system, Coogan and Wright threw a large sheet of green canvas over the vehicle, then covered it with foliage from nearby trees to camouflage it further. It was unlikely, Coogan knew, that anyone would see the van at this time of night, whether from the nearby track or from the air, but it was best not to take chances.

When the van had been camouflaged, he and Wright divided the separate parts of the audio surveillance system between them. Then, with Coogan in the lead, Newman in the middle and Wright bringing up the rear, they made their way through the woods, heading in the direction of Tolan's house.

Emerging from the woods, they saw a white-painted farmhouse to their right, with lights shining from the windows, indicating that some of the inhabitants were still awake. Assuming that the gateway they had passed through was owned by that farmer and that the track that wound through the woods ended at that farmhouse, Coogan cut across the field that lay east of the farm and led eventually to a tree-covered, grassy hill. He led the group up the hill, down the other side and then up a second hill. Crossing the brow of that hill he came to a densely wooded area that overlooked Tolan's big country house.

Though the house was surrounded by high walls that hid it from the main road, this densely wooded hill offered a clear view of the front of the house, the driveway leading to the front door and the neglected lawns at the front and on both sides. The unobstructed view from this sheltered position was necessary not only for eyeball recces but for the line-of-sight path required for the audio surveillance system.

'Perfect,' Newman said.

'So let's get organized,' Coogan said.

After choosing a spot where the branches of the trees gave overhead cover and a hedgerow gave concealment from the front, they constructed between them a one-man OP consisting of a hessian screen with camouflage netting supported on wooden stakes, looped at one end over the hedgerow and pinned to the ground with iron pickets and rope.

Once this basic structure had been set up, the three men used spades and small pickaxes to dig out a large rectangular area suitable for a long-term, top-to-tail OP with one end running under the hedgerow. Two shallow 'scrapes' were then dug in the earth, one for Newman to stretch out and sleep in, the other as a depository for the weapons, ammunition, cold, high-calorie rations (Newman would not be able to cook hot food because the smoke might give away his position), water bottles and other necessary items. The soil from the scrapes was scattered around the ground a good distance away from the OP. The hessian-and-net covering of the OP was then covered, in turn, with grass, gorse and other vegetation torn from the hedgerow and trees. A camouflaged entry/exit hole was cut in the hessian hanging to the ground at the rear of the OP and a camouflaged rectangular viewing hole was made in the vegetation and hessian covering the front of the OP, which overlooked Tolan's house.

With the OP completed, the weapons and other kit, including a David Optical Modulux image intensifier connected to a Nikon 35mm SLR camera with an interchangeable long-distance lens, were placed in the shallow scrape designated as a depository. Then the various parts of the STG audio surveillance system were connected together, with the transmitter and recorders mounted on two metal tripods. The transmitter looked like a large camera and was positioned on the tripod with its lens poking through the rectangular viewing hole on a line-of-sight path to the front windows of the big house below. It was connected by a series of electric cables to the transmitter, which was, in its turn, connected to a tape recorder with headphones.

The transmitter would direct an invisible laser beam onto the windows, which would then act as the diaphragm of a microphone with oscillating sound waves, picking up, as a modulated beam, any conversation taking place inside the building. When the modulated beam then bounced off the window, it would transmit back to the optical receiver placed on the second tripod. The receiver would then convert the modulated beam into audio signals which could be filtered, amplified and converted into clear conversation. The conversation could then be monitored through headphones and simultaneously recorded on the tape recorder for later analysis.

When the audio surveillance system had been set up, Newman strapped his holstered Glock-19 handgun to his waist, checked the weapons and hand grenades in the shallow scrape being used as a depository, placed his camouflaged military binoculars and a cellular phone on the ground directly under the viewing hole, then withdrew a notebook and pen from the depository and placed them on the ground beside the binoculars.

'That's me set up for the week,' he said, turning back to Coogan and Wright. 'Aren't I the lucky one?'

'Rather you than me,' Wright said. 'I'll think of you when I'm watching that gorgeous Russian.'

'Get a heart attack while wanking,' Newman retorted. 'It's all you deserve.'

'Photograph every vehicle, every person coming and

going,' Coogan said to Newman, 'and make sure you jot down every detail, every time, in that notebook.'

'You can depend on it,' Newman said.

'I'll keep in touch,' Coogan said.

'So will I.'

'Okay, good luck.'

'Thanks,' Newman said.

With a nod of his head, Coogan indicated to Wright that they should both leave the OP and make their way back to the parked van. Wright went out first with Coogan just behind him. When Coogan glanced back at the OP, he saw Newman disappearing inside it. Nodding again, indicating silent approval, Coogan joined Wright and together they made their way back through the dark woods, through striations of moonlight, to where the camouflaged transit van was parked.

With Coogan keeping watch beside the track that led from the farmer's house to the distant gateway, ready to signal should anyone come along, Wright quickly brushed the local foliage off the green canvas sheet covering the van, removed the sheet, rolled it up and placed it in the rear of the van, beside a plastic bag containing a home-made Semtex bomb. He then climbed into the driver's cabin and drove the short distance to where Coogan was keeping watch, stopped to let him get in, then drove back with dipped headlights to the gateway. The gate was still locked, indicating that no one had driven through since they had been there. Relieved, Coogan opened the gate, let Wright drive out, closed the gate behind him and clambered into the van again. Wright drove off, heading for Lurgan and the border.

'Well, that was pretty easy,' Wright said.

'Yeah, pretty easy. We weren't seen by a soul. And that OP's in a really good position, practically invisible from the track through the woods and from Tolan's house.

I think Barry will remain undetected until we pull him out of there.'

'Or until we join him for an assault on the house.'

'Right,' Coogan said.

'We're still going to Belfast, not to Antrim?'

'Yes. I'll drop you off and then park the transit van well away from Boris's house. When I complete my task, I'll pick up the van again and drive it back to Armagh. Meanwhile, you can have a good night's sleep and get up tomorrow, fresh as a daisy, to begin your observation of that woman. Try to keep your pants dry.'

Wright grinned. 'Yeah,' he said. 'I know what you mean. You don't see too many like that in Belfast. I mean, she stands out a mile.'

'Well,' Coogan said, 'you're going to get a good eyeful for the rest of this week and your *cock* will probably stand out a mile.'

'That could be true, boss. But if that happens, I'll try to keep it hidden from passers-by to avoid drawing attention to myself.'

'I always knew I could depend on you, Nick. You're a pillar of strength to me.'

'I do my humble best,' Wright said.

Less than half an hour later, they had crossed the unguarded border and were on the road to Lisburn, where the alluvial hills and green glens gave way to modern housing estates, most of them dark and silent at this late hour, with only the occasional light showing. From Lisburn, Wright drove on to central Belfast, coming in via the Newtownbreda Road, then sticking to the roads that snaked along the banks of the River Lagan, its far bank ablaze, even at this late hour, with the lights of the concert hall, the Hilton Hotel and the converted warehouses that formed a mini-city where the river had been converted into a lagoon. Finally, Wright drove across the

Ormeau Bridge and made his way to Fitzroy Avenue in the university area. When he had parked at the end of the road, well away from his own apartment building, he and Coogan climbed down from their respective sides of the van and Wright handed Coogan the keys.

'I'll be off, then,' Wright said.

'Be careful when you follow her,' Coogan said. 'She and Tolan are both used to being watched, so they'll have eyes in the backs of their heads. Also, as we saw too late, Tolan had extra bodyguards hidden near that house by the golf course, so he could have minders following him and the woman at a discreet distance and those minders might end up watching you.'

'I'll be careful,' Wright said. 'And *you* be careful during the next half-hour.'

Coogan nodded. 'I will. Okay, Nick, off you go.'

The instant Wright turned away and started walking along the lamplit pavement to his apartment block, Coogan opened the rear doors of the van, climbed in and closed the doors behind him. Opening the plastic shopping bag on the floor, he pulled out the bomb that he had made in the kitchen of his rented house in Antrim. It was a simple, highly effective device consisting of Semtex plastic explosive, a remote-controlled electrical initiator and a blasting cap with bridge wire. Coogan inserted the detonating cord into the bomb, placed the 'button job' – a remote-control firing device – in his jacket pocket, then put the bomb back into the plastic bag and, holding the bag in one hand, opened the rear doors, slithered out of the van and carefully placed the shopping bag on the pavement. After closing and locking the van doors, he picked up the shopping bag and carried it the short distance to the adjoining tree-lined street where Boris Vasilyovsky's house was.

Coogan hesitated only long enough to check that the

street was deserted. Then he crossed to the side where Boris's house was and walked at a normal pace along that pavement. When he was abreast of the wall of the front garden of Boris's house, he kept walking but dropped the plastic bag containing the bomb onto the pavement and left it there, placed against the wall. Glancing upwards, he saw the surveillance camera fixed to the top of the high gate following him as he walked, but he knew that it could only pick up him and not the bag now resting on the pavement behind him.

Lowering his head to ensure that the camera would not catch his face, only his shadowy figure, he kept walking along the street until the house was well behind him. At the end of the street, he turned left, walked along to the adjoining street, turned into it and went along it until he had passed his own van and had turned the corner that led him back to Boris's street. At the next corner, he looked across the road and saw that his shopping bag was still resting on the pavement against the garden wall of Boris's house.

Coogan slipped his right hand into his jacket pocket and curled his fingers around the button job. He withdrew his fingers from the button job when he saw a young man and his girlfriend coming arm in arm along the street.

Holding his breath, Coogan watched as they hugged and kissed each other on the move, approached the shopping bag, failed to notice it, and continued walking along the street when they had passed it. He released his breath when they reached the end of the street, still on the opposite pavement, and turned left to walk away from him. He waited until they had been swallowed up by the darkness before he curled his fingers around the button job for the second time. He then took a deep breath and pressed the button.

The bomb exploded with a thunderous roar, tearing the night's darkness with a jagged sheet of white flame, shattering the front windows of the house with its blast, and filling the air with boiling smoke and dust out of which hundreds of pieces of shattered brick flew like missiles.

Instantly, Coogan turned away and hurried back to the next corner. He turned that corner and walked to his transit van, parked mere metres away. As alarm bells started ringing in the adjoining street, obviously set off in Boris's house, Coogan drove away from the kerb, travelled the whole length of the street, turned into University Road and then headed for Shaftesbury Square and the centre of town.

'That should give him a sleepless night,' Coogan muttered to himself as he began the journey back to Antrim. 'Let battle commence.'

Chapter Twenty-one

Tolan entered the upstairs private room in his favourite pub in the lower Falls and found Bobby Meehan, Mick Curran, Jack Delaney and Shaun O'Hagan waiting for him, all knocking back pints of stout with whisky chasers, thus proving that they were hard men who could hold it. Someone had already ordered a pint and a whisky chaser for Tolan and he found the two glasses sitting in front of him when he sat down. The room was pretty spartan, with flock wallpaper, a couple of old photographs of the Falls Road as it had been back in the 1920s (not much different from now, Tolan noted) and a single rectangular pine table with six chairs placed around it. Tolan was seated at the head of the table, with Bobby Meehan at his right hand, Jack Delaney to his left and the other two sitting beside them.

Tolan had a good-sized slug of his stout, followed it up with his whisky chaser, wiped his lips with the back of his hand and said, staring grimly from one man to the next, 'Can I take it that you've all heard the news?'

'What news?' Mick Curran asked.

'Ackay,' Shaun O'Hagan said.

'Sure enough,' Jack Delaney added.

'It's already been on the TV,' Bobby Meehan said, 'so how the fuck could we miss it?'

'What news?' Mick Curran repeated, looking confused.

Everyone, including Tolan, stared at him as if he was thick, which he certainly was. Then a couple of them rolled their eyes while Tolan shook his head from side to side in melodramatic disbelief.

'Someone bombed the Russian's place last night,' Tolan explained. 'At least, they left a bomb on the pavement and blew half of the fucking garden wall away.'

'Really?' Curran asked, blinking repeatedly.

'Yes, really,' Bobby Meehan said, his face like stone.

'Anyone hurt?' Curran asked.

'Don't you watch the fucking TV,' Jack Delaney asked, 'or read your newspapers?'

'Well, I . . .'

'Never mind,' Tolan interjected. 'No, no one was hurt. The front wall was demolished and the garden was ruined and all the windows of the front were blown in, but no one was hurt.'

'What about the minders who usually sit out front?' Curran asked.

'They weren't hurt either. Maybe a little deaf, a little scorched, but the blast wasn't that big. It seems that whoever planted the bomb didn't really want to do all that much damage.'

'So what *did* he want to do?' Shaun O'Hagan asked.

Tolan shrugged. 'Sure how the fuck should I know? I only know that something funny's going on. Like, first someone tries to gun me down and Boris denies that it was him; now someone bombs Boris's place with no intention of doin' major damage. Something funny for sure.'

'The fact that Boris denies trying to top you,' Delaney said, 'doesn't mean that he didn't actually do it.'

'True enough,' Tolan said. 'But now someone's bombed *his* place and the bastard's already been on the phone to me, accusing me of doing it.'

'You denied it, nat'rally,' O'Hagan said.

'Of *course* I denied it!' Tolan exclaimed. 'But do you think that Russian bastard really believes me?'

'Any more than you believed him,' Curran said, 'when he denied having attempted to assassinate you.'

'So who the fuck, if it wasn't us, would bomb Boris's place and why would they not do it properly?'

'Maybe they used that small bomb,' Meehan said, 'because they didn't want to damage the houses next door or harm innocent passers-by.'

'That bomb would have hurt anyone passing close to the wall when it exploded,' Delaney informed them, having been the explosives expert for an IRA active service unit and knowing his stuff. 'So if the bomber didn't want to hurt passers-by, he would have used a button job, which would have let him keep his eye on the street and only explode the fucker when it was clear.'

'I don't give a fuck if he used a button job or not,' Tolan said. 'All I care about is finding out who did it and *why* they did it.'

'To start a turf war,' Meehan said, 'between us and the *mafiya*.'

'What?' Tolan wasn't too sure that he'd heard properly, so he stared at his stone-faced second-in-command and waited for clarification.

'It's startin' to add up,' Meehan said. 'First, someone tries to top you and we automatically think it has to be the *mafiya*. Boris denies it and he might be telling the truth but, whether right or wrong, we can't help but be suspicious of him. Next, someone plants a bomb against Boris's garden wall – a bomb big enough to destroy the wall and blow in the front windows of the house and, more importantly, cause enough devastation to guarantee that the police will pay Boris a visit and ask him some questions that he'd rather not be asked.'

'So?' Tolan asked when Meehan, having said his piece, dramatically let the silence linger.

'So we're suspicious of Boris, thinking he might be behind that shootin', and he's suspicious of us, thinkin' we might be behind the bombin'. Now neither side trusts the other and both sides have drawn the unwanted attention of the cops – us because of that attempted assassination attempt; the Russians because of the bombing. Now, since *we know* that we aren't responsible for that bombing, we can reasonably assume that maybe Boris is tellin' the truth when he denies responsibility for the shootin'.'

'Which means?'

'I'd say that someone is tryin' to cause disruption between us and we'd better find out who it is right quick.'

'You don't think Boris was responsible for that attack on me?' Tolan asked.

'Not any more, I don't. It's still a debatable issue, I grant you, boss, but given that bombing, which wasn't arranged by us, I'd say we have an outside agent here.'

'Outside?' Tolan asked, always respectful of Meehan's intelligence. 'How far outside? Would ya be talkin' about a rival Belfast gang or something, someone, further out than that?'

Meehan shrugged. 'That's the million-dollar question. Sure there's plenty in Belfast that'd like to do us down, cause a split between us and Boris – maybe a rival gang, maybe the police – but I don't think a rival gang would give a shit about harmin' innocent passers-by. I don't think, either, that a rival gang would go to the trouble of plantin' a bomb and not make sure it was the biggest fucker they could manage. No, my bet is that it *isn't* a rival gang; that it comes from further and higher.'

'Meaning?'

'The Brits.'

Delaney gave a low whistle.

'Fuck me,' O'Hagan said.

'The Brits?' Curran asked, blinking repeatedly and looking confused.

'Yes,' Meehan said, 'the Brits. They'd have good reason to come between us and set us at each other's throats. More reasons than one, in fact.'

'Ackay, that's right enough,' Tolan said. 'There'll be no secret about the fact that Boris is here to talk with me and they've already got enough problems with crime on the mainland without lettin' us up the ante by joinin' forces with the fuckin' *mafiya*. Sure you're right, Bobby: it could be those bastards huddled up in their pinstripe suits in Whitehall. I think you've got a good point there.'

'I agree with Bobby here,' Delaney said, 'but I have a second reason for doing so. We all agree that the assassination attempt, though it failed, was a professional job. I'd say that suggests somethin' other than a wildcat local gang. Those are the only gangs, boss, that aren't under your control, which means that they're all pretty amateurish. The guys who made that attack on you and planted that bomb were no fucking amateurs.'

Pleased to be so addressed, Tolan offered a bleak smile to Delaney, then turned back to his trusted lieutenant Bobby Meehan and said, 'So if it isn't the work of a local wildcat gang, where the fuck is it coming from?'

'Well,' Meehan said cautiously, 'it *could* be Boris and his lot, it *could* be a local gang, or it could be the work of the Brits – but for the reasons offered by me and Delaney here, I'd bet it's the Brits.'

'We have to find out,' Tolan said. 'We have to find

out who's pulling these stunts *and* why they're pulling 'em.'

'Not easy,' O'Hagan said as he clicked his lighter to ignite a cigarette. He lit the cigarette, exhaled a stream of smoke and said, as the smoke emerged from his pouting mouth, 'Not fucking easy at all.'

The subsequent silence encouraged a lot of nervous activity, including the lighting of more cigarettes, the swilling of more booze and the drumming of fingers on the table. The silence was only broken when Curran, normally slower than all the others, blinked as if struggling to think, then asked, 'You say both operations were kinda professional?'

A few of the men rolled their eyes.

'He doesn't watch TV,' Donovan said.

'Nor read the papers,' O'Hagen said.

'Yes, you dumb cunt,' Meehan said brutally, 'both operations were certainly done by professionals, but what the fuck does *that* prove?'

'Well . . .' Curran began tentatively.

'Yes?' Tolan snapped impatiently.

'Well,' Curran continued doggedly, 'if the jobs were done professionally and the operatives came from outside . . .'

'They could have been local operatives,' Meehan interjected as impatiently as Tolan had just done.

'Ackay, right,' Curran said, knowing that they thought him dumb, so always keen to be agreeable, 'I appreciate that. But if they *weren't* local . . . I mean . . . If they came from outside, like you said they might . . .'

'Yeah, *might*,' Tolan interjected contemptuously.

'. . . then,' Curran continued, hardly hearing, 'they would've had a bit of a problem smuggling weapons and explosives into the city . . . So they might have . . .'

'Yes?' Meehan asked when Curran hesitated again.

Curran wiped sweat from his forehead with the palm

of his hand then, blinking repeatedly, said, 'They might have . . . They probably had to . . . buy the weapons here in Belfast . . . Which means . . .' He shrugged forlornly, as if suddenly confused and embarrassed by his own reasoning.

'Jesus Christ,' Tolan said impatiently. 'Means *what*?'

'Means . . .' Curran began, almost stuttering, then changed his mind and said, 'It means . . .' Then he changed his mind again and said, 'If they bought the weapons here in Belfast, there's only a couple of people doing the selling apart from ourselves . . . If you get what I mean, like.'

At this point, Bobby Meehan glanced at Tolan who returned the glance. Then both men leaned forward in their chairs to stare intently at Curran.

'You mean,' Meehan said, 'that if we question the men doing the selling, we might find out who's been buying recently?'

Curran nodded. 'Aye, that's what I mean, like.'

Meehan turned to Tolan. 'And if we eliminate the straight criminals – the regular buyers – we might be left with a couple of blow-ins and they'd be our men.'

'Fuckin' right,' Tolan said. 'Even better, right now, though others are selling weapons, all but one are doing so with our permission and getting the weapons from us. There's only one man in Belfast who's sellin' weapons and explosives completely outside our jurisdiction. He'll be the cunt we should talk to.'

'Right,' Meehan said. 'So I say let's go and talk to him right now, before he gets wind that we're tryin' to find him and before the bastards he's maybe selling to create more fuckin' mayhem.'

'Right,' Tolan said. 'I agree. Let's do it right now. Finish up your drinks, lads, and let's go for a trip. Since you're no good at anything else, Curran, you can do the driving.'

'Right,' Curran said, happy to be put back in his place. 'Anything you say, boss.'

They hurriedly finished their drinks and then left the room, going down the narrow, dusty stairs one by one, with Tolan in the lead. As Tolan made his way through the packed, noisy pub, heading for the front door, he was gratified to note that the crowd filling up the room, though mostly flushed with drink and practically bawling against the pounding rock music of a live band, parted like the Red Sea to let him through. He walked through like Moses, pushed the front door open and stepped out into the lower Falls, which was still fairly busy at this time of night and brightly lit from its many street lamps.

'Where's yer car?' Tolan asked Curran when they were all bunched up around him, offering the protective wall he had demanded ever since the botched assassination attempt.

'Just across the road,' Curran said, 'in Northumberland Street.'

'We'll walk to it,' Tolan said, then started across the road, weaving between the surprisingly dense traffic with his men still bunched up around him. Once in Northumberland Street, they found the car, a well-maintained Volvo, and piled in, Tolan taking the seat beside Curran, who was driving, and the other three squeezed up in the rear.

'We're goin' to Bangor,' Tolan said.

Nodding wordlessly, Curran made a U-turn, drove back to the Falls, then turned down Divis Street to go through the centre of town and pick up the A2 at the other side of the Lagan. Looking out the window, Tolan saw the bright lights of the new high-rise buildings, soaring above streets that had once been busy at night, filled with their own communities, but now, like the central areas of most cities in Britain, busy only during the day. He felt a twinge of pride at the thought that he practically owned it, that this was his empire.

'Sure, it's a grand wee city,' he said reflectively, to no one in particular. 'You couldn't find much better, like.'

'Right, boss,' Curran said, keeping his eyes on the road as he drove across the river where lights glittered on the old warehouses turned into fun palaces. There were murmurs of assent in the rear, but nothing coherent was said.

'Sure would you not agree, lads,' Tolan persisted, 'that Belfast's still a grand wee city?'

'I'd rather live in Benidorm,' O'Hagan confessed. 'I just can't make a livin' there.'

'I can't really say,' Donovan confessed. 'I've never been anywhere else, so I've no way of making comparisons, like.'

'It's a grand wee city all right,' Meehan said, his voice flat and hard, 'but let's hope it stays that way when the Russians get their share of it.'

'They won't be sharin' it,' Tolan said. 'They'll only be gettin' a cut of it, but we'll still be runnin' it.'

'Let's hope so,' Meehan said. 'Let's hope those bastards don't get ideas above their station and try to take over the whole place. I mean, they've that reputation, like.'

'You think Boris would try that?'

'He might,' Meehan said. 'He's not known for bein' a modest man – that's for damned sure.'

They were now on the A2, taking the Holywood Bypass, and Tolan blinked against the lights whipping past on either side of the speeding car, illuminating the black, stippled waters of the Belfast Lough, which was stretched out on his left and ringed with the silhouetted mountains. That sight warmed Tolan's heart. He wanted to share it with Lara, make her Queen to his King. He wanted to dump Mary and live with Lara Tikhonova in a big fancy house in Holywood. He wanted to fuck Lara night and day, but right here, in Northern Ireland, which he once more loved with a passion because he was convinced again that he owned it. All men needed motivation of some kind and Tolan had his.

'I'll tell you this much,' he said, addressing everyone in the car. 'Depending on what we're told when we get to Bangor, we *might* give Boris his weapons, we *might* let his men into Belfast, but for fucking sure, if he gets above his station, we'll flatten him *and* his men. Sure you can take that as read, lads.'

'Hear, hear,' O'Hagan said.

The others said nothing and Tolan fell silent, content to think of Lara, recalling her naked beneath him, above him, beside him, sweat-slicked and sublime, sexually artful, insatiable, the recollections agitating his loins and making him breathe more deeply than normal. He wanted Lara all to himself, but she still belonged to Boris and this knowledge was confusing his thinking and clouding his judgement. Desiring Lara, he wanted Boris to disappear somehow and (yes, he had to admit it to himself) he had actually been hoping that he could prove that Boris had been responsible for the assassination attempt and thus he, Tolan, would be justified in breaking their agreement and seeking instant, violent retribution. Now, alas, it would seem that Boris was innocent, leaving Tolan with no excuse for turning against him. With luck, something would turn up in the near future, but right now, given yesterday's bombing, he had other fish to fry. He looked forward to doing that.

They were now coming into Bangor, a prosperous holiday town greatly favoured by those in Belfast, though right now, with its many shops closed and the streets rain-drenched, it looked bleak and unwelcoming. Reaching the bottom of the main drag, Curran turned the car along the promenade and drove around the bay, the waterfront lashed by a fierce wind, waves exploding over the low walls and drenching the pavements.

About a half-mile down the road, following Tolan's instructions, Curran turned away from the promenade and took a road that led up into the hills overlooking the bay. There were expensive houses scattered over the hills and the man they were after lived in one of them. When they reached his house, which was a large, two-storey affair set well back among smooth lawns, they noticed that the lights inside were still on. Tolan checked his wristwatch. It was ten in the evening. He instructed Curran to drive another fifty yards or so along the road and then park. Curran did so. When he had doused the car's lights and turned off the ignition, Tolan ordered them all out of the vehicle.

'Okay, Curran,' he said. 'Get yer wee leather bag out of the boot.'

'Right, boss,' Curran said, pleased to be of use, and hurried around to the rear of the car, returning a minute or so later with a small, oil-smeared leather bag in his right hand.

'Let's go,' Tolan said. 'And keep yer fuckin' voices down till we're inside that bastard's house.'

'Is he married?' Meehan asked.

'Separated.'

'Living alone?'

'I hope so, but I can't guarantee it.'

'Okay,' Meehan said.

They walked back the way they had come, turned along the driveway of the house and bunched up around the front door. Meehan rang the doorbell. The door was opened by a burly man with red hair, a freckled face, thin Calvinist lips and steely grey eyes. He was wearing a pair of striped pyjamas and obviously preparing to go to bed.

When he saw who was standing on the doorstep, his steely grey eyes became panic-stricken.

'What . . . ?' he began and was about to slam the door when Meehan, in front, kicked the door open wider and roughly pushed the man back into the hallway of the house. Before he could resist, the others had all charged in and Donovan, coming in last, slammed the door shut. Meehan bunched his fist and slammed it sideways into the side of the man's face, a vicious, expert blow that sent him bowling sideways as Donovan and O'Hagan rushed away to explore the rest of the house, withdrawing handguns from under their jackets while on the move, Donovan taking the upstairs, O'Hagan covering the rest of the downstairs floor. While they were gone, Meehan stepped forward to where the red-haired man was trying to scramble back to his feet and kicked him brutally in the ribs, making him cry out in pain and collapse again, with his hands palms downward on the floor. To ensure that the man couldn't put up a fight, Meehan tramped on the back of both his hands, one after the other, breaking the bones of his fingers, and the man, Phil Wilson, screamed again and twitched as if he'd been hit by a jolt of electricity.

'Don't fuckin' move,' Meehan said, then kicked Wilson again in the ribs to emphasize his point. Wilson gasped and groaned, but remained lying face down on the floor, too frightened to move.

At a nod from Tolan, Curran, still carrying his leather bag, went into the living room. No sooner had he disappeared than Donovan and O'Hagan returned, still holding their handguns at the ready.

'All clear,' O'Hagan said.

'No one upstairs either,' Donovan said.

'Good,' Tolan said. 'Now pick that lump of shite off the floor and drag him into the living room.'

'Oh, Jesus!' Wilson gasped as Donovan and O'Hagan grabbed him under the shoulders, hoisted him to his feet and began to drag him into the living room. Curran was already in there, standing by the dining table. He had opened his bag and was laying a hammer and several six-inch nails on the table. He had also pulled a chair away from the table and turned it around facing the doorway. As Wilson was dragged in and slammed down onto that chair, Curran, blinking repeatedly, removed a small blowtorch from his bag and set it down, fastidiously, on the table, beside the hammer and nails.

'Oh, Jesus!' Wilson repeated.

Donovan, a truly big man, gave Wilson a backhander so vicious that a bloody tooth flew out when Wilson's head jerked rapidly to the side.

'Shut yer fuckin' gob,' Donovan said, 'and don't open it unless Mr Tolan asks you to speak.'

Wilson gasped, almost choking for breath, then licked the blood from his split lip and nodded his head. He did not say a word.

Tolan stepped in front of Wilson. He stared steadily at him, as if taking his measure, then he leaned down and said, 'Still in the business of sellin' weapons, are you, Phil?'

Wilson nodded. 'Ackay.'

'And not weapons that you buy from us, right?'

Wilson nodded. 'Right. But sure you knew that and never questioned it, Paddy.'

'Ackay, that's right enough. Sure I never questioned what you were doing. I let you get on with your wee bit of business as long as you kept yer nose clean.'

'I did!' Wilson said. 'Sure you know I did, Paddy!'

Tolan smiled bleakly. 'I'm not sayin' you didn't, Paddy. I haven't come here for that. I've come here because some boyos have moved into town and they've shot at me and bombed the house of a friend. I don't figure they're local boyos – those wankers couldn't even get that close – so they must be boyos from out of town, if you get my drift, Phil.'

Still gasping, his heart obviously racing, Wilson licked more blood from his split lip and shook his head from side to side, indicating 'No.'

'You don't get my drift?'

'No, Paddy.'

'Well, the drift, Phil, is that those boyos must have come from outside, blow-ins from England maybe, and if they did, they'd have had to buy their weapons right here in Belfast. And since they didn't buy them from us – since they used them *against* us – that means they must have bought them from you. Do you get my drift now, Phil?'

Wilson nodded. 'Yes, Paddy.'

'Good,' Tolan said. 'So what I want to know, Phil – and you'd better tell me, like – is the names of those you've most recently sold weapons to and, in particular, the names of any blow-ins you've sold to. That's what I'm here for, Phil.'

Wilson's grey gaze, formerly steely, widened and glazed over with fear because he knew that if he admitted selling to blow-ins, which was forbidden by Tolan, he would be as good as dead. A shiver passed through him and he sobbed, trying to choke back his tears.

'I never sold to no blow-ins,' he said. 'Honest to God, Paddy. I wouldn't do that. Not blow-ins, Paddy.'

'You swear to that?'

'Yes, Paddy, I swear to it.'

'Let's make sure you're tellin' the truth,' Tolan said. He

stepped back, nodding at Curran who, blinking repeatedly, turned on the blowtorch and lit it as Donovan, grinning wolfishly, pinned Wilson to his chair and O'Hagan picked up the hammer and nails.

Wilson took a long time to break, but he broke in the end.

Chapter Twenty-two

Boris sat on the edge of the bed, listening in a cold fury to the workmen in the living room and out in the front garden who were replacing the windows that had been blown in by the blast of the bomb explosion. They were also cleaning up the debris in the living room, where ornaments had been smashed and paintings destroyed by flying shards of glass. Luckily, everyone had been in bed at the time so no one had been hurt, but Boris was still livid at the damage that had been done.

He had, of course, phoned Tolan immediately, accusing him of organizing the bombing. But Tolan had vigorously denied any personal involvement in it and certainly, at least according to what he had told Lara when blubbering emotionally into her naked breasts, he seemed genuinely to be innocent of it. Nevertheless, Boris still had some residual doubts, though he was keeping his mind open to the possibility of someone other than Tolan being responsible.

As Boris sat there on the edge of the bed, thinking of Tolan naked in bed with Lara, alternately repelled and fascinated by the erotic images that filled his head, Lara was in fact standing right in front of him, checking her latest figure-hugging, blood-red silk dress in her full-length wardrobe mirror as she put on her earrings, prior to going out for yet another afternoon with Tolan.

Quietly studying her, Boris felt a little guilty that he was having her followed by Mikhail, the more so because Mikhail had confirmed that so far she had visited only Tolan when going to town and, apart from that, had only been seen (by Mikhail) shopping on her own. So clearly, to date, Lara had remained loyal to Boris and was, as he had instructed, meeting with Tolan every afternoon of the working week, from Monday to Friday. Now, since Mikhail had been following her for three weeks and had seen nothing unexpected, Boris had not the slightest cause to doubt her. Nevertheless, he was keeping Mikhail on her tail, though he wasn't sure why.

'How do I look?' Lara asked, not turning to face him, but still examining herself in the full-length mirror.

'Wonderful,' Boris said, meaning it, though he realized that, in his anger over what had happened, he didn't sound too enthusiastic.

Lara turned to face him, a catlike smile on her moisturized lips. 'That didn't sound convincing,' she said.

'You know what you look like,' Boris retorted, 'so I don't have to convince you. And humility, I should remind you, my dear, was never one of your virtues.'

'You think humility is a vice?'

'No, not really. I'm just being mean.'

Lara smiled again and nodded in the direction of the living room, where the workers were making a lot of noise repairing the damage. 'Because of that?'

'Yes, I suppose so.'

'You've been through worse, Boris. This is *minor* compared to some of the things you've experienced in the past.'

'Yes, I agree. I'm just mad that I let it happen and that

the police came knocking at my door asking too many questions. I'm also mad because I don't know who did it and like a fool, in my anger, I rang up that idiot Paddy Tolan and accused *him* of doing it. When he denied it, I made it clear that I didn't believe him, but everything he's said about it so far to you – even his anger that I should actually accuse him – indicates that he's innocent.'

'His anger could have been feigned,' Lara said. 'The fact that he's confiding in me doesn't mean he's always telling me the truth. Men like him never tell the *whole* truth, as you know perfectly well.'

'Just how well have you captivated him, Lara?'

'He's enslaved,' Lara said. 'He keeps blubbering about getting rid of his wife and starting a new life with me. For that, of course, he has to get rid of you, so he wants me to do for him what I'm now doing for you.'

'He wants you to pass on what I tell you.'

'Exactly.'

'And presumably you're pretending to do so.'

'Of course.'

'But you tell him nothing important.'

'No. I haven't told him that you're planning to take over his whole city once you get your hands on those weapons. Instead, I've told him that even if you wanted to do that, you could never run this province without an insider's help – in other words, without *his* help. I've told him that your main interest in the weapons is to use them against the London triads. I've told him that if he hands over the weapons as he's promised, you'll only leave a few men here to liaise between him and you. I've told him that once you get the weapons, your main focus will be on London and, eventually, all the major cities of the mainland. I've told him that this province is too troublesome, too enmeshed in British politics and all they imply, for you to want to take it on alone. I think I've done a good job on him.'

'You think he believes you?'

'Yes, I do, Boris.'

Drinking in her full presence, from the tip of her blonde head to the delicate feet in their high-heeled shoes, Boris appreciated once more just how beautiful she was, albeit deadly with it, and realized that if he still had doubts about her, despite what Mikhail had told him, those doubts could be based on a jealousy that he was refusing to recognize. Initially, it had excited him to think of her with Tolan, that undertaker, that lump of slime, knowing just how much she despised him. Yes, Boris had got his thrill not only by making Lara whore for him but by degrading her with a man who he knew filled her with repugnance. But did she still feel that way about Tolan? Did he still make her flesh crawl? Or did the fact that she seemed in good spirits, despite being forced to consort with him every day, indicate that either the sex or some perversity in her (and certainly she was perverse) had let her start to enjoy her afternoons with him? This possibility, which filled *Boris* with repugnance, now haunted his thoughts.

'I promise you,' Boris said with quiet deliberation, 'that you won't have to do this much longer.'

Lara shrugged. 'I don't mind, Boris. I'm used to it by now. I won't pretend that I *like* what I'm doing, but if it helps you and is only for a short while, I'm sure I'll survive it.'

'You didn't feel that way at first,' Boris said. 'In fact, you were very annoyed with me when I first proposed it. I thought you'd hate me for ever.'

Lara smiled and leaned down to kiss him full on the lips, though in what he felt was an almost sisterly manner; not like it used to be. 'I don't hate you,' she said, straightening up again and then walking to the wardrobe to fetch her overcoat. 'I'm no innocent virgin, I wasn't when we first met, and you always made it perfectly clear that we had an arrangement. That arrangement included – how shall we put it? – my keeping some of your business associates happy or, as you put it, softening them up – and that's exactly what I'm doing with Tolan. My initial resentment was only because I loathed him so much – loathed him and *still* loathe him, so nothing's changed there.'

Lara took her overcoat from the wardrobe, put it on, then slung a black leather bag over her shoulder and turned back to face Boris. 'Don't worry, he still makes my skin crawl, but I'm treating this as a job for a working girl. When it's over – and I'll be glad when it is – you and I can return to our normal life. Meanwhile, don't you worry.'

'I won't,' Boris said. 'But please don't relax with him. Don't start taking what he says for granted. The most vacuous-sounding remark, the most innocent, could have a hidden meaning, so I still want to know everything he says.'

'What about the bombing?' Lara asked, indicating with a nod of her blonde head the banging and screeching going on in the living room, where the workers were repairing the damage. 'What's your reaction to that supposed to be?'

'Despite the fact that I think he may have had something to do with it, tell him the opposite. Say that I don't suspect him, but that I suspect outside interference – possibly a rival Belfast gang; perhaps even the British security forces – and that I'm now desperate to complete the weapons transaction and get back to London. Tell him that the sooner I get out of here, the happier I'll be.'

'I understand,' Lara said. Having smeared her lipstick by kissing him on the lips, she was holding up a mirror and carefully restoring her make-up. This task completed, she put the lipstick back into her shoulder bag, then walked up to him and placed her hand on his shoulder. 'I won't kiss you again,' she said, 'in case you mess up my lipstick, but let's have a romantic dinner tonight to make up for all this.'

'I'll fix it up,' Boris said. 'Now go and tell that bastard Tolan what I told you to say and let's hope that this will all be over quickly.'

'Trust me,' Lara said.

She blew him a kiss, then turned away and left the room, leaving the smell of an exotic scent behind her. Instantly, Boris rose from the bed and went to the window of the bedroom to look down on the devastated front garden. He remained there until Lara emerged from the front door and walked down the garden path, stepping daintily and (as Boris observed) sexily around the rubble from the explosion. Then, with the workmen desperately trying (and failing) not to ogle her, she turned right at the mangled remains of the gateway. She was lost to sight as she walked along the street, heading for University Road, where she would pick up a taxi to take her to her supposedly 'secret' tryst with Tolan. Of course, she could have taken a taxi direct from the house but as this was meant to be yet another 'girl's day out' when she could wander alone lackadaisically about the city centre, it had been decided that she should do everything on her own, thus ensuring that Tolan did not suspect her duplicity.

We play children's games, Boris thought. *Do we ever grow up?*

Nevertheless, when Lara had disappeared from view, Boris returned to the bed and pressed one of the buttons on an intercom resting on the bedside cabinet. Mikhail's voice, distorted, metallic, came out of the speaker: 'Yes?'

'She's left.'

'Okay,' Mikhail said. Less than two minutes later, he walked into the bedroom and found Boris pouring a brandy and lighting up a cigar.

'Want one?' Boris asked, raising his glass of brandy.

'No, thanks,' Mikhail said.

'A cigar?'

'No, thanks. If I'm going to follow her as usual, I'd better get going.'

Boris drew on his cigar, letting the smoke out with his breath, feeling confused as he had never felt before but not wishing to show it. He then sat back on the edge of the bed, leaving Mikhail standing. 'Well, Mikhail, my friend – my most trusted friend – is there any point in following her yet again?'

Mikhail looked perplexed. 'What do you mean, boss?'

Boris spread his hands out in the air, showing palms empty except for the cigar smouldering between two fingers. He shrugged. 'Is there any point?' he asked. 'You've been following Lara for two weeks now and confirmed that she hasn't done anything other than see that undertaker Paddy Tolan and, occasionally, go shopping. You've been watching her every day, five days of the week, and never seen her do anything except buy a few trinkets after going to that house, the one near the golf club, where she spends two or three hours fucking Tolan senseless, with luck. It would seem, then, from your observations, and also from what she's told me, that Lara has only done what I asked her to do and has not deviated from that task.'

Mikhail lowered his gaze, looking at his own feet, obviously deep in thought. Then he nodded, not raising his eyes, and said, 'Yes, I suppose you're right. I mean, certainly I haven't seen her do anything to raise suspicion. Apart from shopping, either before or after, she's gone nowhere else but to that house where she has her few hours with Tolan. There's no question about that.'

'So?'

'Pardon, boss?'

'You seem a little doubtful.' Boris said, 'about stopping the surveillance. *Are* you doubtful, Mikhail?'

Mikhail took a deep breath and released it in a slow, unusually loud sigh that struck Boris as being a sign of unaccustomed nervousness. 'Not doubtful,' Mikhail said. 'Her behaviour has raised no doubts. I just think that since *you* had your doubts, you should see this business through—'

'You mean the surveillance,' Boris interjected.

'Yes. I think you should see it through until the weapons have been handed over. Until then, since you had misgivings in the first place, you'll still have them. So it's best that you put your mind at ease by keeping up the surveillance.'

'My mind *is* at ease, Mikhail. It is *now*. It's been two weeks, after all, and you haven't seen anything unexpected, so I've laid all my doubts to rest.'

Mikhail coughed into his clenched fist. He seemed more than a little nervous. Boris assumed that this was because he was sensitive, despite his violent calling, and didn't wish to cause undue embarrassment. Boris respected him for this.

'Spit it out,' Boris said. 'I promise you that, no matter what you say, I won't take offence. What is it, Mikhail?'

'Well . . .'

'Yes?'

'Can I just say, boss, without causing offence, that while nothing I have seen so far has caused *me* the slightest doubt, I still believe that I should keep Lara under surveillance – at least until Tolan has handed over the weapons.'

'Why?' Boris asked him.

Mikhail sighed. 'No specific reason, boss. I just think it's wise, that's all. I mean, I know she's only doing what you asked her to do, but she's now been seeing Tolan every afternoon for five days a week and . . .'

'Yes? Come on, Mikhail, spit it out.'

'Well . . .' Mikhail glanced left and right, up and down, as if wanting to be swallowed up by the floor and disappear for ever.

'*And?*' Boris insisted.

'Well, despite how paranoid it seems, I just think that it won't do any harm to keep all avenues open.'

'Meaning?'

'It's not Lara, boss. I don't believe she would betray you. But she's now been seeing Tolan every day for two weeks and it's clear from what she's told you that he's become obsessed with her.'

'Which is good,' Boris said.

'Good up to a point. Good so long as he gives her information and she passes it on.'

'Which she's doing,' Boris said, actually starting to feel exasperated because he couldn't quite follow Mikhail's logic.

'Yes, boss, she is,' Mikhail agreed. 'I'm not arguing about that at all. But my belief is that we have to keep her under surveillance because she might now be in danger *because* of her relationship with Tolan.'

Now Boris, who respected Mikhail's intelligence, was truly perplexed. '*Because* of her relationship with Tolan?'

Mikhail nodded vigorously. 'Yes, boss. Think about it.' He paused to let Boris think about it, then nodded again and said, 'Tolan thinks he's having a secret affair with Lara. Right?'

'Right.'

'But he also knows that sooner or later Lara will have to leave Northern Ireland with you. Right?'

'Yes, Mikhail. Right.'

'So if Tolan's obsessed with Lara, he's likely to become highly unpredictable. And that could rebound on Lara personally and, in a more general, much more important way, on you and the whole of the *mafiya*.'

Boris, no fool, saw instantly what Mikhail was driving at. 'You mean that his obsession with Lara could make him try to get rid of me? Or maybe, if he *really* becomes obsessed – by which I mean insanely jealous – punish Lara in some way that would hurt us all?'

Mikhail sighed as if relieved that Boris had seen this. 'Yes, boss, that's what I mean.'

'And one of his ways of getting rid of me would be to *not* hand over the weapons, thus compelling me either to go to war with his lot, which could lead to my own downfall, or suffer the consequences from our own organization which would, understandably, not look too kindly upon my failure.'

'Exactly,' Mikhail said.

'So it's best that you keep Lara under surveillance, at least until the weapons are handed over?'

'Yes,' Mikhail said.

A lengthy silence fell between them. Mikhail, still standing, glanced left and right, up and down, shuffling his feet, looking nervous. Boris, who had his sentimental side, which he carefully concealed under normal circumstances, felt a welling-up of deep feeling for his younger friend. He and Mikhail, after all, went a long way back together, had been through a lot together (spilt blood and guts, the anguished cries of the tormented, the hopeless pleading of the damned: Mikhail there, with Boris and all his pals, fully prepared to squeeze the trigger when the indescribable torture had ended) and each of them was *mafiya* first and last, brothers to the bitter end. So Boris, in this time of deep confusion, looked upon Mikhail with an emotion verging on love. And what was love, if not one of the many kinds of trust?

'Yes,' Boris said, feeling positive once more. 'I think you're right, Mikhail. Though we may trust Lara, we certainly can't trust Tolan, and her relationship with him could still produce something helpful to us. So keep following her, Mikhail – keep watching her and let's see what transpires . . . Have I kept you too late?'

'Pardon?'

'She went ten minutes ago,' Boris said. 'Will you be able to find her?'

Mikhail released his breath in another audible sigh. He still seemed unusually nervous.

Perhaps because of the bombing, Boris thought. *God knows, it even made me nervous and that's not my style. What the hell's going on here?*

'Yes,' Mikhail said, 'I'll be able to find her. Her routine never varies, after all: she'll meet Tolan in the Gallery Bar of the Europa Hotel, go back to his love nest by the Belvoir Golf Club, then either leave late and come straight back here, using a taxi ordered by Tolan or, if she leaves early, she'll go shopping for an hour or so and pick up a taxi in town. So if I take a taxi to the Europa right now, I'm pretty sure that I'll see them in the bar. If they're not there, it simply means that they left early to go to the house. Either way, I can pick up her trail, so don't worry about it.'

'Excellent,' Boris said, trying to sound confident, though for reasons he could not understand he still felt uneasy. 'Go to it, Mikhail.'

'I will,' Mikhail said.

When Mikhail had left the room, Boris rose from the

bed and went to the window overlooking the front garden. He watched Mikhail emerge from the house and pick his way tentatively through the rubble from the explosion. He was completely ignored, as Lara had not been, by the dust-covered builders. Boris waited until Mikhail had disappeared behind the adjoining garden wall, on his way, like Lara, to University Road and, presumably, a taxi. Then he went back to the bedside cabinet to pick up his unfinished bottle of brandy.

Boris poured himself an unusually stiff drink and proceeded to drink it. He thought of Lara and Mikhail and Tolan. Without knowing what he was doing, he went back to the window and gazed down again on the devastation caused by yesterday's bomb. That bomb, he knew from experience, had not been meant to kill him. It had, however, been left there for a purpose and he thought he knew what that purpose was.

The bomb was intended to make him suspect everyone around him – and in that, he had to admit to himself, it had been totally successful.

But who had planted the bomb?

Boris wondered.

Then the telephone rang and Boris, in a trance of introspection, automatically picked it up.

'It isn't Lara and Tolan,' someone said. 'It's Lara and Mikhail.'

Then the line went dead.

Chapter Twenty-three

Coogan now lived night and day with the tension of knowing that his time was running out. For the past five days he had been monitoring Tolan's activities in the Falls. He had also been communicating constantly with Nick Wright, who was tailing Lara Tikhonova every afternoon, and Barry Newman, who was keeping Tolan's country house under surveillance from his lonely OP high in the windswept hills of the old 'bandit country' of south Armagh.

Coogan was looking for an opportunity to neutralize Tolan, but so far he hadn't worked out how he could do it. Since the failed assassination attempt, Tolan, clearly frightened, had stopped walking to his office in the Falls and now made the journey in the Honda Accord, driven by a minder, while being tailed by another car, a Mazda 323 saloon, containing another four bodyguards, all doubtless well armed. To make another assassination attempt more difficult, Tolan had stopped showing off by sauntering freely about the Falls, as he had used to do. Now he surrounded himself with a bunch of his hard men. These days, when he entered the bars, bookies and social clubs that were paying protection money, he always did so accompanied by two of his heavies, leaving the others outside to stand guard at the doorways, carefully scan the streets and check those entering or leaving the buildings.

Getting close to Tolan, then, was simply not on the cards and an attempt to shoot at him from a distance with a sniper's rifle would more likely lead to the death of one of his minders or, even worse, an innocent passer-by. Increasingly, therefore, it seemed to Coogan that he would only be able to strike at Tolan when the gangster was outside the city, perhaps somewhere along the road that led from Belfast to Keady in Armagh.

There were, however, surprises. Early in the afternoon of the first day of surveillance, Coogan received a cellular phone call from Nick Wright, who was then on Lara's tail, saying, 'I don't know what the hell's going on, but our Russian beauty didn't go near that house by the golf course. Instead, she went into town, walking all the way, stopping here and there to look into shops, then entered the Europa Hotel.'

'You followed her in?'

'Of course. I'd assumed she was going to the Gallery Bar for a drink, but I got into the lobby just in time to see her taking the lift upstairs, clearly going to someone's room. Naturally, I waited. I was there for three hours. I was expecting her to come down with Tolan, but, boy, was I surprised!'

'Yes?' Coogan asked impatiently.

'Well, she came down alone. I was going to follow her out, but then I realized that she was certain to be going home to Boris at that time, so I just let her go. Then I stayed on in the lobby, watching everyone getting out of the lifts or coming down the stairs. And guess who came out?'

'Just tell me.'

'Boris's second-in-command, Mikhail Kulinich.'

'Good God!' Coogan exclaimed. 'And you're pretty sure that that's who she was seeing upstairs?'

'Well, I watched Mikhail leaving the hotel and then, just to be sure, I waited around for another hour or so. No one else that I recognized came out of the lifts or down the stairs. So unless it was an extraordinary coincidence – Lara and Mikhail being in separate rooms at the same time, each not knowing that the other was there – they had to be seeing each other. I mean, what do *you* think?'

'I think you're right,' Coogan said. 'Keep me informed, Nick.'

Coogan called Newman, who was enduring his grim isolation in the OP overlooking Tolan's house in south Armagh. It was raining, Newman told him. The wind was howling constantly. Newman was cold and miserable and fucked off that he couldn't even make hot soup and had to subsist on cold high-calorie rations. Apart from that, nothing much had happened that first night and, according to the STG laser surveillance system, the house was empty. Next day, Newman said, there were no signs of coming or going at all.

'Fucking boring, I have to tell you,' Newman complained.

'Hang in there,' Coogan told him.

Following Tolan the next day, driving a discreet distance behind him, Coogan was surprised to see that the driver did not take him to his office in the Falls but instead went straight past it and continued on through the centre of town to a new hotel on the banks of the Lagan. Parking his own car a good way behind Tolan's Honda Accord, in the car park overlooking the broad, tree-lined river, directly facing the hotel's imposing entrance, Coogan watched him as he left the vehicle and, accompanied by his two minders, entered the building. Coogan was about to follow him when his cellular phone rang. He turned it on and said, 'Yes?'

'Nick here.'

'What's up?'

'Are you still following Tolan?'

'Yep.'

'So you've just seen him entering this hotel?'

'Yep. That's where you are?'

'Yeah – and guess where the Russian beauty is?'

'You don't mean . . . ?' Coogan began, glancing automatically across from where he was parked to the hotel entrance.

'Yes,' Wright said. 'She went into the hotel and I followed her in and saw her take the lift upstairs. I'd just sat down, preparing for my usual long wait, when Tolan entered and also took the lift upstairs. Shall I stick around?'

'We'll both stick around,' Coogan said. 'Over and out.'

They both waited, Coogan out there in his car, Wright in the hotel lobby, and eventually, about three hours later, Coogan's cellular phone rang again.

'Yes?'

'She and Tolan just came out of the lift together and embraced in the lobby. When they parted, he was joined by the two minders who had escorted him in. She's still standing there, watching him leave. If you look, you'll see Tolan leaving the hotel right now with his two minders.'

Looking across to the hotel entrance, Coogan did indeed see Tolan hurry down the steps with his two minders and make his way back to his car.

'Yes, I see him,' Coogan said. 'What's the Russian beauty doing?'

'She held back to talk to the porter,' Wright said. 'I think she's asking him to get her a taxi, Yes, she's just left the lobby with the porter.'

Looking across at the entrance, where taxis and people were coming and going constantly, Coogan saw Lara and the porter stepping out together. The porter did indeed call for a taxi and Lara slipped into it and was driven away. As the taxi moved off, Wright appeared in the doorway, talking into his cellular phone.

'Did she get a taxi?' he asked.

'Yes,' Coogan said.

'She's gone back to Boris's place,' Wright said. 'What the hell's going on?'

'What's going on is that they've given up the house near the golf course because of that little incident we arranged there.'

'But what about Mikhail, yesterday? Surely that should have been Tolan also.'

'Exactly,' Coogan said.

'So what the hell's going on?'

'I've a pretty good idea,' Coogan said, 'but let's see who she visits tomorrow.'

'Whatever she does this evening,' Wright said, 'she'll be doing it with Boris, so I might as well take the rest of the day off – or the evening, rather. Is that okay with you?'

'Yes,' Coogan said, 'but make sure you're on her tail again tomorrow.'

'You can bet on it,' Wright said.

Coogan turned his cellular phone off and sat there looking on as Wright walked down the steps of the hotel, entered the car park and went to his car, which was parked a good distance away from Coogan. Not waiting for Wright to leave, Coogan drove back to the Falls and cruised around for a bit, looking for Tolan's Honda Accord. It didn't take him long to find it, parked outside one of Tolan's favourite pubs where he often spent most of the evening, emerging only shortly before or after closing time, always surrounded by his hard-faced minders.

Coogan waited. Darkness fell. Tolan did not leave until just before closing time and he was, as usual, in the company of his hard men. Tolan was driven home by one of his minders, followed by another car containing more bodyguards. Coogan followed in his own car, keeping a good distance. By the time he turned into Tolan's street in Ballymurphy, Tolan's car was already parked outside his house, a couple of minders were keeping watch by his front gate, and the second car was pulling into the kerb a good distance along from the house. Coogan drove on down the street, passing both cars, and continued to the end of the road as if just passing through. After turning the corner at the far end, he drove back to Antrim.

He had hardly put his head down on his pillow – or so he thought – when his cellular phone rang. Picking it up, he glanced at his wristwatch, saw that it was seven in the morning, and realized that he had indeed slept all night.

'Yes?'

'Newman here.'

'What's happening?'

'Movement,' Newman said. 'Lots of it. Trucks moving in and out all night, entering by the front driveway but off-loading at a door in the east side. Judging by the light beaming up from it, I'd say that door leads down to a large basement. While the trucks were being off-loaded, other men took up watch positions at the front and rear gates. They were armed with what looked like sub-machine guns. The man who appeared to be giving the orders – I saw him clearly through my night-vision scope – was Tolan's second-in-command, Bobby Meehan.'

'What was offloaded?'

'Wooden crates of various sizes.'

'The kind you'd ship weapons in?'

'Yep.'

'Did anyone enter the building?'

'Yes, Meehan and some others. The audio surveillance system picked up their conversation when they were in the front room. They were just having a drink and a chat while waiting for their minions to complete the offloading. One of them was asking when the handover would take place and Meehan replied that it was supposed to be late the following week, though that date could be moved forward, depending on what happened between Tolan and that, quote, Russian bastard, unquote.'

'Boris,' Coogan said.

'Right.'

'Anything else?'

'Well, I've got it all down on tape and you can hear it when you come out here if you want, but the gist of it seems to be that Tolan and Boris no longer trust each other, with each expecting the other to do the dirty on him and each wondering if it wouldn't be sensible to be the one to make the first move. Meehan's all for making a move and he made a few sarcastic comments about Tolan being turned soft by, quote, that piece of Russian cunt.'

'That's not Boris,' Coogan explained. 'That's Lara Tikhonova. I think Tolan's involved with her.'

'Oh, boy!' Newman exclaimed.

'Anything else?'

'Nope. The last truck made its delivery about four o'clock this morning and then Meehan and all the others left the building. It's empty again and I'm going to have to snatch some sleep, despite the fucking daylight.'

'Only two hours' sleep at a time,' Coogan said, 'so set the alarm on your wristwatch. Have you placed anything around the OP in case of intruders?'

'Yes. A tripwire goes all the way around it, about eight feet out on either side. If someone trips it, it'll set off a soft alarm bell right here in the OP. The intruder might hear the alarm, also, but at least it'll give me time to defend myself. No sweat, boss. Relax.'

'Sleep tight,' Coogan said.

He switched his cellular phone off, got out of bed, attended to his ablutions, had a fry-up for breakfast, then drove back to Belfast to keep track of Tolan. This was the third day, and this time Tolan was driven straight to his office where he spent an hour or so. Then he went out, surrounded by his minders, to spend most of the afternoon doing his customary rounds of pubs, betting shops and social clubs, collecting his protection money.

Coogan followed Tolan by car from his home to the taxi company in the lower Falls; then he followed him on foot for the rest of the afternoon. Tolan did not go to town and Coogan soon found out why. Late in the afternoon, just as Tolan was entering yet another social club, leaving a couple of heavies on watch outside, Wright called Coogan again. Coogan spoke to Wright as he watched the heavies from the far side of the road.

'Coogan here.'

'Wright here.'

'What's up?'

'The Russian beauty went to the Europa Hotel again. I've been waiting here in the lobby for the past three hours or so and she came down about fifteen minutes ago and caught a taxi outside. I stayed on here and I've just seen Mikhail leaving again, having also come down from upstairs. I'd call this hanky-panky, wouldn't you?'

'Yes, I would,' Coogan said. 'And the man she should be with is right here in the lower Falls, conducting his usual business, doubtless thinking that his Russian beauty is with her Russian boyfriend, – the only one he knows about, that is.'

'You think that Russian boyfriend thinks his girlfriend spent the afternoon with Tolan?'

'I'm beginning to think so, yes. I'm beginning to think that he set her up with Tolan and that he's being betrayed. But let's take it to the end of the week and make sure we're right.'

'Right, boss, I'll do the same tomorrow and give you a ring.'

'Yes, please,' Coogan said.

The next day, the pattern was reversed again. Tolan, instead of doing his rounds in the Falls, had himself driven back to the new hotel by the River Lagan and Lara was seen by Wright going in shortly after him. As had happened before, they did not emerge for another three hours or so. They came out of the lift together but then parted as previously, Tolan being driven away by his minders and Lara taking a taxi back to Boris's place.

'The evidence is mounting up,' Wright said, speaking from the hotel entrance on his cellular phone to Coogan, who was sitting in his car in the car park, having followed Tolan there from the Falls. 'If that Lara isn't fucking them both, I'll eat my own dick.'

'I hope you don't have to do that,' Coogan replied, 'and I don't think you will because I'm sure you're absolutely right. The only question, it seems to me, is: how much of this does Boris know about? And my bet, having seen what's going on, is that Lara is fucking Tolan at Boris's behest in the hope of either blackmailing him or literally screwing information out of him.'

'That makes sense,' Wright said. 'But what about Mikhail?'

'Boris certainly would have no reason to give his permission for *that*, so it must be going on without his knowledge, let alone approval. My bet is that she and Boris were already having an affair behind Boris's back and that then, when he ordered her to screw information out of Tolan, she used that opportunity to see Mikhail more than she normally did. Almost certainly, Boris thinks she's seeing Tolan every afternoon, when in fact she's only seeing him a couple of times a week and seeing Mikhail on the other days. I think that's what we have here.'

'Shit,' Wright said, 'this smells like trouble.'

'Not for us,' Coogan said. 'In fact, it could work to our advantage: the spark that blows the whole thing apart.'

'What does that mean?' Wright asked.

'I'll let you know when the time's right,' Coogan said. 'I want you to follow her one last time, tomorrow, and then I'll decide.'

'Okay, boss, I'll do that. So how's Barry doing out there in south Armagh? Is he having a good time?'

'He's had one night of activity,' Coogan said, 'but nothing since then. If I don't pull him out of there soon, I think he'll go mad with boredom.'

'Rather him than me,' Wright said. 'Over and out.'

In fact, Newman *was* starting to go mad with boredom: no movement had been seen in Tolan's country house since that one night when the trucks had moved the crates in.

'It's not fair,' he said on the cellular phone to Coogan. 'That wanker Nick gets to follow the beauty while I suffer in this holiday cottage with nothing to see. I've done four days already and I've one more to go and then I think you should reverse our positions and let *me* do the wanking.'

'I'll do that,' Coogan promised. 'If nothing happens tomorrow I'll pull you out and put Nick in your place. He could do with a holiday.'

'Right on,' Newman said.

On Friday, however, things became more interesting. Coogan drove to Tolan's street in Ballymurphy and waited until the gangster had left his house and been driven off in his car, then followed him and the back-up car, expecting them to go, as usual, either to the lower Falls or the town centre. So he was surprised to find them taking the A504 to Lisburn. Beyond Lisburn, he was even more surprised to find himself following them across the border and all the way to Tolan's country house in south Armagh.

Letting them drive on to the house, Coogan took the turning that led up into the hills above the house. Once there, he drove into the woods and parked where he and his friends had originally parked the transit van, then he made his way on foot to Newman's OP, taking care to look out for the tripwire and step gingerly over it. When he knew he was near the OP (for, indeed, it was so well hidden that he could scarcely discern it) he was careful enough to call out: 'Barry! It's me! Coogan! Don't do anything drastic!' Advancing a few metres more, he saw the rear entry/exit flap being pulled aside and Newman, still black-faced and clearly weary, stared at him.

'Fuck,' Newman said, 'it really *is* you!'

'Yes,' Coogan said.

'Thought I was hallucinating. Thought I'd been here too long.'

'Did you see Coogan arrive?'

'Yep. Meehan arrived before him and they've both gone into the side entrance, the one leading down to the basement of the house where the weapons are kept.'

Coogan dropped to his hands and knees and Newman moved back to let him in. The OP was damp, dark and cramped and Coogan did not envy Newman the four days that he'd already spent here. Crawling past Newman, he looked down on the house through the rectangular viewing hole, his cheek pressed to the side of the STG laser surveillance system. He saw Tolan's car parked in the driveway with a couple of minders standing on either side of it.

'You say he's in the basement?'

'Yep, but the laser system can't pick up anything from there.'

'He's probably just checking that the proper amount of weapons have been delivered.'

'I reckon,' Newman said. 'And that means they're preparing to hand them over.'

'Just what I was thinking,' Coogan said. His cellular phone rang; he switched it on and said, 'Yes?'

'Wright here.'

'What's happening?'

'The Russian beauty and Mikhail have met again in the Europa Hotel.'

'As we expected,' Coogan said. 'So she's seeing Tolan twice a week and Mikhail three times a week. My bet is that Boris thinks she's seeing Tolan every day of the working week.'

'That makes sense,' Wright said. 'So what do I do now?'

'You can relax until the next time I call you.'

'Great,' Wright said. 'Over and out.'

Coogan switched his phone off and looked down through the viewing hole at the big house below. About fifteen minutes later, Tolan emerged from the side entrance with Meehan and a couple of their men. They got back into their car, drove out of the grounds and headed back the way they had come.

'What now?' Newman said.

'Can you bear another day here?' Coogan asked him. 'Just one more day?'

Newman sighed. 'I guess I can manage that.'

Smiling, Coogan turned on his cellular phone and made a call to Boris's house in Belfast. The phone was picked up at the other end and Coogan heard heavy breathing. Coogan spoke before Boris could do so.

'It isn't Lara and Tolan,' Coogan said. 'It's Lara and Mikhail.'

Then Coogan switched his phone off.

Chapter Twenty-four

With his hands nailed to the table, his feet nailed to the floor and his naked back blowtorched, Wilson had sung like a bird, confessing that he had sold a pile of weapons to Coogan who was back in the province with two companions. Despite repeated blowtorching, Wilson had stuck to his original statement that he did not know who the other two men were and had no idea where Coogan was actually staying – when he wasn't screaming in unbearable pain. He did, however, recall, as the non-therapeutic heat treatment continued, that Coogan and his two buddies had collected their weapons in a dark blue transit van and that he, Wilson, had jotted down the van's registration number just in case *he* ever wanted to find them.

When Tolan, who was doing the questioning while Donovan and Curran did the torturing and Meehan and O'Hagan looked on thoughtfully, asked Wilson what the registration number was, he told them, sobbing like a child, that it was in his address book on the bedside cabinet, under 'Coogan' in the 'C' section. Meehan went into the bedroom and returned a few minutes later to confirm that he had found the registration number and jotted it down on a piece of paper that he now had in his wallet.

Tolan nodded in acknowledgement, then continued with his questioning, trying to find out if Wilson knew any more. But Wilson sobbed, 'No!' and kept repeating that single word like a mantra, now practically incoherent with pain, until Tolan finally decided that the pathetic bastard was telling the truth.

At a nod from Tolan, Donovan put Wilson out of his misery by cutting his throat with his own breadknife and they left him there, sitting upright, still nailed to the table and floor, his scorched flesh practically melted off his back bones, blood pumping from his slashed throat, to be found by his girlfriend when she next came to the house. Then they left and started back to Belfast to trace the owner of the transit van.

'That fucking Coogan,' Tolan said as he and the others were being driven by Curran back to the Falls. 'I remember that bastard well. He was with the SAS during the Troubles, one of their best men, working covertly for those cunts in the 14th Intelligence Company and giving us any number of headaches. He was fucking good, I tell you.'

'I thought he worked for you,' Meehan said.

'He did. When the so-called peace came, he was sent back to England. Then the SAS was disbanded and he left the regular army and turned to crime out of frustration. Fucked up in his head, he was, so he came back to Belfast, where crime was virtually out of control, thanks largely to us, and robbed a couple of post offices on his own. When I found out about it, I had him tracked down and brought in and we had a wee chat, like. I explained that if he wanted to rob post offices and the like, he couldn't do it on his own, he had to work with me, use my transport and weapons and give me a cut, and he said, "Does that buy me protection?" and I said, "Yes". So he said, "Okay" and started working for me. He was good

– no doubt about it. That fucking SAS training. But then he started gettin' uppity, went back to working alone, an' when I sent some of my boyos to give him a warning, he told them to tell me to get fucked. Well, what could I do? I mean, he was showing lack of respect. Even worse, he was letting my boyos know it and I couldn't wear that. So I shopped the cunt. Had a chat with the cops. Give 'em all the evidence they needed to put him behind bars and they nabbed him and passed him on to the Brits. They put him on trial and gave him a ten-year prison sentence. It's all the bastard deserved.'

'If he got a ten-stretch on the mainland,' Meehan said, 'how come he's back in Belfast so soon?'

'Only one way he could do that,' Tolan said. 'He must've struck a deal with someone highly placed and got his freedom in return for doing a job here. Now we know who tried to assassinate me. Not Boris. Coogan.'

Though not easily frightened, Tolan had been badly shaken by that attempt on his life and had not gone back to the house near the golf course since. Instead, when he had met Lara for their two most recent trysts, he had done so in a room in that flash new hotel on the banks of the Lagan River, where neither Boris nor his men ever went. He had also surrounded himself with armed minders and had made sure that a couple of them were in the lobby downstairs when he had entered and left. Now the thought that Coogan and his pals might be tailing him gave him the shivers.

'Right,' Meehan agreed. 'Your minders swore they saw three men in that car when it raced away from them.'

'Three men. Correct. Wilson said that Coogan was here with two friends. I'd place a bet on who they are. Throughout the Troubles, when he was with the 14th Intelligence Company, Coogan always worked with the same two men, Nick Wright and Barry Newman, both

SAS like him. So I'd bet that those two are the bastards working with him right now.'

'You think they were sent to Belfast to get us?'

'Ackay,' Tolan said. 'Sure Coogan would only have got out of prison if someone really high up pulled the strings. The bastard that comes immediately to mind is Daniel Edmondson of MI5. He was the brains behind a lot of the covert SAS operations that gave us so many headaches during the Troubles. According to IRA intelligence reports, Edmondson was the one who first sent Coogan to Belfast, so I'd say he'd be the one best placed to send him back here. Also, it's a well-known fact that MI5 is particularly nervous about the growth of the Russian *mafiya*, so they'd certainly be concerned at Boris's presence here in the province. I'd say, then, that Coogan has been sent here to put a stop to our proposed amalgamation with the *mafiya*. So the fucker tried – and failed – to assassinate me and he's still somewhere out there.'

'What about the bombing of Boris's place?'

'Coogan again. I know how that fucker operates. He wanted Boris to blame me for it and then turn against me and, damn it, he nearly succeeded. Right now, no doubt about it, Boris is suspicious of us, thinking we did that bombing, but if I tell him about Coogan and his pals, that should put him to rights. But we still have to track Coogan down and put him into his fucking grave.'

'Fucking right,' Meehan said.

'Where are we going?' Curran asked as he drove them along the motorway through Skegoneil, which was nearly empty at this early morning hour.

'Take us to Jimmy Twomey's place,' Tolan replied, glancing out to see the three channels of Belfast Lough, the inky black water reflecting the lights of the docks and the Isle of Man ferry terminal. 'That clever wee shite should be able to fix us up with what we need.'

'Sure Jimmy'll be asleep by now,' O'Hagen said.

'Or havin' a good wank,' Donovan said.

'Whether his hand's dry or wet,' Meehan said, 'we'll drag him out of his bed.'

'Amen to that,' Tolan said.

They came off the motorway a few minutes later and soon were heading up Divis Street to the lower Falls. About halfway up the Falls, Curran made a left turn into a side street and stopped a few houses along.

'The lights are out,' Donovan said. 'The wee wanker's asleep.'

'Then let's wake him up,' Tolan said. 'Everybody out.'

They all piled out of the car and bunched up around the front door of Twomey's two-up, two-down terraced house. Meehan took hold of the brass knocker and banged it loudly, repeatedly. When there was no immediate response, he banged it again. This time the response came from a man in the upstairs room next door. He pushed his top window down, stuck his head out and bawled, 'What kinda fuckin' racket is that to be making at this time of . . . ?' But his voice trailed off when he saw whom he was addressing. 'Sorry, lads,' he said and hastily closed his window as Meehan banged the knocker even more loudly, and longer.

This time the front door opened a few inches, which was as far as the security chain would let it go. Jimmy Twomey, who was nineteen years old but looked about sixteen, with big brown eyes and a mop of dishevelled auburn hair, his chubby face peppered with acne, peered around the edge of the door.

'What the fuck?' he said.

'Take the door off that fuckin' chain, Jimmy,' Tolan said, 'and let us all in.'

'What's up, boss? Am I . . . ?'

'No, yer not in trouble, Jimmy. We just need some information and we need it right now, so open the door.'

Clearly relieved that he wasn't about to be kneecapped or get a good hiding, Jimmy opened the door and let them all in. Jimmy was four feet, ten inches tall, but in his striped pyjamas, stained around the crotch, he looked even smaller. When O'Hagan, the last of them, had stepped into the hallway, Jimmy closed the door behind him, then yawned and scratched the top of his head.

'So what is it?' he asked.

'We're tryin' to run down the owner of a transit van,' Tolan said, 'and all we've got is a registration number. Do you think you can manage to trace him for us?'

'Sure I can manage anything that's to do with computers, Mr Tolan. Would youse like a cuppa tea while I'm doin' it? I don't keep no drink here.'

'Shit,' Donovan said.

'Might have known,' O'Hagan said.

'We'll do without the tea,' Tolan said. 'How's yer mother these days?'

'Still in the hospital,' Twomey said, 'but not doin' too badly. She likes talkin' to the other ould bags in there and it keeps her out of my hair, like. Do you wanna come upstairs?'

Tolan turned to the others and said, 'Take a seat in the living room and smoke yerselves to death while I'm up there with Jimmy.'

Nodding and gratefully withdrawing cigarette packets from their pockets, the others shuffled into the living room while Tolan and Meehan followed Twomey upstairs to his bedroom. The room was pretty small and you could hardly see the walls or floor for the piles of CD-ROMs, boxes of diskettes, obsolete scanners, printers, modems and all the other paraphernalia of the computer freak. In fact, Twomey was a genius hacker who specialized in breaking into mainframes and stealing information for a wide variety of never-honest clients. One of those clients was Tolan. Twomey's powerful Packard-Bell computer was never turned off and it rested on a table facing his bed. Sitting on the edge of the bed, in front of the computer screen, Twomey held out his left hand.

'Gimme the number,' he said. Meehan withdrew a piece of paper from his wallet and handed it to Twomey who studied it, placed it at the top of his keyboard where he could see it and then proceeded to key in instructions at a remarkable rate of speed. 'I'm hacking into the mainframe computer at the DVLA in Swansea,' he explained as he worked, 'to find the last-registered owner of the vehicle.' He was there in no time at all. Once into the DVLA mainframe, he keyed in the registration number given to him by Meehan and sat back while the computer sorted through the voluminous files. Within seconds, he found what he was looking for. 'So,' he said, pointing proudly to the glowing screen. 'The registered owner of the vehicle is the Glenarm Car-Hire Company based in Antrim city.'

'Fuck,' Meehan said. 'Can you get into the computer of that company?'

'Of course,' Twomey said, grinning to reveal his bad teeth and scratching his head again. 'Sure that's a piece of piss, like.'

Again, his fingers became a blur as he keyed in the name of the car-hire company and let the computer search for it. He found it, but the company's computer system was protected by a security program. 'Fuck that for a joke,' Twomey said and attacked his keyboard again until he was able to bypass the security program and penetrate the system. 'So!' he exclaimed again, pointing to his glowing screen, which showed details of who had last hired the transit van. 'Guy by the name of Brian Glover.'

'That'll be Coogan,' Tolan said. 'He's obviously come here with false identification, but that'll be him all right. Did he take the van back?'

'No,' Twomey said, 'he still has it.'

'Do those details include this so-called Glover's address?'

'Ackay,' Twomey said. 'It's some place in Antrim.'

'Give me the details,' Tolan said.

Nodding, smiling with quiet pride, Twomey clicked his mouse on 'Print' and the details were printed out on his ink-jet. He handed the printed sheet to Meehan, who studied it thoughtfully.

'I know the area,' Meehan said. 'It's not far from the northern tip of Lough Neagh, out near Antrim town. Probably a fucking rented holiday cottage.'

'No rest for us this morning,' Tolan said. 'We're going out there right now to catch that bastard while he's still asleep.'

'I'm with you,' Meehan said.

Tolan placed his hand on Twomey's shoulder and gave it an affectionate squeeze. 'Sure you're a good lad, Jimmy. I'll make sure you're fixed up for this one. Now go back to yer bed and we'll let ourselves out.'

'Okay, Mr Tolan.'

But Twomey was still sitting on the edge of the bed, keying in more instructions to his computer, obviously about to amuse himself by surfing the Net or breaking into another mainframe, as Tolan and Meehan made their way back down the stairs to the living room where the rest of the men were smoking fags and looking weary.

'Get off yer arses,' Tolan said. 'We're going out for another joyride.'

'Jesus,' Donovan said. 'Where to now?'

'Antrim.'

'Fucking hell, boss!' O'Hagen said, looking at his wrist-watch. 'That's a long way away and it's already two o'clock in the fucking morning.'

'Never mind the fucking time,' Tolan said. 'We're goin' out there and we're goin' right now – once we've picked up some weapons from the garage. Come on, let's get out of here.'

Leaving Twomey's house, they climbed back into the car and Curran drove them to the garage behind Tolan's taxi-hire company. In the garage, in one of the old six-foot-deep bunkers formerly used for inspecting the undersides of vehicles, now covered with a locked steel trapdoor, Tolan kept a good supply of weapons. When Meehan unlocked the trapdoor and pulled it open, Donovan went down into the bunker and passed up four Scorpion sub-machine guns and a wooden crate filled with box magazines, as well as spare magazines for the handguns they were already carrying. When he had finished, he climbed out and Meehan closed and locked the steel trapdoor. At a nod from Tolan, Curran opened the boot of their car and raised its false bottom. The men kept their holstered handguns, but the crate of ammunition and Scorpion sub-machine guns were placed in the boot, the false bottom was lowered over them and the boot, which looked empty except for the jack, was then closed and locked.

'Let's go,' Tolan said. He took the seat beside Curran, who was driving, and the others squeezed up together in the rear. Curran, yawning, drove them out of the garage and then headed for the motorway that would take them to Antrim. Tolan closed his weary eyes and had a quick nap. He dreamt that Lara Tikhonova was sucking his cock, that his cock was gargantuan and that Lara's throat was like a great tunnel and it gradually swallowed him, leaving nothing but total, fearful darkness.

He awakened to find Curran shaking him gently by the shoulder, saying, 'We're here, boss. We think that's the cottage.' Looking out, he saw a straight road running past a white-walled, thatched-roof cottage that had clearly been tarted up for holidaymakers. The cottage was not ideally located, being separated from the road only by a modest front garden. There was a closed garage beside the cottage. None of the lights were on. At the far side of the road was a flat field that offered no cover, except for the low hedgerow that ran along the front of it. Another field, rising to a modest hill and with hawthorn trees scattered here and there, was at the back of the house. Curran had parked the car by the side of the road, about twenty yards from the house. He had turned the engine off and doused his lights. Tolan heard the wind moaning.

'You're sure that's it?' he said.

'Yes,' Meehan said from behind him. 'It's listed on the car-rental details as Rushy Glen Cottage, Randalstown, and while you were sleeping we drove around Randalstown until we found it. There's a sign over the door that says Rushy Glen Cottage, so this is definitely it.'

Tolan glanced along the road at the dark, moonlit house. 'You think Coogan's sleeping?'

'Either that or he isn't there.'

'No sign of the transit van.'

'It could be in the garage.'

'Right,' Tolan said, 'let's go up there on the assumption that he's in, but let's hide the car first.'

'There's a gate just farther on,' Curran said. 'I can see it from here. It's set back from that high hedgerow, so we can tuck the car nicely in there, like.'

'Do it,' Tolan said. 'And be quiet about it.'

'You'll have to get out now,' Curran said, "cause I'll have to park so tight against the gate that we won't be able to open the doors on that side.'

'Right,' Tolan said. 'Give me the keys and we'll take the weapons out of the boot.'

Curran took the keys from the ignition switch and handed them to Tolan. He and the others got out of the car and went around to the boot. Tolan opened it and stepped back to let the others remove the weapons and ammunition. When the boot was closed again, Tolan gave the keys back to Curran who turned the ignition on and accelerated lightly, moving forward without using his headlights. When he reached the gate, he went past it slightly, then reversed up against it and turned the ignition off. The area around the gate was dark because of the high hedgerows on both sides and the car was set back a good bit from the road. Curran's door was on the free side of the car and he was able to get out without any bother. When he joined the others, he was given a Scorpion sub-machine gun and some magazines of ammunition. The others were already loading their weapons and Curran did the same. Everyone except Tolan had a sub-machine gun, but Tolan drew his Glock-19 handgun from its holster and held it at the ready.

'You and you,' he said, jabbing the index finger of his free hand at Donovan and O'Hagan, 'go straight around the back of the house to cover the back door. The rest of us will check out the front. Don't try to break in until we do. Okay, let's go.'

They advanced slowly and silently along the road, falling into a single line in order to hug the shadows of the high hedgerow, with Meehan out front, Tolan behind him, and the others strung out behind Tolan. The moon was bright, though with clouds drifting across it. The wind moaned eerily about them. When they had reached the near end of the garden wall, which was only three feet high, they clambered over it and advanced to the nearest front corner of the house. Once there, Meehan dropped low and inched his way along the front wall until he reached the first window. The curtains were open. Raising his head carefully, he glanced in.

Satisfied that the dark room, the front lounge, was empty, Meehan advanced to the side of the front door as Tolan and Curran came up behind him. Still crouched low, he crossed the doorway and went to the other window. He looked in and saw that it too was empty. Turning back, he indicated that Tolan and Curran should remain at their side of the door and prepare to rush in. They nodded their understanding. Glancing past them, he saw that Donovan and O'Hagan had already gone around to the rear of the house. He glanced at Tolan, received his nod of consent, then aimed his Scorpion sub-machine gun at the lock and squeezed the trigger.

The noise splitting the rural silence sounded apocalyptic. The lock was blown to pieces. Meehan kicked the door open and went in crouched low, holding his pistol in the classic two-handed grip, aiming left and right as he advanced. Tolan and Curran followed him as another sub-machine gun roared out back. Meehan raced from the main living room to the adjoining room as Tolan rushed boldly up the stairs. There were two bedrooms upstairs, but both of them were empty. Tolan checked the toilet and it too was empty, so he went down the stairs again as Donovan and O'Hagan, having advanced from the back door through the kitchen, met Meehan coming out of the side room.

'No one down here,' Meehan said.

'No one out back,' Donovan said.

'No one upstairs either,' Tolan said. 'The bastard isn't here.'

'Let's check the garage,' Meehan said.

They all went out together and formed a semicircle around the front of the garage, with the others aiming their pistols at it and waiting for Meehan to blast the lock off. His sub-machine gun roared. The lock was blasted to smithereens. The door was too big to kick open, so Meehan dragged it ajar and looked inside. He saw the dark blue transit van inside, but there was no one there either.

'All clear,' Meehan said. 'But the fucking transit van's here.'

'That means Coogan's coming back,' Tolan said, 'so let's wait for the bastard. I want to talk to that fucker and find out where his friends are, so let's try to take him alive. Bobby and me'll wait in the house. You three,' he said, addressing Donovan, O'Hagan and Curran, 'hide in that field across the road. The hedgerow's low there and should keep you hidden while letting you fire your weapons if you have to. If you see that bastard Coogan arriving, don't open fire unless we do. If you hear gunfire, or if he makes a sudden move, blast the shite to Kingdom Come. Right, lads, get going.'

Without a word, still carrying their Scorpion sub-machine guns, Donovan, O'Hagan and Curran loped across the road, clambered over the low hedgerow, then melted into the darkness behind it. Tolan and Meehan between them closed the door of the garage, then went back into the house, shutting the door with its shattered lock behind them.

'He won't see the smashed lock in the darkness until he gets right up to the door, by which time we'll have the fucker covered.'

'Right,' Meehan said.

Tolan saw a bottle of Bushmill's whisky and a collection of tumblers on the living room table. 'You fancy a drink?' he said.

'Sure,' Meehan said. 'Why not? It might help to keep us both awake.'

'My sentiments exactly,' Tolan said.

He poured two large whiskies and handed one to Meehan. Then he sat on the sofa, which faced the front door, and Meehan took the armchair directly opposite but also facing the front door. Meehan laid his sub-machine gun across his lap and Tolan did the same with his handgun. They drank their whisky and waited.

Chapter Twenty-five

Boris was in hell. He knew exactly what he was going to do and that nothing would stop him. But for the first time in his life he felt tormented by guilt and he couldn't understand why this was so. He was lying beside Lara in the early hours of the morning, listening to her breathing, touched by her lambent heat; he realized that he had cared for her much more than he had imagined and that this caring was what had made her betrayal so painful to him. He would punish her for that.

People sleeping were helpless, at their weakest, defence-less, and he had waited until Lara had fallen asleep, was deep in slumber, only because the shock would be more acute when he woke her and, later, Mikhail. Now he wanted to wake Lara, but something held him back, a ghostly voice in his head, a premonition of disaster. So he lay there beside her, eyes open, staring up at the ceiling, waiting for the right moment.

In fact, there was no right moment. He had always known that. You snatched the moment when you got the chance and that's all you could do and all the rest of it was a matter of luck or of losing and dying. Lara and Mikhail had betrayed him and he felt the pain of it and knew that it was because he had loved them both in different ways: Lara as a woman and Mikhail as a son, though both of them were now beyond the Pale and could never come back to him. Boris knew about the Pale, the dominion of the elite, and he knew that those who were banished from that place never returned. The area outside the Pale was that void in the heart that knew betrayal when it was broken in two. Boris felt that void in himself because his own heart had now been broken.

He lowered his gaze to study Lara. She was radiant in sleep, with the self-containment of a cat and every bit as selfish. Boris realized that he had loved her, that she had been the only love of his life, and that his love for her had made him blind and let her deceive him. He hated her for that, for making his love turn to poison, as it had done with Mikhail, yet he reached out and stroked her blonde hair and heard her purr like the cat she resembled. As if in a trance, he ran his fingers lightly down the side of her face, stroked her smooth, warm cheek, then ran his fingers over her lips and felt them part to receive him. He moved his fingers between her lips and then withdrew them and lowered his hand again. Taking hold of her shoulder, he shook her gently until she awoke. He watched her blinking, the green eyes still sleepy, and he loved and loathed her at once.

'What . . . ?' Lara murmured.

'You betrayed me,' Boris said.

'What?' she repeated, her voice sleepy and hoarse and confused, though still eerily sensual.

'You betrayed me with Mikhail,' Boris said levelly. 'You were fucking Mikhail for pleasure three days a week when you were supposed to be fucking Pat Tolan to obtain information. Don't deny it because it's too late for that. You betrayed me. I know it.'

Shocked, though trying not to show it, Lara blinked

repeatedly and licked her lips, her gaze fixed on the ceiling. She did not deny anything.

'How . . . ?'

'Never mind. It's enough that I know. You and Mikhail were meeting three days a week in the Europa when you were supposed to be in bed with Pat Tolan. You betrayed me with Mikhail and you must have told me a lot of lies about Tolan. So why did you do it and what did you hope to gain by it?'

Lara was silent for some time, wondering what she should say, too intelligent to deny the obvious but clearly thinking that there might be a way out – though, in fact, there was no way out this time. Eventually, with a long drawn-out sigh, she said, almost whispering, 'I don't know why I did it. It just happened, that's all. These things happen between men and women and they can't be explained. I didn't hope to gain anything by it and neither did Mikhail. It was just one of those things.'

'You're lying,' Boris said. 'With you, *nothing* just happens. Mikhail ended up in your bed, between your legs, because you wanted him there. What you want, you get, Lara. But why did you want him? Don't tell me you loved him, because I simply won't believe you. If you seduced him, which you did, you did so for a purpose – and I want to know what that purpose was. So what was it, Lara?'

'There was no purpose,' Lara said. 'You won't believe me, but it was love. Maybe not the kind of love that most women would feel, but as near to love as a woman like me can get and that's what I wanted. It was no more than that.'

'You weary me, Lara. Your lies make my teeth grind. You told me you were seeing Tolan when in fact you were seeing Mikhail so a lot of the things you said that Tolan had told you must have been invented. That could only have been to my disadvantage and you had to know it.

What did you and Mikhail hope to gain? To put me into an early grave?'

'No,' Lara said. 'It wasn't that at all. I only lied so you wouldn't find out about me and Mikhail. I was protecting us both.'

'You told me that Tolan didn't trust me. You encouraged my lack of trust in him. You suggested that he might turn against me before handing over the weapons we so desperately need. You slyly sowed the seeds of discontent between us with your lies and inventions. Were you hoping to see me make a foolish move and bring about my own downfall?'

'No!'

'I think you were. I think that you and Mikhail, when you weren't fucking each other, were plotting to bring about my downfall. Which would, of course, have placed him in my high position in the *mafiya* with you, my scheming little bitch, sitting at his right hand.'

'That's not true.'

'Yes, it is. You will pay for this, Lara. You and Mikhail, you'll both pay the price. Now please get out of bed.'

Boris moved first, swinging his legs off the bed and placing his feet – he hadn't taken off his socks – on the floor. Apart from the lack of shoes, he was fully dressed, wearing trousers with an open-necked shirt, already prepared to go out. Lara lay on in the bed, naked under the quilt, admirable in her determination not to let him see her shock and watching him with that steady, opaque green gaze. His heart went out to her for a second, then he brought the shades down.

'Get out of that bed,' he said harshly.

He flipped the quilt back, exposing Lara's nakedness, and she lay there, letting his gaze roam over her. Then, perhaps trembling, he couldn't be sure, she rolled off the bed and stood beside it. Naked, she was superb, a sight to behold. Staring steadily, boldly, at him, she raised her hands in the air, palms upward, as if to say, 'Here I am. Take me.'

'So what now?' was what she actually said.

'Get dressed,' Boris responded. 'Casual clothing. Denims, shirt and flat shoes will do.'

'We're going out?'

'Yes, we're going out. You, me and Mikhail, all together. One big, happy family.'

Boris saw her fear then, the quick brightening of her green eyes, but she turned away, hiding it from him, and entered the bathroom. Boris put on his shoes, then a windcheater jacket. He opened a drawer and withdrew two compact SIG-Sauer P-228 handguns, holstering one to the left and rear of his waist, the other in the same position at the other side. Ready to leave, he sat on the edge of the bed and waited patiently for Lara.

She emerged a couple of minutes later, dressed as he had instructed in an open-necked check shirt, blue denims and flat shoes. Even dressed as plainly as that, she looked like a million dollars and Boris knew that her loss would wound him deeply.

'Put a coat on,' he said.

Lara went to the wardrobe and put on a black leather jacket of elegant simplicity. Then she turned back to face him. Boris looked for the light of fear in her eyes, but she had managed to quench it.

'Let's go,' he said.

They left the bedroom and Boris led her down the stairs, then through the various rooms of the ground floor to the garage at the rear. A silvery-grey BMW was parked there, with one of his minders, Yuri, sitting behind the steering wheel and another minder, Alix, sitting in the rear. Boris opened the rear door at the side where the seat was free and said curtly to Lara, 'Get in.'

When she had slipped into the seat, Boris closed the door with the lock on, thus ensuring that she couldn't slip out when the car slowed down at a traffic light or elsewhere. He then took the seat beside Yuri and said, 'You know where to go.'

'Yes, boss,' Yuri said.

He drove out of the garage, turned along the street and headed for University Road. The city was asleep at this hour of the morning, though the street lights, neon signs and other vehicles made it seem lively still. As Yuri drove south at a steady, respectable clip, along Stranmillis and Lockview roads, past the Belfast Boat Club, Boris glanced over his shoulder and saw Lara's lovely, impassive face, which was bravely concealing the fear that she must surely be feeling. He had to admire her for that. She had the courage of a lion. When she caught his glance, she deliberately held his gaze and he admired her for that as well. Turning back to the front, he took a deep breath and let it out in a sigh, his sole sign of weakness.

Yuri kept following the roads that ran alongside the river until he was on the outskirts of the city. Reaching an area where there appeared to be no houses, where trees lined the river bank, he turned off the main road and took another, narrow road that snaked between woods and led to a clearing by the river. He doused his headlights, turned off the ignition and applied the handbrake.

'All out,' Boris said.

When Yuri released the automatic locks on the doors, using a button on the dashboard, all of them clambered out of the car. Lara glanced about her, taking in the broad, black river, the trees lining both banks, the stars glittering in an exceptionally clear sky, illuminating eternity. She had a peculiar look on her face and it made her seem unreal. Boris recognized that look. It was the look of those about to be executed. Grimly resolved, he nodded towards the boot of the car and said, 'Drag that piece of filth out.'

Instantly Yuri raised the lid of the deep boot. Then he and Alix reached down into it and dragged Mikhail out. His hands were tied behind his back and were also bound to his ankles, his legs being bent painfully up his spine. A gag had been shoved into his mouth and his face was swollen and bloody from what had clearly been a severe beating. Yuri and Alix, when they had him out of the boot, let him fall to the grassy, muddy ground. Yuri kicked him in the ribs for good measure, then stepped back to let Lara see him. Her eyes widened in shock.

'Take the gag out of his mouth,' Boris said. 'There's no one around here but us. He can sob or scream as much as he wants and no one will hear him.'

They removed the gag from Mikhail's mouth, revealing his split, bloody lips, and he coughed and vomited into the grass. He was shaking all over.

'Keep his hands tied behind him,' Boris said, 'but untie the knot around his ankles and haul him onto his knees.'

Alix, a big man with a pugilist's rough features, untied the knot around Mikhail's ankles, letting his feet fall free. Then he roughly hauled his victim to his knees and slapped his face a couple of times to gain his attention. Mikhail was so badly battered that he was barely recognizable and his eyes, which had once seemed poetic, were now brightly glazed with pain and dread. He was trembling and sweating.

'How do you like him now?' Boris asked Lara. Receiving no reply, only a look of contempt, he added: 'Did you really think that this lump of shit would give you more than I could?'

Lara did not reply.

Boris sighed. 'You have to be punished, Lara. Both of you – you have to be punished and that's what we're here for.'

Lara failed to respond. She avoided looking at Mikhail. He was swaying like one of the bulrushes in the river, but each time he started to fall over, Alix held him upright. Mikhail's clothing was soaked in blood, his nose was broken, some of his teeth were missing, and the sweat was pouring in rivulets down his face to soak his split lips. Apart from his unnaturally harsh breathing, he was making no sound.

'He has to die,' Boris said. Lara did not respond. Boris sighed and shook his head from side to side, as if weary of all this. He removed a handgun from its holster, cocked it and aimed at Mikhail who trembled even more, but mustered up enough courage not to turn away from the gun barrel that was aimed squarely at him.

'You're going to do this in front of me?' Lara said, speaking for the first time.

'No,' Boris said. He nodded at Yuri and Alix. Both men removed their handguns from their holsters and aimed them at Lara. Boris removed his second handgun from its holster and held it out to Lara. 'I won't do it. You will,' he said.

Lara's eyes widened in shock and revulsion and dis-belief. She glanced at Mikhail, almost winced at what she saw, then returned her bright green gaze to Boris.

'This is filthy,' she said.

'Life's filthy,' Boris replied. He raised the handgun in his right hand and aimed it at her while holding the second weapon out to her. 'Take it,' he said, 'or we'll blow your fucking brains out, believe me.' Lara took the handgun from him.

'Cock it,' Boris said. Lara cocked the handgun and said, 'What makes you think I won't shoot you instead?'

Boris smiled and nodded, indicating his two mind-
ers who were still both aiming their handguns at Lara.
'*They*'re why I don't think you'll shoot me. Now shoot
Mikhail, Lara.'

'I can't,' Lara said.

'You can and you will.'

When Lara shook her head from side to side, there were
tears in her eyes. 'I wanted to use him,' she confessed,
'but I also loved him, so you can't make me do this.'

'You *loved* him?' Boris said. 'That's the past tense. Does
love die that easily?'

'You vicious fuck,' Lara said.

'Either he dies or you do. If you die, he's going to
die anyway, so why not save one of you? Save *yourself*, Lara.'

'If I shoot him, you'll let me live?'

'That's the deal, Lara. Then you can live with his death
on your conscience for the rest of your life. That's *your*
punishment, Lara.'

'You evil bastard,' she said.

'Do it, Lara,' Mikhail said. He was on his knees in
the mud, his hands tied behind his back, and he was
trembling with pain and the fear of death, but he still
managed to say that. 'If you don't, that bastard will kill
me anyway, so do it and save your life.'

'True love, indeed,' Boris said with soft sarcasm. 'I
almost respect you again, Mikhail. Almost, alas, is not
enough and what will be, must be. Now kill the man you
love, Lara.'

'For God's sake!' Lara exclaimed.

'Do it, Lara!' Mikhail cried out. 'If you don't, they'll
only kill me a lot slower and you'll have to watch. Shoot
me, Lara! Do it now for both our sakes. *God, Lara,
just do it!*'

Lara took aim at Mikhail. Tears were streaming down

her cheeks. 'Fuck you, Boris,' she said. 'Damn you to hell, I won't ever forget this.'

The handgun roared. Lara's hand jumped up and Mikhail jerked to the side, then twisted around and slammed face first into the mud with half of his head gone.

Lara sobbed and dropped the handgun. Alix picked it up immediately and wiped the mud off it, then gave it to Boris without a word. Lara turned away from Mikhail's prostrate body and walked to the car. She slipped into the back seat. Yuri and Alix rolled Mikhail's body across the ground to the muddy bank, then kicked at the corpse until it splashed into the river.

Boris holstered his two handguns. Then he glanced into the rear of the car to see Lara wiping tears from her eyes. Boris didn't understand her. He had never understood her. He slipped into the front passenger seat, Yuri sat in the driver's seat and then Alix took the seat beside Lara. Yuri locked the doors, turned the ignition and headlights on, then slowly drove away from the clearing.

He drove back to Boris's house and parked in the garage. When they were out of the car, Boris led Lara upstairs to one of the guest rooms. It was not where she normally slept. She normally slept with Boris. Boris pushed her into the room and told her to sit on the edge of the bed. Lara sat there and stared steadily at him. Her eyes were dry now. Even if she still felt fearful, she was showing only contempt and Boris admired her for that as well.

'What happens now?' she asked.

'What do you expect?' he said.

'You said that if I killed Mikhail, I would live. And I expect you to stick to that.'

'I will,' Boris said.

He stepped away from the doorway to let Yuri and Alix in. When Lara saw them, she started to rise off the bed but between them they pushed her back down. Lara screamed in rage and grief, struggled wildly, but was subdued. She was bound hand and foot, though not as Mikhail had been bound, her bonds allowing her at least to stretch out, and a gag was tied around her mouth to make sure she stayed silent. When they were done, they propped her upright against the headrest and walked out of the room. Only Boris remained.

'I'll keep my word,' he said. 'You won't be punished with death. Instead, you'll remain here as a prisoner in this room until I'm ready to deal with you. You'll get food and drink. You'll be able to shit and piss. Every three hours, some of my minders will come in to untie your bonds and let you use the toilet or to give you food and drink, before tying you up again. You'll stay here as my prisoner until the weapons are handed over and I deal with Tolan in my own way and then go back to London. I'll take you back to London with me. Once there, I'll have you taken in the boot of a car to a particularly evil brothel near Manchester. It's a secret brothel used by the worst kind of pervert and it's in the middle of a deserted industrial wasteland. You won't be able to leave that place. It's guarded night and day. You'll be kept there until you're too old, too battered or too demented to be of further use to them. Even then, you won't be killed. You'll just be thrown out into the street. By that time you won't be worth a second glance and, if you've actually managed to stay sane, you'll have only your memories, the most salient one of which is bound to be your killing of Mikhail, the man you professed to love. This is your punishment, Lara. This is your future. You'll have all the time in the world to think about it. Now I'm locking you in.'

Boris left the room, locked the door and went into his

own room. He stared at the wall, breathing deeply and harshly, surprised that his heart was racing, feeling broken up inside. Then, getting a grip on himself, he picked up his cellular phone and put a call through to Tolan.

Chapter Twenty-six

Driving back to Antrim in the early hours of that morning, Coogan felt distinctly unreal, at once pleased and shocked at just how effective his anonymous phone call to Boris had been.

After leaving a disgruntled Barry Newman in the OP in south Armagh, Coogan had wanted to follow Tolan and his cronies back to Belfast, but by the time he had walked back to his car and hit the road, he was far too late to catch up with them. Highly frustrated by the time he reached Belfast, he had driven around the Falls Road area, hoping to see Tolan's car parked somewhere. Failing to see it, he had been about to go home for a good night's sleep when he received a call on his cellular phone. It was from Nick Wright, who was back in his apartment in Fitzroy Avenue, a few streets away from where Boris lived.

'I think you'd better get over here,' Nick had said. 'I don't want to tell you this on the phone.'

Arriving at Wright's place, Coogan was told that his friend had been keeping Boris's house under surveillance as usual, first following Lara back there, then staying out front in his car until Mikhail had also arrived, which was an hour or so later. Wright had got out of his car a couple of times and wandered past the house to see Boris pacing his bedroom with the curtains wide open. He also saw Lara up there with Boris before the *mafiya* boss finally closed the curtains.

By this time it was close to midnight so Wright, satisfied that everyone was at home, drove around to the street behind Boris's house, intending to watch the garage exit for a couple of hours, to check if anyone was coming or going. In the event, he did not have to wait long. About two in the morning, the silvery-grey BMW emerged from the garage with Boris in the front and Lara sitting beside a burly minder in the back. Wondering why they would be going out at such an unusual hour, Wright had followed them at a discreet distance until they stopped in a wood beside the Lagan River, in an isolated area on the outskirts of town.

Parking a long way behind the BMW, Wright had advanced on foot until he could see its occupants in a clearing near the river bank. He saw Boris, Lara and two minders standing around a figure who was on his knees on the ground with his hands tied behind his back. It was pretty dark in the wood but the clearing was moonlit and Wright recognized the kneeling man as a badly bruised and bloody Mikhail Kulinich. He then saw Boris handing Lara a handgun that she aimed at Mikhail while Boris and his two minders pointed their own guns at her.

Lara shot Mikhail and his body was dumped in the river. Then the rest of them piled into the car and drove, back to Boris's house. Wright, shocked by what he had seen, had then gone back to his own place and put his call through to Coogan.

Now, as he drove from Antrim town to his rented cottage near Randalstown, Coogan wasn't sure if he felt pleased or horrified by what Wright had told him. Clearly, Boris had taken note of Coogan's anonymous phone call and, as was the *mafiya* way, had exacted swift and brutal retribution. Clearly, too, he had punished Lara by forcing her to execute Mikhail personally. Nevertheless, Coogan had to accept that he was more horrified by the thought of that woman being forced to kill her own lover than he was by the actual death of Mikhail Kulinich. In fact, Mikhail's death pleased him, since it would certainly weaken Boris when it came to a final confrontation. Even better, Pat Tolan might be encouraged to view Mikhail's abrupt departure from the scene as a weak link in the defences around Boris. If he did – and if, as Wright had deduced from his surveillance, he was seriously involved with Lara – he might then decide to withhold his weapons and instead remove Boris from Lara's life. All in all, then, Coogan was pleased, in his own ruthless way, with the results of his phone call.

Extremely weary now, perhaps exhausted by all that had occurred this day, Coogan slowed down as he approached his rented cottage. The building was bathed in moonlight. A light wind was blowing. Coogan drove up to the house and turned along the driveway to park the car in front of the garage. He was just about to turn off the ignition when he noticed in the glare of his headlights that the door, which at first glance had seemed closed, was actually slightly ajar.

Coogan froze. He studied the door more intently. First he confirmed that the door was indeed slightly ajar. Then he saw that the lock was missing and that the wood around where the lock should have been was a jagged, badly splintered, slightly scorched mess.

Coogan didn't move. With a quick glance, he looked in his rear-view mirror. As far as he could see, the road behind him was deserted. But he knew that the low hedgerow at the far side of the road could hide anyone wanting to gun him down.

Still, he didn't move. He simply glanced left and right, inclining his head only a little, and listened for the slightest sound of movement. He heard only the eerie whispering of the light wind and the rustling of the foliage it blew through.

Coogan glanced back at the house. The lights inside were off and the front door appeared to be closed, though that didn't mean anything.

Coogan stared at where the lock should have been on the garage door and knew that someone had shot it off. He knew that that 'someone' was here – maybe one, maybe more. He was convinced it would be more. Unfortunately, he didn't know where they were.

They could be in the garage.

They could be in the house.

They could be hiding behind that low hedgerow at the other side of the road.

They could be in all three places, preparing to catch him in a crossfire, aiming at him right now.

Fuck, he had to get out of here.

His headlights were still on and the engine was still running, so he went sharply into reverse and shot backwards into the road, swinging the car viciously to the left, its tyres screeching like banshees. He heard the first shots firing even as he ground the gears, going desperately into first, and shot forward again, tyres screeching again, trying to head back the way he had come.

A hail of bullets ricocheted off the side of the car and one of the rear windows exploded.

'Fuck!' Coogan exclaimed.

He was indeed racing back the way he had come, but a dark figure rose up from behind the hedgerow to his left, well ahead of the car, and Coogan heard the deafening roar of a sub-machine gun. Bullets ricocheted again off the car, this time blowing out the window beside him, showering him in shards of glass that made high-pitched whistling sounds as they flew about him. He ducked, wrenching at the wheel again, and realized, too late, that he was skidding and screeching across the road, back towards his front garden. The car smashed through the garden wall, the engine howling dementedly and the bonnet buckling, raising clouds of boiling dust. Then it ground to a shuddering halt, the bonnet wrapping untidily around a concrete post – the corner post of the wall – and the spinning wheels sinking deeper into the churned-up soil as Coogan threw his door open and rolled out.

He struck the ground and kept rolling, keeping his head down, eyes closed, until he was stopped by the gable end of the house. There he wriggled around onto his back and jerked his handgun from its holster even as he sat upright. He heard the roaring of sub-machine guns, the bawling of men. Pressing his back to the wall, holding his weapon in both hands, Coogan peered around the wall and saw Bobby Meehan emerging from the front doorway, crouched low, holding a Scorpion sub-machine gun across his chest, followed closely by Pat Tolan who was preparing to fire his handgun.

Three other men were racing across the road, firing their sub-machine guns while on the move, silhouetted by moonlight, so Coogan raised his handgun, fired and saw one of them spin away.

Instantly, as Coogan saw out of the corner of his eye, Meehan and Tolan threw themselves face down in the garden and fired a few bursts at him from there. They were mere yards away, but the wall protected Coogan and he ignored the two in the garden while firing at the men racing across the road. Another one went down, limbs sprawling, dropping his weapon as Coogan jumped up, turned away and ran alongside the gable end of the house to reach the rear garden. He didn't look back. He was vaulting over the rear wall, looking up to see only the moon and stars, when a sub-machine gun roared right behind him and bullets whipped past him. He struck the ground again, rolled over, still holding his handgun, and rose, facing the rear of the house, firing as he came upright.

He saw Tolan and Meehan, both pressed to the gable end, as another man screamed and staggered backwards, dropping his weapon, a Scorpion sub-machine gun, before convulsing and seeming to vomit as he collapsed.

Coogan didn't wait to see any more. He turned away and ran for it.

He headed along the dark field, running parallel to the road, and heard someone bawling behind him – either Tolan or Meehan.

Three down, he thought. *That leaves two of them. Tolan and Meehan.*

Coogan kept running across the field, crouched low, zig-zagging, hearing the roaring of that sub-machine gun behind him and then – sudden silence. Now he heard his own heartbeat, a clock ticking his time off, just as he heard his own breathing, grotesquely amplified, gasping in his throat. He kept running across the field, through striations of moonlight, deliberately staying well away from the road, intent on losing himself in the dark countryside. There were lots of hills here, rising and falling like great breasts, rings of silhouetted trees around their tops, and he remembered his training, the old SAS ways, the hiking from one trig point to another, one peak to another, and did it that way until he was certain that those behind him had given up. He was as fit as a man his age could be, but his lungs were on fire.

Fuck it, Coogan thought, *just keep going. They'll never find you out here. Those two fuckers are city boys.*

This thought gave him confidence. It was enough to keep him going. He hiked for over three hours, watching the slow glide of the moon, the flitting of clouds across it, the lights of aircraft in flight, the moon's majestic domination of the night as the Earth slowly spun. Coogan crossed hill and glen, never relaxing for a moment, using a pocket compass to keep him on the right track, and came eventually to a road that he knew would lead him back to Belfast. It was not a major road, though it led to the M2 motorway, so Coogan hiked it until he found a small town, more like a village, where he was able to hot-wire a parked car and drive the hell out of there.

He drove under the speed limit, making sure to break no rules, and let the journey back give him time to adjust to the fact that Tolan had obviously tracked him down and knew why he was here. How had he done that? Who had given him that information? It could only have been Frank Cooney or Phil Wilson and Cooney, a trustworthy man, seemed highly unlikely. No, it would not have been Cooney. It simply had to have been Wilson. Also, Cooney had never seen the dark blue transit van and that, as far as Coogan was concerned, was the only item through which he could have been traced. Phil Wilson had seen that van.

My mistake, Coogan thought as he drove into Belfast along the almost deserted M2 motorway, fighting to keep his eyes open because of his lack of sleep. *I should never have let that bastard see my van. That was a dumb thing to do. Either he went to them or they went to him, but either way I was fucked. I should have known better.*

Disgusted with himself, not daring to go back to his rented cottage in Antrim, he drove to Nick Wright's flat in Fitzroy Avenue. When he rang the bell by the main door, he had to wait a long time before Wright, obviously not expecting him, rolled out of bed. Wright yawned as he asked who was at the front door and he yawned again when Coogan informed him.

'Christ,' Wright said, 'what time is it?'

'Just open this fucking door,' Coogan said, 'and stop being an arsehole.'

'Did it click? There you go, boss.'

Coogan entered the building and walked up the stairs to find Wright, looking sleepy in pyjamas, holding the door of his flat open. Coogan walked in. Wright closed the door behind him. Coogan sat on the sofa in the living room and said, 'Jesus, I'm tired.'

'So am I,' Wright said. 'So what's the occasion?'

Coogan told him. Wright raised his eyebrows. 'You mean that bastard Tolan knows we're in town?'

'Yes, Nick, I'm afraid so.'

Wright slumped into the armchair facing the sofa. 'If I have a drink now, I'll be catatonic in the morning,' he said, 'but if you feel like a drink I'll pour you one and I think we both need one.'

'Not me,' Coogan said, 'I need sleep – and that's *all* I need.'

'So what happens now, boss? If Tolan knows we're in town, there's no way he won't find us – he has eyes and ears everywhere. So either we clean this fucking mess up or we get *out* of town.'

'We *have* to clean this mess up,' Coogan said, 'and that's all there is to it.'

'So how do we start?'

Coogan didn't even have to think about it. 'We kill Boris,' he said.

Chapter Twenty-seven

'Sure I had nothing to do with it,' Tolan told Boris as they had drinks in a fancy new warehouse restaurant overlooking an old toll gate along the Lagan River. It was one of those fancy open-plan restaurants with a high roof, timber beams and steel girders, with balcony areas overlooking the vast central dining area filled with potted plants and countryside or river views from most of the windows. There were tables outside as well, but given the unpredictability of the province's weather, Boris and Tolan had opted for a balcony table with its good view of the river. When Boris glanced at the river, he recalled the death of Mikhail and knew exactly what Tolan was talking about.

'What are you talking about?' Boris asked innocently.

'That body they fished out of the river,' Tolan said. 'The one identified as that boyo of yours, Mikhail whatsisname. I swear to you, I had nothing to do with it.'

'Then who did?' Boris asked, since he wanted to place Tolan on the defensive. 'According to the police reports, it was a paramilitary-style execution carried out after a bad beating of the kind also often administered by the paramilitaries. Your own kind, in fact.'

'It wasn't us,' Tolan insisted. 'We know nothing about

it. In fact, at first we thought that *you* might have done it. You know? One of them *mafiya*-style punishments for some infraction or other.'

'No,' Boris said, not wishing Tolan to have an advantage through knowing that dissension was being sown in the *mafiya* ranks. 'Mikhail was one of my most trusted lieutenants and I had deep personal affection for him, so certainly we had no cause to punish him. But you used the words "at first" when saying you thought we might have done it. What's changed your mind?'

'Well, if you didn't do it and we didn't do it, there's only one group that *could* have done it.'

'What group?'

'The fucking SAS,' Tolan said.

Boris, normally calm, was slightly startled to hear that. He knew a fair bit about the legendary Special Air Services, having read about them in newspapers and books not only during the time when they had been highly active but also since they had been disbanded. They had, if anything, become even more legendary since their demise, becoming a major item of popular culture in TV drama, comic books and CD-ROM computer games. But in real life, as Boris knew, they had been ferociously efficient and ruthless at carrying out their military tasks. So, in Boris's view, if the SAS, or some variation of it, was looking into his and Tolan's business, it was not good news.

'I thought the SAS regiment was disbanded,' Boris said.

'It was. I'm not talking about the fucking regiment. I'm talking about a former SAS sergeant, Mike Coogan, who may have been hired by British security to come here and cause disruption between us and, no doubt, put us out of business completely. If that's his brief, he'll be tasked with neutralizing us—'

'Pardon?'

'Putting out our lights, like.'

'Oh. Execution.'

'Right. And I think that's what the fucker's been tasked with.'

'What makes you think that?'

'Because someone attempted to assassinate me – and at first I blamed you. Then someone planted a bomb by your house – and at first you blamed me. Now your second-in-command has been shot in the head and dumped in that very river we're looking at in what seems to be a paramilitary – or military – style execution. Since I happen to know that Coogan's in town with a couple of his old SAS mates, and since I also know that he purchased a lot of illegal weapons here in Belfast, I'd say him and his mates are in town to create mayhem for us.'

'This sounds like bad news,' Boris said.

'It sure as fuck is.'

Boris loathed Tolan's obscene language but he tried not to show it. 'Tell me more about Coogan.'

'One of the best men the SAS ever had. A real fucking hard man. Natural-born killer. During the Troubles, he ran a fucking death squad – there's no other term for it – on behalf of those bastards in the British Army's notorious 14th Intelligence Company. A lot of valuable IRA men, I can tell you, went to meet their Maker early because of that bastard. He was as ruthless as we were, no question, and fucking brilliant with it. Usually operated with the same two partners, both SAS troopers as hard as he was, later identified as Nick Wright and Barry Newman. Since he's known to be here in Belfast with two other men, I'd say that's who they are.'

'You knew him personally?'

'Ackay. I had a personal interest in him during the Troubles because we all knew he was out there, killing off our mates. Even though we managed to identify him through one of our touts, we could never track the bastard down. I kind of admired him, you know? I mean, you had to admire his talent. Then the SAS was disbanded, he left the regular Army and, like a lot of former SAS men, he fucked up in Civvy Street and turned out of desperation or simple boredom to a life of crime. Armed robbery and the like. *Mostly* armed robbery, in fact. Did a few jobs in England, but was soon drawn back to Belfast because the so-called peace is a load of ould shite. Both sides, IRA and Loyalists, are still armed to the fucking decommissioned teeth and thriving on crime and it's easier to get weapons and criminal work here than it is anywhere else in Britain. So Coogan came back here and started workin' for me. We had a little bit of a disagreement and I had the cunt shopped. He got a minimum of eight-to-ten in an English prison and now, after serving only a year, he's back on the streets. What the fuck would *you* think?'

'I'd think he's backed by British security,' Boris said.

'Fucking right,' Tolan said. 'There's no question about it. And he's here to fuck you and me up and that isn't good news.'

'So you think he's responsible for the assassination attempt on you as well as the bombing of my house?'

'Yes.'

'And the death of Mikhail?'

'I'd say that's pretty obvious, wouldn't you? I mean, Mikhail was your second-in-command and his loss is going to be felt by you, right?'

'Right,' Boris said blandly.

'Well, I know how that fucking Coogan operates and picking off our best men one by one would be right up his street.'

'How did you find out about him?'

'I knew that someone was after *me*, at least, and they'd

have had to buy weapons for the task. The only way to buy weapons in this city is to go to people controlled by me, so I found out who the seller was and then found out, through him, that the people buying the weapons had used a transit van. I tracked that van down and found out that it had been rented from a company in Antrim to a pseudonymous character living out in that area. So I got his address from the rental company's computer and went out there last night to put out his lights, not caring if it was Coogan or someone else. In fact, it *was* Coogan – I recognized him instantly – but, unfortunately, the bastard got away.'

'And you've no idea where he is now?'

'No. But I'm pretty sure that now we know he's in town and gunning for us, he'll move his plans forward to complete his task before we manage to track him down. So what I've come here to say is that we have to stick together, stop suspecting each other of treachery, which is mostly caused by him, and get those weapons handed over before he can stop us. Then we link up to form a united front against him.'

Boris wanted to do at least some of that, though he had his own reasons. He certainly wanted to get his hands on the weapons more quickly than originally planned because he couldn't afford to let Coogan stop him. However, he also wanted to advance the delivery date because, despite what Tolan was saying, Boris knew that he could not be trusted and would use the slightest excuse to turn against him and break the agreement they had over the sharing of the criminal profits of Belfast. On top of all that, Tolan was now clearly besotted with Lara and, not knowing of her present plight, would most likely want to get rid of Boris in order to keep her all to himself.

'So when do you want to hand over the weapons?' he asked.

'Tomorrow,' Tolan said. 'Because of Coogan, we now have to do it as quickly as possible and that means tomorrow. Can you get out to south Armagh tomorrow night?'

'Yes,' Boris said. 'What time?'

'Midnight. Under cover of darkness.'

'Excellent,' Boris said. 'What's the location?'

'My place in Keady, near the border with Monaghan. Here's a wee map for you.' He passed a hand-drawn map over to Boris, who studied it for a moment, then folded it carefully and put it into his wallet. 'It's a big house,' Tolan continued, 'with high walls all around it, so you can load up in the grounds without bein' seen by anyone driving past. Not that many people would be driving past in any case; it's pretty desolate out there.'

'Will four trucks do it?'

'Ackay, they'd be grand.'

'We can ship the "groceries" out immediately, as agreed?'

'No sweat. Sure I've already fixed it up. You pick the groceries up at my place, then drive them to a wee cove we often use in Dundalk Bay. There'll be a big fishing boat anchored out there, crewed by men from Dublin, and a smaller boat to ship the groceries out to it. Your men can go with the groceries on that boat. The fishing boat will transport the groceries to a similar cove near Heysham, in England, where they'll find another four trucks waiting for them. Once those trucks are loaded, your men can drive the groceries back to London or anywhere else.'

'And when can I move my twenty key men into Belfast to work with your gangs?'

'I'd say you can start doin' that as soon as you like. Once they're here, we'll work out between us a plan to get rid of that fucking Coogan and his murderous boyos. Let's shake on it, Boris.'

'Yes, let's do that,' Boris said.

He reached across the table to shake Tolan's hand, thinking, *I wouldn't trust this man as far as I could throw him.* Indeed, while he was shaking Tolan's hand, he was thinking that Tolan's big country house, where the handover of the weapons was to take place, would be an ideal spot, particularly at midnight, for Tolan's men to shoot down Boris and his men. If not there, then that 'wee cove' in Dundalk Bay, in the early hours of the morning, would also make a suitably deserted area for a massacre.

Thanks, Boris thought as he released Tolan's hand, *but no, thanks. I'm not about to fall for it.*

In fact, Boris was planning to turn up early at Tolan's house, say at about 2100 hours, with a dozen of his best men, all well armed, to launch a surprise attack on Tolan and his men, ruthlessly exterminate them and *then* take the weapons he had been promised. After that, when Boris had dealt with the triads, not to mention Lara, he would return to Northern Ireland and gradually take over Tolan's territory in the wake of the chaos that the elimination of Tolan and his gang would have created.

Fuck Tolan. The Irishman is a dead man. Boris smiled at the thought of it.

'Sure it's good to see you in such good mood,' Tolan said. 'Tying up this matter's obviously been a good thing.'

'*Very* good,' Boris said. 'Now I'd better go back to my place and start getting organized for tomorrow.'

'Good thinking,' Tolan said. When Boris pushed his chair back, Tolan did the same. 'Sure I've gotta get back myself,' he said, 'so let's walk down together.'

'Fine,' Boris said.

It was an indication of how much trust they actually had in each other that each had brought along three armed minders who were seated at two separate tables nearby. When Boris and Tolan rose from the table to leave the balcony area, the two groups of minders did the same and followed them out, keeping a respectful distance apart while also eyeing each other warily, each group fully prepared to draw its weapons and fire at the other. The tension was palpable.

In the event, nothing happened. But if Boris had any doubts about Tolan's interest in Lara, they were dispelled as he and Tolan walked together down the stairs and out of the restaurant, followed by their respective minders.

'So how's Lara?' Tolan asked, trying, though failing, to sound casual.

'Oh, she's fine,' Boris said.

'Sure I only ask because's she's such a pretty wee picture, a flower in a field in May, and she usually hangs around with you, like.'

'She's gone away for a couple of days,' Boris lied blandly, knowing that Tolan was asking about her because she had not turned up the last time they had been supposed to meet – since she was bound and gagged in one of Boris's guest rooms. 'Just to London to do some shopping at Harrod's. I thought it best that she get away while this business of poor Mikhail is sorted out. As you can imagine, the police have been around asking questions and I thought it best to keep her out of that. So I sent her off with a lot of money for a couple of days.'

'Ah, right,' Tolan said, helplessly displaying his feeling of relief. 'A good idea, I think, and I'm sure she'll enjoy her wee bit of shopping. Sure don't the wimmen like to spend the money?'

'Indeed, they do,' Boris said as they left the restaurant and made their way to the car park.

'She likes London, then, does she?'

'I don't wish to offend the Irish, but I'm sure you'd agree that shopping in Belfast isn't the same as shopping in London – and Lara *does* have expensive tastes.'

Tolan grinned (if his undertaker's grimace could be called that) and tapped the side of his nose to indicate that they were both in on some sort of secret manly knowledge. 'Sure don't I know it, Boris? So when she's comin' back, like?'

'Tuesday,' Boris said.

'The day after we hand over the weapons.'

'Yes, Pat, that's right. She's coming back for the party. We'll have a blow-out – is that what you call it here in Britain?'

'Ireland!' Tolan sharply corrected him.

'Sorry . . . *Ireland*. Is that what they say here when they mean a big party?'

'Blow-out? Ackay, sure that term is fine.'

'Then that's what we'll have,' Boris said. 'I told Lara by phone and she's really looking forward it. Lara likes a good party.'

'Sure don't we all?' Tolan said. 'Ah, well, here we are.' They had come to a halt in the car park by Boris's BMW, with the River Lagan flowing past on their right, between banks lined with hawthorn trees and lush greenery, all washed in the soft light of a northern summer. Boris and Tolan shook hands again. 'Tomorrow night, then,' Tolan said.

'Yes, tomorrow night,' Boris responded. Then he slipped into his car where the door was being held open by Yuri. When Boris was in his seat, Yuri closed the door and went around the front to take his own seat behind the steering wheel. The other two minders, one of whom was Alix, clambered into the rear only after Tolan and *his* minders had walked to the other side of the car park to find their own car.

'Back to the house,' Boris said.

As Yuri drove him back to the city, which did not take very long, he thought with sour amusement of how relieved Tolan had looked when he had told him that Lara had only gone away for a few days. Clearly, Tolan had been greatly disturbed when Lara had failed to show the last time they'd been supposed to meet for a fuck. So it was equally clear to Boris that Tolan would try to get rid of him, if for no other reason than to clear the way for what he hoped would be a long-term relationship with Lara. Tolan was not to know that by tomorrow night he would be dead and that Lara, his beloved Lara, would be on her way to a life of hell on Earth in a brothel used by sadomasochistic perverts. God's justice, indeed.

When he was back in the house in Belfast, Boris went straight up to the guest room where he found Lara stretched out on the bed, flat on her back, her ankles bound together and her hands, also bound together, resting on her stomach. She was wearing the same open-necked check shirt, belted tightly at the waist, and skin-tight blue denims: both items of clothing emphasized the perfection of her figure. She looked like a wet dream made flesh. Still gagged, she could not speak to Boris, but she could hear every word he said.

'I've just had lunch with Tolan,' Boris informed her. 'He's promised to hand over the weapons tomorrow night at midnight and he's told me where it's going to happen: at his big house in a place called Keady in South Armagh. However, unbeknownst to him, I'm going there early with my men to launch a surprise attack against him and wipe him off the face of the Earth. I will then take the weapons and come back here for you. You can rest assured that the next day you'll be on your way to England and a future that you'd rather you didn't have. Tomorrow night, it all ends for Tolan – and it all ends for you. Think about it and weep.'

Boris turned away and closed the door, locking Lara in again. He leaned his back against the door, closed his eyes and gritted his teeth. He was trying to kill the love that had weakened him and let Lara deceive him. He stood there for a long time, his back pressed to the door, imagining her at the other side of the door, bound and gagged, at his mercy. That image of her burned through his brain and filled him with pain.

Boris wanted oblivion.

Chapter Twenty-eight

Coogan broke into Boris's place that night, just after midnight. His first task was to neutralize the electronic security systems and to do this he had had to visit an old friend, after making an urgent phone call, earlier that afternoon. The old friend was Sergeant Major Walter Bannerman, formerly a Field Intelligence NCO, or Finco, with the same notorious 14th Intelligence Company for which Coogan had covertly worked when he'd been fighting the IRA. Though peace had supposedly come to Ireland and the British Army no longer had an official presence on the streets of the city, Bannerman and others like him were quietly doing the kind of work that they had always done, though this time they were involved in a war against the criminalized paramilitaries of both sides and were operating out of the British Army's Northern Ireland Headquarters in Lisburn.

Coogan didn't meet Bannerman there, of course, but at a pub in the Golden Mile. But when he told Bannerman what he needed, which was an electronic blocking device that would neutralize Boris's high-tech security systems, plus a hooked rope for scaling a sheer wall, Bannerman, who had come to town in an unmarked, windowless transit van, placed Coogan in the back of it and drove him straight to the Lisburn HQ. There, in a technical laboratory in the basement of the main building, where experiments were conducted regularly on all kinds of sabotage and surveillance equipment, he gave Coogan one of the two items he needed: a magnetized electronic device not much larger than a chocolate ice-cream bar. With this in his hand, Coogan then followed Bannerman to another department, a kind of quartermaster's store, where he was given a twenty-foot long scaling rope with a curved metal hook in the end. Both items were placed in a black plastic rubbish bag, then Bannerman put Coogan back into the transit van and drove him back to the same pub.

Bannerman did not enter the pub this time but simply dropped Coogan off there, wished him luck and drove away. He had not, at any point, asked Coogan what he was involved in because in his line of business, as he knew from bitter experience, it was often a case of the less you knew the better.

Coogan did not go back into the pub either.

As soon as Bannerman had driven off, Coogan, carrying the plastic rubbish bag, walked back to Nick Wright's house in Fitzroy Avenue. He had spent the night there and decided to remain there, not only because it was close to Boris's house, but also because he did not dare return to his rented house in Antrim where some of Tolan's men might still be waiting for him. Entering Wright's flat, Coogan placed his package on the living-room table and sank into a chair to light up one of his rare cigarettes.

'Smoking kills,' Wright quipped brightly.

'So does this line of work,' Coogan retorted.

Wright nodded at the package resting on the table. 'You got what you wanted?'

'Yes,' Coogan said.

'You're going in this evening?'

'Yes, about midnight. When it looks like all the lights are out. Have you been keeping your eye on the place?'

'Yes.'

'Any movement?'

'No.'

'Any sign of Lara?'

'She hasn't left the house since Mikhail was killed. Not unless she went out while I was following Boris. But, under the circumstances, I don't think that's likely.'

'No, neither do I. Making her kill Mikhail was part of her punishment, but almost certainly it was *only* part of it. The very fact that Boris didn't kill her at the same time is a fair indication that he has something else, something worse, planned for her later. So he's probably keeping her as a prisoner in the house until the time is ripe. So when did Boris go out?'

'Late this morning, just before lunchtime.'

'And where did he go?'

'To that big new warehouse restaurant down by the old locks of the River Lagan.'

'You followed him in?'

'Yes. He met Tolan there. They had lunch together. They both had minders at other tables. Naturally, I couldn't go near them, couldn't hear what they said, but they had lunch and then shook hands and went their separate ways.'

'If they shook hands, they must have come to some kind of an agreement.'

'I'd reckon,' Wright said.

'Like the handing over of the weapons. Now that they know I'm here, that I've armed myself for a job, they'll have put two and two together and come to the realization that I'm here to prevent their link-up with Boris. That'll only encourage them to cement their relationship before I try to do it permanent damage.'

'So the handover of the weapons, which symbolically seals the deal, will take place real soon.'

'Correct,' Coogan said. 'I'd say any day now. So did Boris return to his house after the lunch?'

'Yep.'

'And he was still there when you left the place an hour ago?'

'Yep.'

'He doesn't go out any more at nights, does he?'

'By and large, no.'

'Okay,' Coogan said. 'Let's just make sure of that. I want you to go back there right now and keep an eye on the rear of the house, on the garage, until I show up, which should be around midnight. If you see Boris leaving, with or without Lara, call me here on your mobile.'

'You're going to go in there alone?'

'Absolutely. No point in the two of us running that kind of risk.'

'You'd better get something to eat, then rest up in my absence to ensure that you're as bright as a new pin at the midnight hour.'

'I'll do that,' Coogan said. 'Now get going and don't leave that place until I come and join you.'

'Roger,' Wright said

When his friend had left the flat, Coogan made himself a plate of pasta, which was light but high in energy content. He avoided alcohol. He lay down, fully dressed, on Wright's bed and remained there until darkness had almost fallen, which was after 2100 hours, though he didn't actually fall asleep: he was just resting his eyes.

At 2130 hours he rolled off the bed, undressed, had a hot-and-cold shower, brushed his teeth and then, feeling bright and alert, put his clothes back on. He was wearing black corduroy trousers with a thin black roll-neck pullover, black trainers and a black windcheater jacket. He strapped the only weapon he would take, a silenced Glock-19 handgun with a fifteen-round box magazine, around his waist with the holster positioned slightly to the rear of his left side. Then he picked the black rubbish bag off the table and left the flat to go down into the street.

It was a pleasant warm evening, with the moon on the rise in a sky still faintly tinged by the afternoon of sunset. It only took a couple of minutes for Coogan to walk the short distance to Boris's house, passing from shadow to light under the leafy, rustling branches of the breeze-blown trees. He went first to the front of the house to check if the lights were on or off. All the lights were off, though two bodyguards were sitting on wooden chairs on the front porch, both wide awake.

Satisfied that everyone in the house was in bed, if not necessarily asleep, and not yet concerned about the bodyguards, Coogan walked around to the next street. When he approached Boris's garage, located at the rear of the house, he saw Wright's rented red Volkswagen Golf parked at the opposite side of the road. Coogan opened the door and slipped in beside Wright, though he left the door open behind him.

'Did anyone come out?' he asked.

'Not a soul,' Wright replied. 'And the lights – at least the lights in the rear – went out about half an hour ago.'

'They're all out at the front as well,' Coogan said, 'so I assume everyone is asleep.'

'Except the bodyguards out front,' Wright reminded him.

'With luck I can get in and out without them being aware of it. But since I'm here now, why don't you just drive around to the front, find a parking space within hearing distance of the house and help me sort out the guards if you hear shouting or gunshots.'

'Good idea,' Wright said. 'I'll go as soon as you get out of this car.'

'I'm on my way,' Coogan said. 'But don't start up the engine until I give you a wave.'

'Okay,' Wright said.

Coogan slipped out of the car, closed the door and then made his way across the road, still carrying the black rubbish bag. There was a narrow garden area at the back of Boris's house with a high brick wall running along it to merge with the cornerstone of the wall that angled up to the closed door of the garage. Even from here, lost in the shadows, Coogan could see a burglar alarm and an overhead video camera, attached to the top of the high door frame, moving constantly to and fro to cover the area at the back of the house. Coogan was hidden from the camera by the high wall, but he would be seen as soon as he walked up to the garage door.

He didn't walk. Instead, he dropped to his hands and knees, removed the magnetized blocking device from the rubbish bag and pressed a button repeatedly until a blinking red light came on. The device, Coogan knew, was already sending out a series of silent electronic blips that would short-circuit the burglar alarms and video surveillance systems. Knowing that he was safe so long as the blocking device was operating, he held it against the door of the garage and felt it sticking magnetically to the steel surface. When he released his hand, the magnetic device remained where it was.

Coogan knew that he was taking a chance since even though the video surveillance cameras had been switched off there could be a guard inside the house, instructed to stay awake all night and keep his eye on the video monitor. If that was so, the guard would already have been alerted by the fact that all the electronic security systems had malfunctioned. However, while this was a distinct possibility, Coogan had the feeling that Boris was not the kind of man to take his security that far and was probably content to use the video cameras only during the day, when he could see clearly who was coming and going. He probably depended solely on the burglar alarms at night – and they had just been put out by the magnetized blocking device attached to the garage door.

Deciding to proceed, Coogan waved across the street to Wright who started his car as quietly as possibly, then moved off down the street, soon disappearing around the corner at the far end to go around to the front of the house.

Glancing up and down the street, seeing that no one was coming, Coogan removed the hooked scaling rope from the rubbish bag and placed it on the ground. After carefully rolling up the large bag, he dumped it in a nearby bin. He then picked up the scaling rope, uncoiled it and slung the hooked end up over the top of the high wall. When the steel hook had fallen over the other side, making a slight metallic ringing sound where it struck the bricks, Coogan pulled on the rope until the hook had taken a firm grip on the wall. Then, holding the rope in both hands, he stepped back, swung his legs up in the air, braced his feet against the wall and proceeded to haul himself up the fifteen feet to the top. Once on top of the wall, he hauled the rest of the rope up and threw it down the inside of the wall, thus ensuring that no passers-by would see it. He felt the wind tugging at him.

Standing on top of the wall, Coogan could see the French windows of one of the back rooms, set approximately fifteen feet above the ground, at the far side of the open space above an eight- or nine-foot-wide strip of garden. A black wrought-iron balcony ran the length of the French windows. Like a professional cat burglar (and certainly trained as such by the SAS for this kind of task), Coogan picked up his scaling rope and walked along the top of the garden wall, turned right where it formed an L-shape leading up to the rear wall of the building, and stopped again when he came abreast of the balcony window.

The near end of the wrought-iron balcony was a good six feet away, which was too far to jump even if Coogan could manage to do it silently, which was next to impossible. Frustrated by that approach, he fixed the hook on the rope to the top of the wall, lowered the rest of the rope to the ground and lowered himself down to the garden. Once there, he flipped the rope to release the hook and caught it as it fell to prevent it from making a noise. Then, knowing that this time he could not avoid making at least a little bit of noise, he threw the rope up and expertly tugged at it so that the hook fell, with a light metallic ringing noise, over the edge of the black wrought-iron balcony.

Holding his breath, Coogan waited for a minute or so to see if a light would come on in the room or if someone, alerted by the metallic ringing of the hook, would open the French windows to look out. In the event, nothing happened. Satisfied that whoever was in the room was still asleep, Coogan tugged at the rope to ensure that the hook was gripping firmly. When he was satisfied that it was, he stepped back, swung his legs up, braced his feet against the wall and proceeded to haul himself up to the balcony.

The wrought-iron railing was a good four feet deep, so when Coogan was abreast of it he was able to grab the top of it and raise his right foot to rest it on the helpfully wide ledge that ran around the concrete base of the balcony. Once in that position, he was able quickly to grab the top of the railing with his free hand, then pull himself forward and swing his other leg over the railing. Eventually, with an athletic swing of his body, he was standing on the balcony.

The curtains had been pulled across the French windows, so Coogan could not see into the room. What he could see, however, was that the lights in that room were still turned off.

Turning away from the window, Coogan glanced up and down the shadowy lamplit street, of which he had a panoramic view from his position. He was pleased to note that there was no one out and about.

Turning back to the French windows, Coogan gently tried the handle and confirmed that the windows were locked. Removing a special tool-knife from the side pocket of his windcheater jacket, he pulled out a miniature glass-cutting bit and, working with the utmost delicacy, taking his time and making practically no noise, he drilled a small hole in the window pane by twisting the bit to and fro until the solid glass was a powder that drifted silently to the floor inside the room. Once the hole had been completed, he folded the bit back into the tool-knife and pulled out a miniature glass-cutting blade. Using the blade, again working slowly and silently, he cut downwards from the hole for approximately twelve inches, cut across for another twelve inches, cut upwards for the same distance, then cut across in the opposite direction until he was almost back at the hole. Just before making the final cut, he inserted a tiny hook into the hole. As he made this last cut, he tugged the hook towards him and the square twelve-inch-sided piece of glass, instead of falling into the room to break noisily on the floor, came gently outwards at chest level and he was able to grab it before it fell farther. He lowered it gently to the floor of the balcony, then straightened up again.

After folding the miniature glass-cutting blade back in, Coogan returned the tool-knife to his pocket, then slowly, carefully, reached through the twelve-inch-sided hole in the French window to take hold of the end of the curtain, which covered the inside lock, and pull it a few inches to the side. Lowering himself slightly by bending his knees, he glanced between the curtains and saw that the room was still in darkness. He kept looking, letting his eyes adjust to the gloom, and gradually made out a bed positioned directly opposite the French windows. There was someone on the bed. That person, man or woman, was lying flat on his or her back, hands resting on his or her stomach, face turned up to the ceiling. In the darkness it was impossible to see whether the person was asleep or awake, though something in the posture of the body made Coogan feel that the individual was asleep.

Slowly, quietly, with infinite patience, Coogan reached through the hole cut in the window-pane and groped downwards with outspread fingers to where he knew the lock was. His fingers touched a key. He wanted to sigh with relief, but he didn't dare do so. He simply took the key between his thumb and index finger and, now practically not breathing, turned it slowly but surely.

The key made a slight clicking sound and the lock was opened.

Again Coogan wanted to sigh with relief, but again he didn't dare do so. Instead, he reached across his belly with his right hand and withdrew his silenced handgun from its holster, positioned to the rear of his left side. Holding the pistol behind his back to muffle the sound, he released the safety catch. When he heard it click off (the sound was soft but seemed louder in the silence), he raised the pistol to the side of his face with the barrel turned upwards. Then, trying not to make a sound, he pushed one side of the French windows open and entered the dark room.

The curtains parted before him with a soft rustling and then fell closed behind him.

Coogan froze at that moment. He looked across the room at the bed. He saw that the individual was still lying there, stretched out flat on his or her back, face turned towards the ceiling. Coogan glanced left and right. There was no one else in the room. He advanced to the bed, looked down and saw Lara Tikhonova.

There was a gag in her mouth, obviously tied behind her head, and the hands in her lap were bound with cord. When Coogan ran his gaze over that luscious body – luscious even in a man's check shirt and blue denims – he saw that her ankles were bound also.

Then she opened her eyes.

Coogan saw the eyes widen with shock and disbelief. He lowered his pistol automatically, aiming it at her, about to kill her. Then he remembered that she couldn't make a sound and that, if nothing else, stopped his trigger finger. Instead of killing her, he raised the index finger of his free hand to his own lips, indicating that she should not make a sound. Obviously no fool, clearly not easily frightened, she nodded her blonde head in acknowledgement.

'Don't panic,' Coogan said, not whispering but keeping his voice low. 'I haven't come here for you. I know who you are and I'm certainly not your enemy, so if I take that gag out of your mouth I'll expect you to stay calm and keep your voice down. Do you promise to do that?'

She stared steadily at him – her gaze so steady it was unnerving – then nodded her head.

'I repeat,' Coogan said, 'that I'm not here for you, but if you make a sudden move when I remove the

gag, I'll blow your fucking brains out. Do you understand that?'

She nodded again.

'Raise your head,' Coogan said.

She raised it. Coogan placed his handgun on the bedside cabinet, then used both hands to untie the knot
behind her head. When he had done so, he removed the
gag, let it fall to the floor, then picked up his handgun
again, keeping it aimed away from her.

'You're Lara Tikhonova,' he said. 'Boris's mistress.'

'Yes,' she responded.

'I haven't come here for you,' Coogan said. 'I've come
here for Boris. But if you give me any problems, I'll kill
you. Do you understand that?'

'Yes,' Lara said.

'You were betraying Boris with Mikhail,' Coogan said.
'Why did you do that?'

'Because Boris treated me like a whore,' Lara said, 'and
I won't be treated that way. Because I knew that sooner
or later he'd want to get rid of me and I wasn't about to
lose all I'd gained.'

'So you were going to use Mikhail to get rid of Boris and
then become Mikhail's wife once he'd taken over Boris's
mafiya role.'

'Yes,' Lara said. 'You were obviously watching me.'

'Sure,' Coogan shrugged. 'What about you and Tolan?'

'Tolan wanted me badly and Boris saw that, so he
ordered me to go to bed with Tolan and pass on what
he said. It was no more than that.'

'I believe you,' Coogan said. 'But Boris thought you
were meeting Tolan every day of the week when in fact
you were only seeing him twice a week and seeing Mikhail
the other days.'

'Yes,' Lara said.

'Why was that?' Coogan asked.

'Because Tolan is a loser – no way can he beat Boris – whereas Mikhail could have got me all I wanted. So I went with Mikhail.'

'But it's Mikhail who's now dead and Tolan who's running around out there on the loose, making deals with Boris.'

'I made a mistake,' Lara said.

Coogan actually smiled. 'So what has Boris planned for you?'

'A brothel used by sadomasochistic perverts and guarded at all times. A lot of abuse, with AIDS thrown in for good measure. A life not worth living.'

'That's good cause to hate Boris.'

'That's one of the reasons I hate him,' Lara said.

'And the others?'

'Fuck you.'

'I've come here to kill him,' Coogan said, 'and you've got to help me.'

'How can I do that?'

'By telling me where he is, for a start.'

'Leave this room, turn right and it's the door directly facing the corridor. It's the master suite.'

'What about the other rooms?'

'The only other person who slept here – apart from me – was Mikhail and he, as you know, is dead and buried.'

'What do I do about you? If I kill Boris and just leave, the guards will come in and take it out on you.'

'Then don't leave me here.'

'Why not?' Coogan asked.

'Because you don't want just Boris. You also want Tolan. You're obviously working for the British and that means you must want the whole damned show. I can help you with that.'

'How?' Coogan asked.

'I know all you need to know. I've worked both sides of the fence. Because of Boris, I know everything that you need to know about the *mafiya*; because of Tolan, I know everything you need to know about the Northern Irish underworld. What *else* do you need to know?'

'Not much,' Coogan said.

He turned away from her and walked to the bedroom door. He opened it slightly, looked out and saw nothing but darkness. Closing the door, he went back to the bed and looked down on Lara.

'There *is* something else,' he said.

'What's that?' Lara asked.

'Where and when was Tolan intending to hand over his weapons to Boris?'

'Tomorrow evening,' Lara said. 'About midnight, at his country house near Keady in south Armagh.'

'I know the house,' Coogan said.

'Like you knew I was seeing Mikhail,' Lara said.

'Yeah, like that,' Coogan said.

Lara sighed. 'So what happens now?'

'I'm going to kill Boris. If I succeed, I'll come back for you. I'll take you somewhere safe and let you stay there until I've taken care of Tolan. Then, given a little bit of time, I'll sort you out for good.'

'How?' Lara asked.

'A free ticket to Australia and a good life once you get there.' Coogan knew he was going to have to fight hard with Edmondson for that. But what the fuck.

'It's a deal,' Lara said.

Coogan went to the door, opened it slowly and peered out. He stepped out into the dark and empty landing and padded quietly down it in his rubber-soled trainers, holding his silenced handgun at the ready. He was half-way along it, approaching Boris's room, when he heard someone moving in the room. Something clicked – a switch – and then striations of light beamed out obliquely from around the door frame.

Coogan froze instantly.

Clearly, Boris had just left his bed and turned on the light.

Coogan stayed motionless for a long time. At least, it seemed like a long time. Eventually, his breathing constricted with tension, he advanced along the landing and stopped again when he came to the door. He pressed his ear against it. There was no sound from inside. He curled his fingers around the handle, turned it and quickly pushed the door open. He rushed into the room.

A man was kneeling on the floor by the window, illuminated in the moonlight, his hands clasped under his chin, his silvery-grey head bowed.

He seemed to be praying.

When Coogan burst into the room, the man raised his head and then turned around, shuffling on his knees, to let Coogan see him.

Coogan recognized Boris.

'Who are you?' Boris asked.

'You don't want to know,' Coogan said.

'You're Coogan,' Boris said. 'You have to be. You can't be anyone else.'

'So what?' Coogan asked.

'Did you harm Lara?'

'No.'

'Please don't,' Boris said. 'There's no way she can harm you, after all. It's me and Tolan you want.'

'That's right,' Coogan said.

Boris was in his pyjamas, on his knees on the floor, and he spread his arms out to either side with the palms turned upwards and trembling, as if making an offering.

'I'm tired,' Boris said. 'I was *always* tired. Now put me

out of my misery, Sergeant Coogan. Some day you'll be tired, too.'

'Have a rest,' Coogan said.

He fired a single shot, the sound muffled by the gun's silencer. Boris, his eyes widening in surprise, fell back against the wall beneath the window, then toppled sideways, as if in slow motion, to fall face down on the floor.

'Jesus Christ,' Coogan muttered.

He turned away and left the room, walked back along the landing, then went back into the room where Lara Tikhonova still lay stretched out, bound hand and foot, on the bed.

'Don't say a fucking word,' Coogan said. 'Just stick close to me.'

He untied her bonds to let her slither off the bed. She tried to stand up and promptly fell back again, grunting with pain though she kept her mouth shut.

'It's your circulation,' Coogan said. 'You've been tied up too long. Just give it a couple of minutes, massage your legs a bit and you'll be okay again. Get up when you can manage it.'

Coogan went back to the door, holding his handgun at the ready, and waited there, keeping watch until Lara's circulation had returned to normal and she could roll off the bed and stand behind him.

'We're going down those stairs and out the front door,' Coogan whispered. 'And no fucking bodyguards are going to stop us. Now stick close behind me.'

'I will,' Lara said.

Coogan went down the stairs, treading carefully in the darkness, holding his handgun at the ready, and felt Lara right there behind him, breathing against his neck. He tried not to think about that (her body outstretched, her green eyes drawing him in, her full breasts and flat belly and broad hips and long legs, the full lips and the flowing blonde hair and the expression that said, *I've known every fucking man in the world and you're no different, mister*) as he padded stealthily across the rooms of the ground floor to reach the front door. Once there, he froze again. Lara's body pressed against him. He reached behind him with his free hand, pushed her away from him, then reached down and quickly turned the door handle. Then he kicked the door open, splitting the silence.

The bodyguards reacted quickly, though not quickly enough. Coogan heard the chairs squeaking as the guards pushed them back. Then he stepped out onto the porch, looked left and squeezed the trigger, looked right and squeezed the trigger again.

There was very little noise. The handgun made a coughing sound. The man on the left looked surprised, staggered backwards and then collapsed; the man on the right glanced down at his bloody chest, said, 'Shit!' and then dropped dead.

Coogan turned to face Lara, placing a finger to his lips. Lara nodded, understanding that she should be silent, and Coogan turned away from her. He led her down the porch, across the garden, out to the street, and saw Nick Wright's car, the red Volkswagen Golf, parked farther along the road. He led Lara to it and introduced her to Nick Wright. Then he pushed her into the back of the car and took the front seat beside Wright.

'I have reason to believe,' he said, shocked by the sound of his own voice, 'that Tolan's men won't be waiting for us in Antrim, so let's go there right now.'

'Where the fuck do you think they'll be?' Wright asked.

'In Armagh,' Coogan said.

Starting the Golf's engine, Wright drove Coogan and Lara all the way back to the rented house in Antrim.

There was only one day left.

Chapter Twenty-nine

I n the dark early hours of the morning, Wright drove
along the road that led to Coogan's rented house in
Antrim and parked a good distance away. Leaving
Wright and Lara in the car, Coogan went the rest of the
way on foot, clambering over the gate where Tolan's men
had previously parked their car (the car was gone) and
then making his way silently along the edge of the field
to come abreast of the low hedgerow facing the house.
There was no one hiding behind the hedgerow.

Coogan kept going, advancing at the half-crouch to
ensure that he was hidden from the view of anyone in
or around the house. When he had passed the house,
where he was definitely out of view, he loped across
the road to come up on the building from the side. He
checked the garage and found it empty, except for the
transit van which covered the camouflaged hole in the
ground where his weapons were hidden. Tolan's men
had not found the weapons.

Leaving the garage, he checked every side of the
house from outside, peered through all the windows
and, seeing no sign of anyone inside, gingerly stepped
in through the open door, not needing to use his key
because the lock had been blown off by Tolan's men.

He checked upstairs and downstairs, but found no one there.

Satisfied that Tolan's men had left, he went outside again and waved for Wright to drive up to the house. Wright did so. He let Lara out. Then he reversed and drove back the way he had come to tuck the car into the gateway, not wanting it to be seen out front. Then he joined Coogan and Lara inside the house.

'They did no damage, apart from the doors,' he said, amazed.

'No,' Coogan said. 'They must have left shortly after I fled, maybe thinking I'd tell someone they were here – the police or the army. Either that or they simply had to get to Armagh to arrange for tonight's handover of the weapons. They won't know that Boris is dead, so they'll get ready to receive him as planned. We'll be there waiting for them.' He turned to Lara, who was standing beside him. 'How do you feel?'

'I'm okay,' she said. 'A bit tired and shaken, but okay.'

Her green gaze was steady, opaque, disingenuous, framed by the golden-blonde hair, above the slightly parted luscious lips. Coogan realized that he wanted her. What man *wouldn't* want her? That had always been her blessing and her curse: the male eyes hungrily watching her. Coogan nodded and turned to face Wright, trying to neuter his feelings.

'I don't think they'll come back,' he said, 'but we can't take a chance on it, so you and I will take turns at watch, two hours on, two hours off. You, Lara, try to sleep. We'll be leaving here in the morning. We'll drop you off at a hotel in Antrim town and come back for you later, when we've done what we have to do.'

'You're going to kill Tolan.'

'Yes.'

'Good,' Lara said.

She slept in the upstairs bedroom. Coogan and Wright stayed downstairs, taking turns at watch until the dawn broke. The morning was uneventful. No one came to the house. When Lara awoke and came down the stairs, she was wearing the same clothes that she had worn yesterday, the check shirt and denims, but she still managed to look like a million dollars.

They had breakfast at the kitchen table – a fry-up for the men, toast and marmalade for Lara – then Lara sat on the sofa and smoked a couple of cigarettes while Coogan and Wright loaded the rest of their weapons into the transit van. When they had completed their task, Wright took his place behind the driving wheel and Coogan went back inside for Lara. Silent and smoking a cigarette, she was sitting in a shaft of morning light that fell on the sofa. The mere sight of her gave Coogan a hard-on.

'We're ready to leave,' he said.

'I don't have money,' Lara replied. 'Or my passport or anything else. We left the house too quickly for that.'

Coogan went to the Welsh dresser and opened a drawer. He pulled out a fistful of notes and handed them to her. 'If we don't come back,' he said, 'that should keep you going for a week or two. After that, it'll be up to you.'

'I'm sure I'll survive,' Lara said.

'I'm sure you will,' Coogan said.

They left the house, closing the smashed front door as best they could, and clambered up into the transit van with Lara squashed between Coogan and Wright. Wright drove them to Antrim town, which was sleepy this overcast morning, and eventually they found a small hotel for Lara to stay in. Coogan stuck to her until she had booked in, practically shoulder to shoulder with her, aroused by her presence.

'You've enough money there,' he told her, 'to buy any-thing you'll need over the next few days – clothes, make-up, a travelling bag – whatever. Go shopping. Relax. If we're lucky, we'll see you here tomorrow morning.'

'Good luck,' Lara said. 'You'll need it.'

'Thanks a lot,' Coogan said.

He left her there in the lobby and returned to the transit van, which was parked a good distance away. Wright drove them out of town, along the east side of Lough Neagh, then on across the border to Lurgan and from there to Armagh and then to Keady. The sun came up, burning through the thin clouds, and the countryside looked lush and inviting, all its horrors concealed.

When they arrived at Keady, Wright took the turn-off that led into the hills above Tolan's house. He parked the transit van in the woods, where he had parked it before, and remained in it while Coogan advanced to the OP on foot, calling out his own name to ensure that Newman didn't mistake him for one of Tolan's men. Newman emerged from the OP, still black-faced, clearly exhausted, and said, 'I can't take much more of this, Coogan. There's nothing happening down there and I'm going crazy with boredom up here.'

'We've come to join you,' Coogan said. 'Tolan's handing the weapons over tonight and we're going to take him out. Boris is dead, but Tolan doesn't know that, so he's bound to turn up with his gang. This is your last day up here.'

'Thank Christ,' Newman said.

He helped Tolan and Wright unload the weapons and carry them to the OP. When the transit van had been emptied, they camouflaged it as they had done before, then returned to the OP. The STG laser surveillance system was still set up on tripods in front of the viewing hole, but as it was no longer needed they dismantled it, took the separate pieces back to the transit van, then set the General Purpose Machine-Gun up in its place.

'You get the GPMG,' Coogan said to Newman. 'You, Nick,' he added, speaking to Wright, 'will be in charge of the SMAW and I'll expect you to take out their vehicles with it.' He was referring to the Shoulder-launched Multi-purpose Assault Weapon that fired High Explosive Anti-Armour rockets, or HEAA. 'I'll have the Barrett Light .50 rifle and we'll all have our usual personal weapons. Now we wait and watch.'

They sat with their personal weapons on the ground beside them: Heckler & Koch MP5 sub-machine guns and M16 rifles with high-powered European SS109 shells. They all had Glock-19 handguns holstered around the waist and there were hand grenades dangling from their webbed belts.

It was a long wait. They passed the time listening to pop music on the radio and were relieved to note, when the news came on, that there was no mention of Boris.

'His *mafiya* friends are probably keeping the news of his death secret,' Coogan said, 'until they can sort something out.'

'They'll be looking for Lara,' Wright said.

'Probably. But they're not likely to think of looking in Antrim town. Almost certainly they'll think she's either hiding out in Belfast or has already taken a boat or plane out of the country. Lara's safe for the moment.'

'Safer than we are,' Newman said.

'That's a fact of life,' Coogan said.

Time dragged on, the sun shifted across the sky, and eventually, at 2135 hours, they saw a line of saloon cars coming along the darkening road. Instantly, Newman took his position behind the GPMG and Wright hurried out of the OP to kneel beside it with the bulky SMAW pressed to his shoulder and a good supply of HEAA rockets at his feet. Picking up the Barrett Light .50 rifle and an MP5 sub-machine gun, Coogan also left the OP to take up a position beside it.

The line of cars, six in all, drew abreast of the front wall of the house, which was about fifteen feet high and thirty metres long, and stopped when the first car was at the gate. A couple of men in grey suits and black shoes got out of the first car to open the gate.

'Go for the cars,' Coogan said, 'before they get into the grounds behind that wall. *Go for it now!*'

The sharp crack of Wright's SMAW split the silence and the HEAA rocket flew towards the first car, its trajectory clearly marked by a trail of thin, whitish smoke. The rocket just missed the car, but it struck the wall beyond it, exploding with an ear-splitting roar, spewing boiling clouds of black smoke and dust across the road to obscure the first couple of cars. Instantly, the roaring of Newman's GPMG was added to the bedlam as he raked the area in front of the gate, striking one of the two men, who convulsed wildly before collapsing, and encouraging the other to frantically push his side of the gate open and rush into the grounds behind the high wall.

All of the cars jolted forward, practically ramming each other as the first one made a screeching sharp left turn and started through the gate. Wright fired his SMAW again and another HEAA rocket slammed this time into the first car and blew it apart, with pieces of red-hot metal flying off in all directions and yellow flames bursting out from the exploding engine.

With the entrance to the property blocked by the burning car, the other drivers frantically turned their vehicles this way and that. But then Newman started raking them with sustained bursts from his GPMG. Windows were smashed and bullets ricocheted in every direction. Two of the cars crashed into each other. Another slammed into the wall. A third went into a screeching skid, its tyres smoking, and then practically leapt off the road to smash into a tree trunk. Only when men started spilling out of their vehicles did Coogan open fire with his Barrett Light .50 rifle.

His first bullet struck a man struggling to get out of an open rear door and it punched him back into the car with his legs kicking wildly. Another man came out firing his handgun on the move; Coogan's second shot blew his chest apart and made him somersault backwards to the ground. Coogan was looking for Tolan but hadn't seen him yet. So he fired at anyone he could get in his sights and struck a few more. Then a silver-grey Honda Accord, about halfway along the line, raced out of the boiling smoke and headed straight for the car blazing in the middle of the gateway. It crashed into the blazing car, clearly doing so deliberately, and kept going until it had pushed the burning car aside and could race on into the grounds behind the high wall.

That was Tolan, Coogan thought.

Tolan's car having cleared the gateway, other cars were now making screeching turns in the swirling smoke and racing into the grounds of the property. Some men, having already left their vehicles, fired back up the hill with handguns and Scorpion sub-machine guns. Newman's GPMG roared again, raking the area, and two of the men firing convulsed in clouds of spewing, swirling dust before the stream of bullets picked them up and then slammed them back down to the ground. When the last of the undamaged cars had gone through the gateway, a couple of men pushed the gates closed.

'Get that gate!' Coogan bawled at Wright.

Instantly, Wright took aim at the gate with his SMAW and sent a HEAA rocket shooting down the hill. It exploded with a deafening roar in the middle of the gates, blowing them apart and sending buckling, red-hot pieces of metal flying out in all directions, one piece neatly slicing off the head of a man still in the road.

'Let's go!' Coogan yelled.

Lowering the Barrett Light .50 rifle to the ground, he picked up an MP5 and started slithering down the hill. Men were firing up at him and some bullets whistled past to thud into the ground above and behind him. Wright discarded his SMAW and also picked up an MP5, then followed Coogan down the foliage-strewn muddy hill. Newman gave them covering fire, raking the open gateway with bursts from his GPMG and keeping the men trying to fire at them pinned down.

Reaching the bottom of the hill, covered with mud and twigs and with an equally messy Wright bunched up behind him, Coogan took cover behind the trees lining the road. He looked across to where the mangled remains of the gates were lying in the dirt. Some of Tolan's men were still firing up the hill, shooting wildly and blindly, from behind the protection of the high wall. From where they were positioned, those men could not see Coogan, so he hurled an incendiary grenade, saw and heard the explosion, then raced across the road, advancing crouched low and zigzagging as the smoke swirled between the two gateposts. He burst around one of the gateposts, firing sustained bursts from his MP5 while still on the move, and saw at least two of the men behind the wall go down. As Wright's MP5 roared to the left of Coogan, Newman's GPMG fell silent and Tolan's men, some still stumbling out of their cars, which had braked in front of the house, retreated, firing their weapons, into the building.

Coogan and Wright crossed the lawns, both crouched low and zigzagging, both firing on the move, until they could take cover behind the cars parked in the driveway.

A window was smashed upstairs and a sub-machine gun roared, the bullets ricocheting noisily off the car behind which Coogan was hiding. Wright glanced up, took aim and fired a burst from his MP5. More glass exploded, someone bellowed and the sub-machine gun at the window stopped firing. Other men, however, were shooting from the ground-floor windows at both sides of the main door, so Coogan threw two more hand grenades, one at each window, and they both smashed through the windows and exploded inside, causing black smoke to pour out through the shattered glass as men inside screamed and cursed.

Coogan jumped up and ran across the driveway to press himself against the wall beside the closed front door. Wright tried to do the same, but he didn't get far: a sub-machine gun roared from inside the house and he was knocked off his feet. He dropped his weapon, spun around and crashed in a quivering heap in clouds of dust on the gravel of the driveway. He was still alive, though. His body was twitching. Someone inside the house saw that movement and put another burst into him. His body convulsed, rising briefly off the ground, then collapsed, shuddered and was still.

Coogan fired a short burst at the lock of the front door, blowing it to pieces. Then he kicked the door open and rushed inside, crouching low and firing blindly left to right while still on the move. The bullets stitched along the walls, making plaster explode in swirling clouds of white powder, and two men, one at either window, were caught in the fusillade. One dropped his weapon, which clattered noisily to the tiled floor, and flopped forward to hang over the window frame, the glass having been blown out. The other remained where he was, still on his knees by the second window, his sub-machine gun still held in his frozen grip, the barrel resting on the window frame, his head lolling to the side, held upright by the stock of the weapon as blood spurted from the jagged hole in his temple and formed a pool on the floor around his knees.

Thinking of Wright lying out there on the driveway, of the final burst that had killed him, Coogan felt no sympathy for the men by the windows. He had no time, anyway, to dwell upon their fate. Instead, he glanced left and right, taking in the huge lobby, a grand staircase in the middle, doorways leading off in three different directions. He was wondering where to go, upstairs or downstairs, when a man stepped out from one of the doorways and fired a couple of shots from his handgun.

Coogan dropped to the ground, rolled over two or three times, came up firing a sustained burst from his MP5 and saw the man do a Saint Vitus' dance before sliding down the door frame. Coogan jumped up and ran across the lobby, still looking for Tolan.

He found Meehan instead.

The short, stocky killer stepped out from the side, from a hidden doorway, holding a pistol in the classic two-handed grip and pointing the barrel at Coogan's temple, mere inches away from it.

Coogan froze automatically.

'You're fucked,' Meehan said, 'you dumb shite. Here's one for all of us.'

Coogan heard the shot. The sound filled his whole head. He blinked and opened his eyes to see Meehan staggering sideways, staring down in disbelief at his bloody chest and then looking up again. He was looking at Barry Newman, who had come up behind Coogan. The last thing that Meehan saw in this world was the smoke drifting out from the barrel of Newman's Glock-19 handgun.

Meehan sank to his knees. 'Well, fuck me,' he said as

he let his pistol fall noisily to the floor and swayed on his knees. 'Who'd've thought . . . ?' Then he coughed up a mouthful of clotted blood, fell face down and died.

'Fuck *you*,' Newman said.

Another shot rang out. The bullet ricocheted off the wall just behind Newman's head. Then a second shot rang out and made a hole in Newman's face. He staggered backwards and went down like a felled tree.

Coogan, though shocked, threw himself instantly to the side, into the hidden doorway, then peered out to see Tolan firing a second wild shot before turning away and disappearing into another room.

'You fuck!' Coogan exclaimed, boiling up with revulsion and rage when he looked down at Newman. 'Fuck you, let's end it!'

Coogan went after Tolan, moving slowly and carefully, crouching low, weaving constantly, advancing along a corridor that came to a junction, one corridor to the left, another to the right, with an open door opposite leading into another room near the rear of the house. Coogan smelt smoke and cordite. The walls appeared to move in and out. The short corridor seemed to form a dark tunnel that went endlessly downhill. He knew that this was an illusion, the result of high levels of adrenalin surging through his system, and he tried to keep a grip on himself as he entered the room straight ahead. He was following the sound of footsteps, two men, maybe three, and when he passed through that room, which was filled with buckets and mops, he found himself in a dazzlingly white-tiled kitchen that overlooked the rear gardens.

The back door was open. He saw Tolan running out. He was being protected by the man, broad-shouldered, dark-suited, who stepped out from behind a fridge-freezer and took aim at Coogan with his handgun. Coogan fired first, a short burst from his MP5, and the man dropped his weapon, staggered backwards and then fell through the doorway. Coogan jumped over him, leaving the house, entering the gardens, and saw Tolan racing into the woods at the far end of the lawn.

You cowardly shit, Coogan thought.

He followed Tolan into the woods, crouching low, racing from one tree to another, always waiting for the punch of that invisible fist that would tell him that he'd been hit before he had even heard the shot. In fact, he did hear a shot. The bullet whistled past his head. Coogan saw Tolan turning away, about to run again, and he fired a short burst from his MP5. He heard Tolan cry out and saw him jerk upright as if whiplashed. Tolan pushed branches aside and let them fall back behind him. He disappeared temporarily from sight, though he was making a lot of noise.

Coogan followed him and saw blood on the green leaves, which told him that Tolan had been wounded, though how badly he could not tell.

Coogan kept following Tolan through the woods, tracking him by the sound of his thrashing progress, and came eventually to a broad, sun-stippled lake hemmed in by more trees. Tolan was circling the lake, slipping in and out of shadow. He glanced back over his shoulder, saw Coogan and fired a single wild shot from his handgun. The bullet whistled past Coogan's head, ricocheting off a branch behind him. He stopped advancing, raised his MP5 and fired a short burst at Tolan.

The woods around Tolan exploded, spewing broken branches and leaves, with dirt spitting up around his feet before some of the MP5's bullets found him. He screamed and fell down, rolling onto his back and staring disbelievingly at his smashed, bloody ankle. Then he rolled onto his belly and slithered forward like a snake.

Coogan went after him.

Tolan was crawling frantically through tall grass, his body covered in mud and blood, when Coogan approached him from the rear, crouching over and holding his MP5 at the ready. When he heard Coogan drawing near, Tolan attempted to crawl away more quickly. But his loss of blood, now draining out of him to mix with the mud, had weakened him too much.

'Ah, fuck!' he cried out in anguish and dread. 'Ah, Jesus! Oh, Christ!' His face fell into the mud. He shuddered visibly and rolled over, finally coming to rest on his back as Coogan came up to him. Tolan raised his handgun. 'Get away,' he bawled, 'ya bastard!' He fired a single shot as Coogan fired his MP5. Tolan's bullet went winging off into the wild blue yonder while Coogan's short burst cut across Tolan's belly to make him spasm and cry out. 'Ah, God, no!' he bellowed, his weapon wavering in his hand, the barrel gradually tilting downwards. Then he frantically kicked his feet, trying to push himself backwards, as Coogan came up to stand over him and look down upon him.

The pistol fell from Tolan's hand, slipped off his torn, bloody belly and splashed into the mud that his thrashing had churned up around him. He stared at Coogan with eyes widened and glazed by terror, his lips dribbling spit, then waved his hands frantically in front of his gaunt face, deathly white under its streakings of mud.

'Get away from me!' Tolan bawled. 'Fuck, ya bastard, get out of here! You're a fuckin' mad animal and ya should be put down and oh God oh Jesus the pain you fuckin' caused me ya fuckin' cunt. Get away! Leave me alone! Leave me in peace, ya fuckin' bastard ya shite! *Don't shoot me, for God's sake!'*

'You're dead,' Coogan said. Then he fired a short burst into Tolan's bloody chest, into his racing heart, making it stop for all time.

Tolan spasmed as if jolted by a burst of electricity. Then he coughed blood and collapsed like a burst balloon and at last moved no more.

Coogan knelt beside him. He checked that Tolan was truly dead. When he had confirmed that, he stood upright, sighed, turned away and walked back to the house.

There was still a lot of work to be done and he was on his own now.

Chapter Thirty

C oogan was standing on a windswept bluff overlooking a vast white beach that curved away,
dreamlike, around the rugged coastline north of
Larne. The sea was calm and iridescent, its gentle, azure
waves peaked with white foam. The only person down on
the beach was Lara and she was waiting for him.

Coogan started down, taking the narrow, winding
track, feeling the light wind tugging at him, hearing
the lonesome cries of the seagulls. It took five minutes
to descend all the way, though it seemed longer than
that, and as he crossed the beach to join her, his shoes
sinking into soft sand, he noted that she had pinned her
blonde hair up on her head and was wearing absolutely
no make-up. She didn't need make-up. She was flawless
without it. She was wearing a simple gaberdine coat
belted tightly at the waist, black leather boots and a
light green silk scarf that hung down her front. She
looked impossibly beautiful.

'Hi,' Coogan said, stopping directly in front of her. 'Long
time no see.'

She smiled slightly. 'Only a week, Coogan, though it
seems a lot longer than that.'

'A *lot* longer,' Coogan said. 'Come on, Lara, let's walk.'

They fell in side by side, then began walking along the flat white beach that seemed to stretch out for ever. The white-capped waves were so gentle that they seemed to sigh.

'So Tolan's dead,' Lara said.

'Yes,' Coogan replied.

'I read about it in the papers,' Lara said, 'though it wasn't what I expected to read.'

'It never is, Lara. That story was a nice little piece of disinformation put out by my friends in British security.'

'Very clever, your friends. Making all those dead bodies appear to be the result of a firefight between two rival gangs from the Belfast underworld. No mention of British security, the *mafiya* or former SAS men. Just IRA terrorists who'd turned to crime when the peace came in and then slaughtered each other over a drugs deal. Oh, yes, they were clever!'

'No mention of Boris, either,' Coogan reminded her.

'Of course not. They wouldn't want the public to know just how close their country had come to being taken over by the Russian *mafiya*. Boris's body has been spirited away. Boris never existed. The world works in mysterious ways.'

Coogan caught her sideways glance, her steady green gaze, and he knew that, although he hardly knew her, he still wanted her badly. She would know that, of course, because she could read her men, but he was hoping that her knowing it would encourage her to let him take care of her. He wanted to fly away with her.

'What happened to your two friends?' Lara asked him. 'Were they just described in the reports as two more Belfast gangsters or were they spirited away like Boris was?'

'I took care of them,' Coogan said. 'I did a lot of work

that night. I couldn't afford to let Wright or Newman be found – to be identified as former SAS men – so I demolished the OP, removed all traces of our presence there, then drove the transit van back down to the house and picked up both of their bodies. I then drove back into the hills where the OP had been and spent half the morning digging a double grave and putting them into it. When I filled the graves in, I sprinkled the soil with local foliage and left it looking as though the ground there had never been touched. Now they're just two of the many unmarked graves scattered all over the old bandit country.'

'Amen,' Lara said.

Coogan noted the sarcasm, but decided not to respond, wanting only to let her know that he would help her as he had promised to do. A new life in Australia was what he had promised her and that was exactly what he wanted to give her. Him and Lara together, in Australia – far away from Ireland, from England, from Europe – far away from the people who might destroy them because they knew too much. Coogan didn't trust Edmondson. He didn't trust M15. He didn't trust the British government and he didn't trust a single soul in Belfast. He was on his own now and so was Lara – and he wanted to tell her so.

'Come away with me,' he wanted to tell her, 'and I'll protect you for all time. I doubt that I love you – I'm not capable of love – but I want you with a singular passion and I'm willing to work for it.'

That was what he wanted to tell her, but the words would not come out, so he simply walked beside her along the vast white wind-blown beach, waiting for the right moment.

'Have you grieved for your friends?' she asked him.

'What does that mean?' Coogan replied.

'Did you feel any pain when they were killed and you buried them out there?'

'I don't think so,' Coogan said.

'You don't . . . *think* so? What does that mean? You don't know what you felt?'

Coogan nodded. 'That's right.'

'Do you know what love is, Coogan?'

'I know what it's supposed to be.'

'And that's something you've never experienced?'

'No, I don't think so.'

'What about your wife, Coogan?'

'She was sexy. That's why I married her.'

'You have kids?'

'Yes.'

'You love them?'

Coogan shrugged. 'I don't know. I mean, I like them when I see them – I feel *something* for them – but, in truth, if you asked me if I miss them, I'd have to say no. I like to live on my own . . . At least I did . . . Until I met you.'

She stopped walking and he stopped as well when she turned in towards him. 'What does that mean?' she asked.

Coogan hesitated, but at last the words came out. 'I promised you a new life in Australia,' he said, 'and that's something I think I can arrange. You're not safe here, Lara. You won't be safe in London. You won't even be safe back in Russia because the *mafiya* will hunt you down. They're bound to think you killed Boris. That means they'll kill you. As for British security, they won't want any witnesses, which means that you and I are both in danger. Let me protect you, Lara. I'll do that just to have you. I can get us to Australia before anyone finds us and once there we can live a better life than we'll get anywhere else. That's what I came here to tell you.'

'I *called* you here,' Lara reminded him. 'I phoned you up and arranged this meeting.'

'Yes,' Coogan said. 'Because I'd promised to look after you if I got back in one piece. But by the time I got back you'd moved on, leaving no message behind. You were frightened and you hid elsewhere for a week and then eventually called me. Why was that, Lara, if not to seek my protection? Well, that's what I'm now offering you.'

Lara smiled and walked on, going slower this time, kicking the sand up with the toes of her boots, first the left, then the right. She seemed almost girlish at that moment and maybe she knew it.

'Why do you want me, Coogan? Because you love me?'

'I can't promise you that.'

'No, you're not the loving kind, Coogan. It's just not in your nature. You can *want*; you can't love.'

Coogan sighed. 'What's the difference?'

'There's a lot of difference, Coogan.'

'I want you enough,' Coogan said with conviction, 'to try to get you anything you want. So what *do* you want?'

'I want something I love.'

'And what's that?'

'I love seashells,' she said.

They stopped again. Lara pointed at the sand. Coogan looked down and saw the white-foamed wavelets sighing over some seashells. He smiled, thinking that maybe he *could* love her. Then he bent down to pick up a seashell. When he straightened up again and turned around he saw the handgun.

Lara was holding the handgun and aiming it at him.

'You're not the loving kind, Coogan. *Mikhail* was the loving kind. He was a gangster and he had his cruel streak, but at least he loved me. I'd never been loved before. *Wanted*, yes, but not loved. Wanted so much that they were blubbering all over me, but without showing a single shred of love. Beautiful women are *never* loved; they're desired, but never loved. Beautiful women rarely see the side of men that makes most men human. Mikhail loved me, Coogan, loved me more than he loved the sex. Tolan wanted me like you want me, Coogan, and I won't be had that way. So how can you help me, Coogan? You've already robbed me blind. You told Boris about Mikhail, about *me* and Mikhail, and in doing so you sentenced him to death and that sentence was carried out. *You* killed Mikhail, you bastard, because you don't know what love is; because you're no more than a killing machine who takes his pride from his murderous skills. You killed Mikhail and, in doing so, you also killed me – or what life I had left in me. So fuck you, Coogan. Damn you to hell. And that's just where I'm sending you. The waves will wash you away.'

Coogan felt it for the first time, which was also his last . . . the punch of that invisible fist that would tell him he'd been hit before he had even heard the shot. The invisible fist hit him: he was dazed and staggered backwards, but managed to keep himself upright as the sound of the shot, which came an eternity later, resounded in his head.

He stared at Lara in disbelief, thinking, *Why? I could have loved you.* Then the ground seemed to sink beneath his feet as the sky reeled and scattered. Coogan felt the sand beneath him. The grains of sand became his skin. He licked his lips and blinked and saw the sky and Lara's face filled it up. She was looking down at him.

'We're both dead,' she informed him. 'We always were. Now go to hell, Coogan.'

Lara shivered. She seemed to tower above Coogan. Her blonde hair was the peak of a mountain in the golden light of sunset, disappearing in drifting clouds. Coogan went with the clouds. He went through Lara and beyond her. He looked back down and saw Lara on the beach, walking into the sea. She had a pistol in one hand. She let it fall into the water and she kept walking into the sea for as far as she could. She kept walking and then she started swimming and the sea washed her clean. She decided to dive. She wanted to see below the waves. A skein of golden-blonde hair was briefly visible in the water, then a wave that was as gentle as it was quiet swept those few strands away. The sea rolled on for ever.